S0-AZT-066

This book is dedicated to the nuns I have known
and loved, to those who have left and those who
have chosen to stay.

I have seen all this with my own eyes,
Heard with my own ears and understood.

Job 13:1

The Good Sisters

Kathleen W. FitzGerald, Ph.D.

2nd Printing
June 2002

Whales' Tale Press
P.O. Box 27
Lake Forest, Illinois 60045
1-800-914-1887
www.goodsisters.com

Library of Congress Cataloging In Publication Data

FitzGerald, Kathleen W.
     The good sisters.

     I. Title
PS3556.1833G6   1981   813'.54   81-66079
ISBN 1-882195-04-3   AACR2

All of the characters in this book are fictitious,
and any resemblance to actual persons is purely
coincidental.

Book Cover Design By *Alexander & Walsh*

Permission granted to quote from the following (All
Rights Reserved):

"The Gambler," words and music by Don Schlitz.
Copyright © 1977 Writers Night Music.

"Smoke Gets in Your Eyes," by Jerome Kern and Otto
Harbach. Copyright © 1933 T. B. Harms Company.
Copyright renewed. International copyright secured.

Copyright © 1981 Kathleen Whalen FitzGerald
All rights reserved

Published by:
Whales' Tale Press
P.O. Box 27
Lake Forest, Illinois 60045

Preface to the Second Edition

The Good Sisters is a butterfly caught in amber, stopped in time and space forever. You can hold the lovely butterfly up to the light and see the startled look on her face as she was caught in the sticky flow. You can toss her in your bottom drawer with your old college yearbooks and pressed prom roses, embarrassed at such innocence. You can wear her around your neck, tied through with a black velvet ribbon, to mourn the passing of her beautiful days and grace-filled ways. You can try to release her, but the amber and the butterfly have become one.

There is a story about Daniel Moynihan and Mary McGorry mourning the death of their friend John Kennedy. Daniel said that they would never be young again, never laugh again. Mary assured him that they indeed would laugh again, but that to be Irish was to know that the world would always break your heart.

At this time of the reissuing of "The Good Sisters", the Catholic Church has broken the hearts of her people, the People of God, as we were called after Vatican II. Bad, sick priests have hurt our children. The sexual abuse of children by priests first came to public attention in 1985, but this issue did not reach the tipping point until January of 2002, seventeen years and thousands of children later.

The scarlet-robed hierarchs are toppling like palm trees in a hurricane, their shallow roots exposed for all the world to see. Shabby priests, their consecrated hands locked in handcuffs, are shunted off to prisons. Shamed, humiliated and suspect themselves, good priests watch their felonious brothers from the sidelines, praying for the courage to get out of bed in the morning.

Lawyers, judges, prosecutors, accountants, public relations specialists, reporters, diocesan spokesmen. Priests, priests, priests. Bishops, archbishops, cardinals. These people are mostly men, the *yang* or masculine energy source. *Yang* is about power, force, leadership. Left to itself without the softer *yin* of the female, we end up in chaos, abuse and betrayal.

Where are the women? We are grieving. Mourning the rape of our little children. Mourning that we trusted the men in the church to care for our children. To be honest and caring and gentle and brave. Like the good priests who are suffering because of their unfaithful brothers.

We are waiting in the wings to take our proper place as full persons with the People of God.

The second coming of *The Good Sisters* is synchronous with the dearth of the female, of the *yin* in the church. It harkens us back to butterfly times in the church, when every playground and classroom in America was filled with dedicated women in brown, white, blue, gray and black habits, chalk dust on our veils and long wooden rosaries swinging from our belts. We thought it would last forever. When "The Good Sisters" kept the men in balance, the likes of Msgr. Desmond Ryan, Father Jack O'Mahoney and Father Danny Doyle didn't even think of abusing a child.

At St. Paul's Parish in the late 50's, it seems that it took seventeen women with their hidden *yin* to keep the three men of the masculine *yang* in check. We didn't know anything about these matters then, but they were to come and come they did with the force of a charging hurricane, a plague of locusts, a crackling forest fire.

In the 60's Pope John XXIII opened the stained-glass windows to let in the fresh air and thousands of us hurled ourselves through the open casement, away from the confines and unnaturalness of convent life. Those who stayed took off their veils and began living in more natural environments and sought jobs beyond the classroom. Today, the nuns are older and fewer, with the younger ones in their late 50's.

One elderly nun stood on the steps of her mother house, threw out her arms and screamed, "Where are the young nuns?" There was no answer.

As you read *The Good Sisters*, you will be coaxed back to a time when the church was clear and predictable, a Ferris wheel circling through the liturgical year at the same speed and rhythm as the year before and the year after. People changed but the roles remained. Everyone was replaceable, or so we were told.

Maybe not. Perhaps in the near future, some young scholar will draw correlations between the downward slope of the reduction in the sheer number of nuns (*yin*) and the ascending vector of child abuse by men (*yang*). Where will the next source of female energy in the church be drawn from to hold in check the solitary male? As women we still may not fully participate, toe to toe, with the men, and we are unwilling to return to our sweet, silent cloister. It doesn't work now and it really didn't work then, despite the image that we all colluded to project.

We will never again see the likes of *The Good Sisters*. Unlike our alma mater, we can't go back there, because that life has also blown through the open casement, the once-starched curtains, torn and stained, cracking in the wind.

However, you do need to return, if only in your memories, to the good nuns who educated you well, disciplined you perhaps too harshly, picked you up when you fell, kept your secrets when you asked her, and who prayed for you in a cold and dark chapel while you slept. Perhaps today she is a mother, a grandmother. Perhaps she is still single or divorced. Perhaps she is in a wheelchair at her motherhouse, her hair thin and white, her boney fingers curled around a small black rosary.

And if you were fortunate enough to know *The Good Sisters*, one may well hold your young face or your young name in her old heart. She remembers you fondly, perhaps with regret for her harshness or exhaustion. I know that good sister sends to you blessings across the years, for how could she not? Now hold that beautiful butterfly caught in amber up to the light of day and understand what it was all about.

Kathleen Whalen FitzGerald, Ph.D.
June, 2002

1980

She slipped out of bed quietly so as not to disturb her husband. He had been at the hospital late the night before and she wanted him to sleep longer. She put on her robe and walked slowly down the stairs. Patrick was already up, watching "Sesame Street" in the front room. She waved at him and went into the kitchen to make coffee. It was going to be a hot day, so she left the blinds slightly closed.

August 4. Twenty-one years ago today, she thought, Marce died. She'd be fifty-six. Maureen smiled to herself, for Marce would always be young, as young as she was when she died. I'm forty-one; Marce never saw her forty-first birthday.

Maureen sat at the kitchen table, listening to the water squirting through the top of the coffee-maker. A sleek, scarlet cardinal was pecking at the birdfeeder. She looked at Patrick's half-eaten bowl of cereal. Cheerios floated in the milk. Twenty-one years ago today . . . how very different life was then.

The coffee was finished. She went to the cupboard, pulled

out a deep blue mug with a white sand dollar painted on the side, and poured herself a cup of strong coffee. She snapped on the radio. Kenny Rogers sang:

> You've gotta know when to hold 'em
> Know when to fold 'em
> Know when to walk away
> And know when to run.
>
> You never count your money
> When you're sitting at the table.
> There'll be time enough for counting
> When the dealin' is done.

Know when to walk away, she thought to herself. I walked away, I ran, and it was time. Marce's dealing was done, over, cut so painfully short. Maureen smiled, thinking of Marce, the gambler, the free soul, who never counted her money, her days, her weeks. She just lived them, abandoning herself to the flow of life and the pain of death.

"Mommie, can I have my breakfast?"

"Come here, Marcy, give Mommie a big hug."

The little three-year-old ran into her mother's arms, burying her soft brown hair in Maureen's neck. Marcy planted a big, wet kiss on Maureen's cheek and scampered off her lap to check the birdfeeder. Maureen filled her daughter's Snoopy bowl with Raisin Bran, placed it on the table, and put Marcy into her chair. Marcy lifted her pajama top. "Look, Mommie, only these many more chicken pops left." She then attacked the Raisin Bran.

Little Marcy, another of God's free spirits. Will I ever tell her how she got her name? Maureen stared at the cardinal.

"What's you thinking about, Mommie?"

"Just another lady, Sweetheart. She got very sick and she died. She was my friend."

You never count your money, when you're sitting at the table. There'll be time enough for counting, when the dealing is done. It was all over. Those many days and weeks and years, living that strange, hard life. Yet would it really ever be over? How can I tear all those memories out of my heart? Maureen poured herself another cup of coffee, humming to herself, "You've gotta know when to hold 'em; know when to fold 'em . . ." They'll never go. I'll always hold them.

And secretly, she never wanted those memories to leave.

Cast of Characters

Sister Kevin Mary: age nineteen, newly professed sister. The former Maureen Barrett, trying to make sense out of convent life and the demands of Obedience.

Sister Theodore Marie: age forty-four, called "Theo," giggles a lot, somewhat withdrawn from the community, more involved with her own family.

Sister Helen Francis: age thirty-two, the Superior. Referred to as "Sister." Attractive looking, enjoys her status.

Sister Jean Martin: age thirty-five, called "Jean" or "Jeanie." Small, intense, moody.

Sister Maximillian: age thirty-six, called "Max." Big, tough, masculine.

Sister Mark Stephen: age twenty-one, called "Mark." From a wealthy family. Cynical, suffering no illusions about anyone.

Sister Clare Elliot: age twenty-two, called "Clarabelle" or "Clare." Sloppy; sets herself up for criticism, misunderstanding. Loved by kids.

Sister William Ann: age twenty-three, called "Willie." The perfect nun—kind, honest, straight.

Sister Julia Mary: age twenty-eight, called "Jules." Bright, well read, quick-witted.

Sister Frederick Ellen: age twenty, called "Freddie." Kind, sympathetic, hard-working.

Sister Agnes Patrick: age seventy-four, called "Aggie." Irish immigrant, hard of hearing, self-sacrificing.

Sister Lucy: age sixty-one, called "Sister Lucy." A former Superior. Very formal, takes Sister Helen Francis's place when she is away.

Sister Marie Marcel: age thirty-four, called "Marce." Face contorted in a sneer. Totally free soul.

Monsignor Desmond P. Ryan: age fifty-two, Pastor of St. Paul Parish, accomplished golfer and singer.

Father Jack O'Mahoney: age twenty-eight. Sandy-haired, muscular priest, dedicated to the priesthood.

Father Dan Doyle: age twenty-four. Dark, curly-haired priest; spends most of his time with school kids.

Margaret: laywoman, cook at the convent for noon meals.

Hilda: laywoman, housekeeper at the rectory.

1.

Her stomach tightened, as if a fist were grabbing her insides; she'd better go to the bathroom again before they got to the station. The conductor walked quickly through the car, announcing "Chicago—63rd and Englewood, 63rd, Chicago, Englewood" as the train slowed. She lowered her eyes, focusing on the back of his shiny black pants.

She reached into her deep sleeve and pulled out the note card: white with a thin yellow border, the initials S.H.F. embossed in the upper left-hand corner. She stared at the proud, lacy script. She had never seen anyone write quite like that. The bold up-and-down strokes ended with tight little curlicues. The capital letters began with a great flourish, managed an extra loop, and came down with a crash on the little vowels next to them. She held the paper to her nose, trying to name the obtrusive fragrance sprayed on the paper. She had memorized the note, the pale blue ink fixing itself within her:

7

August 4, 1958

Dear Sister Kevin Mary,

I have just received word from Mother Jeremiah that you have been assigned to St. Paul Convent for the forthcoming school year. We want to welcome you to St. Paul's for your first year on mission. It will be a year of learning and of hard work, but we do manage to squeeze in some fun now and then.

There are seventeen of us here at St. Paul's. As you may know, you will be the youngest. I believe that you already know Sister Mark Stephen and Sister Frederick Ellen from the Novitiate.

You will be in our prayers on August 15, as you take your first vows in the order. Monsignor Ryan will offer Mass for you at the convent that morning.

Some of us will be at the Englewood stop to meet you on August 16. I won't be wearing a red carnation, but I am sure that we will know each other.

Best wishes as you conclude your Novitiate and prepare to take your vows.

Sincerely in Our Lady,
Sister Helen Francis

Sister Kevin Mary folded the note, jammed it back into her sleeve, and stood to get her cloak down from the rack overhead. She had folded it precisely: the high collar snapped, shoulders meeting, folded inward twice, and then over and over four times. It fell out without a wrinkle. She lifted her veil and placed the new black serge cloak around her shoulders, snapping the second snap.

She looked out the window and saw five groups of nuns waiting for their new members. Sister Kevin Mary looked around at her four companions, who were as nervous as she. There was an uneasy feeling in her chest. They had to say good-bye after two solid years together—twenty-four hours a day, seven days a week. She didn't want to cry and make a fool of herself in front of the new nuns. They quickly hugged each other good-bye as the train jerked to a halt.

The nuns lurched forward, grabbing the round metal handles on the back of the seats. The big steel doors slid open and they tried to make the jump off the high steps with as much dignity as they could muster. The conductor had offered his hand, but they did not accept. Near occasions of sin could come when you least expected them.

A short nun with flared nostrils and thick, arched brows approached her. She extended her hand. "Are you Sister Kevin Mary? I'm Sister Jean Martin from St. Paul's. We're over here." She motioned to two other nuns standing beside a long wooden baggage cart. Despite the heat of the August afternoon, Sister Jean Martin's hand was cold and lifeless. Sister Kevin Mary followed her over to the other two.

She looked at the older of the two and said, "Good afternoon, Sister. Are you Sister Helen Francis?" The older nun giggled, "No, I'm just me. This is Sister." Sister Helen Francis extended both her hands and took Sister Kevin Mary's hand in hers.

"Welcome, welcome. It is so good to finally meet you. This is Sister Theodore Marie and I know you've met Sister Jean Martin. It really is hot, isn't it? Have you ever been to Chicago before?"

"Once, when I was twelve, Sister."

Sister Helen Francis turned to Sister Jean Martin. "Jeanie, where did you park? Why don't you and Theo get the car, and I'll wait with Kevin."

Sister Kevin Mary had forgotten to go to the bathroom before the train had stopped but was too embarrassed to say anything to her new Superior. Perhaps it would not be too far to the convent. She picked up the gray canvas suitcase her mother had bought at Sears and followed the Superior to the curb.

Sister Jean Martin pulled the long black station wagon up beside them and stopped abruptly. Sister Kevin Mary opened the door for her Superior, lifting the bottom of her habit into the car so the door wouldn't close on it. She opened the back door, put her suitcase in the back of the wagon, and sat down next to Sister Theodore Marie.

They drove down the narrow, curved drive of the station. Broken beer bottles, newspapers, potato chip bags had blown up against the high black stone walls that banked the drive. Two little boys with butch haircuts jumped against the wall to get out of the way of the big station wagon, throwing an empty can at the rear window as the car passed. Sister Jean Martin muttered "damn brats" and stepped on the gas.

Sister Kevin Mary tried to follow the conversation but wanted to get a good look at Chicago. She was glad she hadn't been sent to some little Podunk place in the sticks. She looked up at the electric sign over the bank: South Shore National Bank. Time: 2:47. Temperature: 93 degrees.

She could feel sweat roll down under her headband. She counted the layers of clothing: a bra, undershirt, slip, habit, scapular, collar, cloak. Seven layers; 93 degrees. O Sacred Heart of Jesus, have mercy on the dying. This is nothing compared to the pains of Purgatory. The sweat rolled from under her arms down into her bra. Two years ago today, she probably would have been out on Jerry Killeen's twenty-six-footer. Dear God, don't let me think of that stuff.

She looked over at Sister Theodore Marie, who had been staring at her. Sister Theodore Marie was in her middle forties. Not very good-looking. Rather tall and heavyset. She wore thick wireless glasses that seemed to grow out of her colorless eyes. Her nose was long and short at the same time. Her skin had no particular color—it was just sallow and murky. A big brown mole was on the left side of her lips. It looked like a chocolate chip growing out of her face. Sister Theodore Marie giggled a lot and addressed everything to the Superior, even though there were two others in the car. On the outside, she didn't seem like a giggler, but Sister Kevin Mary didn't really know what nuns were like. She would soon find out.

"Jeanie, please pull over. I've got to run into that Clark station on the corner. Please, Jeanie." Sister Theodore Marie looked at the Superior, for Sister Jean Martin gave no indication that she was about to stop. Sister Helen Francis turned to Sister Jean Martin and said in her deep, calm voice, "Pull over, Jean. Theo has to make a stop." Sister Jean jammed on the brakes, pulled into the Clark station, and snapped off the motor. Sister Kevin Mary had to use the bathroom but decided to wait. She could tell that Sister Jean wasn't too happy with the delay and didn't want to make her madder.

Sister Theodore Marie came out of the washroom in less than a minute. She plopped on the seat, giggled, and pulled out from under her cloak a long, white corset. "Oh, Sister, this was just killing me. I thought I was going to die. Thanks so much, Jeanie." She giggled again.

Sister Jean rested her head against her hands that were encircling the steering wheel. She made no move to turn on the car. "Do you have any more projects, or can we get started? I've wasted my entire day with this trip," she snapped, abruptly started the ignition, and tore out of the Clark station. Sister Helen Francis turned and winked at Sister Kevin Mary; Sister Kevin Mary smiled back at her Superior. She still had to go to the bathroom.

Sister Theodore Marie placed the long corset on the seat between her and Sister Kevin Mary. The six little metal garters bounced up and down every time they hit a bump. Part of the corset was resting on Sister Kevin Mary's new cloak. The corset had large yellow stains on it. She was afraid if she moved it off, she would hurt Sister Theodore Marie's feelings, but she didn't want an old corset on her new cloak. The garters bounced up and down, and Sister Theodore Marie giggled again.

Sister Kevin Mary brought her arm in from her lap and pulled the heavy serge cloak about her. She sat up straight, drawing the cloak out to the side. Slowly, as Sister Theodore

Marie looked out the window, Sister Kevin Mary's fingers, covered by her cloak, reached the corset and shoved it gently off to the side. She gave it one more little shove as it cleared her cloak. The garters jumped up and down as Sister Jean raced on the expressway out to St. Paul's Convent. Sister Kevin Mary thought she would burst if she didn't get to a bathroom. The sufferings of the present day are not to be compared to the glory which is to come. Dear God, get me to the toilet.

She recognized the smell. Shalimar. Sister Helen Francis had on Shalimar. She touched her left sleeve and felt the note card. S.H.F., white and yellow. Did she squirt the paper with Shalimar, or does everything she touch turn to Shalimar? Sister Helen Francis's cloak was not made of serge but of some light silky material. She seemed so poised and confident.

Sister Helen Francis was attractive, not pretty, for her nose was rather shapeless. Her skin was good—firm with a slight dust of peach. She was too feminine to have a ruddy complexion but too strong and confident to look like a China doll. Her large brown eyes did not project sensitivity—just strength and control. Perhaps confidence. She seemed very young for such a big job.

As they exited the expressway, Sister Jean adroitly negotiated the cloverleaf, passed under a viaduct, and within seconds pulled into a long drive. On the left was the school: a two-story, L-shaped, Dijon mustard yellow brick school. A tall, handsome, middle-aged priest stood, one leg propped against the flagpole, hands in his pockets. He wore a starched, long-sleeved white shirt without a collar, black pants, black shoes. He was bald with a baldness so natural that one could not imagine him ever having had a head of hair.

As the station wagon came to a halt in front of him, he gave a piercing cry and began dancing around on one foot, holding the other one in his hands. Sister Jean, the driver, jumped out of the car. Monsignor Ryan burst into laughter and walked over to the back window to meet the new nun. Sister Jean got back in the car and slammed the door.

Sister Helen Francis introduced the new nun. "This is Sister Kevin Mary, Monsignor. . . . This is Monsignor Ryan, Kevin."

"How do you do, Monsignor?"

"Why, I do very well, Sister. And how do you do, Sister Kevin Mary? Are they treating you all right? Just let me know if they give you any trouble."

He winked at Sister Helen Francis; Sister Jean stared at the Dijon bricks; Sister Theodore Marie giggled. Sister Kevin Mary had to go to the bathroom immediately but smiled cordially at Monsignor Ryan, focusing on the initials DPR embroidered on his shirt pocket.

Sister Helen Francis said warmly, "Stop over after," as Sister Jean turned right, behind the yellow brick rectory, the orange brick church, and pulled up in front of the convent. She honked three times, calling the nuns to meet the new addition.

A narrow sidewalk ran from the parking lot alongside the church to the convent. More Dijon mustard. Sister Mark Stephen, whom she had known in the Novitiate, came running out of the convent, down the sidewalk, and grabbed Sister Kevin Mary's arm and began to introduce her to the rest of the community—so many names and faces. She absolutely had to get to the bathroom or embarrass herself permanently. And she could hardly look at Sister Mark Stephen, for she had one of those "things" on.

They call them "aprons," but they are not really aprons and are not the habit, she thought. They are nurses' uniforms—thin little short-sleeved nylon dresses to which is sewn about ten inches of nylon material to lengthen them. Over these "aprons" is worn the scapular, a long, narrow garment that goes over the head and hangs down in the front and the back. It is called *scapular* from the Latin, *scapula,* for shoulder.

Sister Kevin Mary had been warned over and over again not to wear one of those aprons: "Brides you are and brides you shall be." She had prostrated herself on the floor to ask for the habit of the order. She had waited so long to be able to wear it—that long, beautiful flowing dress—the habit. During the Novitiate, Sister Duns Scotus, the novice mistress, had told them again and again not to dress as a woman of the world but always to be garbed as a bride of Christ in the habit of the order. And now, less than twenty-four hours after she had made her first vows, she was going to have to throw down the habit and wear an "apron." She heard Sister Helen Francis say to Sister Mark Stephen, "Get her out of all those clothes and give her one of your aprons."

Sister Kevin Mary felt that she was going to faint. The heat, the nuns, that crazy priest, her bladder, and now "aprons." "Where's the john? I'm dyin' to go," she muttered to Sister Mark Stephen. They went up the stairs, entered the convent, went down the long, gray-tiled hall and up more stairs to the second floor. Sister Kevin Mary went into the bathroom and snapped the door of the narrow stall closed. She felt like she was going to pass out.

As she left the bathroom, something wet touched her heels. There was water on the floor. Her scapular had fallen into the toilet and was dripping wet, leaving a delicate trail of water behind her. Sister Mark was waiting. "Honest to God, the least you could do is to go to the bathroom properly the first day you get here," she roared. She grabbed Sister Kevin Mary's arm and led her to the small room they would be sharing that year.

"Take off that stuff, Kevin."

"I can't."

"Yes you can."

"Honest, Mark, I just can't. You know what Sister Duns Scotus said about those things." Sister Kevin Mary tried not to let Sister Mark know that she felt Mark was a traitor. Sister Mark had been a year ahead of her in the Novitiate and had received virtually the same training from Sister Duns Scotus— she had been told not to wear those things.

"Take your stuff off. They'll all think you're nuts. It's 105 in the shade. What does D.S. know, anyhow? Sister told me to get you comfortable."

"I won't be comfortable in one of those things."

Her new Superior was telling her one thing; she had been told another thing in the Novitiate. "When the Superior commands, God commands, and that's all there is to it," Sister Duns Scotus had drilled into them. She forgot to tell them what to do when the Superior commands them to do stuff that they had been told not to do.

And since when did Mark start to call Sister Duns Scotus "D.S.? She was getting just like the rest of them. Worldly.

Mark Stephen was turning into a smart ass. A worldly, smart ass nun.

"OK. I'll put it on."

Sister Mark smiled wisely. "You'll catch on, kid. You can't live here like we did in the Novitiate. That was a Never-Never Land. This is the real thing, Kev. Grow up and just trust me. Would I tell you to do something wrong? By the way, how is Sister Duns Scotus?"

"She's going to have another operation on her heart," Sister Kevin Mary said softly, implying that it was all Sister Mark's fault for calling her "D.S." and wearing an "apron."

"That's too bad. She looked like hell when I saw her this summer. She gave me one of her funny looks. I was going over to see her, but I didn't have time." Sister Kevin Mary felt utter contempt for Sister Mark. She looked down at the floor.

"Are you going to wear that scapular with tinkle on it?"

"Get off my back, will you, Mark? This is sure a great welcoming. I'd like to get out of here, right now."

"I'm sorry, Kevvie. It's just that you're so new. Guess I just want you to get toughened up so they don't hurt you too much."

Sister Kevin Mary looked around the small bedroom. Two small beds, maple, early American with a carved acorn on each poster, were against the walls, about twelve inches apart, under the one large window. The bedspreads were orange cotton with vertical ribbing—the kind that was advertised in the Sears catalogues for boys' bedrooms. There was a tall maple chest and a maple desk with a straight back chair; both to be shared. No rug. A small closet. Near the doorway, a small porcelain sink with two towel racks and a medicine cabinet with a mirrored door caught her eye.

"Why is this sink here?"

"Where are you going to wash your face?"

"I thought there'd be a room with a bunch of sinks, just like the room with the bunch of toilets."

"This is it. You can hang your socks and towels on the bars. Take the one on the left, OK?"

Sister Kevin Mary began to unpin her veil and remove some

of the seven layers of clothing. Sister Mark reached into the closet for an apron. She drew out a soft veil—a small, black nylon scarf that was pinned to the starched headgear. Sister Kevin Mary could feel her face redden, for this was her first betrayal, all in the spirit of obedience. And this was the first time in two years that her arms had shown, so white for the middle of August.

She heard someone climbing the stairs, two at a time. It was Freddie. Sister Frederick Ellen, her old pal from the Novitiate. Sister Frederick Ellen was six months ahead of her; she had come out the previous Christmas, immediately after her profession. With her typical bombast, Freddie charged into their room, threw her strong arms around Sister Kevin Mary, and planted a big kiss on her cheek.

"Kevvie, it's so good to see you. I've been counting the hours 'til you got here."

"Oh, Freddie, am I glad you're here!"

"I see you're in an apron. It's really not so bad."

"I feel like a rat."

Sister Mark looked first at Sister Frederick Ellen and then at Sister Kevin Mary. "It won't kill you."

"Mark, she just got out. Don't be so rough on her."

Sister Kevin Mary felt like an ass—compromised, immature, awkward.

"Did Jean Martin pick you up?" asked Freddie.

"Yeah."

"Isn't she a doll? So sweet and kind."

Sister Kevin Mary didn't want to speak unkindly about any of the nuns. She looked at the sink sticking out of the wall. "Things are different than I had thought," she said softly, to no one in particular.

Sister Frederick Ellen shouted down the hall, "Clarabelle, Clarabelle, come and meet Kevvie."

Sister Clare Elliot came out from her room. She was wearing only her slip. Her headgear was crooked and stained with perspiration. Her thick glasses rested at an angle on her face. She stuck her fingers inside her gimp, that soft cotton cloth that encircled the face and enclosed the stiff, starched headband.

Sister Clare's gimp was frayed and thin about the ears. Her slip was torn under the arms. The straps of her bra fell off her shoulders.

"Hi. I'm Clare Elliot. It's nice to see you. I'm sweatin' like a June bride."

"Hi. Think I remember you from the Novitiate. You were two years ahead of me."

"Yeah, well, I gotta get some of this stuff off. God, I think I'm goin' to die. We were at Field's for hours. Glad to see you've gotten an apron already. Wouldn't D.S. just flip? See ya 'round, Kevvie."

Sister Kevin Mary felt the anger come up around her eyes. Another one called her "D.S." That was one thing she was never going to do. They could make her wear an apron, but no one could make her call Sister Duns Scotus "D.S."

She was glad there were so many young nuns there. Freddie was twenty already, Mark was twenty-one, and Clare must have been twenty-two. Sister Kevin Mary was going to be twenty in October—nineteen for just two more months.

Sister Frederick put her arm around Sister Kevin Mary and led her out of the room. She turned to Sister Mark. "Let's go down and get a Coke. Clarabelle, we'll be downstairs when you're ready."

The three young nuns, all in their aprons, went into the small, square kitchen. Three of the walls were lined with overhead white metal cabinets. The floor was a nondescript green; the counter tops were lemon yellow, finished with a thin metal edging. A large white refrigerator dominated the kitchen.

They fixed themselves large tumblers of Coke with plenty of ice. Sister Kevin Mary had not had a Coke in two years. The taste was so familiar, like a taste of home. They took their drinks into the community room, the one room in the house with an air conditioner. The community room was the main living room, rectangular with blond wooden bookshelves at the west end and a piano at the east. There was no carpeting, just the same gray tile that ran down the hallway. The chairs and sofas were a nubby avocado green with maple arms and legs, a

prosaic interpretation of early American. The south wall—
mostly windows—was covered with venetian blinds. In the
center, below the windows, was a radio/hi-fi, early American.

Sister Kevin Mary tried to remember whom she had met: the
Superior, Sister Helen Francis; the driver, Sister Jean Martin;
the nun with the girdle, Sister Theodore Marie; and then there
were Mark, Freddie, and Clarabelle. She sat back in the chair.
Her body felt strange. The fleshpots of Egypt, that's what this
is. He who condemneth little things shall fall, step by step. The
Coke tasted so cold, so sweet. The air conditioner blew cur-
rents of cooled air around the room, drying the perspiration on
her face, on her neck, under her arms. The foam rubber
cushions held her tenuously, for she could not give in to their
softness. Her thighs and ankles tensed so as not to succumb to
the pleasure of the flat rubber pillows.

It was half past four, nearly time for Matins and Lauds. Sister
Kevin Mary turned to Sister Mark. "Do we get back into our
habits for chapel?"

"We're not prayin'. Just say your own. This is still vacation,
and besides, it's too hot."

Sister Frederick, her shoes off and feet on the couch, became
somewhat solemn. "Don't worry, Kevvie, we're not going to
the dogs. We usually just say them privately during these few
weeks before we go back to school. . . . By the way, did Sister
tell you what grade you're going to have?"

"No. What am I going to have?"

"She'll tell you soon enough."

"What grade am I going to have, Freddie?"

"I'm not free to say."

"Honest to God, Freddie, tell 'er what grade she's going to
have!" shouted Sister Mark.

"You're going to be in first with me and Willie."

"First grade?"

The bell rang for dinner. They put their glasses in the sink
and went into the refectory. All the nuns had on their aprons
and soft veils. There were two long, joined gray formica-top
tables; Sister Helen Francis sat at the head of the tables and the
sixteen others, eight on each side, sat according to age, oldest

first. Sister Kevin Mary was at the end, at the place near the kitchen door. Across from her sat Sister Frederick; next to her was Sister Mark; across from Sister Mark was Sister Clare.

Since this was vacation, no one read a. designated spiritual book. They stood, said grace in English, were seated, and began to talk. Each nun opened the little drawer in front of her place and took out her own placemat, dishes, and silverware. Two servings, one for the head table and one for the second table, were brought in from the kitchen.

Sister Kevin Mary looked incredulously at the heaping plate of hamburgers and cheeseburgers, with two kinds of cheese— Swiss and cheddar—in bakery buns, not Wonder Bread buns. There were enough for all. (In the Novitiate, there would have been five servings for eight nuns: The first two could act as if they didn't know there weren't enough and take a whole one; the next five had to share; the last one usually got a whole one, or at least a big half.) The degrading habit of counting the portions to see how many were missing was going to come to an end, she thought.

The hamburgers were plump and juicy and stuck out all around the fresh buns. There were plenty of tomatoes—big, red, sexy tomatoes—and onions, olives, catsup, mustard, relish. And more tall Cokes. They didn't even buy those little six-ounce bottles. There were two baskets of chips, plain and wrinkled.

Sister Kevin Mary's hand trembled as she shoved the big cheeseburger—Swiss cheese on a poppy seed bun, tomatoes and onions—into her mouth. Juice from the hamburger ran down the sides of her mouth, but she didn't take time to wipe it. Freddie was saying something to her about "D.S.," but Sister Kevin Mary was too busy to get angry. The potato chips were crisp and salty; the second Coke tasted as good as the first.

Sister Clare had scratched her ear with her left hand and spread mustard all over her gimp—her frayed and dirty gimp. Some of the juice from the hamburger squirted onto her thick glasses, and half her potato chips were off her plate. She sat far back from the table and dropped food in her lap.

The nun who was serving went back to the kitchen and

returned with another plate of hamburgers and cheeseburgers, all cheddar this time. She could not refuse, although she was mildly stuffed. Sister Frederick cut a cheeseburger in half, took one half, and left the other. Sister Kevin Mary took the other half, in memory of all those times she had gotten only a half of something that was too small to be cut in the first place. The bowls and platters were cleared from the table. The server emerged again from the kitchen with a tray of Good Humor bars. Nothing was left but the papers and sticks.

As the last remnants of the meal were cleared from the table, the server brought out four large plastic bowls with a rubber spatula. Each nun scraped her own dish, emptied her glass and cup, and passed the scraping bowl to the next nun. The server then brought these to the kitchen and returned carrying a large tray with a rubber basin full of hot, soapy water. There was a pink plastic dish mop with a foam rubber head for washing the dishes, a dish towel, and a dishrag. The dirty dishes had been piled next to Sister Mark. The tray was shoved in front of Sister Kevin Mary to dry the dishes.

The dishes were thin, grayish-white china with pale blue flowers—Noritake. Not at all like the heavy white Novitiate dishes with the red band made in Steubenville, Ohio. Sister Kevin Mary was cautious not to break or chip any of the lovely dishes that Sister Mark was so quickly stacking up on the tray. As she would dry them, Sister Frederick would pass them back to the nuns, and each would put a clean set into her drawer. They never got rinsed, but the water was hot and sudsy and they got dried well.

The four trays with the basins of dirty water were returned to the kitchen, emptied, dried, and stacked up for the next meal—all very methodical and efficient. Sister Frederick was emptying the basins when the server, a heavyset nun in her middle twenties, stuck the sudsy dish mop in her face. "Kiss Grandpa, Freddie. Kiss Grandpa." Sister Frederick wiped the dirty suds from her face, telling the nun she was disgusting. The nun went away chuckling to herself.

After they said grace after meals, Sister Helen Francis announced that they would have night prayer at 8:15. Sister Kevin

Mary wondered why she had to announce that they would have night prayer, for night prayer was what they did every night, wasn't it? By the patronizing looks on their faces, she could tell that this little show of piety was for her benefit. Sister Jean sent a benign scowl in her direction. Sister Kevin Mary resolved not to get tangled up with her, not if she could help it.

Some of the nuns went down to the basement recreation room to watch the Huntley-Brinkley newscast. She and Sister Frederick went on a short tour of the school, walked around the church property, and ended up on the convent stoop. They didn't talk much.

"Freddie?"

"I know, Kevvie. Just take it easy. Everything is just not what you'd expect, I know. One day at a time, OK? You know what Desi tells Lucy, 'Take it tizy, take it tizy,' Kev."

Sister Kevin Mary did not respond. She didn't need to. Freddie understood. It was just so different from the Novitiate. The nuns all seemed so, well, maybe worldly. They really had it pretty soft. All those hamburgers and Cokes. And no prayer and wearing those aprons. Don't let me turn out like that, dear God. Now I sound like the Pharisee, "Thank God I am not like the rest of men. . . ." Her head was spinning. The bell for night prayer was a welcome relief.

Sister Kevin Mary's place in chapel was next to Sister Mark. Everything was done by age. Eat, sleep, pray according to when you were born. The Superior began night prayer with the Sign of the Cross: "In the Name of the Father, and of the Son, and of the Holy Ghost, Amen. . . ." The words sounded so good and reassuring. The order is bigger than these nuns; the Church is bigger than the order; God is bigger than the Church. So what did that mean? All she knew was that it was Wednesday—St. Paul's Convent outside of Chicago, and she was where she belonged. That's all that mattered.

With the ending of night prayer, three of the nuns shot out of chapel. The bell for profound silence, marking the end of the day's conversation, did not ring immediately afterwards, as it usually did. One more aberration. Sister Kevin Mary could hear the nuns talking again down in the basement. She finished her office, which she had missed. But she really hadn't missed it. They just didn't say it. With a spirit of rectitude, she made the venia.

It felt funny making the venia without her habit on. The floor was cold and hard against her bare arms. As she prostrated herself before the Blessed Sacrament, she asked God to take the sacrifice of her life, in a spirit of obedience and generosity. And humility.

Sister Kevin Mary walked quietly up the stairs to their room. She pretended that the bell had rung. She was tired from all that talking, all those nuns. She adjusted the blinds, took off her clothes, and put on her nightgown, robe, and nightcap, for her head was always to be covered as a sign of virginity. She went down to the shower room.

The shower felt good—a cleansing of the body and the spirit. Which had taken the worst beating? She felt uncomfortable from all that food. She wasn't used to hamburgers and Cokes anymore, and she had really made a pig of herself. She washed her hair, all one and a half inches of it. Her head felt like her brother Marty's. She looked just like him, but he'd never know that. She dried herself vigorously and got into her thin cotton gown. She put her new nightcap back on, buttoned up her robe, and headed for the door of the shower room.

Her eye caught a scale in the corner under the window. She hadn't weighed herself since she'd left home. One hundred twelve pounds. Not too bad. She had been 118 when she entered. She never wanted to get up that high again. She left the shower room, feeling rather thin and very clean.

Sister Helen Francis's light was on in her room. Sister Kevin Mary had to pass her room and since the bell hadn't rung, she thought she would say hello.

Sister Helen Francis was sitting at her desk writing. Sister Kevin Mary recognized the stationery. As she knocked softly, the Superior raised her head. Sister Kevin Mary fell to her knees, for that was the position a nun assumed when she spoke to her Superior, for she was usually asking for something— permission to do something, a penance, advice. In the Novitiate, the novices always addressed Sister Duns Scotus on their knees. Besides, with her heart problem, it was less of a strain for her to speak to them if they were closer to her.

"Sister Helen Francis, I don't know your rules around here, but if you will just tell me what you expect, I'll be happy to conform."

"We just want you to get adjusted, Sister. Don't worry about the rules. You know what they are, and I'm not unreasonable."

"I'm sure you're not, Sister."

"You know, we're not on schedule now. The nuns have been in summer school. A few have been in the hospital. We just need a break before getting back into the school routine."

"I'm sure you do, Sister."

"Did Sister Frederick tell you what grade you'll have?"

"Yes, first, Sister." Sister Kevin Mary blushed, for she didn't know if she should have been told already or if she should have waited for the Superior to tell her.

"You'll have some good help. Sister Frederick is turning out to be a real strong teacher, and Sister William Ann will be with you, too. She is a marvelous teacher. You can learn a lot from Willie."

"Yes, Sister."

"Well, if you have any problems, don't hesitate to ask me anything, and I'm sure that all of the nuns would be more than happy to help you with anything."

"Yes, Sister. Thank you, Sister."

"Good night, now."

"Good night, Sister."

Sister Kevin Mary walked slowly back to her room. It was just not the same talking to this new Superior. She sniffed at her nylon robe to see if any Shalimar clung to it. Sister Helen Francis's room was not like the rest of the nuns' rooms. In the first place, it smelled better—Shalimar. On her desk, there was a small milk glass lamp with a white and yellow ruffled shade; on the rest of the desks were brown, metallic fluorescent lamps. The Superior had an oval rug of the most delicate lemon shade. On the bed was a lovely white quilt with little yellow rosebuds; her sheets were the exact shade of yellow as the little roses. The rest used white sheets.

Sister Mark was downstairs watching a movie on television

with the rest of the nuns. Sister Kevin Mary was glad to be alone. She climbed into bed, read a few paragraphs from the *Imitation of Christ,* and began her rosary. The fourth of the day. She fell asleep within minutes.

She slept fitfully. The night was filled with bizarre images, amusement park distorted-mirror images of nuns and priests, of Sister Duns Scotus taking off her girdle in chapel, of hamburgers and drive-in restaurants. And Jerry Killeen was there with his twenty-six-footer at the Yacht Club; he was there dancing; he was there driving his convertible. She sat up with a bolt. Her heart was racing and pounding in her head. Where was he? That black curly hair and those thick lashes. Where was he? Was he in her room? She looked over at the next bed— it looked like a boy was sleeping next to her. Brown crew cut. On the little carved acorn, Sister Mark had hung her nightcap. Her rosary was lying on the pillow next to her face.

Sister Kevin Mary reached for her own nightcap, which had fallen on the floor. She had to go to the bathroom—all that Coke. She walked quietly down the long gray hall. In the light from the two night-lights, plugged into the wall, the young nun saw only distortions of herself. Although most of the bedroom doors were shut, they were not very thick, and the sounds of the nuns snoring sounded in the hall. Someone was shouting in her sleep; someone was moaning. She went quickly into the bathroom.

As she left the bathroom, a large figure without a nightcap or robe was racing down the hall. Sister Kevin Mary didn't know if she should wait and hold the door open or get the hell out of there. She let the door close and walked quickly back to her room. The other nun shot into the bathroom. Before Sister Kevin Mary reached her room, she could hear the nun vomiting, the sounds of her retching echoing through the empty tile bathroom and down the hall. Sister Kevin Mary shut her bedroom door, climbed back into bed. She pulled the covers over her head and grabbed for her rosary.

2.

Thursday morning—7:40 A.M. The bell rang much later than Sister Kevin Mary was accustomed to. The air was hot and sticky, and her nightgown soaked with perspiration. She dressed quickly, walked into chapel, and prostrated herself in front of the Blessed Sacrament.

> I, Sister Kevin Mary, make profession and promise obedience to Almighty God, to you Reverend Mother Mary Jeremiah, and to your lawful successors, according to the rule and constitutions of our holy order, 'til the hour of my death.

She stood, genuflected, and knelt in her place by the window. It had been less than forty-eight hours since she had made first profession. The vows she made were not until death but only for a year; in her heart, it was for keeps.

She was now a professed Sister. She was now under vows— Poverty, Chastity, and Obedience. Poverty, so that I may be emptied of all earthly possessions and filled with the love of

God; Chastity, so that I may love not one, but all; Obedience, to do the most holy will of God, not my own. Those two long, wonderful years at the mother house were over; the work had been done—she had been transformed from a silly high school girl into a religious, a nun, a sister. Day after day, filled with silence, prayer, and mortification of the senses. Dying to the world so that I may be filled with the grace of God.

She thought of her Profession Day—just last Tuesday. This was only Thursday. Her crowd, the twenty-two nuns she had been with for two years, walked slowly to the altar of the old Baroque chapel, the chapel of the Mother of God. The Novitiate Choir was chanting the *Magnificat,* the prayer that the Virgin Mary said to her cousin Elizabeth when she told Elizabeth that she was with child.

> My soul doth magnify the Lord
> And my spirit rejoices
> In God, My Savior,
> Because He hath regarded
> The lowliness of His handmaid
> And henceforth all generations
> Shall call me blessed
> For He who is mighty
> Hath done great things to me.
> And holy is His Name.

As the voices of the choir filled the chapel, all she could think as she walked down the aisle was, "Get the hell out of here before it is too late! Just get the hell out of here! Run for your life, kid!" She proceeded more steadfastly to the altar, kneeling before Mother Jeremiah, placing her hand on the Rule Book, and promising to obey. Sister Duns Scotus, the Novice Mistress, standing next to Mother Jeremiah, quickly slipped off Sister Kevin Mary's white veil and placed on her head the heavier black veil of a professed sister.

It was her wedding day; now she was joined forever to the Bridegroom. She was a Spouse of Christ, a Bride forever; she would wear the veil every day of her life to remind herself and the world that she was His Bride, fixed in time in an irrevocable union with Him. In five more years she would make profession until death and receive the ring, that small gold band that would truly bind her forever to the Eternal Bridegroom—if she had proven herself worthy.

Monsignor Ryan cleared his throat as he came out of the sacristy. His large pink head sat incongruously on top of his shoulders; the thin white vestments blew slightly in the breeze from the small fan at the bottom of the altar steps. With a twinkle in his eyes, he periodically looked up at Sister Helen Francis. He finished the Mass in less than seventeen minutes, for he had a golf game at 9:30 and wanted to get out on the course before it got too hot.

After Mass and breakfast, Sister Frederick took Sister Kevin Mary over to the school. School started in two weeks. There were bulletin boards to decorate, books and materials to pass out, kids to divide up. And then she had to find out how to teach them. She was going to have fifty-six kids that year. Sounded like a lot to her, but fifty-six was probably not too many. All you have to do is teach.

The work of the Lord, workers in his vineyard. The vineyard looked so different when you finally got a close look at it. In her mind Sister Kevin Mary could still see that picture of the Biblical folks with flat straw baskets, picking grapes. The vineyards of the Lord. "Come, follow me and I will make you fishers of men." Throwing the big nets over the other side of the boat and coming up with little people in the nets. The work of the Lord. Dear God, help me to bring the little children to you. "Let the little children come unto me, for of such is the kingdom of heaven." Dear Holy Mother of God, give me the grace to bring the children in my care to the arms of your loving son. May I never get in their way. May I never be a scandal to them. May they see you, dear Mary, in me, in my love for them.

Sister Kevin Mary looked up and down at the long rows of tiny blond wooden desks. How do you teach? During a three-week period in the Novitiate, from 1:45 until 2:30, before she made her daily Holy Hour, the novices were given a third grade arithmetic book. They did all the assignments and checked their accuracy against the teacher's manual. That was the sum total of their professional preparation for teaching. To be concerned about the technicalities of teaching only showed a lack of Faith and Trust. If God called you to teach, His Grace would be there, for He did not abandon those whom He called. Hard work, obedience, and being open to receive His Grace were all that were needed.

But what do you really do when the kids get there? She saw some teacher's manuals on top of the teacher's desk. She thumbed through them; they all looked too complicated. Well, she could always read to them. God, she was really going to have to teach them all day long. She hadn't really thought about that. It was always presented as such an abstraction; there was nothing abstract about those fifty-six desks that would soon be filled with fifty-six children.

She began to finger her rosary as she walked over to the windows. Monsignor Ryan was driving into his garage. He parked, left his clubs in the trunk, and walked over to school. Sister Kevin Mary waved to him. He saluted and began marching into Sister Helen Francis's office.

Three minutes later, Sister Helen Francis's voice came over the PA. "Mrs. Thornton wants us to honor her with our presence this afternoon. She has an area there that is badly in need of attention. I told her we would be there at one o'clock." Sister Frederick burst into Room 103, Sister Kevin Mary's new classroom.

"Did you hear that, Kevvie? We're going swimmin' this afternoon."

"But she said the lady needs attention or something like that."

"Her pool needs attention and she likes to see us running around without our habits. Besides, she's not in any condition to go swimmin'."

"What's wrong with her?"

"You'll see."

"I can't go, Freddie."

"Yes, you can, Kevvie. Sister wants us all to go. Why can't you go?"

"My legs."

"What's the matter with your legs? Everyone has legs. Mrs. Thornton has legs. What's wrong with yours?"

"I look like my father. She took away our razors. I'll just die if anyone sees me looking like this. I look like an ape-woman. I can't go."

"Oh, for God's sake, you can use mine. Just go over early for lunch, take a shower, and shave your legs. You'll look gorgeous."

"Do I have to ask permission?"

"For what? Going swimming? Shaving your legs? Eating lunch? Breathing?"

"For borrowing your razor."

"Oh, for God's sake, Kevvie. This is not the Novitiate. You can even have your period without asking. Just go into my medicine cabinet. My razor is on the bottom shelf. Don't clog up the drains."

After lunch, the nuns got their bathing suits and towels and headed for the cars. A nun went over to the rectory to borrow Monsignor Ryan's Catalina—license plate DPR 1. As they were going out the back door, one of the older nuns dropped on her knees before Sister Helen Francis. The nun was quite elderly and somewhat hard of hearing. Sister Helen Francis, bending over, nodded benignly and then helped the nun to her feet, embarrassing her. The elderly nun turned and walked quickly into the chapel.

Sister Mark backed the station wagon out of the garage, and the younger nuns all piled into it. The older ones went in the Catalina. As they drove out of the drive, Sister Mark turned to Sister Kevin Mary. "Welcome to the Nobodies, Kevvie."

"Mark!" said Sister Frederick, telling her to shut up.

"She ought to get the lay of the land as soon as she can, Freddie. There are Somebodies and Nobodies. You're a Nobody, Kevvie. Just in case you thought you were Somebody. A first class Nobody. A real special Nobody."

"Cut it out, Mark. Just cut it out. We don't need that stuff today. Ignore her, Kevvie," Sister Frederick said kindly.

The two black cars drove south for eight miles and turned off the main road, through the massive iron gates, and headed up a long, evergreen-lined drive. An elegant Tudor mansion was at the end of the drive. The butler met them at the cars and told them to go right back to the pool, that Mrs. Thornton would be out to see them shortly. As they passed the long French doors leading out to the patio behind the house, a small black maid in a white uniform waved respectfully.

There was a beautiful, rectangular pool—not Olympic size but very long—with a diving board at one end. Behind the pool was a white pool house, done in Florida greens and yellows. The pool house had a large center room, three bedrooms, a kitchen, and a bathroom. Above the toilet was a little framed notice: "We aim to please. Please aim." It showed a picture of a man going to the toilet, getting it right in and looking very pleased with himself.

The fifteen nuns quickly changed from their habits into their bathing suits. It was all accomplished with the utmost of speed and modesty—behind chests, in the bathroom, bedrooms, and closets, under towels. Those who were not quick or adept waited until they could change alone in the privacy of a bedroom.

The refrigerator was well stocked with pop and beer, cheese and fruit. Alongside the pool were lounge chairs, both recliners and straight-backed, all in yellow and green to match the interior of the pool house. One of the nuns grabbed a cold Budweiser and headed for a chair. "Watch it, Marce," shouted the Superior. "Just relaxin', Sister Helen Francis. Just relaxin'," said the nun, whose face seemed twisted in a sneer.

Sister Helen Francis was down at the shallow end of the pool. She pretended to be swimming, but her feet were on the ground all the time. She then hung on to the sides and kicked gracefully. Her suit was white with little yellow rosebuds. She looked very attractive. Her skin was well tanned. Sister Kevin Mary looked at her Superior—a picture of health. Poor Sister Duns Scotus was coming apart at the seams with her hard, ascetic life. "Some of the nuns have been in summer school and some have been in the hospital." She wondered where Sister Helen Francis had been all summer.

Off the board, Sister Mark did a perfect jackknife dive, entering the water without a ripple. She came to the surface, breathed easily, and climbed out of the water. Up on the board again, she looked straight ahead, pointed her fingers, ran to the end, sprang high in the air, somersaulted twice, and shot straight into the water without a splash.

Sister Mark was formerly Muffy Meldrum. She had been in the AAU diving finals the summer before she entered the convent. The Meldrums were a prominent Kenilworth family. Her father, Mark G. Meldrum, had played quarterback at Notre Dame in the early thirties and had gone to Harvard Business School after that. He began his own manufacturing company which made millions during the war. The Meldrums were socially prominent. Both husband and wife frequently had their pictures in the paper for museum or charity benefits. The Cardinal consulted with Mr. Meldrum on financial matters for the Archdiocese. They had six children who attended private Catholic schools and spent their summers at the Onwentsia Country Club in Lake Forest—one of the few Catholic families admitted.

Sister Kevin Mary dove in modestly and came up where Sister Frederick was holding on to the side. She asked her why the older nun had knelt down at the doorway and had not come with them. Had she done something wrong? Weren't they all supposed to be together?

"Are you talking about Aggie? Poor Aggie, she'll never get near water. Haven't you heard about Aggie?"

"No. What's her real name?"

"Sister Agnes Patrick. Even the kids call her Aggie. She was on the Titanic, coming over from Ireland. She was supposed to have been a nanny for a wealthy English family who was coming over here for a visit. The kids and the wife and Aggie were getting into a rowboat, but the father shoved Aggie out so he could be with his family. Women and children first, but that didn't mean nannies. They never saw that family again, but as soon as Aggie got to her sister's in Chicago, she ran right down the street to the convent and told them that she wanted to be a nun. Guess some guy was waiting for her back in Ireland. She never bothered to let him know. She figured that God had spared her life, so the least she could do was join the convent. Aggie is scared to death of water, and every time we come here, she asks to stay home. She waits until the last second. Maybe she thinks she can do it. She never has. Poor Aggie."

They looked up to see a plump woman in her early sixties walking hesitantly across the lawn. Her knees seemed to lock with every step, throwing her body slightly forward. She jerked back about four inches with every step. Her eyes held a fixed stare and she smiled as if she were in mild pain and were trying to conceal it.

She was wearing a flowered, zip-up-the-front housecoat and men's black leather slippers. As she approached the pool, Sister Kevin Mary could see that her stockings were rolled around her knees, donut fashion. Her fuzzy gray hair was knotted in a tired bun, her face round and blotchy, with innumerable white hairs shooting out of her chin.

Mrs. Thornton had just returned from England, or she had just returned from sailing to England. She never got off the boat. Mr. Thornton disembarked, stayed in London for eight days on business, and joined his wife back on the ship just in time for sailing.

She sat down next to Sister Marie Marcel, who was drinking a beer. Mrs. Thornton was holding a drink in a tall, thick jelly glass, with two olives at the bottom. Perhaps she felt more comfortable seeing the Budweiser in the nun's hands. And the three cans on the ground next to her chair. A few of the other nuns were enjoying a Coke and approached Mrs. Thornton to thank her for letting them use the pool. Mrs. Thornton's eyes were fixed on a blue hydrangea bush next to a birdbath, but she managed to smile and nod as they spoke to her.

She reached into her housecoat pocket, took out a crushed pack of Camels and a handful of kitchen matches. She offered the nun a Camel; the nun declined. Mrs. Thornton struck the wet cement with a match but had trouble finding the end of the Camel hanging from her mouth. Sister Marie Marcel took a fresh cigarette, lit it, and gently handed it to Mrs. Thornton. Mrs. Thornton nodded and smiled. Three sparrows splashed in the birdbath. Mrs. Thornton rose, extended her arm in a flat, jerky wave, and began her journey back to the main home. The maid lowered a shade on the second floor.

Sister Mark was working on her back flip. She was entering the water too soon, making a large splash. She stood at the end of the board, her heels extended beyond it, toes taut. Her arms were stretched out in front of her, eyes straight ahead. She bit her lower lip, lunged up and back, flipped twice in the air, and entered the water perfectly.

Sister Clare had been doing cannonballs, somewhat recklessly. The nuns shouted at her to be careful, but she just laughed, swam to the side of the pool, jumped up, and began again. She would stand on the grass, run as fast as she could, jump high in the air over the pool, circle her legs with her arms, and hit the water, bottom first. The impact was shattering. Water sprayed 360 degrees around the pool. Unwittingly, she landed with the full force of her weight on Sister Mark, who had begun to surface after her dive.

Sister Marie Marcel threw down her Bud, raced to the edge of the pool, and made a shallow dive. She swam underwater, reached Sister Mark, and brought her quickly to the surface. She pulled her out of the water, placed her face down on a towel, and began pumping her back. Sister Mark coughed, choked, and belched up water and air as she tried to hold her neck and shoulders. Sister Marie Marcel looked up at the nuns standing over Mark. She seemed to be laughing cruelly all the time. Her left eye was half-closed, like Robert Mitchum's. She frightened Sister Kevin Mary.

In the meantime, Sister Clare, unaware of what had happened, did another cannonball. As she came to the surface, all eyes were glaring at her. Sister Mark weighed 104 pounds; Sister Clare, 174.

"God, my neck, I think it's broken. I can't move my neck."

"Take it easy, Mark," said Sister Marie Marcel softly.

"You make me sick, Clarabelle. Why the hell don't you watch where you're going?" snarled Sister Jean.

Sister Frederick had tears in her eyes. She didn't know whom she felt the worst for—poor Clarabelle, always doing the dumb thing; poor Mark, she'll be crippled. They'll be so nasty to Clarabelle. Sister Kevin Mary wanted to run.

Sister Helen Francis was already in her habit. Another nun had driven the station wagon across the lawn and stopped next to where Sister Mark was lying. Sister Frederick had gotten one of the beach robes hanging in the pool house and put it on Sister Mark's shoulders. It was a bright peach, red, and purple terry cloth and smelled like martinis.

"My neck, my damn old neck. I can't leave with this old rag on. My neck is killing me. Take this robe off me, Freddie."

"You're wearing that, Mark," said Sister Helen Francis in her deep, calm voice. "And you're going to the hospital with me. I'm sure it is nothing, just a little pull. You are to keep that robe on, Mark."

"What about my head?"

"What about your head?"

"I can't go. I look like a boy. I feel like a fool."

"Sister Frederick, get Mark's headgear."

They drove off for the hospital, Sister Mark dressed in her pink bathing suit, Mrs. Thornton's robe, and her headgear. They placed her on the back seat and drove slowly, assuredly, back across the grass and onto the drive. The maid closed the French doors. Sister Clare had changed back into her habit and was standing next to the birdbath, saying her rosary. A statue of St. Francis of Assisi affixed to the edge of the birdbath smiled up at her, his face covered with bird droppings.

Within a few hours, they were all back at the convent. Sister Mark had a sprained neck that caused her considerable pain. Many of the nuns would not look at Sister Clare. Sister Mark was put into bed; someone brought her tea and toast.

Sister Clare spent an hour and a half in chapel. Her eyes were red, and her fingernails were chewed down. She left the chapel, walking slowly down the long gray halls. Her eyes followed the patterns on the floor so she didn't have to take any more dirty looks. She slowly climbed the stairs and walked into Sister Mark's room and up to her bed. Sister Kevin Mary was half asleep in the next bed.

Sister Mark was sleeping, for she had been given some painkillers at the hospital. She opened her eyes and saw the cannonball standing beside the bed.

"Clarabelle."

"Oh, Mark, I'm so sorry. I could kill myself. I never meant to hurt you."

"Clarabelle, don't worry. I could have hit you just as easy."

"Mark, they're all so mean to me. I didn't mean to do it. Honest to God, I didn't."

"Ignore 'em, Clarabelle. They're just a bunch of damn asses anyway."

"I know, Mark. I just would never want to hurt you. Is it OK? I mean, do you think you'll be all right?"

"Forget it, Clarabelle. I'm just glad to get some extra sleep. And tea and toast in bed."

"Good night, Mark. Hope you'll feel better in the morning."

"Good night, Clarabelle. Incidentally, why don't you lose some weight?"

"Go to hell, Mark, OK?"

"Good night, Clarabelle."

3.

It was Labor Day, 1958. The heat of late summer, mixed with wax, disinfectant, and Murphy's Oil Soap, announced the beginning of a new school year. The next day, the school would fill with more than 2,000 students, and the sisters and lay teachers were working in their classrooms to be sure everything was ready. The mood had suddenly shifted, there was a new seriousness, preoccupation. Conversation among the nuns became shorter, clipped.

Many of the younger nuns who had been helping the older ones get books, prepare class lists, and clean classrooms were now attending their own classrooms. A few of the older ones were back in the convent, ironing the habits of the younger nuns; no one would be found wanting on the first day of school.

Sister Kevin Mary was sitting at her big wooden desk, looking over her class list. Fifty-six entries: twenty-four girls, thirty-two boys. Eight boys named Mark; four Johns; four Richards. Mary Sue; Mary Ellen; Mary Kay; Mary Kay; Mary Kay; Mary Beth; Mary Therese; Mary Ann. Three Patricias; three Karens. Her teacher manuals were stacked in front of her: *Fun with Numbers*; *Reading Readiness, #1, #2, #3*; *Writing by Kittle*; *Jesus Loves Me*; *Songs to Grow With.* They made no sense to her at all.

She heard Sister William Ann's quick footstep in the hall. She was singing:

> When I was young, I had no sense;
> I bought a fiddle for eighteen pence.
> The only tune that I could play
> Was "Over the Hills and Very Far Away."
>
> So early in the morning
> So early in the morning
> So early in the morning
> Before the break of day.

Sister William Ann taught one of the three classes of first grade. No lay teachers were assigned to first grade because it was such an important year for a child and only a nun could handle it. There were three nuns that year: Freddie, herself, and Sister William Ann, who was three years older than they were.

Willie pulled up a little reading chair next to the teacher's desk and began going through some of the teaching manuals. The children were coming only for a half day that week, so they only had to plan three hours of class time, from 8:30 until 11:30. Sister William Ann helped Sister Kevin Mary plan her schedule for the first day of school:

8:30-9:00	Introduce teacher—write "Sister Kevin Mary" on board. Call off kids' names. See who didn't show up. Send list to office.
9:00-9:30	Talk about Catholic School. How important. How lucky they were. Differences between public and Catholic schools. Go over some of the rules.
9:30-10:00	Bathroom, water. Take kids outside. Show them where they are to line up. Difference in bells (long, short).

10:00-10:20	Numbers. Use patterns alongside cork board; 1-10. Have individuals count up to 10. Count various objects in room. Show them number book. Explain object/number/word.
10:20-11:00	Reading Readiness. Alphabet. Sing alphabet song. Point to letters. Use children's names to pick out various letters—"M" for "Mark." Colors. Write "red," "blue," "yellow," on board. Have kids spot objects of same.
11:00-11:15	Story (The Little Engine That Could).
11:15-11:30	Review what we did. Go over rules. Get ready to go home. Teach the sign of Cross. Say Hail Mary.

Willie smiled a broad, protective smile, squeezed Sister Kevin Mary's shoulder, and told her that she was sure she would do just fine. The kids were darling, and she knew that they would love her.

"You have younger brothers and sisters, don't you, Kevvie?"

"Eight of them—three girls and five boys."

"You've had lots of practice with little kids. Don't worry your pretty little head about a thing. You'll be great."

Sister Kevin Mary blushed. She could feel the perspiration run down her arms and behind her headband. "How come there are so many more boys than girls, Willie?"

"There has to be. Boys get killed in the war. It turns out even in the end. I've got to go, Kevvie. My brother is coming. I'd like you to meet him. About noon." Sister William Ann replaced the chair, turned quickly, and returned to her own classroom, humming:

> When I was young, I had no sense;
> I bought a fiddle for eighteen pence.

Sister Kevin Mary wondered if she would ever be like Willie. So poised, so confident, so kind. She seemed like the perfect nun. She knew how to teach, she knew about those manuals, flashcards, books. She was so good to everybody and didn't seem to be in the turmoil Sister Kevin Mary was in. Maybe in a few weeks, after school starts, I'll be like Willie. I'll know what I'm doing. When things settle down, I won't feel like I'm on a tightrope. I'll understand all the nuns better. I'll get used to the kitchen and the way they do things here. I'll stop thinking about the Novitiate and Sister Duns Scotus. I'll be a good nun. I'll stop judging everyone and everything. Dear God, grant me stillness of soul in Thee. Let Thy mighty calmness reign in me. Rule me, O Thou King of Silence, King of Peace.

"A penny for your thoughts, Kevvie." Sister Kevin Mary looked up. Freddie stood next to the desk, her arms loaded with fourth grade books for Sister Agnes Patrick, who was home ironing.

"I've got to get Aggie out of that basement in this heat. Come on home, and we'll get a bite of lunch. Aggie's been ironing all morning. You ready for tomorrow, Kevvie?"

"I hope so. Willie went over the stuff with me. I'm a nervous wreck. Never thought this day would really come."

"Let's go eat. Don't think about it."

They walked back to the convent. The nuns who taught the upper grades were already home, making sandwiches for themselves. Freddie ran down to the ironing room, unplugged the iron, and made Sister Agnes Patrick come up for lunch. The older woman's thin, wrinkled face was flushed. Freddie told her to sit down and began making a ham sandwich for her. Aggie sat near the head of the table, near the Superior's place, for she was the oldest nun there. The big nun, Max, kicked Aggie's chair out for her.

"Come on, Aggie, take a load off your feet. What are you doing—running a Chinese laundry down there? Sit down, Aggie."

Sister Agnes Patrick blushed, thanked Sister Maximillian for getting her place ready, and plunked down heavily on the small refectory chair. Everytime Sister Agnes Patrick sat down, Sister Kevin Mary looked the other way, because she thought Aggie was going to land, face down, on the floor. Sister Agnes Patrick aimed for the chair, crossed her legs before she sat, and landed heavily on the edge of the chair at such an angle that it looked as if she would crash onto the floor. She began to eat in silence. The nuns tried to bring her into the conversation, but Aggie just smiled pleasantly and concentrated on her sandwich and cup of tea.

Sister William Ann raced up the back steps, threw open the screen door, and tripped on the small throw rug at the entrance, falling over the three large, empty milk bottles the milkman had not yet picked up. Books, papers, pencils, a jar of paste, a cigar box of new crayons were all over the floor, among the broken glass. Willie's chin was cut deeply; her elbow and leg were both bleeding.

The nuns threw down their sandwiches and ran to the back hall. Willie looked up impishly and began to laugh at herself as Max, the big nun, picked her up. Aggie blessed herself. "Sweet Jesus, help that poor child." Sister Kevin Mary began picking up the glass while Freddie went for the broom. She could hear Willie laughing all the way up the stairs to her room.

Sister Jean Martin stood against the kitchen door with her arms folded, surveying the mess. "Honestly, that nun is so clumsy. She's going to get herself killed one of these days. Watch that glass, Kevin. Honestly, you'd think she was old enough to watch where she was going." Sister Jean Martin returned to her ham on rye. Sister Agnes Patrick came up from the basement with a plastic bucket filled with suds and a green squeegee mop. She began to scrub the floor. Freddie took the mop away from her. "Please Aggie. Sit down and eat your lunch. Let Kevvie and me clean up this mess."

The front doorbell rang. It was the Sullivans—Father Jimmy Sullivan and his mother, Cornelia Mary Sullivan. All three of Mrs. Sullivan's sons were priests, and three of her four daughters were nuns. Sister William Ann, Margaret Sullivan, was her youngest. Besides the three nuns and three priests, a slew of aunts, uncles, and cousins were also priests and nuns. The Sullivans frequently had their pictures in Catholic newspapers and magazines, often with Mrs. Sullivan sitting in the middle, the hub of the wheel.

Sister William Ann, who had changed into her habit, ran

down the back stairs and hurried through the parlor doors to greet her mother and brother. The other nuns had already gone into the parlow to say hello to the Sullivans. Mrs. Sullivan noticed the large Band-Aid on her daughter's chin.

"Margaret, what in the world happened to you? Look at your chin!"

"Just a little scratch, Mom. Not to bother."

The big nun, Max, looked down at little Mrs. Sullivan. "Your daughter almost tore a hole in the wall. She landed on the milk bottles, full force. You ought to see her legs."

"Let me see your legs, Margaret. You never know when an infection will set in. You have school tomorrow." She turned to the young priest with her. "James, go into the other room. I want to see Margaret's legs."

Big Max stood, arms on her hips, smiling at Sister William Ann. "Willie, do what your mother says. We don't want you limping over to school tomorrow."

Sister William Ann unfastened her black stockings, propping her leg up on the ottoman. Mrs. Sullivan knelt down, inspecting her daughter's wounds. She lifted the Band-Aids off to see if the wounds had been cleaned properly. Mrs. Sullivan looked up at Sister Maximillian. "They look all right to me, Sister. Did you dress these wounds?" Max nodded.

Mrs. Sullivan turned to her daughter. "Margaret, you are just going to have to learn to slow down. You know, dear, you are a nun now. What would the people think if they saw you falling all over the place? Do try to be a lady, now, won't you, sweetheart?

Father Jim Sullivan came back into the room. "Come on, Margie, pull up your pants. Let's get the show on the road. I've got to be back by 7:30 tonight. Grab your purse, Ma."

The Sullivans headed down the front steps, Sister William Ann holding Father Jim's hand, both singing,

> When I was young, I had no sense;
> I bought a fiddle for eighteen pence.
> The only tune that I could play
> Was "Over the Hills and Very Far Away."

So early in the morning
So early in the morning
So early in the morning
Before the break of day.

Mrs. Sullivan smiled to herself as Father Jim pushed the front seat forward for Sister William Ann to get in the back, helped his mother into the front seat, and closed the door firmly. They headed off to Elgin to spend the last holiday of the summer with Monsignor Sullivan, their uncle. The rest of the family was on their way, from the north and from the west sides of the city. By 2:30, they all would be there. The rest of the nuns returned to their ham on rye.

After lunch, the nuns piled into the black station wagon and drove out to the Thorntons' for the last swim of the summer. Sister Helen Francis did not join them, but remained home to finish some work with the pastor, Monsignor Ryan.

It was 5:00 before they got back to the convent. Monsignor Ryan and Sister Helen Francis were sitting in the community room, enjoying the air conditioning. He asked the nuns if they were thirsty on this hot, dry Labor Day afternoon. Some of the nuns giggled; Sister Jean Martin rolled her eyes; Aggie blushed. Sister Kevin Mary couldn't understand these strange responses to a simple question.

Sister Julia Mary headed for the kitchen and began filling glasses with ice. She was a plump nun, not yet thirty, with a round, soft face that came to a point at her chin, like a heart. Her large hazel eyes were streaked with melancholy and filled easily with tears when she spoke.

There was a set of tall, thin tumblers, with little yellow roses painted on them. There were twelve squatty old-fashioned glasses, each with yellow roses. Monsignor Ryan had brought over two quarts of Seagram's Seven Crown Whiskey, a bottle of Canadian Club, a frosted bottle of Gordon's Very Dry Gin, and a bottle of Smirnoff's Vodka. There were little dishes of lemon and lime wedges, lemon twists, green olives, little white onions, cherries.

In the sink sat a large plastic bag with clear ice cubes. To the left of the sink were Monsignor Ryan's mixers: Coke, 7-Up, club soda, tonic water, Tom Collins mix, and a pitcher of water.

Sister Julia Mary knew each one's favorite and told Monsignor Ryan what was called for as she handed him each glass. Freddie motioned to Sister Kevin Mary to help her serve the drinks.

Monsignor Ryan looked up at Sister Kevin Mary standing at the kitchen door. "What'll you have, Kevvie?"

"Just a Coke, Monsignor, thank you."

"What? And your name is Barrett and you drink Coke?"

Sister Mark Stephen was drinking a Coke. He didn't seem to mind that. What was wrong about wanting a Coke?

"I'd really just like a Coke, Monsignor," said Sister Kevin Mary, looking to Sister Julia Mary for some help.

Sister Julia Mary whispered to Monsignor Ryan, "Just give her a 7 and 7."

"That's right, Jules. A 7 and 7 for the new nun."

Monsignor Ryan poured 7-Up into the glass, topping it off generously with Seagram's Seven Crown. He took a thin black swizzle stick, stirred the drink quickly, and handed the cold glass to Sister Kevin Mary, the ice cubes still spinning.

"May God reward you, Monsignor," said Sister Kevin Mary, feeling like an absolute ass. She avoided Sister Julia Mary's eyes, turned, and made her way into the community room.

Sister Helen Francis, the Superior, looked up from her Tom Collins as Sister Kevin Mary came into the room. "What's the baby drinking today?" Sister Kevin Mary looked behind her to see to whom the Superior was speaking.

Sister Mark Stephen stated flatly, "She's talking about you, Kevin. Didn't you know? You're the baby this year."

The baby? I don't believe this. This just can't be real. She actually called me a baby in front of all these nuns. I am nineteen, going on twenty. I'm the oldest of nine kids. I was never a baby. Dear God, they never told us about this.

"I'm drinking 7 and 7, Sister." She sat down with a thud next to Max. The amber drink was sweet and bubbly. She sipped it at first, then took three big gulps and finished it off.

"Baby," God, that's just awful. What if my mother hears about that? I still can't believe it.

Monsignor Ryan and Sister Julia Mary joined the others in the community room. He turned toward Sister Kevin Mary and, noticing her empty glass, shouted, "Barrett here tried to make us think she was a Coke drinker. Look at *her* glass!" The nuns all laughed heartily at Sister Kevin Mary and her empty glass. He turned to Sister Julia Mary. "Jules, get her another one before you sit down. "Thank God they didn't send us another party pooper this year."

Max turned ceremoniously to acknowledge Sister Mark Stephen's social position. Sister Mark Stephen stared at the Van Gogh reprint, picked up her Coke, and drank deeply.

Clarabelle, responding poorly to friction of any sort, spilled her 7 and 7 on the tile floor. As she started to grab for it, her foot hit the bowl of peanuts, dumping them into the sticky drink.

Monsignor yelled into the kitchen, "And fix another one for Clarabelle."

Freddie got up quickly and came back with a damp cloth. Clarabelle tried to help, saying, "I'm so sorry, Sister. I'm so sorry, Sister. I'm so sorry." Sister Helen Francis looked away.

Sister Julia Mary came in with two fresh 7 and 7s. She handed one to Sister Kevin Mary and the other to the nun sitting next to Clarabelle, so Clarabelle wouldn't spill it. Clarabelle muttered, "May God reward you, Sister," to Sister Julia Mary and attempted to smile apologetically at her Superior. Sister Helen Francis was looking at Monsignor Ryan and didn't notice.

Monsignor Ryan moved to the piano, motioned to Sister Mark Stephen to accompany him, and began to sing:

> They asked me how I knew
> My true love was true.
> I of course replied,
> Something here inside,
> Cannot be denied.
> They said someday you'll find,

All who love are blind,
When your heart's on fire,
You must realize
Smoke gets in your eyes.

So I chaffed them and I gaily laughed
To think they could doubt my love.
Yet today, my love has flown away,
I am without my love.

Now laughing friends deride,
Tears I cannot hide,
So I smile and say,
"When a lovely flame dies,
Smoke gets in your eyes."

Sister Helen Francis cradled her Tom Collins in her hands, looking intently at Monsignor Ryan. Aggie's face was deep purple, either from embarrassment or from her 7 and 7. She began to finger her rosary. Sister Kevin Mary began her second drink and resolved to drink it slowly. She listened intently to the words of the song, wondering why a priest would want to sing a song like that. She stared at his red face, imagining smoke curling up from his heart and into his eyes. His entire face was screened with smoke, as she drained the last of her 7 and 7. He sang again, "When a lovely flame dies, smoke gets in your eyes."

Sister Julia Mary and Freddie had begun to refill the glasses. When they returned to the community room, Monsignor Ryan lifted Sister Kevin Mary's drink off the tray and, bowing deeply, handed her another drink. She thought that this one tasted stronger, but it really didn't matter. She was doing what she was told. Monsignor wanted her to drink 7 and 7. The Superior calls me a baby. Maybe this is my test so she won't do that to me anymore. 7 and 7. 7-Up. Seven sacraments. Seven days of the week. Seven continents. Snow White and the Seven Sacraments. Dopey, Sneezy, Grumpy, Baptism, Confirmation, Poverty, Chastity, Extreme Unction, Marriage, Hold Orders,

Sleepy. Dear God, everyone looks like rubber. The lamp is bending. Monsignor Ryan's head is on fire. Sister Kevin Mary turned to Max. "Ask Sister if the baby can leave. I'm going to throw up, Max."

Max and Freddie took Sister Kevin Mary up to her room. Sister Mark Stephen glared at Monsignor Ryan, at Sister Julia Mary, at the Superior. She put down her Coke with a bang, excused herself, and went upstairs to see how Sister Kevin Mary was doing. She was already asleep.

4.

The moon was still bright in the sky when Sister Mark Stephen rang the small brass rising bell—5:10 A.M. September 6, 1958. Sister Kevin Mary blessed herself, rose immediately, and began to dress. Pulling on the long black stockings gave her the same revulsion she always felt. Her legs disappearing into nothingness; she was disintegrating from the chin downward. She had hoped that she would have outgrown this horrible feeling by the time she made her First Profession. She tied her black shoes with determination and walked quickly down to chapel.

It was still dark outside; the thin amber chapel lights served as a gentle transition from the world of sleep into the real world. Sister Kevin Mary made the venia, stood, moved into her place next to Sister Mark Stephen. The first real day. This was going to be it. They were finally acting like nuns now. It felt so much better. She could hear one of the nuns out in the kitchen filling the coffee pot.

"In the name of the Father, and of the Son, and of the Holy Ghost. Amen," began Sister Helen Francis. The Hebdomadarian, the one who led the prayers for the week, started the morning prayers, "O my God, I place myself in Thy divine presence." The rest of the nuns joined in: "O my God, I believe that Thou art here present; I adore Thee, and I love Thee with all my heart. . . ." They said the Our Father, Hail Mary, Apostle's Creed, The Confiteor, The Guardian Angel prayer, and completed with a long prayer to the Sacred Heart of Jesus.

The sisters reached for their Office Books in the small rack suspended from the pews in front of each of them. The Hebdomadarian opened the chanting of the morning Office: *Prime,* the first hour; *Tierce,* the third hour; *Sext,* the sixth hour, *None,* the ninth hour. The ancient words and customs and habits were comforting, thought Sister Kevin Mary as she made a medium inclination toward the center aisle at the Minor Doxology:

> Gloria patri, et filio, et Spiritui sancto.
> Sicut erat in principio, et nunc, et semper,
>   et in saecula saeculorum. Amen. Alleluia.

How she loved the Latin, its precision, its predictability, its rules and cadences, its esoteric grammar and rhetoric, its majesty, universality. Juvenal, Plautus and Terence, Suetonius, Augustine. The timelessness of the Church, the timelessness of the Latin language: to be so young, yet to be an intrinsic part of Antiquity. It was good and right.

> Levavi oculos meos in montes
>   unde veniet auxilium mihi.
> Auxilium meum a Domino
>   qui fecit caelum et terram.

I have lifted my eyes to the mountain, whence help shall come to me. My help is from the Lord, who made heaven and earth. I look to you, Dear Lord, to help me with my first day of teaching. You indeed made heaven and earth, You will have no difficulty in assisting me as I lead the souls of Your children to You. I have no help but Your divine grace.

After the Office, the nuns chanted the *Angelus,* then knelt for the prayer at the beginning of meditation. They sat during the half-hour meditation, and the Hebdomadarian read one of the three points of the assigned meditation every ten minutes: 6:00, 6:10, 6:20. At the end of meditation, Father O'Mahoney, the tall, sandy-haired young priest, came out on the altar and began Mass. He was finished in twenty-five minutes. Two nuns left the chapel immediately after Mass and began getting the breakfast on the table.

Sister Helen Francis tapped her ring three times against the pew. The nuns rose in silence and proceeded to the refectory, senior sisters first, immediately behind Sister Helen Francis. The Hebdomadarian blessed the food in Latin, and the reader, sitting next to the buffet, began a review of the morning meditation.

She then pulled out the *Lives of the Saints and Blessed of the Order,* as the nuns began to butter their toast and crack their soft-boiled eggs in silence. She read:

Blessed Bertrand of Garrigua (Confessor):

Born at Garrigua, France, he was one of the first disciples of Our Holy Founder. He had the gift of tears and always prayed for the souls in Purgatory and for poor sinners. About 1230, he died in the odor of sanctity at LeBouchet. In 1881, Leo XIII confirmed his cult.

Practice: Pray earnestly for the souls in Purgatory.

Prayer: O God who to our Holy Patriarch thou didst join Blessed Bertrand, Thy Confessor, as a companion and illustrious imitator, grant us by his pious intervention so to follow his footsteps as to attain to his reward. Through Christ Our Lord.   Amen.

The nun who was serving returned from the kitchen with a fresh pot of coffee as the reader began to read *Keys to the Third Floor.* Someone relieved the reader so she could eat her breakfast. Sister Kevin Mary grabbed a third piece of toast before it went back to the kitchen and lavishly spread it with Smucker's raspberry jam. She lifted her cup for more coffee. She'd need plenty of energy for her first day in the vineyard.

After dishes, she went back to their room to make her bed and get ready for school. She sat down at the desk and reviewed the plans she and Willie had made yesterday. There was a sharp knock on her open door. Max stood, black briefcase in hand. "Good luck, kid. You'll knock 'em dead."

"May God reward you, Sister," said Sister Kevin Mary, ineptly.

"Take it easy. I remember my first day of teaching. It won't be so bad. See ya' at lunch, kid."

"Thanks, Sister." Sister Kevin Mary smiled at Max. She then cleaned her teeth and left for her classroom. It was 7:50; the first bus was due in at 8:10.

Sister Kevin Mary unlocked her classroom door. As she was turning the key, Aggie walked up to her and squeezed her arm, whispering, "God bless."

Sister Kevin Mary smiled shyly at the elderly sister. "May God reward you, Sister." She watched Aggie move unsteadily down the long hall. She went into her classroom, opened the windows, straightened two of the front seats, checked for chalk and erasers, and began studying the class list: Ambruster, Mary; Armstrong, Michael; Ashcroft, Linda. Freddie ran into the classroom, threw her right arm around Sister Kevin Mary's shoulders, saying nothing, and gave her a squeeze. Sister Kevin Mary looked up. "Thanks, Freddie, thanks." Freddie gave her another squeeze and ran out to her own classroom across the hall.

She returned to the list: Backman, Paul; Bafalis, Karen; Baggett, Mathew; Bailey, James. She heard Willie approaching. ". . . I bought a fiddle for eighteen pence, the only tune that I could play . . . All ready, Kevvie? Do you know what you're doing?"

"I'm all set, Willie. Thanks so much."

"Let me know if you get in a jam. And Sister Helen Francis is just wonderful. Don't hesitate to ask anyone for help. You'll be just great, Kevvie. Don't worry."

"I'm scared, Willie. Thanks again."

Willie turned on her heels, wrapping her rosary beads around her fist. "So early in the morning, so early in the morning . . ."

Sister Kevin Mary stood, looking out the window onto the playground. Monsignor Ryan, Sister Helen Francis, and Father O'Mahoney were directing the children and their parents. A little boy clung to his mother's skirt. She shifted the baby in her arms, bent over, kissed him, and gently directed him into his classroom. As he walked up the steps, she took out a piece of Kleenex and wiped her eyes. She took the baby's arm, and they waved at her son going into school.

Carmody, Peter; Clark, Robert; Crangle, Mark; Cummings, Mary Pat. A loud scream pierced the hall. "I won't go in there! I won't go in there! I want to go home this minute!" Sister Kevin Mary looked up to see a short, balding father pleading with his son to go into the classroom. "Tony, the Sister is waiting for you. You'll have lots of fun, Tony. Please go in there, Tony."

"Take me home, Daddy! I want to go home! I have to see Mama."

Tony's father raised his eyebrows in helplessness at the strength of will of his six-year-old son. "Sister, ah, Sister, this is Tony Mariani. Sister, can you get him in there? He's got to go to school, Sister. Tony, do what the good Sister says, Tony."

Sister Kevin Mary took Tony's hand, telling him that she had a very special seat all picked out for him. She quickly scanned the desks, looking for the name cards that began with the Ms: Murray, Murphy, Marmet, Mariani.

"Tony, this is your special place. You'll be able to see everything and to make new friends."Tony refused to sit, but stood, lower lip hanging out. He quickly turned to locate his father. Mr. Mariani had disappeared. Tony let out a sharp wail, "I want to go home; I want my Daddy. I gotta get outta here."

Sister Kevin Mary bent over, looked Tony Mariani straight in the eyes, and said coldly, "Sit down, Tony." Tony sat down quietly.

The classroom quickly filled with first-graders. Sister Kevin Mary had to ask some of the mothers to kindly leave the room. One gave her a ferocious look as if she were stealing her child.

Sister Kevin Mary squeezed her rosary and closed the door firmly. She returned to her desk and sat down. God, what do I do now? She looked down at the class list. She had read it fifty times. I got to get up and teach. I got to get up and teach. The fifty-six children were silent. They were staring at her. She stared back at them. Her throat felt parched. She stood, scraping her chair, banging it against the chalkboard. Her face reddened. The children continued to stare. Some looked frightened.

A mother with red frizzy hair was trying to look in the windows. Monsignor Ryan headed in the mother's direction, so Sister Kevin Mary was not going to have to pull the shades in her face. She couldn't talk. Her mouth was dry. "Hot pipes" her brother Marty would call it. She thought she'd dash out to the hall for a gulp of water before she started; as she turned, her rosary beads caught on one of the knobs of a desk drawer, pulling the drawer out of the desk. It landed upside down on the floor. Pins, chalk, rulers, crayons, Band-Aids rolled all over the floor. The children stared. A little girl near the back was close to tears. So was Sister Kevin Mary.

She put the pieces of her rosary on her desk, picked up the drawer, and walked decidedly out to the hall. The children didn't move. The little girl was in tears, sobbing audibly. A large blond boy in front of her told her to shut up—he couldn't hear what the nun was saying. The nun was saying nothing. She returned to the classroom, wiping the water from her lips. She cleared her throat, stared at her class, and walked back to her desk to find out what she was to do.

> 8:30-9:00   Introduce teacher—write "Sister Kevin Mary" on board. Call off kids' names. See who didn't show up. Send list to office.

It was 8:45 already. The only thing she had done in fifteen minutes was to get a drink of water. She'd better get going. Her knees were weak, and her throat had dried up on her again. She moved to the center of the classroom. The kids were still staring at her. The blond boy shoved his elbow on the little girl's desk again as she continued to sniffle. "Just plain shut up, will you? I'm going to tell on you. I mean it, just shut up!" Sister Kevin Mary stared at him. He smiled back, proudly.

"I'm your teacher this year. This is my name." She walked to the chalkboard, picked up a stick of yellow chalk, and wrote "Sister Kevin Mary" in script on the green blackboard. The class continued to stare.

A little boy jumped up from the fourth row, holding himself. "I gotta go pee-pee. I gotta go pee-pee." She walked back quickly, opened the door to the little bathroom at the rear of the classroom, and motioned for him to go in. As she closed the door, four little boys raced to the back, hoping to be next into the sanctuary of the bathroom. Sister Kevin Mary told them to get back to their seats. The big blond boy had remained in his seat. He smiled at her proudly.

It was 9:00, time for the talk about Catholic schools. She looked soberly at her class, imitating the way Sister Duns Scotus would address a room full of novices, explaining to them the ramification of their vows. "This is St. Paul School. It is a Catholic school. Not a public school. Things are different here. You are lucky to go to a Catholic school. To St. Paul's. Does everyone understand?" The class nodded. The little girl had her head down on her desk. Just as well.

That didn't take too long. "9:30-10:00. Take kids outside. Show them the bathroom. . . ." It was only 9:05. That would have to wait. She'd go ahead to "Numbers, 10:00-10:30."

"Everyone look at the side. Count the numbers inside the large green circles. Now, everyone, 1, 2, 3, 4, 5, 6, 7, 8, 9, 10. Good. Does everyone understand? Good. OK, now, OK, here we go." She remembered that the alphabet was next so she didn't have to check it out on her desk.

It was only 9:08. She was just faster than Willie. She had been pretty fast in everything she ever did. She'd just be a fast teacher. "OK, now, OK. Look up at the front. See the letters? OK, now, we'll just say the alphabet, OK? Everybody see where I am? OK, here we go, A, B, C, D . . . X, Y, Z. Good, good. OK, now, see, you know your alphabet. OK, OK, now, I'll just see what's next. Just sit right there, OK, now?"

She walked back to her desk. God, it was supposed to be 11:00. She had finished all that stuff in less than fifteen minutes. What was all the fuss about? She sat down at the desk. The children continued to stare. She stared back. The little boy jumped up again and ran for the bathroom. The big blond boy looked disgusted. My God, I've got these kids for two more hours. What am I going to do?

She walked over to the window, breathing deeply of the hot September air. She wanted to go home and see her mother. The children were looking at her. A few began to giggle. Another child was beginning to cry. The blond boy stood and walked confidently to the door to get some water. Sister Kevin Mary turned on her heels, stared him in the eyes, and told him to sit down. The little girl behind him smiled sheepishly. He told her to shut up as he passed her desk.

Sister Kevin Mary faced the class again. It was 9:17. They hadn't even been there for an hour. She put on her best Sister Duns Scotus expression. "OK, now. Just sit. Sit right in your places. OK, and I'll be right back. No one is to move, ya' hear? OK, now, I'll be right back."

She tore out of the room, down the hall, and knocked on Sister William Ann's door. She motioned for Sister Kevin Mary to wait a moment at the open door. She heard Willie talking to her class: "Boys and girls, I am a Sister. My name is Sister William Ann. Can you say that?" The class responded in unison, "Sisssterrrr Willlllliammm Annn."

That's right, boys and girls. Would anyone like to say my name alone?" As she walked to Sister Kevin Mary, she pointed to various children who stood and carefully said, "Sister William Ann."

"What's the matter, Kevvie?"

"I'm done."

"You can't be. It's not even 9:30."

"I'm done, Willie. I did everything you said. What'll I do now?"

Sister William Ann avoided Sister Kevin Mary's eyes. She turned to her class. "Boys and girls, this has been a long morning. Put your heads down on your desk, and Sister will be right back. I don't want to hear even a tiny little peep out of you. Sister will be right back."

Sister William Ann raced down the hall, walked to the back of Sister Kevin Mary's classroom, opened a locker, took out a stack of manila paper, placed some on the first desk in each row, telling the first child to go to the end of the row and to give each student one piece of paper. She then told them to take out the crayons in their desks and to draw a picture of their families for Sister Kevin Mary. She then told Sister Kevin Mary to come to get her when that was finished.

Within seconds, bedlam broke out. Three little boys charged for the bathroom. Seven others were out of their seats.

"I broke my yellow."

"What way should the paper go? Mine is crooked."

"Do we do our mother or father first?"

"Do I do my sister? She died."

"Sometimes my grandmother comes to live with us and sometimes she doesn't. Should I put her in?"

"My daddy moved out this summer. Is he still part of our family?"

"I can't draw noses."

Sister Kevin Mary stared at the boys and girls. They were no longer looking at her. In a loud, controlled voice, the way Sister Duns Scotus used to do when she was agitated, Sister Kevin Mary said, "Just plain do it. Just draw them and don't ask any more questions. OK, now, just do it. Does everyone understand? Just do it. Do it, OK, now?"

Sister William Ann returned three more times that morning to give the first-graders in Room 103 various assignments. Sister Kevin Mary had completely lost face. She was embarrassed in front of the kids, in front of the other nun, in front of herself.

The children were in line to be dismissed at 11:25. The buses had been waiting for fifteen minutes. Parents were trying to look through the windows at their children. The class was straining to find their parents. The big blond boy, whose name was Peter, pushed, sending four little boys to the floor. He looked up innocently, then turned quickly to the boy behind him, trying to place the blame on him. God, she had had it. She

took them out to the playground. The kids ran for their parents
or older brothers and sisters. Sister Kevin Mary went back to
her classroom, closing the door behind her. Then she wouldn't
have to see anybody. Or anything.

She finally packed up her papers and headed over to the
convent. The rest of the nuns had gone home for lunch. She
walked heavily up the back steps. The nuns were all sitting
around the refectory table. She heard Willie telling a funny
story: "And I looked up, it was only twenty after 9:00, and
there was Kevin, all finished for the day. "I'm done, Willie. I
did everything you said. What'll I do now?" The nuns laughed
heartily.

Sister Kevin Mary's throat ached. Her head hurt. Her feet
hurt. Her soul hurt. She closed the door of the chapel and knelt
down at her place. The hot tears rolled down her cheeks. She
buried her face in her hands and began sobbing loudly. She
couldn't stop. She couldn't breathe. She couldn't teach. She
couldn't stop crying.

Someone knelt beside her. She felt a thin arm around her
shoulders that were shaking with each sob. It was Aggie. She
whispered, "Now, Sister, you wouldn't want to be gettin' a big
head the first day in the classroom, would ye now? The Lord
lets us be humbled, for it's His gift to those He loves. You're
cocky enough, don't ya' know, little Kevin? You go in and eat
now, and someday you'll be a good teacher, and, maybe, you'll
even be a good nun. God bless, dear. Go and eat, and leave the
praying to me. Go on with ye."

5.

Monsignor Ryan motioned for Sister Kevin Mary. Her arms were full of papers, teaching manuals, and an assortment of apples, early fall flowers, and other gifts from the children. The abstraction of teaching was becoming a cloudless reality, It was plain hard work. Those manuals, plans, papers to correct, conversations with parents—nothing the least bit abstract.

She hurried over to the small group of nuns standing by the sacristy door. Monsignor Ryan began singing loudly, "Here she comes, Miss America." Sister Kevin Mary felt anything but Miss America. She waved at Monsignor to let him know she was coming as fast as she could. A big red delicious apple fell from her arms and began to roll down the drive toward the gym. She let it go, poverty or no poverty. She'd drop everything, lose her veil, and probably trip if she attempted to pick it up.

"Sister Kevin Mary, I'd like you to meet Father Doyle. Dan was just ordained a few weeks ago. The Cardinal thought I could break him in. Dan, Sister Kevin Mary."

"How do you do, Father," said Sister Kevin Mary.

"Hi, Sister."

They both began to giggle like teenagers. The heat, the books, nuns and priests and priests and nuns. Kids and papers and now this. Sister Kevin Mary felt herself go weak in the knees. She knew she was blushing furiously and couldn't control it. And she couldn't stop giggling. She dug her nails into the palms of her hands, with difficulty, since her arms were full. And she laughed harder and harder. The young priest was laughing harder. Tears rolled down his face as he jammed his fists into his black pants pockets, stiffened his shoulders, trying to gain his composure. Monsignor Ryan looked down on his curly black hair, scowling at the bizarre behavior of this newly ordained priest. Father Doyle continued to giggle, uttering, "Dear Jesus, dear Jesus," between gasps of air.

Sister Mark walked up to Sister Kevin Mary and reached for some of her things. "She's had a long day. I've got to get her home. Bye, Monsignor. Nice to meet you, Father."

Father Doyle had taken out a handkerchief and was wiping his forehead and upper lip. He waved to the two nuns as they headed for the back door of the convent. Sister Kevin Mary was still giggling.

Sister Mark put Sister Kevin Mary's things down on the refectory table. Sister Kevin Mary went into chapel to try to compose herself. In a few minutes, she came into the kitchen, still grinning.

"What in the world happened to you two out there?"

"I just never thought that would happen! I felt like I was going to faint."

"You sure made a fool out of yourself, Kevin."

"I know it, Mark. I totally came unglued. It was that priest." What's the matter with him?"

"There's nothing the matter with him. That's the trouble. . . ."

6.

The following day was the annual Archdiocesan Elementary and Secondary Teachers' Institute held at the Amphitheatre. Some of the Superiors were having lunch at the Stockyard Inn. Each of the nuns was given $2 for lunch: hot dog stands were situated throughout the Amphitheatre. The keynote address was being delivered by Monsignor McManus, Superintendent of Schools. Various workshops, dealing with such topics as the *Development of Faith in the Primary Grades*; *Simplified Long Division for Fourth Graders*; *The Role of the Lay Teacher in the Upper Grades,* were on the agenda. Sister Kevin Mary had planned to attend the ones directed at reading readiness techniques, seatwork ideas, and faith development. She, Sister William Ann, and Sister Frederick Ellen were going to attend together since they all taught first grade.

As the black Chevy wagon pulled in front of the Amphitheatre and the nuns got out, Sister Marie Marcel, the driver, turned to Sister Kevin Mary and told her to stay in the car with her. She had to park and would have to walk back alone. Sister Kevin Mary moved over toward the passenger door, for she had been squeezed in next to her by the other nun in the front seat. Sister Marie Marcel stepped on the gas, passing group after group of nuns, in various habits and colors. She turned out the drive, passed first the large parking area, then the smaller one, finally the area beyond the Amphitheatre reserved for overflow and kept going.

She drove east to South State Street, turned north and headed for the Loop. Neither spoke. Sister Kevin Mary pretended to be absorbed in the sights. Sister Marie Marcel turned on the radio. Sister Kevin Mary cleared her throat. Where are we going? Monsignor McManus will begin his talk. We're not going to the convention. It's twenty minutes to ten. The nuns will be looking for me. God, she scares me.

"Nice day, huh?"

"Yes, Sister."

"You been in the Loop before?"

"A long time ago, when I was twelve."

Sister Marie Marcel turned into a small parking lot, handed the keys to the attendant, told him that they'd be back in about three hours. Sister Kevin Mary straightened her cloak and grabbed her rosary beads hanging from her belt. They headed down a side street, turned onto the main street marked Wabash Avenue, and walked together in silence. Sister Marie Marcel turned into a restaurant, Johnny's Steak House. The hot September air, the smells of the dirty street, and charcoal steaks made Sister Kevin Mary lightheaded.

She remembered with clarity Sister Duns Scotus speaking to a room full of novices: "Sisters, we do not eat in restaurants; that is for the people of the world. We do not eat in public; we are not a part of the public. We do not eat in front of our families; we have left our families. When you eat, you eat in a convent with your Sisters. Is that absolutely clear, Novices?"

When her Aunt Mamie brought to the Novitiate seven dozen of her buttery Christmas cookies, Sister Kevin Mary did not take one. Aunt Mamie was deeply hurt, but Sister Kevin Mary stuck to her principles and tried to make her understand that now everything she had belonged not to her, but to the community. "What's *mine* is *ours*, Aunt Mamie." Aunt Mamie tried to understand; she couldn't, but she respected her grandniece's respect for the rules.

The air in Johnny's Steak House was cool but thick. Over the dark mahogany bar was a fluorescent clock: 11:14. Monsignor McManus's talk was nearing the end. The nuns would be breaking up to go to the individual conferences. A plump woman in a green satin dress looked up with surprise at Sister Marie Marcel. "Oh, Sister, it's so good to see you back. Same place?"

As the nuns followed the woman in the green satin dress, Sister Kevin Mary turned her head quickly to see if Sister Duns Scotus was in Johnny's Steak House. The woman ushered them to a semicircular booth with a round table covered with a white linen cloth. A single red rose matched the red velvet of the seating. Sister Kevin Mary tried to slide in; her black cloak caught the edge of the cloth and, as she moved in, the cloth moved with her. The fresh rose toppled into the little silver sugar bowl; knives, forks, and spoons landed on the floor and back into the booth. She looked up quickly to see if Sister Duns Scotus was there. God was punishing her for this.

The plump woman in the green dress began to laugh with Sister Marie Marcel. "She just got out, Millie. Thought I'd show her around. She's really the All-American girl, Millie. Not used to Johnny's this early." Millie laughed hoarsely as she motioned to an old black man to clean up the mess. Oh, Dear God, all these people waiting on me. I am the handmaid of the Lord, the servant of His people. I ought to be doing the cleaning and waiting. Dear God, please forgive me. Please get me out of here.

"Oh, Millie. I forgot to introduce you. This is Kevvie. Sister Kevin Mary. She's from Grosse Point. Kev, this is Millie O'Malley. Millie takes good care of us."

"Right, Sister. How do you do, Sister Kevin Mary. Welcome to Chicago and a very special welcome to Johnny's. What can I get you?"

"Oh, just a Coke, Millie. How do you do, I mean."

"Millie, get her a 7 and 7. She can really polish 'em off. I'll have my regular. Thanks, Millie."

Millie shouted to the man behind the bar, "George, a 7 and 7 and a very dry Tanqueray martini. Three olives. Right, Sister?"

Sister Marie Marcel opened her cloak, sat back contentedly, waiting for her very dry martini. "Just relax, kid. Take it easy. You've been going at it pretty strong lately. Just relax."

"Yes, Sister. It's cool in here."

They sat in silence until Millie brought the drinks. Sister Marie Marcel raised her glass. "To Monsignor McManus." Sister Kevin Mary raised her glass, whispering, "To Monsignor McManus." She took a little sip and put the glass down. Real nice and slow, little baby sips. Baby, oh God. Baby sips for the baby. The baby eats at Johnny's Steak House, folks. Don't you know, this is why I entered the convent. To be a baby and to eat at Johnny's.

"How do you like it at St. Paul's, Kev? It's one of the best places to be sent. Monsignor is real good to the Motherhouse. Did Mother Jeremiah know you very well?"

"I cleaned her room, Sister."

"That explains it. Bet she liked you. She doesn't send any fools to Monsignor Ryan."

"I didn't see her very much. I had to get in and out when she wasn't there. I really don't know her."

"She knows you. That's all that matters, kid."

Sister Kevin Mary took a long sip of her 7 and 7, rechecking the door to see if Sister Duns Scotus had slipped in. Did Sister Marie Marcel have permission for them to be there? Is she like my Superior, because she is one of the older nuns? Does she think I'm a pushover and won't tell? A jellyfish that just goes along? Did Sister Helen Francis tell her to take me here to loosen me up? Do the rest of the nuns know about us? If I ask her if she has permission, she might get mad. Dear God, I just want to get out of here. Is this God's Holy Will for me? Am I where I'm supposed to be? Am I carrying His Holy Word by my presence here? She took another long drink. Am I a scandal to the order? To the Church? What's the right thing?

Sister Marie Marcel motioned to Millie. She lifted her right index finger, making a double circle in the air. Millie returned to the bar. Johnny's was beginning to fill up. A middle-aged couple came in, holding hands. Sister Kevin Mary tried not to watch them holding hands. She thought of Father Doyle. Groups of businessmen were seated, nudging each other as they observed the two nuns in the round booth. Sister Kevin Mary stared at her empty 7 and 7 glass. Millie returned with more drinks and asked Sister Marie Marcel if they were ready to order. Order, the Holy Order. I promise obedience to the rule and constitutions of our Holy Order. Ready to order, Sister?

"Yes, Millie. I'll have the filet, medium rare. Baked potato with sour cream and chives. And the Caesar salad for both."

Millie turned to Sister Kevin Mary. "What would you like today, Sister?"

"I'll have a chicken salad sandwich, please, Millie."

"Give her what I ordered, Millie. That OK, kid?" smiled Sister Marie Marcel.

"Yes, Sister. Thank you, Millie."

Sister Kevin Mary took a deep breath and looked Sister Marie Marcel right in the eyes. She had been consciously avoiding her since she got to St. Paul's. She was always smirking, laughing derisively, cynical. She had money, her own transistor radio. She wore black loafers, no undershirt. You could always see her elbows and even her armpits when she raised her arms.

When the rest of the nuns went into town, two by two, Sister Marie Marcel was always up there by herself—in the bakery, in the radio shop, in the bookstore or card shop, buying something. The Rule said the nuns were to go out together. Sister Marie Marcel ignored the fine points of that Rule.

She always had money. She spoke to the Superior almost disrespectfully. Not exactly disrespectfully, but kind of intimately. She kidded Sister Helen Francis all the time. She let her know that she didn't take her seriously. They had entered together, so they had known each other for at least ten or twelve years. And whenever someone said something funny at the table, she always gave that scornful, cynical smirk. The left side of her lip curled up; her left nostril curled up, like she was always smelling something bad. She called Monsignor Ryan "Big Balls." A strange name for a priest. Why would she call him "Big Balls"? Maybe because he was always playing golf? Big Balls? She ought to call him "Little Balls."

A young Spanish waiter with a thin, dark moustache wheeled a cart up to their table. He looked lewdly at Sister Kevin Mary. They were about the same age. She looked down. He began to mix the salad with great style. With a long, thin knife, he deftly sliced and chopped vegetables, throwing them into the big plastic salad bowl. They would never be able to eat all that crap. Cheeses, anchovies, green peppers. He took two long wooden spoons, tossing the greens feverishly. When he was finished, he cracked a raw egg and threw that in.

Sister Kevin Mary felt nauseated. She took a deep breath, rechecked the door to see if Sister Duns Scotus was standing there with Mother Jeremiah, and took another gulp of her drink. He threw the salad into two big wooden salad bowls, winking at Sister Marie Marcel. She looked up with her smirk. "Gracias, Ramon."

Turning to Sister Kevin Mary, she said, "Garbage up, kid. It's the best Caesar salad in the Loop. Right, Ramon?" The waiter clicked his heels and pushed his cart back into the kitchen.

Sister Marie Marcel tore into her Caesar salad. Sister Kevin Mary found a small piece of lettuce, two whole mushrooms, a few other pieces that looked harmless enough. A basket of hot rolls appeared with a little black kettle of freshly whipped butter. Sister Marie Marcel tore off a chunk of a roll, smothered it with butter, waved for another martini, and said to Sister Kevin Mary with her mouth full of food, "You ever notice my face, kid?"

Dear God, should she be polite and say that she never noticed the curled lip, the upturned nostril, the half-shut left eye? Should she be honest and simply say, yes, why certainly she had noticed? Sister Kevin Mary cleared her throat. "Pardon me, Sister?"

"My face. Have you ever noticed my face? The way it looks?"

"Yes, I have."

"I've got Bell's Palsy. It looks terrible, I know. Can't do

anything about it. I've been getting terrible headaches lately."

I didn't know that, Sister.''

"Yeah, I got it a long time ago at Saint Hilary's when I slept in front of a fan. The next morning I woke up and my eye was closed like this. Then my nose and mouth. They can't seem to do anything about it. Had surgery last summer. They took out a chunk of my skull. Didn't do a damn bit of good. Gotta go back to the doctor's this afternoon. Appointment's for 1:00. We'll make it back on time to pick them up. You having a good time, Kevvie?''

"Great time, Sister." Dear God, how I've misjudged this nun. She really isn't sneering. Dear God, forgive me.

"Sometimes I frighten people, the way I look. They just have to get used to me. It's these damn headaches. Sometimes I have to leave school. The kids are pretty good. Kids understand, if you give 'em half a chance. They know when I've got a headache. They understand."

"I didn't know what was the matter with you, Sister. I'm sorry."

"Don't be. Just enjoy your steak. Want anything? And call me 'Marce.' ''

The two nuns finished their lunch, brushed the crumbs from their laps, and went over to pay Millie. She told them that the two gentlemen in the corner had picked up the tab. Sister Marie Marcel motioned for Sister Kevin Mary to follow her to their table. She introduced herself, thanked them, and headed out the door. They walked north on Wabash. Sister Marie Marcel turned into a textbook store, bought some books on South America for her class, and pulled out a crisp $20 bill. They walked past DePaul University. It looked Catholic, but the only Catholic colleges she had ever heard of were Notre Dame and the Jesuit colleges. Then Sister Marie Marcel went into Favor Ruhl. She didn't like the chalk on display and asked if they had any better. The manager went into the back room and came out with a narrow box of pastels with an oil base, imported from France. She took three boxes, paying for it with another new bill.

They passed Kroch's & Brentano's bookstore. Sister Marie

Marcel went in and bought three paperbacks and two magazines about racing cars. They proceeded north on Wabash and turned into the Pittsfield Building. She went into the cigar store and bought some gum. They got on the elevator at 12:55 and walked into the doctor's office at 12:59. The receptionist greeted her and ushered her into an examination room. Sister Kevin Mary started to follow her in for the Rule stated that the *Sisters shall not go to the baths—or be examined by a doctor—fewer than two or three together*; another fine point of the Rule overlooked. Sister Marie Marcel told her to sit down. She wouldn't be long.

After twenty minutes, she emerged from the examination room, made another appointment, thanked the receptionist, and the two nuns left.

"He wants to change my glasses. Gave me some new eye-drops. Also thinks if I had a muscle relaxer, I wouldn't get these damn headaches. It's something new. Called 'volium' or 'vulium.' Something like that."

"Sure hope it helps, Sister."

"Marce."

"Marce. OK, Marce, I hope you feel better."

"Thanks, kid."

7.

A beautiful October morning. Friday, October 4, the Feast of St. Francis of Assisi, the gentle saint. Sister Kevin Mary's morning meditation focused on the simple prayer:

Lord, make me an instrument of Thy Peace.
Where there is hatred, let me sow love;
Where there is doubt, faith;
Where there is despair, hope;
Where there is darkness, light;
And where there is sadness, joy.

Divine Master, grant that I may not so much seek
   to be consoled as to console;
To be understood as to understand;
To be loved as to love.
For it is in giving that we receive;
It is in pardoning that we are pardoned;
And it is in dying that we are born to Eternal Life.

The central theme of the Novitiate had been to surrender completely so that the Grace of God could flow freely through you and into the lives of others. A channel, an instrument. Getting out of the way of the love of God, letting God do with you what He wanted. Sister Duns Scotus said to them a million times, "Don't be turning and twisting and trying to fix things up. Surrender and let the Grace of God take you over and use you as He sees fit."

She thought of herself as hallowed out of self. The handmaid, waiting on the desires of the Lord and not even mindful of her own self-will. That was the essence of religious womanhood: a passivity, a surrender, a selflessness, the supple clay to be molded by the Lord.

Her family, the Barretts, was coming in from Detroit that evening, taking the kids out of school at noon. They would be here for dinner, their first meal in a convent. How different it would be to see her family now that she was a professed Sister. As a Novice, she had always felt slightly tenuous: the habit of the order and the white veil as a public statement that she was just a beginner, still learning, new at this business of being a nun. Now she wore the black veil to signify the irrevocability of her vows. Would they notice her sense of commitment, her wholeness? Would God use her now as His channel of Grace?

She floated through the morning class, as smooth as butter, she thought. Most of the days were pretty choppy: three reading groups—flashcards, charts, and books for each group— as well as the three teacher's reading manuals. The smart kids, called the "Baby Jesus" group, had already started to read, or at least develop a basic vocabulary: come, see, go, David, Ann, up. It was sensitive to call the groups by names other than I, II, and III. This way, they would not know if they were smart or dumb, fast or slow. "Baby Jesus" group was first; "Blessed Mother" was second; "St. Joseph" was third. Good theology, too.

For lunch she had tuna casserole, two hot buttered rolls, a tossed salad with poppy seed dressing, three cups of coffee, and a nice big slice of German chocolate cake. Seemed as if she were permanently starving. It was such a relief to eat well, to be able to keep up her energy for the job of teaching. She got on the scale the night before—120 pounds, up eight pounds in less than two months. Her belt notch moved forward. She wasn't worried; the appetite would taper off as soon as she got this teaching business down pat.

After lunch, she washed her dishes and stopped in the chapel for a short visit on her way to playground duty. Sister Marie Marcel was in her place, sitting down, holding an ice pack on the back of her head. Her eyes were closed. Sister Kevin Mary asked God to help her get better. Maybe that new medicine would help her soon. It seemed to have slowed her down a bit.

The edge was off her voice and off her step. She seemed to be getting a little more mellow. Maybe the headaches were taking the starch out of her. Please God, give her some relief.

The thought flashed through Sister Kevin Mary's mind that perhaps God was punishing Sister Marie Marcel for being the way she was—all that money, her transistor ("Transistor Sister" the kids called her), talking to the Superior the way she did. Oh, God, forgive me for judging. May I not seek so much to be understood as to understand. Anyhow, help her not to suffer. Don't let her be in so much pain.

Footballs, jump ropes, races, bloody knees, bloody noses, torn pants and shirts—lunch duty. Sister Kevin Mary tossed the football to some of the boys for a few minutes, then went over to the girls so their feelings wouldn't be hurt. She turned the jump rope and they coaxed her to get in and jump. She jumped into the center and began jumping in perfect time. Within a minute, she could feel the tuna casserole, coffee, and poppy seed dressing on their way up. "That's all, girls. Sister has to go check on the boys again." She breathed deeply and tried not to think of the German chocolate cake.

"Sister, Sister, Michael has been hurt!"

"Sister, Michael's eyes look funny!"

"Michael is going to die, Sister! He hit his head!"

Sister Kevin Mary tore over to the boys' part of the playground. Michael Spivak, a pasty-looking little boy, was lying on his back, holding his head. "Dear God, not Michael. Please,

Dear God." She bent down, picked him up, and headed for the clinic. This was the day the school nurse was off; the school secretary covered the clinic as well as the office on Fridays.

Mrs. Spivak had written a long letter the first day of school explaining Michael's condition. He had brain surgery twice before the age of three for some rare form of epilepsy. If he hit his head or received a bump of any kind, he could easily go into a coma. He had to be kept awake. ". . . Do not let Michael go to sleep if he injures his head. He must be kept awake. If he goes to sleep after hitting his head, he may go into a coma and suffer severe brain damage. Please keep him awake at any cost."

Sister Kevin Mary placed Michael on the cot in the clinic and walked quickly into the bathroom for a cloth. She ran the cold water, rinsed out the cloth, and placed it on his head. "Michael, Michael, this is Sister. Open your eyes, Michael. I don't want you to go to sleep." Michael opened his eyes slightly, then closed them again. She slapped his cheeks gently, "Michael, wake up. You know you're not to go to sleep. Wake up, Michael." He opened his eyes, smiled faintly. "OK, Sister, I won't go to sleep."

The bell rang on the playground. She'd have to leave Michael and go and get her kids. "Michael, I have to bring the class in. I'll be right back. Keep your eyes open."

Sister William Ann had gotten Sister Kevin Mary's class in line. The three first grade nuns stood squarely in front of their classes, a silent warning that despite the fact that it was Friday afternoon, it was business as usual at St. Paul's. Very serious business. She turned to Sister William Ann. "Willie, I've got a real sick kid in the clinic. He could go into a coma. The nurse isn't here today."

"Get your kids settled and tell Sister. She is just wonderful at a time like this. Keep calm, Kevvie. If you need me, come and get me. Sister Helen Francis will know what to do."

"OK, Willie. I'm just worried about the kid. I'll tell Sister Helen Francis right away."

Sister Kevin Mary brought her class in, said afternoon prayers, passed out a Kittle review sheet, and told them to begin printing their letters: I, T, E, F, and L—all based on the straight line. "And be careful not to go above or below the dark green line."

"Yes, Sister," chorused the first graders. She quickly left the room to check on Michael. He was asleep.

"Michael, Michael, wake up. Wake up . . . This is Sister . . . Michael, wake up." She slapped his cheeks and shook his thin shoulders. The little boy opened his dark eyes and closed them heavily. She shook him again and ran for some more cold water for the cloth. "Michael, you just can't sleep. Open those big, brown eyes, Michael Spivak. Do you hear me, Michael?" Michael began to smile slightly as he opened his eyes. "Michael, please don't go to sleep. I'm going to get Sister Helen Francis. Keep those big eyes open, Michael." Michael smiled back sleepily.

Sister Kevin Mary heard no sounds from her classroom and decided to leave well enough alone. As she came into Sister Helen Francis's office, Mrs. Burke, the secretary, motioned that the principal was in. Three of the bigger eighth grade boys who seemed to be a permanent fixture there were in the inner office where Sister Helen Francis had her desk. A handsome, more mature boy was seated comfortably on the edge of her desk. The three boys looked up arrogantly as the young nun asked to speak to her Superior. Sister Helen Francis told her to speak in front of them—they had been assigned to the office and knew what was going on.

Sister Kevin Mary refused to look at the three poachers, squatters on land that was not theirs. "Sister, I have a little boy, Michael Spivak. He hit his head. There is something wrong with him. He can go into a coma. I have to keep him awake. His mother wrote me at the beginning of school. I'm just afraid he'll go into a coma. I don't know what to do with my class."

Sister Helen Francis looked disgusted. The boys understood. "Those Spivaks. She's nothing but a troublemaker. The kid will be OK, Sister."

"Yes, Sister. But she was very specific about not letting him go to sleep."

"A good sleep never hurt anyone."

"Yes, Sister."

Sister Kevin Mary left the office. The boys snickered as she
walked past them. Mrs. Burke looked up from her typewriter
blankly, the good, vacant expression of a loyal secretary. She
went back into the clinic. She could hear her class starting to
get noisy. Fifty-five six-year-olds left alone. What would you
expect? Michael Spivak was fast asleep. She took his shoulders
and shook him hard. "Michael, Michael, wake up right now!"
He raised his eyelids. "OK, OK."
"Please, Michael, stay awake." Dear God, don't let him die.
What is Your Holy Will for me? Again, Sister Duns Scotus, her
constant internal companion, spoke: "When the Superior commands, God commands, and that's all there is to it." God thinks
Mrs. Spivak is a troublemaker. God thinks the kid will be OK.
God wants Michael to go to sleep. God wants Michael Spivak
to go into a coma; that's why his mother wrote to me. Dear
God, I just don't understand. And people think we have such a
simple life.
By the time she got back to Room 103, twelve kids were out
of their seats, two girls were fighting to get into the bathroom,
erasers were flying, three boys were drawing horses on the
blackboard, on top of the seatwork directions. Sister Kevin
Mary bellowed, "Get to your places. This very minute. Fast."
The kids flew. "Boys and girls, Michael Spivak is sick. Put
down your pencils and let's say a prayer for Michael." Dear
God, help me know what to do. Please answer the prayers of
the kids.
The children then took out their religion books and began
coloring. Sister Kevin Mary returned to the clinic. Michael was
in a deep sleep. She couldn't wake him. She went back again to
the office, walking straight back to the inner office. Monsignor
Ryan had joined the group. Sister Kevin Mary acknowledged
the pastor but directed herself to her Superior. "Sister Helen
Francis, I can't wake Michael up." The boys looked at each
other smugly. Monsignor Ryan didn't understand what the
young nun was talking about.
"Just let him sleep, Kevin. The kid is probably tired. And
who is watching your class, Sister Kevin Mary?"
"Michael Spivak is going into a coma. His mother warned
me. You know, you could have a lawsuit on your hands if

anything happens to Michael. You really ought to be apprised of the position you are taking. You are dealing with a child's life. The child is going into a coma and might die. They'll sue. They'll sue."

Monsignor Ryan reached for the phone, buzzed three numbers, and shouted at the housekeeper, "Hilda, send Doyle over here immediately . . . where the hell is he? . . . Damn it to hell!" He slammed the phone down, turned to the boy sprawled on the chair next to Sister Helen Francis. "Bill, get out to the baskets and tell Father Doyle to get in here fast." He turned to Sister Kevin Mary, "Thanks, Sister. We'll take care of Michael. Stay with him until Doyle gets here."

Sister Kevin Mary turned quickly and headed back to the clinic. They knew her father was a personal injury lawyer, and they knew she knew what she was talking about. If her father was a milkman, Michael Spivak would probably die. I know that I did the right thing, Dear God. I'm always using my father for something or other. Guess it's OK this time. She wanted to smash Sister Helen Francis in the face but got rid of the thought faster than she'd get rid of an obscene one.

She could hear Father Doyle come into the school, trailed by a string of fifth grade boys. Monsignor Ryan told him to get his car quickly, back it up to the office door, and take a kid home. "OK, Father, sure, right away," said Father Doyle breathlessly. Sister Kevin Mary was holding Michael Spivak in her arms on the cot in the clinic. Sister William Ann had gone into her room to cover until she got back. Within two minutes, Father Doyle came into the clinic. Monsignor Ryan looked disapprovingly—the young priest in a yellow shirt, stained with perspiration, his face red and streaked with mud. Father Doyle bent over to pick up the boy.

"Hi, Sister."

"Hi. I'm glad you're taking him home. What an afternoon."

"The little guy will be all right. What's his name?"

"Michael," said Michael drowsily.

"Well, Michael, you're just going to have to wake up and tell me how to get you home. I need a good pilot. Eyes open, Michael."

Father Doyle carried Michael out to his car. Monsignor Ryan

opened the door, gave Father Doyle directions, and he and Sister Kevin Mary headed back to school. As they walked up the steps into school, he turned to her. "You know, Barrett, you did the right thing. As a matter of fact, you did one helluva job. Thanks, kid."

"May God reward . . . I mean, thanks, Monsignor."

She felt exhausted as she walked down the hall to her room. She could hear the kids out of their seats again. Guess I'm still Rini Barrett—I'm still my father's daughter. He'd be proud of me, she smiled. Little push, little threats. Stupid people need to be twisted. How her father hated dumb people. Well, not just any dumb people, but dumb people who were in charge. They usually mixed their stupidity with arrogance, he always said. He never wanted his kids to be dumb, to act dumb, to give people the impression they were anything but sharp, on their toes. He was harder on the boys, but the girls got the message just as clearly. The Barretts are not dumb; and, in fact, smarter than most.

After school, Sister Kevin Mary asked permission to call Mrs. Spivak. The boys were back again, poachers, knowing every damn thing that was going on in the school. And in the convent as well. Mrs. Spivak said that Michael seemed to be somewhat more alert but she was watching him. She thanked Sister Kevin Mary for taking care of him, commenting on the nice young priest who brought Michael home.

"Yes, Mrs. Spivak, Father Doyle is very nice. The kids love him."

"He's rather nice-looking, don't you think, Sister?" asked Mrs. Spivak.

"I guess so. I really hadn't noticed," lied Sister Kevin Mary. "He's a very kind priest, and that's what really matters, Mrs. Spivak. If you think Michael is better, send him Monday. If not, one of your older ones can come down and get his work. Tell Michael I asked for him."

She reported to Sister Helen Francis that Michael was more alert. Sister Helen Francis gave her an "I-told-you-so" look and thanked Sister Kevin Mary for taking care of it. The poachers smirked. Those little fruits can go to hell, she thought to herself, as she left the office in a hurry. She was beginning to sound more like her father by the minute. She cleared her desk, washed the boards, and straightened the chairs. She knew her mother would want to see her classroom, so she left some fresh flowers that the kids had brought. She locked her door and went home quickly to prepare for her family.

As she was passing the back of the church, Father Doyle stepped out of the sacristy. They both blushed but seemed to share a common determination not to lose their composure again. She thanked him for taking Michael home and reported that he was somewhat better. Father Doyle cleared his throat and said hesitantly, "What's with your Superior and those kids in her office all the time?"

"I don't know, Father. I guess they have been assigned there to help with stuff."

"By whom?"

They both began to laugh. Sister Kevin Mary knew that she shouldn't be laughing with a priest about her Superior. That wasn't exactly what they were laughing about. She didn't know why they laughed every time they spoke and why her knees always felt like they were going out on her. She told him that her family was on its way from Detroit; he said he'd play basketball on Saturday with her brothers.

"He's giving me a hard time for spending so much time with the kids. I wasn't made a priest to sit around at cocktail parties and play golf every day. My ma'd kill me if she thought I'd do that. And Hilda, sweet, charming Hilda is crabbin' because I bring the kids in for a Coke and chips. She wants that place to look like a museum and me to sit like a statue, run over to church, eat my dinner, run back to church, go to bed, run to church. She runs that place, you know. Just like a museum."

"Does your mother live around here?"

"Yeah, 87th around Seeley. She runs a tavern, 'Danny Boy's,' with my two uncles. They came over after my father was killed. I wanted to be a fireman like him, but she'd break my legs. And the uncles would, too. 'Danny, me son,' she'd say, 'now yer mother knows that the Lard wants ye on the altar, and not killin' yourself for a bunch of cullards like yer father.

Not another Daniel Vincent Doyle is goin' to burn hisself to death, not if I can help it, yer not.' And so Daniel Vincent Doyle will be burning himself out in the service of the Lord. Amen. Alleluia."

They both laughed, a little less self-consciously. He said to send the boys over to the rectory the next morning. Hilda could just lump it. And if her family would like to borrow his television set for the weekend, he'd set it up for them in her classroom. She thanked him shyly and continued on to the convent.

She showered, changed her habit, made another round of the nuns to invite them to meet her family. She was in chapel, saying her Office privately, when she heard the big Buick wagon pull into the back. She genuflected quickly and flew out the back door to greet the Barretts. Little Kevin, her favorite, who was only three years old when she left home, was the first one out of the car, squealing, "Rini, Rini," as he ran to her arms. She scooped him up, threw her arms around him, and kissed his fuzzy blond neck.

"Kevvie, how I've missed you! Give me another hug! Quickly!" Kevin squeezed his sister again, and she put him down gently. Her mother, Lillian Barrett, stood with tears in her eyes. "Maureen, my little Maureen. Look at you. Dear God, Jack," she said, turning toward her husband, "she's a real nun now. Oh, Maureen, I can't believe it." The Barretts had not seen Maureen since July. They were not allowed to attend her profession of vows for it was the most sacred of ceremonies and having the laity present, even if *family,* somehow contaminated the purity of the occasion.

The four other boys—Jackie, Marty, Tom, and Pat, ages thirteen to eight—had climbed out of the back of the wagon and were clamoring around their big sister. She noticed that Jackie's face was broken out but decided not to say anything to him. Not just yet. She looked into the car and saw Molly, seven years old, looking out the window. In every new situation, Molly hid. She went over to the car. "Where's my little girl, Molly babe?" Molly looked down at the floor and suddenly lunged into Sister Kevin Mary's arms, burying herself in her soft habit. Her father, Jack Barrett, unable to wait any longer, put his strong, dark arms around his eldest daughter, who was holding Molly. "Congratulations, honey. I knew you'd make it. They good to you here?"

"Yes, Daddy. They're great. The nuns are just beautiful. You'll love Monsignor Ryan. I just love it here." Jack Barrett smiled proudly at his daughter, giving her an extra squeeze for good luck.

Sister Kevin Mary felt a sharp thud in the middle of her back. "Hi, Doll," whispered Peggy in her best Bogey voice. "Come with me to ze Cazzbaah, Dahling Rini." Sister Kevin Mary grabbed her arm, twisting it behind her sister's back. "Say 'Uncle,' Peggy Babe, say 'Uncle.' "

Peggy said, "Uncle, aunt and forty-two cousins," continuing the ritual greeting. With that, they rubbed elbows and gave each other a swat on the bottom.

"Peggy, stop doing that to Maureen. She's a nun now. I don't want to see that anymore, Margaret, do you hear me?" stated Lillian Barrett in her most authoritarian voice.

"It's OK, Mom. She's still my sister, aren't you, Peggy?" Peggy nodded victoriously, for Rini hadn't forgotten the greeting. Ann, who used to be called "Annie Bannannie" before she grew too sophisticated for such crudity, approached her older sister, with a skeptical look across her face, and gave her a light, somewhat cool, hug. "Hi, Annie, I mean Ann," Sister Kevin Mary said softly. Maureen was eighteen months old when her sister was born; Ann couldn't say "Maureen," but managed to call her "Weenie." Jack Barrett hated the thought of a daughter called "Weenie," so he quickly began calling her "Rini," and Rini stuck.

With the official greeting over, Sister Kevin Mary brought her family around to the front door and led them into the parlor, newly decorated with white French provincial furniture. On the walls were four undersized reprints of Parisian street signs, framed in white. The large sofa curved under pink sheers and came to the end where the heavy brocade drapery began. In front of the couch was a round pink marble coffee table with a thick crystal ashtray and three Hummel angels.

Two pink brocade wingback chairs were on either side of the door, creating the image that once you got in there, you'd be trapped. Sophisticated Ann took one look at the room, uttering, "How gauche!" to anyone who cared to hear her.

"Ann, none of that here," warned her mother. Jack winked at his daughter, rolling his eyes around the room in disbelief. Sister Kevin Mary knew how they would feel about the decorations, yet this was hers now. In fact, she was no longer of the Barretts, but was of the Order and of this community at St. Paul's. They shared with her and she shared with them. One for all and all for one; what's yours is mine and what's mine is yours. Our common poverty includes poverty of taste, she surmised. God, they never taught us that. Help me not to feel embarrassed, Dear God. So many of the nuns were so proud of this room. They came from simple people and would never have aspired to a room of this elegance. When Sister Helen Francis first redecorated the parlor, the nuns were oohing and aahing over the furniture. As she and Sister Mark turned to leave the room, Mark whispered, "Nice crap. Can't wait to show my mother." Aggie knew what the two "rich girls" were up to and shot a stern look in Sister Kevin Mary's direction. Sister Kevin Mary began to laugh, but Aggie's look stopped her short.

Since it was Friday evening, the nuns had changed into their aprons and were performing their "obediences," jobs assigned for the year by the Superior and done in a spirit of Holy Obedience. Sister Kevin Mary's obedience was the laundry. The other nun who did it with her told her not to even think about it but to enjoy her family. She'd do it alone. Aggie went down to the basement to help Sister Kevin Mary's partner, leaving her own obedience until Saturday.

Dressed in their aprons, the nuns came into the parlor to greet her family. Her brothers began to laugh, for the same community taught at their parish grade school in Detroit, and if ever they caught a glimpse of a nun's elbow or of a wisp of her hair, they felt very clever. Now the nuns just looked like nurses with little veils on. Marty, only eleven years old, was sent out to the car by his father; Jackie, Tom, and Pat got the eye. They snapped out of their hysteria and dutifully stood and greeted each nun as if she were standing in front of his class.

Sister Theodore was the first one in and giggled as she met Sister Kevin Mary's parents and brothers and sisters. She kept calling them Mr. and Mrs. Barclay. Ann fixed her eyes on the three Hummel angels until Sister Theodore left the room. Her mother smiled, "She seems like a very nice person, Maureen." Sister Kevin Mary addressed her mother righteously, "They're all nice, Mom. The nuns are really great. I'm glad you're getting a chance to meet them. They're all so good to me."

She was dying to tell Peggy about the time Sister Theodore ran into the gas station and shed her girdle, plopping it on the seat touching her. (One of Peggy's lines was: "I bought me a living bra and now I don't know what to feed it.") She didn't know if she'd tell Peggy or not. Maybe that would be disloyal. Peggy was still a kid and had the nuns in school; she didn't want her to think any less of them. Actually that's all Peggy would need; she'd probably call her "Corset Cora" or something for the rest of her life. "How's Corset Cora? Tell her to *snap* to. Tell her not to be so *bound up* with the things of the world. Tell her to 'always look for the silver garter.'" No, that would just give Peggy too much ammunition. She had enough by herself.

The table in the other parlor was set for ten places. The second parlor, a small room, had lost all its walking space when the leaves were put into the table. Sister Jean Martin, the worst cook in the house, was the cook for the evening. Whenever she cooked, she came to the table and absolutely refused to eat: it was never clear if her food was inedible or whether the demands of the kitchen were unbearable. The Barretts crowded around the table as Sister Kevin Mary brought in the food. Molly looked up at her sister and said, "Rini, aren't you going to eat with us? It isn't any fun eating here alone." Lillian Barrett explained the rules to her daughter. Sister Kevin Mary would have to eat with the rest of the nuns in the refectory. Sister Kevin Mary returned to the kitchen for more food, thinking of Johnny's Steak House.

Poor Sister Jean Martin, thought Sister Kevin Mary. She just

hates to cook and it shows. I wish it wasn't her turn tonight.
The breaded shrimp were curled into stony little circles; the
green peas had turned a strange khaki color; the tossed salad
was nothing but large chunks of browning, tough iceberg
lettuce; the salad dressings were standing in their old, greasy
bottles. She had an odd way of mashing potatoes: cook them in
their jackets, wait until they cooled, peel them, mash them,
then put them in a pan and heat them up. Sister Kevin Mary
knew that if she suggested a simpler way to prepare mashed
potatoes, Sister Jean would snap, snarl, and snipe for the rest of
the night. Guess it really doesn't matter how you fix them.

She brought the food in, avoiding Ann's eyes. Kevin said the
potatoes were good, and her father muttered something about
it was nice of the nuns to feed all of them. Pat and Tom
pretended they were playing marbles with the shrimp. Marty
belched loudly, whispering, "It's just the pea balls, folks,
nothing to worry about, just the pea balls." His father told him
to leave the table. Sister Kevin Mary left her family, joining
the nuns for a dinner of greasy melted cheese sandwiches and
greasy potato chips. The nuns commented on how cute her
brothers and sisters were; the ones who hadn't met them
promised to do so in the evening.

After clearing the dishes from the parlor, Sister Kevin Mary
brought out a jelly roll, the kind that everyone in her family
hated. Peggy looked up at her sister. "Rini, enough is enough.
Is some nun out there trying to poison us? God, a jelly roll.
Remove it, Slave, and wait until I beckon. You realize, you
might lose your head for this offense! Away with you!" Even
Ann broke into a smile at Peggy's clowning.

"I'm sorry. I'm so sorry. We eat such great food here. It's
just the nun in the kitchen tonight. She hates to cook. I wanted
it to be so good tonight," stammered Sister Kevin Mary. Her
mother looked up, surprised. "Why, Maureen; everything has
been just lovely. That poor Sister has been on her feet all day
with a classroom of kids, and now she has to cook for the likes
of us."

Her father grabbed her wrist. "It's been just great, honey.
Don't get upset. Just to be with you is worth anything."

After dinner they all went over to the school. The kids wrote on the board, sat at her desk, opened the books, and snapped up the window shades. Jack and Lillian beamed at their daughter, who was just a silly kid such a short time ago.

"Sister Kevin Mary, I know your real name," shouted Jackie.

"Sister Kevin Mary, I know what your hair looks like," roared Marty.

"Sister Kevin Mary," joined in Tom, "I know that you used to like boys and they liked you."

The Barretts were surprised by a knock on the classroom door. Sister Clare Elliot, back in her school habit, walked into the room to greet the family. "Hi, Barretts. Don't tell me your names, I'll just forget. How many of you are there?" Peggy smiled as she looked at the disheveled nun with the thick glasses, veil askew, poster paint smudged on her habit. "I'm a mess," she continued. "We were making Japanese kites all week and painted them today. Gotta get back and clean up the mess. Anybody want to come with me?" Peggy told her that she'd go with her; Molly trailed along. As Sister was leaving, she turned to Sister Kevin Mary. "See ya' at home, Kevvie. Nice family. Bye. Bye."

Sister Kevin Mary's face reddened at having her family hear what they called her. Ann, leaning against the doorjamb, smiled, "So it's Kevvie, is it? From Rini to Kevvie in two short years. Not bad."

Lillian Barrett turned to her daughter. "Ann, I've had just about as much of your smart mouth as I'm going to put up with. We just don't need that sarcasm in this family. What the nuns call each other is none of your business. Do you understand?" Ann nodded and apologized to her sister.

The weekend of October 5th was the ROTC military ball at the University of Detroit, and Ann had had to break her date to come to Chicago to visit her sister. She was not about to let anyone forget the sacrifice she was making for family unity. Ann Barrett never approved of her sister entering the convent in the first place. When Maureen told her that she was going in, all Ann said was, "You're nuts." The two sisters never again discussed Maureen's choice.

The Barretts stayed at a local motel, eating a huge breakfast
that would last them until they got to downtown Chicago.
They were going to try to visit a number of museums that
Saturday. The boys played basketball with Father Doyle, getting their clean clothes dirty. When Father Doyle brought the
Barrett boys into the rectory for some Coke, Hilda snapped at
him. When he told her who they were, she became sweetly
maternal, solicitous so the Barrett boys would be impressed and
would tell their sister and she would tell her Superior, who
would tell the pastor, and her position would be solidified.
When she ran down to the pantry to bring up some more chips,
Father Doyle told the boys to ignore her because she was
nothing but a pain in the butt. Pat, doubling over with laughter, spilled his Coke as Hilda came into the kitchen. She shot
Father Doyle a dirty look for having caused the mishap. He
winked, speaking to the boys in a low, intimate voice, "Come
on, partners. Let's hit the trail. You gotta go check out the fish
and mummies this fine Saturday morning. No more play."

Lillian Barrett cleaned up the boys and headed them toward
the back of the wagon. There wasn't room for all the Barretts,
since Sister Kevin Mary had to take a companion, so Peggy
decided to stay back at the convent to help Sister Clarabelle.
The rest got into the car and headed for Chicago.

Ann didn't care if she stayed there and helped the third grade
nun, or went to bed, or looked at the damn crap in the
museum. Nothing really mattered that weekend. Sister Kevin
Mary felt a heaviness that her sister had such a little sense of
sacrifice. It was plain—Ann was filled with self-love, self-will,
just plain selfishness. All she thought about was herself. Ann
wanted only to be understood, not to understand; she wanted to
receive, not to give. Take, take, take, that was Ann ever since
she came into the world. How could we be sisters, from the
same parents? Maybe we didn't have the same parents, Sister
Kevin Mary thought. She looked quickly at her mother and
banished the thought before her mother read her mind.

By the time the Barretts went through the Museum of
Science and Industry—the coal mine, the submarine, the
chickens, the dollhouse—had hot dogs and Cokes, Jack Barrett

solemnly announced that he couldn't look at one more exhibit or display or show, or whatever. He sat down and the rest continued on to the "baby room." As the Barretts studied the fetuses in various stages of embryonic development, Lillian Barrett walked up to her daughter. "Maureen, this reminds me, how are your periods? Do you still get those awful cramps?"

"Mother!!!"

"Maureen, I want to know. I brought up some more Gelprin for you. I went to Dr. Carney last week for my checkup. He asked about you and your cramps. Under no circumstances are they to do a hysterectomy on you. Do you understand, Maureen? Dr. Carney said that it's all the rage—nuns coming to doctors with women's problems. They throw 'em in the hospital and whip out everything. They figure they don't need 'em, and they'll shut them up."

"Mother, I'm not going into the hospital. I haven't even seen a doctor."

"How are your cramps?"

"Bad."

"Just remember what Dr. Carney said. Remind me to give you that medicine when we get back to the convent, Maureen."

"OK, thanks, Mom. You know, two nuns in the house had hysterectomies over the summer. I never thought of it that way. Thought it was just like a spare tire that you didn't need and were better off without. I need some more medicine."

Sister Kevin Mary stared at the "Fetus at nine months— Viable." It didn't look like a little mouse or chicken anymore. It was a baby. Her hand rested on little Kevin's blond head as she thought of how her womb really was a spare tire, never to be used. She didn't need it. Dear God, I'll never have a baby like little Kevin. Not only will my womb be empty, but my arms will never hold a child of my own. Just a sterile old maid, just like Aunt Mamie. Empty, alone, unused. Always a Sister, never a mother. Or a wife. Dear God, I am a *chaste virgin*, not a sterile old maid. That does not apply to me. But Aunt Mamie is a chaste virgin and she is still an old maid . . . I'll be an old maid.

She knew how Sister Duns Scotus would have shot down those remarks, twirling her random thoughts into cohesive, comprehensible units of reasoning, distinguishing between voluntary chastity and that imposed "by the nature of the personality or by circumstances." But your arms and your womb were just as empty, whether life dealt you the bitter blow of "blessed singlehood" or God blessed you with a vocation of a nun. O, Sweet Jesus, how can I be an instrument of your love and peace if I am full, if my arms and heart are full of another person? I have freely and generously chosen to be empty so that You can breathe and sing through me. Keep me chaste and empty forever.

"Rini, you're hurting me. You're squeezing my head, Rini," said Kevin, looking up at his sister, staring at the fetus. She took his hand and led him down to the mummy room.

By the time they returned to the convent, Sister William Ann had prepared a beautiful standing rib roast, complete with baked potatoes, fresh green beans, a jello salad, strong black coffee, and homemade apple pie. Sister Kevin Mary felt proud of the dinner. Just leave it to Willie—everything she does is perfect. Not too little, not too much.

Before they left for the night to go back to the motel, Peggy told Sister Kevin Mary that she wanted to ask her something in private. "Does Sister Clarabelle get into trouble, Rini?"

"Why do you ask such a funny question, Peggy?" asked Sister Kevin Mary, trying to throw her sister off the trail.

"I don't know. I just get the feeling that she gets into trouble. It's not that I think she's dumb. She's smart, but not in the right way. I mean, why is her classroom away from the other third grades, down in the basement of the old building where no one else goes? And I heard that principal talking to her like she was an idiot. I bet the kids just love her. Did you see that ugly classroom? She's got it fixed up just beautiful— Japanese kites hanging from the ceiling. She's got every wall painted a different color. Kids' stuff all over the place. Bet the kids love her and that principal hates her. She's just the type, right, Rini?"

"I really don't know, Peggy. I'm sure the kids love her."

"Yeah, but just look at the way she looks. She doesn't look neat and trim the way nuns are supposed to look."

"Peggy, I'm sure Sister Helen Francis respects Sister Clare Elliot just as much as any of the rest of us."

"OK, Rini. I know you can't say, but just don't lie. Nuns aren't supposed to lie." The sisters returned to the parlor together, Peggy looking the wiser for the confrontation, Sister Kevin Mary the lesser.

After Mass the following morning the Barretts came back to the convent for brunch. After many kisses and tears, they were on their way back to Detroit. As they pulled out of the drive, Sister Kevin Mary gasped, "Oh, I forgot to ask my father about his cases."

That evening, Sister Kevin Mary knelt beside Sister Helen Francis's desk, thanking her and "May God Rewarding" her for letting her have such a wonderful visit with her family. She asked for the use of a new typewriter that her father had brought her, explaining that she hadn't *asked* him for it—he just brought it. The nuns didn't ask to *have* things, because they had given up the right to own anything through their vow of poverty: They could *use,* not *have* things. Permission to *use* was conferred by the Superior.

Sister Helen Francis allowed Sister Kevin Mary to *use* the new typewriter, commenting on what a wonderful family she had. She thanked her again for everything and rose off her knees. "By the way, Sister, why don't you call Mrs. Spivak before the night is over?"

"Yes, Sister, I will, Sister. May God reward you, Sister."

Sister Kevin Mary called Mrs. Spivak, reported the call to Sister Helen Francis, and immediately went to chapel to make up the prayers she had missed, thanking God for her family and asking God to make Ann more generous. Sister Marie Marcel, dressed in her nightgown and robe, opened the door of the chapel. Her left eye was nearly closed. She walked slowly, almost in a daze. "Sorry, kid. I just couldn't get down to meet your folks."

"That's OK, Marce. How ya' feelin'?"

"Hard to tell. Head hasn't hurt much today. Must be that

new medicine. But I feel like I'm talking slower. Guess that doesn't matter, as long as the head doesn't hurt. Take it easy, Kev. Sorry again that I couldn't get down. I thought you'd understand."

"I do, Marce. Just take real good care of yourself."

Sister Kevin Mary finished her night prayers, undressed, showered, and typed a letter to her family on her new type-writer. She said so much of what there wasn't time to say during this marvelous weekend. She reminded them that she would be home next August, not really that far off in the mind of God, whatever that meant. Just ten months.

She climbed into bed and began her final rosary. She fell asleep, trying to remember how Father Doyle looked, lifting Michael Spivak out of her arms last Friday afternoon.

8.

The end of October brought a drop in temperature and a bite in the early morning air. Sister Kevin Mary heard the high pitch of the rising bell, blessed herself, and as she sat up in bed, knew that she was never going to make it through the day. Nauseated, lightheaded, cramps. Her periods were getting harder and harder. She was grateful that her mother had brought her medicine, but even that wasn't having the effect it used to have.

She dressed, and as she pulled up her heavy, black stockings, she knew she was going to throw up. She made it to the bathroom, cleaned herself up, and decided to get excused from morning prayer. She knocked on Sister Helen Francis's door, and as she opened it, the early morning blast of Shalimar brought a fresh rush of water brash to her mouth. She knelt quickly at Sister Helen Francis's feet, asking to be excused. Sister Helen Francis asked her if she needed anything. She said no, that she had some medicine from home and that she just wanted to get back to bed.

As she rolled over, she could hear the morning prayers begin.

Within minutes, the nuns were chanting Office and Sister Kevin Mary had fallen into a deep sleep. Two hours later, she was awakened by Sister Mark Stephen cleaning her teeth and making her bed. Mark asked her if she wanted anything from the kitchen and wondered if she were going to school. Sister Kevin Mary said she thought she'd make it, took two more Gelprin, and began to dress. She went to Sister Helen Francis again, thanked her for letting her stay in bed, drank a cup of coffee, and left for school. She was still lightheaded, a bit nauseated, but the cramps seemed to have let up a bit.

As the children began to fill up the classroom, Sister Kevin Mary knew that it was going to be a long morning. The kids came up to her with their homework, tales of the previous evening, to which she delivered a perfunctory response.

"My mommie had a new baby last night."

"Oh, that's nice."

"We had pizza for dinner, and my daddy got mad that it had little fish on it."

"That's too bad."

"Sister, I forgot my homework."

"Bring it tomorrow."

As the morning dragged on, her cramps intensified. She loosened her belt, but it still felt as if something were stabbing her from within. Her knees and thighs ached. Her headband cut into her forehead, forcing her eyes into a squint. Her head ached. She loosened her collar, hoping the nausea would go away. The class was noisy, picking up on her irritability and magnifying it. She thought she was going to scream or vomit or faint, or all three at the same time. She gave them an assignment and went down to the office. It was only 9:45.

Mrs. Burke, efficient Mrs. Burke, was clicking away at her typewriter outside Sister Helen Francis's office. Sister Kevin Mary asked if the principal was in, and Mrs. Burke nodded in three even, clicky nods. Sister Kevin Mary went in, anxious to speak privately to her Superior. Two of the three poachers were entertaining Sister Helen Francis with details of a basketball game. She was giving them her undivided attention; the poachers did not acknowledge the young nun at the door either.

God, I'm invisible. I'll turn into a pool of blood and just see how damn invisible I am. Do I interrupt the poachers or just throw up all over the floor and let them clear it up? Sister Helen Francis, laughing wholeheartedly over the funny story of how the ball seemed to perch on the rim of the basket for minutes and how the coach was fanning the air to push the ball in, finally turned to Sister Kevin Mary. "Yes, Sister? Can I help you?"

"I'd like to speak with you privately, Sister, if you don't mind."

The poachers looked knowingly at each other and smiled at Sister Helen Francis as she walked somewhat suggestively in front of them. One of the boys crossed his legs quickly.

"Ahh, I've really got cramps bad, Sister. I just hate to have to say this, but I really don't think I'm going to make it through the day."

"Why don't you go home, Sister? You can't teach in that condition. Get the work out, and I'll send down an eighth grade girl for the rest of the day. Tell Willie that you're going home. Do you need anything, Kevin?"

"No, Sister. May God reward you, Sister. Thank you, Sister. I'm so grateful. Thank you, Sister Helen Francis." As she walked unsteadily out of the office, she wondered at the difference between obedience and obsequiousness. Her father would know. She had a feeling she was the latter: obsequious. Kiss ass. But she just had to get home or die on the spot. She returned to her class, outlined their work, and went home and got into bed.

There was a sharp knock on the bedroom door. It was Sister Helen Francis with one of the short yellow rose glasses. She said that Monsignor Ryan had sent this over for her and it would make her feel better within minutes. Sister Kevin Mary sat up quickly, trying to make sense out of what her Superior had just said to her. Monsignor Ryan? Monsignor Ryan? What did he have to do with her cramps? Did one of those creeps in the office say something to him? Sister Helen Francis just simply would not have told him that she was having her period. Oh, my God, I never even liked my father to know when I got it, although he could hardly not have known. The big box of Modess became a permanent fixture in the Barretts' bathroom until the boys started to ask questions; then Lillian moved it into the linen closet, hiding it behind the beach towels.

Obediently, obsequiously, Sister Kevin Mary drank the clear, thick liquid. It was sweet, like peppermint. She thanked her Superior for coming all the way over with that for her, smiling appreciatively. Within minutes, she felt relaxed and warmed, unmindful of the fifty-six children pushing their crayons in Room 103.

During the lunch hour, Mark came up to see if she could get anything for her. She had another glass of the peppermint liquor for Sister Kevin Mary to drink.

"She wants you to take this. Drink up, Kev."

"Mark, I just don't understand how Monsignor Ryan would know that I have cramps."

"You've got to be kidding! He knows every damn thing that goes on over here. She tells him everything. I bet he has a big chart on his wall: Sisters' Menstrual Cycles. When it's your turn, he pulls out his big bottle of Schnapps, brings it over, and give you your monthly allotment. So drink up. Don't question. Go along. Be a good nun. Right, Kevvie? Do what your Superior says. Drink your Schnapps, have your period, and go to sleep."

Sister Kevin Mary finished the second glass of Schnapps as the lunch hour bell rang. She could hear the playground fall into an immediate silence. Sister Mark closed the door, returned the glass to the kitchen, and hurried over to her own classroom. The second bell rang and kids got in line as she pulled the covers up and fell back asleep.

At about 2:20, Sister Helen Francis knocked on her door. She was smiling wisely, for good old Monsignor Ryan's Schnapps did more for her than Dr. Carney's pills. After inquiring as to the state of her cramps, Sister Helen Francis asked her if she felt well enough to drive her to St. Gregory's, a neighboring convent. Sister Helen Francis did not drive. She had to see the Superior about some form for the School Board. School wasn't out yet, but the nuns were covering her class and Cynthia

Perkins, the eighth-grader, had everything well under control.

They spent a few hours at St. Gregory's, and on the way home, Sister Helen Francis mentioned that Monsignor Ryan was celebrating the twenty-fifth anniversary of his ordination to the priesthood on November 18th, the week before Thanksgiving. She wondered aloud what the school ought to do to celebrate for him. Sister Kevin Mary didn't know if she was just supposed to sit there quietly and listen to her Superior think or if she was supposed to think with her, for her, in spite of her, or whatever. Sister Helen Francis turned to her. "Do you have any ideas, Kevin? You must have done some things in the Novitiate for Mother Jeremiah's Feast Day. Can you think of anything?"

Humility consists in the truth, thought Sister Kevin Mary. So here goes. "Well, Sister, maybe I could write something or other. I did a lot of that in high school and in the Novitiate. Maybe something like a play or something like that?"

Sister Helen Francis raised her eyebrows. "My luck, Kevvie. That's great. Is that why your father brought you that typewriter?"

"Yes, Sister. He thinks I have a talent and shouldn't let it go to waste."

"I agree completely. I always wished that I could be able to write. You know, I'm an English major—Renaissance poetry. Take my orals this summer for my Master's degree. What I wouldn't give to be able to write. Think I'm just too inhibited. Or maybe not inhibited enough," she laughed.

Sister Kevin Mary laughed politely, thinking of the three poachers in her office. No, Sister, you're not one little bit inhibited, at least from what I can see. Maybe a little bit of inhibition, holy inhibition, that is, dear Sister, would be a little healthy. Sister Helen Francis had turned at an angle so she could face Sister Kevin Mary behind the wheel. The remnants of the Schnapps, a fresh blast of Shalimar mixed with the excitement of having her Superior show a little interest in her writing made Sister Kevin Mary slightly lightheaded again.

The car swerved, almost sideswiping a station wagon full of kids. Sister Helen Francis laughed loudly, thinking Sister Kevin

Mary had done that on purpose. Sister Kevin Mary grew red in the face, for if she told her it was an accident, the Superior would feel reproached and maybe get mad; if she pretended that she did it on purpose, her Superior might keep it in reserve to use it against her sometime when she wanted to be considered responsible. God, I never know what to do anymore. I never know what to be or what to say.

"So, Kevin, are you going to work on something for us to use? I'd feel so much better thinking that someone was working on something. You know, Monsignor Ryan is a very special person to our community. He is good to the parish, good to the school, good to the nuns. I want this to be the very best we can do. If you need extra time at night, let me know. If you need extra help with your obedience, let me know. I want you to give this your all, Kevin. It's for Monsignor Ryan, and he deserves our very best."

"Oh, may God reward you, Sister. I'm really so very honored to be able to do this for you, and for Monsignor Ryan, of course. I write pretty fast, so I don't think I need any time off. I'll get it done. And you know, Sister, if you want to change anything at all, feel free to do whatever you want with it. I'm just so honored, Sister. May God reward you."

"I just envy your talent, Sister Kevin Mary. Thanks so much for your generosity. And I'd like it probably by the end of the first week in November, if that's not too much trouble."

"No, Sister, not at all. I'll try to have it to you before that. I'm just really happy to be able to do it."

For the next three weeks, Sister Kevin Mary was at her typewriter every spare moment she had. By the time Sister Mark got home from school each afternoon, Sister Kevin Mary would be at their desk, working out scenes, dialogue, gestures. The theme of the celebration was a trip around the world, with each class representing a different country. Costumes were specified and the music and dance of each ethnic group were woven into the fabric of the narration. Sister Mark, a musician, assisted Sister Kevin Mary with the musical parts, providing the names of songs and dances. Periodically, Sister Kevin Mary would keep Sister Helen Francis informed as to how far she had gotten and when she could expect it to be finished. Sister Helen Francis was surprised with the progress, and she kept telling Sister Kevin Mary not to put too much pressure on herself.

After the entire draft of the play had been written, Sister Kevin Mary retyped it and proofed it meticulously. Sister Mark read the final version the evening Sister Kevin Mary finished typing it. "Kevin, this is absolutely fabulous. God, there's been so much work put into this. Ryan'll love it. I sure hope Sister appreciates all your work. You know, you couldn't have paid to have this written. It's really great, Kevvie. Congratulations. You did a beautiful job!"

"Thanks, Mark. I really feel good about it. At least I know that I did my best. And Sister can change it if she doesn't like it."

"She'd be a fool if she touches one word. It's just great!"

Sister Kevin Mary placed the fifty-three-page manuscript of the play, *Around the World for Monsignor Ryan,* on top of Sister Helen Francis's desk before she went to school. Sister Helen Francis had already left, so Sister Kevin Mary knew that she wouldn't see it until lunchtime, or even perhaps after school. She went to chapel, thanking God for her gift, her talent for writing, asking Him to let her always use it in His Holy Service, for the glory of the Church and for the order. She asked God to keep her humble in the face of her talent and not to allow His free gift to her to be used as a source of pride or arrogance. Talents were not to be hidden under the proverbial bushel but were to be used to glorify the Creator, the source of all creativity. Her human hands and mind shared in the very creativity of God himself. With a final prayer for humility and generosity, Sister Kevin Mary genuflected and left for school.

She stayed after school, slowly cleaning up the room and correcting three sets of papers. She wanted to give Sister Helen Francis plenty of time to read the play before she got home. Sister Kevin Mary knew that all the nuns would be surprised that it was so good. She bit her bottom lip, hoping that this display of intelligence and maturity would bury forever any and all reference to her as the "baby." It was 4:20, time to get home, see Sister Helen Francis, talk with her for a short time until the bell rang for *Matins* and *Lauds* at 4:45. Sister Helen Francis's door was closed, so Sister Kevin Mary decided to clean up before prayer.

At 4:47, the bell rang for prayer. The nuns opened their bedroom doors and headed for the stairs that led to chapel. Sister Helen Francis's room was at the top of the stairs. She came out and motioned for the nuns. As they gathered around her bedroom door, she began to speak. Sister Helen Francis's face was slightly flushed and she was smiling. Sister Kevin Mary's heart jumped, for she knew the Superior loved her play and was going to announce it publicly before prayer. Sister Kevin Mary grabbed her rosary, waiting for the honor that was soon to come her way.

"Nuns, I just wanted to show you this. I just finished this little play for Monsignor Ryan's anniversary. Been working on it for weeks now. I'll leave it on my desk. I want you all to read it when you have time. Just remember to put it back. I don't want all my work to be lying at the bottom of someone's briefcase."

Sister Kevin Mary stared at her Superior. Mark's mouth dropped open. She turned with disbelief to Sister Kevin Mary. Sister Kevin Mary's face was reddening, her eyes filling with tears. She turned quickly and ran down the hard metal stairs, genuflecting slightly and making her way to her place before she fainted. She swallowed hard, locking her back teeth together so she would neither cry nor faint.

"I absolutely do not believe what just happened," whispered Mark. "Did she say what I think she said? This is the most incredible thing I've ever seen. This place is crazier than I thought."

"Don't Mark . . . Please, don't."

"That woman is stark, raving mad."

"She's the Superior, Mark."

"Tough toenails. She's crazy . . . evil, bad, and crazy."

Sister Helen Francis came into the chapel last, genuflected gracefully, and opened the evening prayers with the Hail Mary, chanted in Latin.

Sister Kevin Mary focused on the Latin, trying to regain her composure, trying to surrender herself to the Holy Will of God as manifest through her Superior. *Te Deum laudamus:* We praise you, O God, we acknowledge Thee to be the Lord. Dear God, are you testing me? Did I really write that? Maybe I just imagined it . . . Dear God, is this Your most Holy Will, that I should accept this with generosity and humility? Is this what my vow of Poverty means, that I have given up all my worldly rights, my rights to my work, my right to call my work my own? Does my work now belong solely to the order as manifest by my Superior? The Lord chastiseth he whom He loveth. Dear God, how could You love me if You make me feel so horrible?

She wondered what her father would make of all of this. He would say something about the violation of her property rights. Or maybe it was a breach of contract issue? Or maybe something about freedom of speech. She stole my work, plain and simple. She knew that Jack Barrett would know what the issue was, but how would he feel about his daughter, so meek and mild, letting that woman walk all over her?

Laudate Dominum de caelis: Praise ye the Lord from the heavens; praise Him in the high places. *Laudate Dominum!!! Laudate Dominum!!!* Praise the Lord. Oh, ho, ho. Praise the Lord and pass the ammunition. I'm going to smash her pretty little face. *Laudate Dominum,* spray some Shalimar in her eyes. I hate her, hate her, hate her! My father would have been so ashamed of me, slinking past her like a dog with his tail between his legs. Yes, Sister. No, Sister. Three bags full, Sister. Full of all the crap that you dish out to me day by day. *Laudate Dominum:* Oh, ho, praise the very Lord on His high and mighty throne. Maureen Barrett is no longer going to kneel and take what that woman dishes out, especially with the three Goddamn little poachers smirking and sneering at me. *Laudate,* Dear God, forgive me, but I don't have to make a royal ass of myself to be a good nun. I don't have to take that stuff morning, noon, and night. *Laudate,* Lord, *Laudate.* God, I'm getting my anger back. My temper that they rammed out of me, hour by hour. *Laudate,* Dear God.

She looked up. The nuns had finished the Office and rosary and were already in the refectory. When Sister Kevin Mary came into the refectory the reader had begun the evening reading. She refused to make the venia, prostrating herself on the refectory floor to ask silently the community's forgiveness for being late. She pulled out her dishes, placed them deliberately on the cotton placemat with little yellow roses painted in the upper left corner.

9.

The windshield wipers strained back and forth, arching toward the center of the window like nuns inclining at the *Gloria* of the Office. The rain landed on the roof of the car in loud thuds. Sister Kevin Mary felt like she was inside a crowded, steamy drum. Three nuns in the back of the wagon were singing, "Over the River and Through the Woods to Grandmother's House We Go." In the second seat, two nuns were working the *Trib* crossword puzzle; another was saying her Office.

In the front seat Sister Marie Marcel, driving, sat tensely at the wheel. Sister Kevin Mary sat next to her. By the door was Sister Theodore with two large grocery bags on her lap. She was on her way to visit her mother and sister on the North Side. In the bags were some schoolwork for her to do while she visited and some sewing that her mother was going to do for her. The nuns in the front did not speak.

Sister Kevin Mary stared at the wipers—slap, slap, slap. She knew how the window felt. It was Friday, the day after Thanksgiving—the most incredible Thanksgiving of her life, of her twenty years. Sister Theodore had not emerged from her room all day. Migraine, she said—"I've gotta head, I've gotta head," she would walk around chanting. Her dark eyes were blacker than usual. There was no giggling, just Ben-Gay, ice packs, staggering down the hall to the bathroom.

The day before Thanksgiving, Sister Mark and Sister Kevin Mary had walked back to school after lunch. "Be sure not to miss what is going to happen today after school, Kev."

"What, Mark? Something good?"

"Just don't miss it. You'll see."

At two o'clock, she saw Sister Helen Francis crossing the playground, heading for the convent. Two of the poachers were carrying her little black briefcase. Ten minutes later, the poachers returned to school without Sister Helen Francis.

At 2:45, the fifth-graders were on the playground, waiting for their buses. School was not dismissed until 2:55. Sister Theodore did not wait with her class but walked quickly, almost ran, over to the convent. That morning she had made breakfast (it was her cook-day), and Sister Kevin Mary figured she wanted to get a head start on the evening meal. Or perhaps she had a headache and wanted to lie down before getting dinner.

School cleared out quickly that Wednesday. Everyone was anxious to get home, change clothes, and begin the Thanksgiving holiday. As she came into the convent, there was a clatter of pots and pans, voices raised, doors slamming.

"This is my cook-day, Sister! I'm making the dressing! It's my day, and you know it as well as I do!" shouted Sister Theodore.

"I'm making the stuffing, Theodore. That's been the tradition here for three years, and it is not going to stop just because it's your day. I make the stuffing for Thanksgiving, is that clear?" said Sister Helen Francis in her deepest, most articulate voice.

"If I don't make the stuffing, you won't see me around this damn place. I'm good enough to scramble eggs and make toast, but not good enough to make the dressing. I'm sick of this stuff! Do you hear me—just sick and tired!" screamed Sister Theodore as she threw down her apron and ran up the stairs. Sister Helen Francis made the dressing.

The station wagon swerved slightly. "Damn, Sam," muttered Sister Marie Marcel as she straightened the wheel. The wipers continued their hypnotic rhythm. The nuns in the back were singing the "Twelve Days of Christmas." It was 9:20. "Around the World in Eighty Days" was being shown at 10:30 A.M. for all the nuns in the city. The card, posted on the bulletin board since November 10, read:

Special Thanksgiving Showing
Michael Todd Theatre, Chicago
Around the World in Eighty Days
For all religious in the Archdiocese of Chicago
10:30 A.M., Friday, Nov. 27, 1958
Please be on time.
A Happy and Blessed Thanksgiving.
Monsignor William McManus
Superintendent of Schools

"Cat got your tongue, Kev?" asked Sister Marie Marcel.

"I don't know, Marce. Guess I just feel kinda quiet today. Sorry."

"No problem, kid. Nothing wrong, is there?"

"No, honestly, I just feel a little quiet."

What a lie, she thought. Everything's wrong. This week had been so much fun with the kids in school. Pilgrims, Indians, the Mayflower, Plymouth Rock. Thanking God for the many blessings. She thought of St. Thomas Aquinas: "Gratitude is the sign of a noble heart." Yet life in the convent was not as she expected. They had so much food, food, food. Baskets of fruit, homemade cookies, pies, cakes. Fannie May candy until it came out of her ears. She was now up to 129½ pounds, 17½ additional pounds in three months. The people in the parish lavished them with food. "A little something for the Good Sisters!" "Happy Thanksgiving to the Dear Nuns!" "For the Good Sisters at St. Paul's."

Then the day actually came, and it was just horrible. A big, gluggy breakfast after Mass, then the Thanksgiving meal at 3:30. Her family had called around 2:00. Everyone was there. The image of her family at home for Thanksgiving unnerved her. She refused to think about them, for she had to keep herself together at least until dinner. Sister Theodore had been in her room all day, pouting. Sister Helen Francis refused to go up and see her. By 5:00, half the nuns were in bed, too stuffed to move.

It was just so lonely. We don't really love each other. The Rule of the order said: *The first purpose for which you have been brought together is that you dwell in unity in the house and that you have but one soul and one heart in God.* Dwell in unity, community, union with each other. See these Christians, how they love one another. See these nuns, how they ignore one another and dislike one another. No one really cares what happens to anyone else. Spiritual isolates, seventeen women rubbing elbows, praying together, working together, living so very close together. Seventeen women who really don't give a damn for each other. No real compassion, no real feeling, no real love.

The wipers cleared away the rain only long enough to see for a moment, then the water covered the window, and again the wipers lunged at the rain. Day after day, the same heaviness, the same thick void, the same lovelessness. Slap, slap, slap. Get through today, get through tomorrow, get through the day after tomorrow.

Sister Theodore directed Sister Marie Marcel down a side street, around a corner, and to the third house on the left. Sister Theodore handed one of the large grocery bags to Sister Kevin Mary so she could get the door opened. Sister Kevin Mary got out and followed her up the steps to her mother's house, carrying one of the bags. The rain splashed on the bags. A bunch of celery, two cans of peaches, a bottle of wine, a box of Fannie May candy, and six altar candles dropped out of the bottom of the bag onto the steps. Sister Kevin Mary looked at the steps, then up to Sister Theodore, who was ringing the bell.

"I'm sorry, Sister. I'm so sorry, ahh, the bags just got wet."

Before Sister Theodore could answer, the door opened. A plump woman in her late thirties stood at the door. Two young

children were hanging from her skirt. She looked exasperated
at her sister, the nun. "Oh, Shirley, don't tell me you brought a
bunch of junk here again. I've told you, we don't need that
stuff. Celery, lettuce, a bunch of rags. Please, just come to see
us and leave that stuff at the convent."

Sister Marie Marcel honked. The woman smiled at Sister
Kevin Mary. "Just go, Sister. I'll get one of the kids to clean
this up. I just wish she wouldn't bring us all that stuff." Sister
Kevin Mary nodded apologetically and ran down the steps to
the car. The movie was going to begin in thirty-five minutes.

They parked and joined hundreds and hundreds of other nuns
filing into the theater. The popcorn machine was clean and
unlit. No one was selling candy. Ten-thirty in the morning,
seeing a movie with a house full of nuns. There was just
something wrong with that. She felt embarrassed, awkward.
People don't go to a show at 10:30 in the morning. Not with a
bunch of nuns. It smelled like a church without the popcorn and
only the musty, damp smell of habits. As she went into the
aisle, she genuflected, thinking she was in church. The nuns
from St. Paul's laughed as they sat down, trying to decide how
they could view the movie around the wide veils of the nuns
ahead of them.

The movie began, the giant balloon lifted off, as the magnifi-
cent theme song, "Around the World in Eighty Days," filled
the theater. The clear, fresh blue skies, real people, real blood.
She looked down the aisle—twenty women on her left, thirty
women on her right, and millions ahead of her and millions
behind. Dear God, I can't believe this. I'm beginning to disinte-
grate. She ached for home, for the people who were her own,
who cared, really cared, and didn't just create an image of
caring.

Something about the balloon and the music and the freedom
uncorked something churning around and around inside her.
The tears—hot, salty, fast tears—rolled down her face. She felt
as if she were being strangled—that they were all jumping on
her chest. She pulled out her handkerchief, the large man's
handkerchief, and blew her nose softly.

Sister Marie Marcel whispered, "You OK?"

"Yeah, think I've got an allergy. Makes my nose run."

She thought again of the play for Monsignor Ryan, *her* play that *her* Superior had taken credit for, and she began to cry harder. The play was exactly as she had written it—not a word, dance, or song changed. The program read: "Around the World for Monsignor Ryan, by Sister Helen Francis." And after it was all over, Monsignor Ryan asked everyone to give Sister Helen Francis an extra round of applause, since she was responsible for writing such a wonderful play.

The nun on the other side looked at her strangely. The nun ahead of her began shifting in her place. Get ahold of yourself, Kevin, she said to herself. Get ahold of yourself, Maureen. You're just crackin' up. You're just losin' your holy marbles. You're a nun now, kid. *To dig I am not able, to beg I am ashamed, but what I have I give.* My life, my love, my feelings. I just hurt so much inside. Maybe this is why the people give us so much stuff. Maybe they secretly know how much we ache inside. Maybe they really know what it's like. The pain and the hurt and the loneliness. The coldness and selfishness. This is what the Lord wants from me, the sacrifice He expects from those He has called to His service. Dear God, make me generous and grateful for what I have. Thank you for my vocation, for the order, for my community. Maybe we really just love each other but don't know how to show it. Or, maybe we really hate each other.

The lights went on abruptly. Nuns grabbed for their shawls and cloaks and purses. As they left the theater and walked down the street, Sister Marie Marcel leaned over to Sister Kevin Mary. Her lip was curled and the eye was almost completely closed. She smiled. "It gets better, kid. I know the first year is hard. I know, it gets better."

Sister Kevin Mary's eyes filled with tears all over again. "When, Marce, when?"

"Who knows? But it does. It gets better."

A large green bus turned the corner, splashing water from the street all over the two nuns. "Son of a B!!" shouted Sister Marie Marcel. "Let's go home, kid."

10.

Sister Kevin Mary pulled her shawl tightly around her shoulders as she hurried across the playground. The early December sun bounced off the blacktop, reflecting the chips of ice embedded in its surface. The school windows were covered with a thin layer of frost, which she knew would melt as soon as she turned up the thermostat.

Yesterday, November 30, was the first Sunday of Advent, the beginning of the Liturgical year, and the start of the preparation for the great Feast of Christmas. Despite the cold and the winds, there was a sense of a new beginning in the air as if the Church were ahead of nature, bypassing the death of winter and anticipating the freshness of spring.

Advent was a time of penance and foreshadowed the greater penitential season of Lent, yet it was not as solemn or severe. Advent was only four weeks long, and although the nuns would fast and receive no mail or phone calls, there was a sense of excitement and joyfulness that was missing during Lent. Maybe it had something to do with kids and Christmas, with birth, not death. Father O'Mahoney had delivered the sermon at each of

the Masses yesterday. He spoke of the joy of Advent, the joy of
the Liturgy, and the joy the Church was experiencing, not only
because of the beginning of the Church year, but because of the
new pope, John XXIII, who seemed to personify the joy of
Christianity.

Father O'Mahoney spoke of the irony of Christianity, of how
a helpless Child was sent to redeem mankind and of how an old
man, chosen as an interim pope, was speaking of renewing the
Church. The pope was calling for a council to be held in Rome
within a few years that would bring new life into the Church.
He said he wanted to open the windows to bring in fresh air.

The young priest with the sandy hair, smiling at the congregation, reminded the people that God chose the weak things of
the world to confound the strong. The fat little Italian pope,
whom no one expected to do anything except keep the Chair of
Peter warm until a more suitable pope was chosen, would
perhaps change the course of history as did the Child of
Bethlehem. He said that, while certainly Pope Pius XII had
been saintly and had suffered greatly for the Church, the new
pope would show us another side of the Church, not a Church
suffering but a Church joyful.

The pope was a simple priest from the hills of Sotto il
Monte, who never forgot his beginnings. He was a joyful priest
who, aware of his girth, raised the salaries of the men who
carried him on his throne because they had to work harder. He
was a pope who had no illusions about the Church and was not
overly impressed with Rome. When asked how many people
were working at the Vatican, the pope said, "About half."

Under the first grade bulletin board of the Nativity scene,
Sister Kevin Mary had placed on a small table an Advent
wreath. It was made of pine branches and four candles—one to
mark each of the four weeks of Advent. Each morning, after
prayers, the class would light one of the candles and sing the
Advent hymn:

> O come, O come, Emmanuel,
> And ransom captive Israel
> That mourns in lonely exile here
> Until the Son of God appear.

Rejoice, Rejoice! Emmanuel
Shall come to Thee, O Israel.

The morning classes were lovely. Perhaps the kids had picked up on her mood, or perhaps they were just a little sleepy from the long Thanksgiving weekend. They seemed to understand, in some simple way, that Christmas was on its way and they were to prepare their hearts for the Savior. They had not yet been exposed to the pre-Christmas hysteria. She would downplay Santa Claus and emphasize the mystery of the Nativity. In its own way, the first grade at St. Paul's would resemble the Advent season in the Novitiate—quiet, reflective, joyful.

At noon, there was a notice from the principal taped to the refectory door. There would be a fire drill at 2:45. Children were to be dressed in their winter coats and ready to leave school. The bell would ring; they would file out but would not return to school. Instead they would get on their buses. The classes would not be told in advance; the nuns were to tell the lay teachers.

Sister Jean Martin filled her plate in the kitchen, stopped to read the notice, and walked defiantly to the table, placing her plate down with a thud. "This makes me sick. It's always the last period. I have math planned right up until the last minute. With these kids in this school, you can't spare one minute! Parading around on the playground when they should be doing their work! This is utterly ridiculous!"

Max looked up. "Jeanie Beanie, you know she has to do that every month. Besides, we'll get rid of the little monsters that much faster. Maybe we'll even have a real fire, ha! ha! ha!"

Sister Jean Martin placed her hands on her hips. "Listen, Max, if there ever were a real fire, it would be out in a second. There's no such thing as a school fire. With those fire trucks clanging in and out of there all the time, I can hardly teach. All they'd have to do is come across the street. Ask Marce!"

Sister Marie Marcel laughed. During the warm weather when the windows were open, the metal latch on the rope of the flagpole across the street at the fire station would bang, keeping her and everyone else awake. Sister Kevin Mary looked out one night, around midnight, and saw Sister Marie Marcel across the street at the fire station, in her nightgown, securing the rope. This seemed to be her habit whenever it was a windy night.

Sister Jean Martin did her dishes, banging the silverware and plates. "I'll tell you one thing. If I'm ever a principal, we'll have *one* fire drill the *first* day of school and *one* the *last*. It's an utter waste of time. It just makes me sick."

At 2:45 sharp, the fire bell blasted down the empty halls of St. Paul's school. Sister Kevin Mary had completely forgotten to have her class ready. The children panicked, ran for their coats, screaming, holding their faces, and pushing each other. One boy ran down the aisle for his coat, pushing and knocking whatever was in his way. Sister Kevin Mary tore after him, lifted him to eye level, and shook him, shouting, "Keep calm, Robert! Keep calm!! Everyone keep calm!!!" She put him down, shouting to her class, "Get your coats. Get in line! Let's go. First ones out—move quickly. No running!! Hurry up!! Keep calm!! Move fast . . . keep calm . . . no talking!!"

The rest of the school was on the playground, a hundred feet away from the school building, when Sister Kevin Mary came out with her class. Sister Helen Francis was on the playground with Monsignor Ryan and the Fire Marshall, who was holding his stopwatch. The fire trucks had pulled into the playground within seconds of the alarm. The 2,000 St. Paul students stood in perfect silence, waiting for the second bell to announce their dismissal. Sister Kevin Mary looked sternly at her class, and felt that her knees were going out on her. It wasn't their fault that she had forgotten to get them ready. It wasn't their fault that she had panicked. With her expression, she tried to deflect the blame onto her class, and as she did, hated herself for her cowardice.

The second bell rang; she motioned for them to stand still. "Boys and girls, you did a really good job. Sister forgot to tell you to get your coats on. I'm sorry. It was my fault. But, you know, if it were a real fire, we wouldn't have time to get our coats on, you know."

The class smiled. "Yes, Sister." They loved it when she was wrong and told them so.

"All right, boys and girls, you did a good job. We'll just forget your homework tonight. You can go now." Smiling, the class went to their buses. Sister Kevin Mary walked over to Sister Helen Francis to apologize.

Before she could say anything, Sister Helen Francis smiled at her. "Did you forget, Kevin?"

"Yes, Sister. I was just so involved with the spelling. I'm so sorry, Sister. I didn't mean to do that."

"Don't worry about it. It's just something we have to do. Try to remember next time, OK?"

"Yes, Sister. I'm really sorry."

Sister Kevin Mary walked quickly back to her class. The desks were covered with the children's work. She went to each place, putting away pencils and crayons, gathering the almost finished papers, and straightening the desks into orderly rows.

Willie came into her room quietly humming, "When I was young, I had no sense. I bought a fiddle for eighteen pence. . . . nice going, Kevvie. Your kids would be burned to a crisp by the time you'd get them out."

"Oh, Willie, I feel like an ass. Don't know why I forgot that. The kids panicked. So did I. Took one kid and shook the livin' daylights out of him. I'm so embarrassed."

"Next time, I'll send a kid in to remind you. Sister wasn't mad, was she?"

"No. She really wasn't at all. I told her I was sorry. The poor kids didn't know what to make of it. And that damn bell scares ya, anyhow."

The two nuns walked together back to the convent, singing, "When I was young, I had no sense. . . ." They hung up their shawls and went into the kitchen for a cup of coffee. Because it was Advent, there were no snacks put out after school; they would have to wait for dinner to eat.

Sister Jean Martin, wearing her apron because it was her day to cook, was slicing the remnants of a ham for dinner. Her movements were abrupt and noisy, for she was still angry about the disruption in her teaching schedule. In addition, cooking put her out of sorts. "The whole thing just infuriates the hell out of me, if you want to know the truth, Willie," she said to both nuns.

"Oh, Jeanie," commented Sister William Ann. "It wasn't so bad. We got out early. Just look what happened to Kevin. Imagine how *her* poor kids felt."

Sister Jean Martin scowled at Sister Kevin Mary. "If people would just think what they were doing when they were doing it, these things wouldn't happen. If people would only concentrate and keep their minds on their own business, these things wouldn't happen."

Sister William Ann winked at Sister Kevin Mary, grabbed her by the sleeve, and headed her toward the refectory where they could drink their coffee in peace. Sister Jean Martin continued to bang around in the kitchen, muttering to no one in particular. They finished their coffee, washed the cups, and went to their rooms until it was time for prayer.

At 4:43, the bell rang for prayer. The telephone also rang. The nun who was "on doorbell" for the week answered the phone and called Sister Helen Francis. It was from Monsignor Ryan. She took the call, telling the Hebdomadarian to start the prayers, for she might be delayed with Monsignor. At 4:45, the Hebdomadarian began *Matins* with Psalm 94:

> Come, let us praise the Lord with joy
> For God is a great Lord
> And a great King above all gods.
> For the Lord will not abandon His people,
> For in His hands are all the ends of the earth,
> And the heights of the mountains are His.

The nuns, chanting the verses in Latin, concluded with, "He is the Lord, our God, and we are His people. . . ."

Sister Helen Francis came into the chapel and slowly genuflected. Her face was drawn. She tapped her ring on the wooden pew, interrupting the Office. "Monsignor Ryan just called. There was a terrible fire in a Catholic school, Our Lady of Angels, this afternoon right before dismissal. Nuns and kids are dead. Just terrible. Pray for them. Pray for their parents. Classrooms were wiped out. Pray for them. It was in the city. They think almost a hundred are dead."

The nuns knelt. Aggie gasped for air and began crying. The

Office continued in a subdued tone. Freddie left the chapel. Some of the nuns wiped their eyes. The Office concluded with an Advent prayer to the Blessed Virgin, who became the Mother of God through the message of an angel.

After prayer, the nuns quickly congregated in the refectory, wanting to know more of the details. The phone had rung all through prayers, with parents calling to know if the nuns had any information. Sister Helen Francis said that, despite the fact that it was Advent, they would fill their plates in the kitchen and go down to the recreation room to watch the news on television.

The nuns sat, watching pictures unroll before their eyes of parents clinging to each other, priests walking among the dead giving the Last Sacraments, firemen, hoses, trucks, screaming and crying children, ambulances, stretchers, doctors, nuns, nurses. The phone continued to ring; the nuns took turns running up the stairs to answer it.

There was talk of the fire starting in a stairwell in a corner of the building, of boxes and dirty rags, of heavy smoke, and of firemen who couldn't get their ladders across a fence. A father, still dressed in his work clothes, tears streaming down his face, spoke of catching children who jumped out the window but that he couldn't make his own son jump. His son wouldn't jump. The other kids jumped. His kid wouldn't jump but went back and was burned to death. He saw his kid looking right at him. He begged him to jump, but he wouldn't jump. A priest put his arms around the distraught father and led him away.

Documentation of the tragedy continued to flood the television screen. Pictures of classrooms with charred desks, spellers and geography books opened to their lessons, shoes burned and frozen, coats hanging from hooks, books and mittens unclaimed. The phone continued to ring, parishioners calling to tell the nuns that their children were hysterical and afraid to go to school the next day. More pictures of the church, of Mayor Daley expressing his shock and offering consolation to the families of parents identifying a child by a shoe or a ring.

Sister Jean Martin said little, cleaned up the dishes and retired early for the night.

The phone rang late into the night and began again shortly

after 6:00 the next morning. Parents, unable to console their children, were asking the nuns what to tell them. Some of the children refused to come to school. Many of the parents who had children in Room 103, Sister Kevin Mary's room, were especially concerned, for they had heard that there had been a fire drill and the first grade was not prepared. The nun had screamed and shouted at her class; the students were shoving and pushing at each other. The first-graders were having nightmares about burning in school, and Sister Kevin Mary was not getting them out.

The nuns who answered the phone, trying to cover for Sister Kevin Mary, said that there had been a mix-up, signals had gotten crossed. They could not very well tell the parents that she was new and didn't know what she was doing. Parents were encouraged to send their children to school and were told over and over again that the school was safe, that St. Paul's emptied out in ninety seconds (except the first grade), and that the fire station was right across the street.

That morning, when the final bell rang for the start of classes, less than half the room was full. The two other first grades had many absentees, but not as many as Room 103. The children, noting the empty desks, looked accusingly at their teacher. They didn't trust her anymore; she couldn't even get them out for practice—what would she do in a real fire? Or, as Sister Duns Scotus used to tell the Novices, "If this is what you do in the green wood, what will you do in the dry?"

After they said morning prayers, Sister Kevin Mary took a match and lit the Advent candle, singing, "O come, O come Emmanuel." A little girl burst into tears at the sight of the fire; a boy ran back to the bathroom; someone else ran for his coat. She knew she would have to talk to them about the fire. She could cut the tension with a knife. Teaching was useless until they got some of this settled.

"Boys and girls," spoke Sister Kevin Mary softly, "I know that you are upset. That was a terrible thing that happened yesterday at Our Lady of Angels."

Hands shot up. Kids began speaking at once. Some were standing in the aisle.

"That almost happened here, Sister!"

"My daddy said that it wouldn't have happened in a public school!"

"One kid had a sore throat and stayed home. He didn't die, but the other kids in his room died."

"There's three kids dead and no one knows who they are!"

"The nuns couldn't save them. The nuns got killed, too."

She let them continue for a few moments. Dear God, help me to say the right thing. I've caused so much of this by my carelessness. If I had used my head yesterday, they wouldn't be so upset. Dear Mother of God, tell me what to say.

There was a knock on the classroom door. Sister Kevin Mary walked over to the door. Father O'Mahoney was standing there. "Hi, Sister. Thought you might be having some trouble with the kids. Can I be of any help?"

"Dear God, yes! They think I'll let them die. They're mad at me. I forgot about the drill yesterday, and it was bedlam in here. Please say something to them, Father."

As the priest came into the room, the first grade stood, greeting him in a chorus, "Good morning, Father."

"Hi, kids." He looked at the empty desks and asked the class where everyone was. They told him that they were afraid to come to school. Those who were there seemed proud of themselves for having the courage to show up. He spoke to them of a loving Father in heaven who protected and cared for His children on earth. The class was not taken in and challenged the priest's theology.

"Yeah, Father, so how come He let all those kids die?"

"That's not right, Father. God couldn't stop that fire."

"We coulda burned in here yesterday. Sister didn't get us out on time."

Father O'Mahoney shot a look of helplessness at Sister Kevin Mary. His powerful hand was rubbing the strong chin that jutted out from his face and seemed to have a life of its own.

"Well, kids, if you won't believe that God loves and protects us, I'm sure you won't believe something else about Sister Kevin Mary." The class bit the bait, shouting at the priest to tell them a secret about their teacher.

"Well, she asked me not to tell you this, but I think that you should know it. You know, nuns are people, just like you. They weren't always nuns. They used to be girls. Well, before Sister Kevin Mary became a nun, she was a fire-lady and rescued lots and lots of kids in fires. There was one day when she carried out four kids all at once. Look at her big, strong shoulders. She's not a weakling. And you know yesterday, when you weren't ready for the fire drill? She did that on purpose, for whoever heard of kids being dressed and ready for a fire?"

The class turned toward their teacher, standing at the back of the classroom with her hands under her scapular. They began to smile at her—expressions of disbelief, pride, and forgiveness all mixed together. Some of the kids began to giggle. Someone ran to the bathroom. Two of the boys pretended they were squirting water on a fire. Some were embarrassed. They all began to giggle. Father O'Mahoney was laughing loudly; tears were rolling down Sister Kevin Mary's cheeks.

Trying to regain her composure, she walked back up to the front of the room and began to thank the priest. "That's OK, Sister. Just say three Our Fathers and three Hail Marys, and keep up the good work," he whispered, feigning what he would say in the Confessional. She closed the door after him and returned to her class.

After school that afternoon, Sister Mark Stephen, who taught sixth grade, stopped in the first grade room on her way home from school. She told Sister Kevin Mary that she and Marce had been listening to her transistor and had heard that the batallion chief was trying to determine the cause of the fire. Apparently some kids had been emptying the wastebaskets before school was dismissed and didn't see anything, but one of the nuns was out in the hall and saw the smoke. She didn't ring the fire alarm because she couldn't find the Superior to ask permission.

"She couldn't find the damn Superior to ask her if she ought to ring the bell! She couldn't find the Superior to ask her if a hundred kids ought to burn to death! She couldn't ask permission to act responsibly! I find that so incredible, Kevin. Some nuns are such asses, such total asses. God, they think that they have to give up all common sense in the name of Holy Obedience. I'm just so angry at such stupidity! I can't understand it, can you?"

"I can . . . I can understand. Let's get out of here."

The two nuns walked home in silence, Sister Kevin Mary thinking about Michael Spivak, who would have gone into a coma if she hadn't spoken up. She realized she couldn't assert herself to challenge her Superior when Sister Helen Francis took credit for writing *her* play. She didn't know what she would do. She didn't know who she was anymore. She didn't know what to think, how to act. The green wood and the dry wood. She never even really understood what that meant.

As they came in the back door of the convent, Aggie was hanging up her shawl. She waited for Sister Kevin Mary to make a short visit to chapel and motioned for her to come down to the basement with her. They walked into the pantry. Aggie reached behind the freezer, pulled out a bottle of Miller's beer, and poured out a few ounces for Sister Kevin Mary in a little flowered jelly glass. You'd never be an alcoholic if you never drink alone, thought Sister Kevin Mary. Aggie knew what she was thinking. "Just drink up. It's good for what ails ye!!"

11.

One by one, the nuns came into the community room, laden with gifts from the children. The ones who taught the primary grades received more than those who taught the upper grades. When the students got older, they were more discriminating with their affection, using the traditional Christmas gift either to reward a favorite teacher or to punish a less favored one. If they didn't like the nun, she didn't get a present. In the younger grades, the students did not have that option; their mothers bought the gifts and they delivered them.

Sister Marie Marcel, "Transistor Sister," received more gifts that any other nun in the upper grades, but she left the presents in school, primarily not to embarrass the other nuns. She walked home slowly through the light snow, stood by the community room door to acknowledge the others, whispered "Merry Christmas, nuns," and made her way slowly up to her room. The headaches were back, suddenly. They had practically ceased for the last six weeks. She had cut down on her medicine, for it slowed her down, made her feel sluggish. Her speech was beginning to slur.

A mountain of wrapping paper, boxes, tissue, string, ribbon, and cards grew in the center of the room. Sister Kevin Mary had never received so many things: pens, Yardley soap—violet and sandalwood—statues, candy, stationery, books. She opened a slender box: a thick gold pen and pencil set, worth well over $100, from the Carmodys. She had discussed with them the possibility of keeping Peter Carmody back another year. They had been so cooperative, supportive, "Whatever you think, Sister; you're the boss. Whatever you think is best for Peter. We'll stand by your decision." Obviously, the Carmodys did not want Peter failed. She closed the slender black leather case with a bang and dropped it on the floor. Mark looked at her. Sister Kevin Mary uttered under her breath, "My Christmas bribe."

Mark smiled. "That's how the Carmodys get their kids through school."

Gloves, scarves, gift certificates to Marshall Field's, six records of the singing nun, *Dominique, nique, nique*. Homemade cookies, fudge, candy, cakes, pies, bottles of wine, sherry, brandy—"Just a little something for medicinal purposes for the Good Sisters"—hams, turkeys, jams and jellies, cheeses. The nuns made lists of who received what, so they could send thank you notes. Food was piled up on the refectory table; the Procurator, the nun whose job was to shop and plan the menus, began to wrap and label the food for the freezer.

Sister Kevin Mary looked at the heap of sweets. Dear God, I'll be a tub of lard, she thought. Up to 134 pounds already—put on 22 pounds and Christmas hasn't even started. They were calling her "Chubby Checkers." Her chin was broken out. She didn't know if it was from all the sweets and greasy food or from nerves. Probably both.

Advent disintegrated. The kids had been impossible the last week of school. Baby Jesus had definitely taken a back seat to Jolly Old St. Nick. O come, O come Emmanuel was usually preceded by someone giving a good, loud "Ho-ho-ho." God knows she had tried to focus on the spiritual, but society was so materialistic that it was difficult to do so. It was impossible to prepare the heart for the coming of the Savior while the good things of the world bombarded the children. If society would not listen to her words, it would at least see her life, garbed in the holy habit that spoke of purity, innocence, and penance, a life that far transcended this earthly one. She sat among her presents, thinking nostalgically of the stark purity and simplicity of the Novitiate, when the bell rang for *Matins* and *Lauds*.

After prayer, the nuns silently filed into the refectory for High Chapter. The Hebdomadarian intoned the *De Profundis,* the penitential psalm, *Out of the depths I have cried to Thee, O Lord.* Aggie, the oldest Sister, began the pardon, facing the crucifix and bending over in an inclination:

> Reverend Sister and Reverend Sisters: I most humbly ask God's pardon and yours for having offended you by my want of diligence, by my pride and presumption, by my careless words and deeds, by my impatience and disobedience, and by all my negligences. I beg of you to pardon me all these faults and to pray for me that I may become better, and in return I shall also pray for you.

Each nun, in turn, recited the pardon prayer. When they were finished, Sister Helen Francis declared in her most eloquent tone, "May God forgive us our faults. On account of the great solemnity of the feast, it is not customary to confess the faults, but we will humble ourselves before God and say the *Confiteor.*" The nuns inclined, saying the *Confiteor* in Latin. High Chapter concluded with the blessing on the meal.

The nuns sat, took out their dishes, while the reader read the life of the Saint for the following day and some passages from the assigned spiritual book. There was a tension in the air. Christmas was only two days away, school was out, and there was much to do to get the convent and the church ready for the great feast. Sister Helen Francis interrupted the reader with, "*Benedicamus Domino,*" to which the nuns responded in a rush, "*Deo Gratias!!*" Thank God we can talk.

After dinner, Sister Helen Francis announced that there would be no night prayer and that the bell would not ring for Profound Silence that evening. *The Bells of St. Mary's* was on television at 8:00; those who wanted to watch it should come down to the recreation room ready for bed. Vacation had started. Christmas Eve was tomorrow, and there was lots of work to do. She didn't want everyone exhausted on Christmas day. They needed a break.

After dishes, the nuns assigned to the church went over to begin preparing the altar for Christmas. Some of the nuns were ironing the altar linens in the basement. The nun in charge of the altar boys went over to her classroom to check the red cassocks and line up the freshly ironed surplices. Each mother had washed and ironed her son's surplice and returned it to school for the Midnight Mass. The Procurator put away more food; the doorbell rang every ten minutes with still more. She groaned every time she heard it ring. The Advent fast was still in effect, so all the goodies went into the freezer. Sister Helen Francis went over to the priests' house to work with Monsignor Ryan.

Sister Kevin Mary went upstairs to visit with Sister Marie Marcel. She knocked softly on her door. No answer. She knocked again. Still no answer. She opened the door. Sister Marie Marcel was lying still in the darkened room, the light from the hall falling on the end of her bed. "Marce . . . Marce, you OK?" Sister Marie Marcel did not answer. She seemed to be in a deep sleep. Sister Kevin Mary closed the door quietly and went downstairs to help the Procurator.

That evening, Sister Kevin Mary sat, enraptured by Bing Crosby and Ingrid Bergman. The scent of pine branches and fruitcakes, the flickering of the Christmas lights, Father Bing Crosby crooning "Silent Night." The excitement of her first Christmas out on mission was too much. She was tired, so very tired, and confused. She was a failure with Advent—Santa Claus had won the hearts of her class; Baby Jesus was freezing in the manger for all they cared. High Chapter seemed a farce. All the nuns cared about was dinner and talking. They really didn't care about Christmas. Sister Marie Marcel could rot away upstairs, for all they cared. She began to sob, and a flood of feelings and thoughts and emotions poured out in one great burst of tears.

Sister Jean Martin looked at her disgustedly. Mark told her to be quiet. Sister Helen Francis said in a loud voice, to no one in particular, "What she needs is something to really cry about!"

Sister Kevin Mary ran up to her room, threw herself on her bed, and continued to sob. She couldn't breathe and found herself gasping for air. They were all downstairs, so she could cry as loudly as she wanted. It was all just so horrible. Not at all the way she thought it would be. If only she had been sent to a holier place, where the Superior was different, where things were taken seriously, where the pastor wasn't such a clown. She thought of the Novitiate and the beauty of the life that she had experienced there. The silence, discipline, penance, the joy and sacredness of life. She thought of home and the warmth and love they shared. She cried harder, wanting to be home, wanting to be a good nun, wanting to see and experience just a small glimmer of love and caring. The nuns were so selfish, so self-centered. Jean Martin scowling, disapproving, moody, black. Everyone had to tiptoe around her.

She thought of her Superior. What a fake! What a sham! Screwing around with the priests, and with those damn kids in her office, flirting with the men in the parish. God, how she embarrasses me. I have to kneel at her feet, ask her permission to write letters, to take phone calls, to take a bath. She is the last person in this place who should be the Superior. She isn't even a good nun. God, how I hate her! I can't believe that You speak to me through her. She's so mean to Clarabelle, takes advantage of Aggie, takes advantage of me. And I'm the bigger fool for letting her do this. Dear God, is this what You want from me? Is this Your Holy Will? The tears came with greater force, her eyes were burning and she was shaking all over. I'm fat and pimply and horrible and crying all the time. Dear God, help me. I just hate this so.

She didn't hear the knock on the door. Sister William Ann came into the room, sat on the edge of the bed, and placed her hand on Sister Kevin Mary's shoulder. She said nothing but sat quietly until Sister Kevin Mary looked up.

"Hard times, Kevvie?"

Sister Kevin Mary nodded and began to cry again.

"I know, Kev. I know. It is hard. Things just aren't what you expected. I know. I know. I know what you're going through."

"Willie, it's just so awful. The nuns are so awful and hateful. Jean Martin and Sister. Then I judge them badly, and I hate myself for that. I wish I were back in the Novitiate. I wish I were home. We never treated each other like this at home. We didn't even have vows. We were just a family."

"I know, Kev. But *we* are a family, too. We do try, you know. We do love each other, but it's hard for women to show that to each other. We do the best we can. We're just people, just plain, ordinary people—some smart, some not so smart; some weak, some strong. You know, Kev, you're stronger than most. You come from a good, loving family. I do, too, but many of the nuns have never experienced what you or I have. They never have known love. You've been loved and respected all your life. Maybe it's just your turn to give some of that back and maybe not expect too much in return."

"Willie, I just don't think I can stand this. It's just rippin' out my insides. I can cut the hatred in this house with a knife."

" 'Where there is hatred, let me sow love,' right, Kevvie? Did Sister Duns Scotus ever say that it would be easy? Did you make profession to have a warm, loving life? If you want affection and love, maybe you shouldn't be here. Maybe you ought to go and get married. Maybe this life really is too hard for you."

Sister Kevin Mary began to smile. Bottom line. If you can't stand the heat, get out of the kitchen. "I want to be a nun, Willie. I want to be a good nun."

"And you are a good nun, Kevin. A real good nun. You give so much to all of us. And you don't even know that. You're good to Aggie, to the kids. Your kids love you. You're better to Marce than anyone in the house. This is what giving is all about, Kev. Giving until it hurts, getting nothing back. Nuns *give*; they don't *get*. You're tired. The first year is hard, trying to make sense of everything, trying to learn how to teach, trying to figure out who you are. Why don't you get some sleep? To hell with Bing Crosby. Get some sleep. There's lots of work to do tomorrow. Besides, Santa Claus won't give you anything if you're not a good girl."

"Thanks, Willie. I just feel so rotten. Thanks so much."

Sister William Ann squeezed her hand and left the room. Sister Kevin Mary climbed into bed, thinking of the women downstairs watching television, the women with whom she had chosen to spend her life. Clarabelle, always getting into trouble, always setting herself up for criticism, Clarabelle the victim; Mark, so cynical, never suffering disillusions for she has no illusions about anyone or anything; Freddie, sympathetic Freddie, giving until it hurts; Max, rough, tough Max, who acted like a man and who frightened her; Aggie, simple, loving Aggie, Aggie with wisdom and age and humor; Willie, the perfect nun, how she wanted to be like Willie; Jean Martin, who had nothing at all good about her and who made everyone's life miserable; Theodore, who did the best she could (if she weren't a nun, what would she be?); Marce, her own person, probably a good nun in her own way; Julia Mary, hysterical, up and down, fun, crazy, so intelligent. Help me to accept my Sisters, Dear Lord. Help me not to judge. Help me not to make demands on them that they can't meet. Help me to give, for You have given me so much.

Alone in her room, she began her rosary. She turned in bed, facing the rectory. The thought of the nuns seemed to pale as she remembered Father Doyle, Danny Doyle, alone in his room. What a waste, she thought to herself, what a waste!

12.

December 24th had been a long day. A long, long day. The church had been decorated with mounds of poinsettias, more altar linens were washed and ironed, the altar boys had practiced, and the doorbell rang constantly with more gifts for "The Good Sisters." The priests were exhausted from hearing confessions all day long. Last-minute gifts were delivered to the doctors and those in the parish who had been especially good to the nuns. Three of the nuns came down with the flu and were taken to Dr. McCarthy for shots. Marce said it was pure Russian vodka that he so unmercifully injected them with, a leftover from his days as a Navy doctor.

The nuns had their own community traditions to observe: the reading of the *Kalendarium,* placing the Nativity within historical context; the black fast; the silence until noon. Sister Helen Francis was preparing the stuffing for the turkey; Sister Theodore was pouting because she didn't get into the kitchen first. Sister Marie Marcel didn't get out of bed and she didn't eat; her head hurt too much.

After lunch, the nuns received the mail that had been collected and saved since the first day of Advent. As Sister Kevin

Mary read the Christmas cards from the nuns who had been in the Novitiate with her, she read between the lines. Some of them were experiencing what she was. "Is this what you thought it would be? I'm in a state of total surprise." A nun from Arizona wrote: "If I knew then what I know now. . . ."

Still another wrote: "Not really sure that I'm going to make it. Maybe I can hang on until summer school. Going to set up an appointment with Sister Duns Scotus. She never told us any of this." Her best friend, stationed in Detroit, wrote: "I'm going to have to do some serious thinking about my life. I hope retreat is good. I need a good retreat."

The letters from her friends were unsettling, disquieting. Maybe they're all experiencing what I am. Maybe this is what it's really like, and I haven't just hit a bummer. Maybe this is what I'd meet wherever I'd go. Letters from her mother described how the house looked, what the kids were getting for Christmas, how happy she was that Maureen was so settled and happy with "all those beautiful Sisters." She quickly closed her mother's letters, feeling that she had projected a lie to her mother and her mother believed the lie. And she had never lied to her mother before. Her father sent her a large check which she immediately turned in.

The nuns met in the recreation room at 8:00 P.M. that evening to open their presents from Sister Helen Francis, a lavish display of either her affection for them or of her ability to obtain money from the pastor. Perhaps both. Gifts from home were opened at the same time.

After opening the presents, the nuns went to their rooms for a short rest. She had a funny dream about her mother, dressed up in the habit, and her father yelling at her to take it off. Her mother kept saying, "But, Jack, you know I must wear this for Christmas. It's your Christmas present." The bell to get ready for Midnight Mass rang at 10:45 P.M. The nuns who were responsible for the church and the altar boys had taken a nap but went over early to be sure everything was ready.

At 11:15, the nuns filed into the first three rows of the church for the start of the Christmas carols. Sister Kevin Mary felt slightly sick to her stomach. For dinner, they had eaten prime rib, baked potatoes with sour cream, rich pecan pie with whipping cream, three glasses of heavy red wine. Maybe it was just the flu coming. Maybe she was just tired. Maybe her dream was upsetting her.

There were three priests on the altar. The Mass went on and on and on. Father O'Mahoney looked green. All week before, when he was not in the confessional or with the altar boys, he had been bringing Communion to the sick. He had lost weight. Father Doyle had gained weight. Monsignor Ryan looked tan and rested.

By 1:10 A.M., four of the altar boys had left the altar. The Mass continued until 1:40—they had been in church for over two hours. After the Mass, two of the nuns left immediately to begin breakfast; the rest stayed in the church to give thanks, to put away the vestments and altar vessels, and to hang up cassocks and surplices.

The three priests joined the nuns for breakfast: baked grapefruit, sausage, Canadian bacon, eggs, coffee cake, toast, all preceded by champagne, which Sister Julia Mary had chilled in the snow before going over to Mass. She opened the bottles on the back stoop, which raised the eyebrows of some of the more devout parishioners who had remained for a long thanksgiving. She said, "I could care less what they think." She said that frequently, giving herself *carte blanche* permission to do pretty much what she wanted.

Sister Kevin Mary had to leave the table—it was all too much, too late. In the Novitiate they had gone to bed immediately after Midnight Mass so they could get up for early Mass on Christmas Day. At St. Paul's, the nuns did not have to go to any more of the Masses; their obligation had been fulfilled for the day. She could hear Monsignor Ryan singing, ". . . Yet today, my love has flown away, I am without my love. . . ." She knew that Sister Helen Francis would be blushing, trying not to look at him. Sister Julia Mary was probably pouring drinks for the more hearty. She wondered if Father Doyle had gone home. She wondered if he missed her not being there. As she fell asleep, with her rosary in her hand, she wondered who had thought to bake grapefruit. It was horrible.

She felt that she had just gotten to sleep when someone was shaking her shoulders. She turned and faced the wall, hoping the interference would go away.

"Kevin, can you get up? We've got to get Marie Marcel to the hospital right away!" It was Sister Helen Francis in her nightgown and robe, standing over her bed.

O, Dear God, not Marce. What happened to her? This is Christmas Day, dear Mother of God. Please don't let anything happen to her!

"Oh, yes, Sister. I'll get dressed right away."

Sister Kevin Mary sat up. Mark's bed was empty—Mark had gotten up, dressed quietly, and had gone over to the early Mass to play the organ.

She dressed quickly and went down the hall to Sister Marie Marcel's room. Sister Helen Francis was pinning on Marce's headgear; Aggie was kneeling down, tying her shoes. They helped Sister Marie Marcel downstairs while Sister Kevin Mary went to get the station wagon. The eight o'clock Mass was just letting out. The people greeted her as she walked quickly past them on her errand of mercy.

Dr. McCarthy was waiting for them as they pulled up in front of the emergency room door. Sister Marie Marcel had not gone to him for her headaches but had seen a specialist downtown. Dr. McCarthy met them with a look of "I'm good enough in an emergency? Where is your fancy specialist now?" Sister Helen Francis smiled her most appreciative smile. "Thank God you were home, Tom. Sorry to have to call you at this hour. She's in an awful lot of pain. She can't keep anything down."

Tom McCarthy took one look at Sister Marie Marcel and frowned thoughtfully as he took her hand. "She's dehydrated. Got to get the IVs started." He called for the head nurse. "Margie, get Sister here into a private room." Margie ran for a wheelchair. "Yes, Doctor, of course, Doctor McCarthy."

Dr. McCarthy motioned for the two nuns to sit down. He asked how long she had been like that, what the "specialist" had said, what the diagnosis was. Why was her face so distorted? What about that eye? Was it always like that? How long had she been bothered by those headaches? How long did they last? What kind of medicine was she on? How could she teach?

Sister Helen Francis fielded the questions with style and grace, impressing the doctor with her medical terminology. She didn't know what kind of medicine she was on—something new that seemed "to take the wind out of her sails." Sister Helen Francis laughed, "You know Marce, Tom. She could afford a little calming down." Dr. McCarthy didn't think it was so funny.

Sister Kevin Mary didn't know if she should tell him what Marce's new medicine was. Would that be like contradicting her Superior? Would that be a putdown? One-upmanship? Should she sit there like a ninny and not say anything when she knew what the medicine was? Oh, Dear God, here I go again.

"Ah, ah, Sister, ah, I think it was something like 'volium' or vulium.' They are little yellow pills, ah, I think. Yeah, something like that."

"Is she on valium, Sister?" asked Dr. McCarthy curtly.

"Yes, Doctor, that's it," answered Sister Kevin Mary directly. She avoided Sister Helen Francis's eyes. Sister Helen Francis raised her eyebrows.

"Listen, why don't you two go up there and see that she's in bed. I've got to get some fluids into her. We're going to knock her out with some morphine. She can't go on like that. Her eyes are black. No fluids in her. The kidneys could go. Got to get them started. I'll see you up in her room."

Dr. McCarthy found out Sister Marie Marcel's room number and directed the nuns to the second floor. They didn't speak in the elevator. Sister Kevin Mary didn't know whether Sister Helen Francis was mad at her for knowing about the medicine or just worried about Marce. As they walked into Room 222, a nurse was trying to unpin Marce's headgear. Sister Helen Francis walked swiftly over to the bed, whipped out the pins without jabbing Marce's throbbing head, and handed the pins and the headgear to Sister Kevin Mary. They lowered Marce onto the pillows. The nurse took her blood pressure and temperature, listened to her heart, carefully marking each reading on the designated line.

Within minutes, another nurse wheeled in a tall metal stand with a colorless bottle hanging from a center hook. She slipped a hollow needle into Marce's arm, attached it to a long plastic tube hanging from the bottle, and adjusted the flow of the liquid by a small gauge on the tube. She returned with a hypodermic. "A little something for the pain, Sister." Sister Marie Marcel opened her right eye, smiled faintly. "Transistor Sister, eh?" The two nuns, standing next to the bed, laughed. Sister Marie Marcel fell asleep.

Dr. McCarthy came into the room. He said that he had spoken to the neurologist who had been seeing Sister Marie Marcel and that she definitely had Bell's Palsy. He didn't understand the acceleration of the headaches, but if the Michigan Avenue neurologist said it was Bell's Palsy, then it was. He said they would keep her sedated so she could get enough rest to throw off the headache and get some fluids back into her system. He wanted to keep her in the hospital for a while so she'd get some rest, and he'd be able to watch her. He told the nuns to go home; there was nothing they could do. He wanted her to sleep. His grandchildren were coming over after the ten o'clock Mass to open their presents, so he had to get home, too.

Sister Kevin Mary looked at the nun, at Marce, who appeared ravaged with pain. She was in a deep sleep, although her face still seemed contorted. She looked like ashes, yellow ashes, lying against the white pillowcase. A small wooden crucifix hung over the hospital bed. The walls were a pale green. The sides of the bed had been raised, reminding Sister Kevin Mary of her little brother's crib; her parents had raised the sides so he wouldn't fall out. She had a fleeting image of Sister Marie Marcel falling out of bed, the tubes and bottles crashing on top of her, the crucifix hanging sideways. She closed her eyes tightly, trying to dispel the image. Sister Helen Francis motioned to her. As she turned from the bed, she touched Marce's foot, sticking up through the white blanket. Dear God, please take care of her—it's Christmas Day, Christmas Day in the morning—please don't let anything happen to her.

As the two nuns walked slowly down the long white corridor, they heard carolers singing, "We wish you a Merry Christmas, we wish you a Merry Christmas, we wish you a Merry Christmas and a Happy New Year!"

13.

The harsh January winds shook the thin chapel windows; inside, the flames of the fourteen candles flickered. She was thankful for the cardigan her mother had sent for Christmas. She wore it under her habit and looked bulkier than ever. She had gained another four pounds over vacation.

The house had been quiet that morning. First Sunday. Retreat Sunday. Tomorrow would be the fifth of January. Vacation was over and back to school, thank God. Too many people with too much time on their hands. Too many women. She remembered when she was a senior in high school, a few months before she entered the convent, telling her mother that she didn't like girls as much as boys. Her mother looked up from the dishes and said, "Well, Maureen, you're making a helluva decision." She was going to be spending the rest of her life with women—morning, noon, and night—and she didn't like girls.

That morning began with the Office and meditation—the first time since New Year's Day. The Superior thought that they didn't have "to overdo it" during vacation. Breakfast in silence, and after breakfast they had the Chapter of Faults, "Where the Sisters shall accuse themselves simply and humbly of external faults against the Rule and Constitutions and religious decorum." Each Sister, in turn, inclined toward the large crucifix, stating in a low tone:

> Reverend Dear Sister, I humbly confess that I have not rightly observed our Holy Rule and Constitutions but have in many ways transgressed them. Especially do I acknowledge myself guilty of the following faults:

Sister Kevin Mary, taking her turn after Freddie, confessed her faults:

> Not answering bells promptly
> Making mistakes in the Office and reading
> Coming late to chapel
> Not paying attention to the reading at the table
> Wasting time
> Not using proper titles
> Forgetting to ask permission
> Presuming permissions and failing to report them

She concluded with:

> For these and all the other faults committed against our Holy Rule and Constitutions, I humbly beg of you, Reverend dear Sister, a deserving penance according to the traditions of our Holy Order.

She knelt and then prostrated herself on the refectory floor, while Sister Helen Francis told her to say a decade of the Rosary for the Holy Souls in purgatory. When she rapped her ring against the table, Sister Kevin Mary stood and walked humbly back to her place. She could feel her face turning red as she was bolted back into the reality of their lives, the monastic reality of discipline, tradition, and rule.

After the Chapter of Faults, Sister Helen Francis announced

that the Carmelite who was supposed to come for the Holy Hour and sermon was not able to make it because of the weather. Father O'Mahoney would be over at 2:00. She reminded them to have their lesson plans on her desk by 4:45 and said that no extensions would be granted today. They responded, "Yes, Sister," in unison and left the refectory.

The bell rang within fifteen minutes. It was Monsignor Ryan, who had come over to expose the Blessed Sacrament. The nuns quickly gathered in the chapel. The candles were lit and the crib set surrounded by red and white poinsettias was turned on. After the Blessed Sacrament was positioned in the gold monstrance and placed on top of the tabernacle, Monsignor Ryan left. The nuns began the first part of the rosary.

After the rosary, Sister Kevin Mary left chapel, deciding to make her Holy Hour around noon. As she walked past Sister Marie Marcel's room, she could hear Sister Helen Francis speaking. "Do you want me to get a lay teacher in there or not? You're going to have to be the one to let me know." Sister Kevin Mary couldn't hear the answer. She went to her room and began her lesson plans for the week. She was anxious to get back to school, to see the kids, to thank them for all the stuff they had given her for Christmas.

At 11:30, she decided to go downstairs for a cup of coffee. The silence was beginning to get to her. She felt jumpy, hungry. Well, she was always hungry, so what else was new? She had three cups of coffee and two pecan rolls left over from breakfast and went into chapel for her Holy Hour. A whole hour. How am I going to make it? I'm getting out of practice. During the Novitiate, an hour each day wasn't long enough. It's all just slipping away, slipping away from me.

She began reading the *Life of Christ* by an Italian Jesuit, Romano Guardini. On the cover was a picture of the face of Christ with red, black, and yellow streaks. She couldn't get into it. Too abstract. And she hated to read things that were full of Scriptural references. It broke up the text, distracted her. She tried to read it, skipping the italicized parts from the Bible, but that distorted the meaning.

Sister Kevin Mary sat back on the seat, watching a curled

poinsettia leaf move ever so gently. She closed her eyes, trying to recollect herself and trying to stop the pounding and pounding inside of her. Dear God, grand me stillness of soul in Thee. Let Thy mighty calmness reign in me. Rule me, O Thou King of Silence, King of Peace. Take the knots out of my stomach. Help me to be like Willie, so calm, so sure of herself, such a good nun. Help me to stop thinking about Father Doyle. Hold me close to You, Dear Lord. I feel myself slipping away. Hold me dear God, hold me.

She heard Freddie clear her throat in the seat across the aisle. Poor Freddie, she hasn't snapped out of what happened to her on Christmas yet. She seems so sad lately, melancholy. Keeps calling herself a dumb Pollack. Fated, ill-fated. She even got the wrong name. She was supposed to be "Sister Bruno Marie," after her mother and her father. When they got the habit and their religious names, the bishop got the cards mixed up: Elizabeth McCurdy walks around with Mary Petrowski's parents' names, Bruno and Marie; and Mary Petrowski is called by the names of the McCurdy children, Frederick and Ellen.

On Christmas Day, the doorbell rang just as the nuns sat down for their Christmas meal. The nun "on doorbell" answered it and reported to Sister Helen Francis that Mr. Petrowski was there. Freddie, profoundly embarrassed, went to greet her father. The nuns were not to have company on Christmas Day. Freddie had asked Sister Helen Francis if her father might come because it was going to be a hard day for him. Sister Helen Francis said no, that wasn't customary. He could come on the twenty-sixth.

Mrs. Petrowski had died on Christmas Day when Freddie was a Novice, just two days before her first profession. She had made her vows privately on Christmas night and left the next morning for Chicago to be with her father. Freddie was their only child for they had married late in life. Freddie told Sister Kevin Mary that her parents "had to get married." When she was getting her papers ready to enter the convent, she discovered that her parents were really married in July and not on March 7, the date they celebrated. Freddie was actually born six months, not nine months, after they were married. She was so proud of them: "Probably the only way my grandmother would let him go . . . he had to make an honorable woman out of my mother . . . and they were both in their *early forties!!* Isn't that a riot, Kev? My folks had to get married! Wonder where they did it? In the back seat of a car? Can't you just see 'em?" The two nuns laughed hysterically, thinking of her two gray-haired parents fornicating their way into marriage.

Bruno Petrowski stood in the parlor, the snow melting on his thick gray hair and on his stooped shoulders. His breath smelled of whiskey, and his eyes were filled with tears. His daughter walked into the parlor, threw her arms around her father.

"Daddy, Daddy. You came!"

"Moja Droga!! Moje Drogie Czoreczko!!!"

"Oh, Daddy, I know. I know it's a bad day for you! But she said you couldn't come, Daddy. I'm not supposed to see you today."

"Moja Droga!!! What could I do? My heart is breaking, and I'm all alone without your mother. Moja Droga, Moja Droga!"

Freddie took her father's coat, made him comfortable, and went back to the kitchen to get him something to eat. She stopped at Sister Helen Francis's place and told her that she had told her father not to come, but he had come anyway. Sister Helen Francis told her not to worry and to get her father something to eat; she understood that it was a hard day for him. Sister Kevin Mary helped Freddie get some food for her father. Freddie was not allowed to eat with him, but she and Sister Kevin Mary sat and watched him. He tried to eat but couldn't.

"Mary, I don't need food; I don't want food. I just want your mama back. I'm so lonely." He turned to Sister Kevin Mary. "You understand, don't you, Sister?"

"It must be hard for you, Mr. Petrowski. I know how I felt when my grandmother died. I know it hurts."

Freddie looked straight at her father. "Daddy, you look so tired. You've lost more weight. Just look at your pants, hanging from you like an old man's. You gotta eat."

"Mary, I am an old man. I'm sixty-four years old; my life is spent. I'll never have any grandchildren, you're gone, your mother is gone . . . so what is there to live for? I'm tired and so lonely, Mary. You wanta come home? You wanta leave this place? No, you got your life in this place, and my life is all over."

"And you're drinking too much again, Daddy. I can tell."

"Now, Mary, don't start on me. It's all I got left."

Mr. Petrowski began to cry, wiping his eyes and blowing his nose with a big, white handkerchief. Sister Kevin Mary looked at Freddie with a "shall-I-leave?" look. Freddie shook her head; she needed some help with her father. The two nuns took Bruno Petrowski out for a walk in the high snow, making their way into the village to look at shop windows, anything just to distract him. They brought him back to the convent for fruit-cake and coffee before he left for the train that would take him back to the North Side and his little butcher shop on Belmont. Bruno the Butcher, the neighborhood people called him.

After Mr. Petrowski left, Sister Frederick Ellen went to the Superior to tell her again that she hadn't encouraged her father to come, that she really understood the rules and didn't want to disobey. Sister Helen Francis looked up from her paper. "I know that, Sister. You've told me that twice. You know, there are just certain things that you shouldn't ask about. Think about that, Sister, and Merry Christmas." Freddie related that conversation to Sister Kevin Mary later that evening. Neither of them understood what she meant.

Sister Kevin Mary stared at the Blessed Sacrament, thinking of how these nuns had become so much a part of her life, like the little spokes radiating out from the center of the gold monstrance. Freddie and Mr. Petrowski, Aggie, dear Aggie, and Marce, who seemed to be doing a little better since she had come home from the hospital. The headaches were gone, but she seemed rather distant. Not her old self at all. It was only 12:15. Forty-five more minutes to go. She flipped open the Guardini book again. The print was too small, too many italics, the paragraphs too long. She decided to say the Litany of the Blessed Mother. That ought to take five minutes.

"Holy Mary, Pray for us; Holy Mother of God, Pray for us; Mother most chaste, Pray for us; Mother most pure, Pray for us; Mystical Rose . . . Tower of David . . . Tower of Ivory . . .

House of Gold . . . Queen of the Most Holy Rosary . . . Queen of Peace."

The door of the chapel banged open. Sister Julia Mary walked through, catching her rosary on the doorknob. She picked up the broken beads, dropped them noisily on the pew, and knelt on both knees before the Blessed Sacrament. This seemed to be one of her "up" days. As a matter of fact, she had been up all during the holidays, her hazel eyes flashing, her step lively, her speech rapid.

She liked Sister Julia Mary, liked her very much, but felt completely out of her league. They called her "Jules" or "Jewel." She was the brightest, the most articulate, the sharpest nun at St. Paul's. Most of the nuns read *Our Sunday Visitor* and *The New World;* Jules read *Commonweal, America, The Saturday Review, The New Republic.* And *The Imitation of Christ* in Latin, because she didn't care for any of the translations. Felt they distorted the original meaning—"contaminated it," she said.

The rest of the nuns spent hours correcting papers, making lesson plans, decorating their classrooms. Jules never seemed to be bothered with those things, saying, "Work expands to fill the time allotted for its completion . . . Parkinson, the English economist, you really ought to read him, Kev . . . get away from those grubby, little papers you seem so fond of . . . Here, read this! Read that! Do you want the double acrostic this week? . . . You know, Galbraith makes sense with his theories on public wealth, don't you agree? . . . What do you think of Kerouac? . . . And this *Loneliness of the Long-Distance Runner* is intriguing. What do you think? . . . *The Ugly American?* You haven't read that? Take it," and she would reach into her crowded bookcase for another book.

Jules was exciting. She made Sister Kevin Mary stand tall, think, develop. She'd try out her new words on Jules. "No, Jules, that isn't feasible."

"Oh, *feasible,* is it? What's wrong with *plausible,* Kev?"

She was exciting but also a little scary. Each night she went to her room with a glass full of ice cubes. What would she want with a glass full of ice cubes? And when she wasn't up, she was very far down. Depressed, melancholy, black. "My black Irish soul is surfacing, I can feel it," Jules would say, and she would go into herself at a depth that no one could touch.

One day, Sister Kevin Mary was outside the convent, cleaning the exhaust pipe for the dryer. It was on the side opposite the walk and next to the fence where no one ever went. She looked up and saw Jules' windowsill lined with beer cans and whiskey bottles keeping chilled in the snow. Her room smelled musty. At first, Sister Kevin Mary thought it was from all her books, but now realized that she was spraying it with Lysol to kill the smell of booze. Her bedroom walls were covered with funny little spray marks that shone when the light hit them at a particular angle.

Jules and a small group of the older nuns, including Sister Helen Francis, began congregating in the French provincial parlor in the evenings during vacation. The bell didn't ring, so they could talk all night. The Seagram's Seven and 7-Up appeared nightly on the counter in the kitchen. A certain selectivity appeared to be at work, since Mark, Clarabelle, Freddie, Willie, Aggie, Theo, and she were never invited. And the parlor door was closed. The Somebodies and the Nobodies, Mark called them. "Isn't it great to be a Nobody, Kev?" When she would go to bed at night, she could hear the Somebodies down below, Jules laughing louder and harder than all the rest. Sister Kevin Mary felt betrayed. Jules was her friend; they did crossword puzzles together, shared books, improved each other's vocabulary, yet she wasn't good enough to join the Somebodies. Maybe they thought she was too young, too innocent. But then, if she joined the Somebodies, how would Freddie and Mark, Willie and Clarabelle feel? They usually watched the late-late movie, made popcorn, drank Cokes or root beer. Just what Nobodies usually do. And they didn't laugh nearly so loud.

Jules was reading her Bible, Monsignor Ronald Knox's translation—"more lucid," Jules explained. Sister Kevin Mary thought that she could detect the beginning of a "down," perhaps by the way she came into the chapel, the way she dropped the broken beads. God, "there is nothing hidden that shall not be revealed." No secrets from each other; the slightest shift in a mood is five points on our personal Richter scale. A mudslide of the mind; earthquake of the emotions. Someone looks out of the corner of her eyes and ten people notice. Maybe that's what's the trouble with me, she thought, no real privacy. I'm just so totally naked to all these strangers, no place to hide. Maybe I'll grow up to be transparent, 138 pounds of transparency.

It was only 12:25. Thirty-five more minutes to go for her Holy Hour to be up. Then an hour break, then the priest would be over. Then more prayers, listen to his sermon, more prayers. She thought she heard a funny noise coming from behind her. Sniffling or choking. She and Jules were the only ones in chapel. She didn't want to turn around and embarrass her. Maybe she just had a cold. She heard Jules making funny noises, painful noises—half choking, half sighing.

Sister Kevin Mary couldn't stand it. She turned around in her place. Sister Julia Mary was kneeling, holding her face in her hands. "Kevin," she gasped, "I think I'm going mad."

14.

As she walked down the hall, a few of the children were already in school, sitting on the floor and pulling off their snowy boots and snowsuits. Little puddles of water were forming in the hall. The janitor would mop up the floors around 9:00, after all the classes were filled. She greeted the boys and girls, unlocked the door, and prepared for the new year, 1959. Perhaps things in school would go a bit smoother, she wouldn't always feel so unprepared, in such a dither. She'd have to study those manuals better to find out what she was doing.

Three little boys hung up their coats and took the large fish tank down the hall to the utility closet to change the water. Every day during the vacation, Sister Kevin Mary had come over to school to change the water and feed the five small goldfish. Each week, different boys were assigned to the fish. It was too big a job for the girls; they got to dust her desk or straighten the books and papers.

Within a few minutes, they came back into the room, the water in the large round tank steaming. The five fish were on the surface, lying on their backs, bumping into the pieces of fish food that had not yet dissolved.

"Sister, the fish were cold. We made the water nice and hot for them!"

"Yeah, Sister, now they won't catch cold. We warmed them up!"

The boys beamed at their sense of protection for the cold, little fish. One of them looked puzzled at the immobile fish. "But something's wrong, Sister. They're not moving."

"Yeah, I think there's something wrong, boys. You know, fish like cold water."

"Are they dead, Sister?" one little boy asked, his bottom lip beginning to quiver.

"I think they are, boys," Sister Kevin Mary said softly. "But I think you tried to do the right thing. You just didn't know that it would hurt them. I'll take care of the fish, and you go to your seats."

One of the boys started to cry. Another put his head down on his desk. Sister Kevin Mary walked into the bathroom and threw the fish down the toilet. She came back into the class- room with the empty bowl, putting it quietly in the back locker.

A little girl, observing the scene, walked swiftly up to the boys. "You're so smart. You killed the fish. You killed *our* fish. You're murderers, just plain old murderers, and I'm going to tell the rest of the kids."

The boy lifted his head from his desk and took a swing at her blond head, telling her to mind her own business. Sister Kevin Mary walked down the aisle, grabbed the girl by her shoulder, and placed her firmly in her own place, telling her to take out her crayons and begin her work.

Now what do I do? Get into some theology about what has a soul and what doesn't? Talk about serious matter, sufficient knowledge, and full consent of the will—the prerequisites for a serious sin? Let it go? The less said the better? Punish the poor kids? Everyone loves a scapegoat. She decided to let it pass and go to Woolworth's after school and buy some new fish.

She looked out the window and saw Father O'Mahoney

going into the sacristy door for the 8:15 Mass. Jack O'Mahoney, so priestly. He loved being a priest. The way he says Mass, the way he talks with the kids, the way he thinks. Not full of himself like Monsignor Ryan; not soft like Father Doyle. He was strong without being stiff, intelligent without being an intellectual. She was glad the Carmelite priest wasn't able to make it for the retreat yesterday. Actually, Father O'Mahoney had never addressed the nuns by themselves—it was good to get to know him.

He had spoken to them about their vocations: to be the flesh and blood representatives of the Church; to be the very heart of the Mystical Body of Christ on earth. A religious vocation from the Latin, *vocare*—to call. A calling to the life of service in the Church. She loved to think back on the time when she first felt the stirrings of Grace within herself. She was sixteen years old—smart, popular, the "all-American girl." She dated lots of boys, mostly from the local Jesuit high school and then the Jesuit college in Detroit. She could never really get serious about any of them. On a level deeper than she realized, she knew that she was different, singled out for more important things than the rest of her classmates. She felt drawn toward the nuns who had taught her, drawn to a life of sacrifice, of prayer and mortification, of study and silence.

She loved the habit, the life of living in a religious community, but most of all, of saving souls and teaching. She would manifest the life of Christ within herself, through her vows of poverty, chastity, and obedience. Obedience, the very crux, the nucleus of her life. So many times Sister Duns Scotus had reiterated: "Obedience should always be prompt, joyous, willing, and simple, without any opposition, discussion, or complaint."

She said a simple prayer of thanksgiving for the grace of her vocation, asking always to be faithful to her vows. Sister Duns Scotus had frequently warned them against infidelity: "An unfaithful religious is a cancer on the Mystical Body of Christ." That never failed to make her shudder. The very thought of turning her back on her vows was intrinsically repugnant. She would remain the faithful bride, vigilant against the first sign of treason from within.

She began the class that first day of the new year with an increased sense of her own vocation, of her purpose, focusing on the grace of a vocation and not on the nitty-gritty of teaching. It would all fall into place, if only her faith were greater.

Sister Kevin Mary began the story of Jesus getting lost in the temple. There had been so much of the Christmas story with angels, wise men, shepherds; it was now time to get on with the boyhood of Jesus. Christ's purpose on earth was to do the Will of His Father who had sent Him, even if that meant forgetting about Mary and Joseph, His parents on earth. The children seemed somewhat disturbed. Forgetting about your parents? She went on with great emotion about Mary looking for Jesus and Joseph looking for Jesus, and their coming together, saying, "I thought he was with you . . . No, he's not. I thought he was with you. . . ." She would spare no feeling, for she knew only too well that fathers and mothers had to be foregone to do the Most Holy Will of God.

The boys and girls looked at her with fright, identifying with the lost Christ child, knowing how His parents felt, even if He had some other stuff to do. She was a master, holding their supple feelings in her wise, masterful hands. As she looked across the room, the way Sister Duns Scotus used to sweep the room with her penetrating eyes, Sister Kevin Mary saw a little boy, sitting on the toilet, green corduroy pants down around his shoes. His mouth was open as well as the bathroom door, for he was not about to miss one word of the drama. Dear God, if I shout at him to close the door, all the kids will turn around and see him. If I walk back there, they'll see him.

The teacher, trying not to watch, related to the class the utter surprise when Jesus found out that his mother and father had been looking for him. The class began to laugh, the tension broke, as she said in her best delivery, "How is it that you have sought Me? Did you not know that I must be about My Father's business?" The children began to laugh, not quite understanding what the story was all about, but just that they knew what it felt like to be lost and found. The boy stood, turned, bare-bottomed, to flush the toilet, and then pulled up his corduroys, zipping them tightly as he walked to his place. No one in the class had noticed, and Jesus returned home with His parents.

The children began to color the picture in their religion books that depicted the Scriptural event. Sister Kevin Mary walked up and down the aisle, feeling that she had delivered the best performance of her life, despite the visual disruption. And she had spared the child embarrassment. The nuns were calling her Sarah Bernhardt, picking up on her tendency to dramatize the ordinary. She reflected on the fact that really good teachers were good actresses; they had a natural ability to hold the attention of the class. She could do that. Fifty-six kids, held spellbound by her words. She always knew that she would be a good teacher. Sister Duns Scotus was right: "Trust in God, don't get in His way, and you will be given the grace to do what you have to do."

Later that afternoon, Sister Helen Francis sent a note around to all the teachers, carried by one of the poachers. It said that Sister Carlotta, the community supervisor, had just called to say she would be visiting St. Paul's the next day to evaluate the teachers. Sister Kevin Mary signed the note with a smile, knowing that Sister Carlotta would be duly impressed with her performance in the classroom. She'll probably think that I've been teaching for years. Maybe I get this from my father, the way he gets those juries to eat out of his hands.

At 3:10, Willie came bouncing into her classroom, humming, "When I was young, I had no sense . . . I bought a fiddle . . ." Sister Kevin Mary looked up, always happy when Willie came in.

"Hi, Kevvie! God, Carlotta's coming tomorrow! She picks the absolute worst time of the year. We'll work on your stuff as soon as we get home, OK? You've got to be ready for her or she'll cream ya!"

"No sweat, Willie," said Sister Kevin Mary. "I'm in real good shape. I really know what I'm doing. Don't think you have to bother. I can handle Carlotta; don't worry." She smiled to herself, thinking of the high level of professionalism that she brought to Jesus getting lost in the temple.

"OK, Kev. It's your show. But if you change your mind and want to go over anything, please don't hesitate to let me know.

That's what I'm here for." She turned to leave, singing,
". . . The only tune that I could play was Over the Hills and
Very Far Away."

The nuns reacted somewhat hysterically to the news that the
supervisor was coming. Intimidated, that's what they are. I
don't teach for a supervisor; I teach because I have been
assigned by my religious superiors. The technicalities of the
trade can be learned, polished; that's not what really makes a
teacher, a religious teacher. It's commitment, dedication, love.
Sister Kevin Mary knew that she was not lacking in any of
those areas.

A schedule was posted on the refectory door. Sister Carlotta
would be picked up at St. Ignatious Convent at 7:30 A.M. and
would be at St. Paul's by 8:30. She would start her visitation at
9:00; at 10:10, she would be visiting the first grade, Room 103.
Sister Kevin Mary looked confidently at the notice, made a
short visit to chapel on her way to school, feeling somewhat
irritated at the nuns, with their stories of "Carlotta this" and
"Carlotta that." Sister Kevin Mary taught for the Greater
Glory of God, and not for Sister Carlotta.

At 10:10 sharply, her classroom door opened. Sister Carlotta
entered the room, clipboard poised in her left arm. The children greeted the supervisor. She told them to be seated, that
she had heard such wonderful things about them, and that she
wanted to see how well they were doing. What a phony,
thought Sister Kevin Mary. She wants to see how well *I'm*
doing. The kids can't be fooled like that. The class went back
to work. Sister Carlotta told Sister Kevin Mary to begin her
reading groups.

Sister Kevin Mary called the Blessed Mother group to the
small reading chairs at the front of the room. They took out
their workbooks and came to the chairs. One little girl tripped
over a chair. Sister Kevin Mary could have killed her. She told
them to open their books and to begin reading, just where they
had left off the day before.

Sister Carlotta quickly looked up from the teacher's desk.
Sister Kevin Mary wrote "play" on the board, telling the class
that was their new word for the day. Then she called on the

little girl who had tripped to begin reading. Sister Carlotta stood abruptly, walked over to Sister Kevin Mary, and asked in a low voice, "What are you doing?"

"Teaching reading, Sister."

"Is this the way that you do it?"

"Yes, Sister, every day."

"What about the charts, your presentation, the flashcards, the board work? Where is your presentation? How do you do it?"

"That's all too complicated. I just do a little bit of this and a little of that, Sister."

Sister Carlotta pursed her lips, staring in disbelief. "Boys and girls, I've made a terrible mistake. This is the wrong room. I'll have to come back tomorrow." She turned to Sister Kevin Mary. "And I'll see you after school! This is an absolute disgrace!" The class stood and said good-bye to Sister Carlotta as she hurried out of Room 103.

Sister Kevin Mary thought she was going to faint. Dear God, I don't believe this happened to me. O, My God, this is just terrible. She could feel her eyes fill with tears. She sent the Blessed Virgin Marys back to their seats with an assignment and headed down to the office, hoping that she would not end up in a heap on the freshly mopped floor.

Sister Helen Francis was alone; the poachers were back in their classrooms while the supervisor was there. Sister Kevin Mary knocked loudly on her open door and walked in.

"Oh, Sister Helen Francis. Sister Carlotta just left my room. She's mad at me. I've disgraced you. I've disgraced myself. I'm so sorry. I thought I knew what I was doing . . . Willie wanted to help me . . . I'm so sorry . . . I was just too proud . . . I've disgraced all of us . . . I'm so sorry."

"Sister Kevin Mary, what are you trying to say? I don't understand."

"She's mad at me. I don't know how to teach . . . She wants to see me after school . . . I disgraced you, Sister. I'm so sorry."

Sister Kevin Mary stood, sobbing at the end of Sister Helen Francis's desk. Sister Helen Francis walked over to the door, closed it, and began to smile.

"Kevin, it just can't be that bad. Carlotta loves to do that to the new teachers. I remember when I came out, she took me to my principal, telling her she was going to send me back to the motherhouse that very afternoon. It just can't be that bad. If you are having trouble, just ask her. That's what she's here for. And you didn't disgrace me. And you didn't disgrace yourself."

Sister Kevin Mary continued to cry, knowing that she had lost face forever, feeling for the first time in her life that she was incompetent, a failure.

"What are you going to do, Kevin? Stand there and cry for the rest of the morning? Go home and get a cup of coffee. I'll watch your class for a few minutes. Go and wash your face. You're not a disgrace. Go on home now and relax." She smiled kindly at the young nun, leading her out of her office.

During the lunch hour, Sister Kevin Mary avoided Sister Carlotta. She told Willie what had happened, knowing that her humiliation was now complete. In her "pride and presumption," she had arrogantly refused help, doing a disservice not only to herself, to the class, but to the nuns with whom she lived. Now St. Paul's would have a bad name, just because of her cockiness, her pride, her self-will and lack of humility. Willie told her that she was sorry; there was not even the slightest trace of "If-only-you-had-let-me-help-you" on her face. Willie's face was blank.

After school, Sister Carlotta came into Room 103 and began explaining the procedure of teaching reading. They went through the teacher's manuals, charts, flashcards, workbooks, and readers. Sister Kevin Mary then had to pretend she was teaching a reading group, with Sister Carlotta one of the students. At 5:30, having missed Matins and Lauds, they went home for dinner. The following morning, Sister Carlotta would come back to see if Sister Kevin Mary had learned how to teach, to give her a chance to redeem herself.

Sister Kevin Mary asked for permission to keep her light on after 9:30. She had to go over the lessons for the next day. She just couldn't blow it again. Sister Helen Francis said of course, not to worry, she would do just fine. Sister Kevin Mary thanked her, feeling irritated at her Superior, for Sister Helen

Francis never seemed to take anything seriously. That night she dreamed of trying to teach reading, and all the kids were trying to go to the bathroom and wouldn't listen to her. And the fish were bubbling in vats of hot water as she turned the flashcards, flipped the charts, and dropped the readers. When the bell rang at 5:10 the next morning, she felt tired, irritable, slightly nauseated.

She made her way over to school early, hoping she would slip on the ice and break a leg. The early bus came too early. She had no time to go over her lessons again before Carlotta came in to harass her. Maybe she would be assigned to cook for the rest of her life, like the foreign nuns at the motherhouse who couldn't teach. She'd spend the rest of her life slopping around with potatoes and carrots and cabbage. They'd all know that she just couldn't cut it; she couldn't make the grade. "Poor Sister Kevin Mary, she's been here for twenty-eight years, with her head stuck in an oven, flour caked under her nails." She tried to concentrate on the teacher's manual, snapping at the early birds to let her do her work; they had work to do, didn't they?

Timothy Moore, the little boy who had gone to the bathroom in front of God and everyone the previous day, made his way up to her desk cautiously. He plunked a large yellow grapefruit on her desk. It was wrapped in dark green cellophane, with a little card, "To my teacher, Sister Kevin Mary, Love, Timothy," written in his own handwriting. She looked up at the little boy.

"Hi, Sister. My grandma sent these from Florida. I wanted to bring one for your breakfast. My mommie said I could." Timothy beamed at his teacher, knowing that a gift out of season meant so much more.

"Thanks so much, Timothy," she said softly. Sister Kevin Mary walked to the blackboard and began to write the words for the Blessed Mother group with chalk. She swallowed hard, knowing if she gave in to the lump in her throat, the tears would flow until noon.

15.

The January snow gusted across the playground. The blacktop looked like a moon crater, tire ridges and footprints frozen in place. The children sitting in the row by the window had their sweaters buttoned tightly; the blast of heat coming from the radiators under the drafty windows did little good.

Fourteen of the children were absent, and Sister Kevin Mary didn't feel very well. Asian flu or something like that. All the nuns had received flu shots from Dr. McCarthy in October, and afterwards felt sick for a few days. She was achy, lightheaded, and her ears and throat hurt. The kids were annoying her; she was probably annoying them. She looked at the clock: 1:40, only an hour and twenty minutes to go.

There was a knock on her door—one of the eighth grade poachers with a note from Sister Helen Francis. The note read:

Nuns:

Since we all have the flu, we will go to bed early tonight. Say your prayers privately. Margaret will put out the dinner. Eat when you want. Everyone is to be in bed, feet off the floor, by 7:00. Lights out by 7:30.

She signed the note at the bottom, handing the note back to the boy, who had a slight smirk on his face. He probably knows what Margaret is putting out for dinner, she thought.

School emptied out quickly. The nuns brought home no schoolwork—the job for the night was to go to bed. Many went into chapel to finish their Office for the day; some took their Office books to their rooms to say their psalms in bed. The back door flew open and Clarabelle, glasses frosted, sneezed her way to the closet, dropping sets of papers and two teacher's manuals. "Damn Sam!" she muttered to no one in particular.

Freddie came out of chapel as Clarabelle began coughing. "Clarabelle, why'd you bring home all that stuff? We're supposed to go to bed. You sound terrible!"

"I didn't know anything about it. How'd you hear?"

"She sent a note around. Didn't you get it?"

"Are you kidding? You know I don't exist down in that hole."

"Clarabelle, I'm sure Sister just forgot. She doesn't feel well, either. Let your stuff go and get to bed."

Freddie picked up Clarabelle's papers and books, while Clarabelle genuflected in the chapel, grabbing her Office book.

"Yippee!!!!" shouted Clarabelle, as she ran up the stairs, rounded the corner, and raced to their room, Freddie following. As she dove into bed, fully clothed, a loud thud shook the house, the mattress hit the floor, cracking the wooden supports, and the maple frame splintered into pieces under the impact of Clarabelle's dive.

Freddie rushed into the room to see Clarabelle, glasses shattered, veil askew, lying on top of the rubble. Mark and Sister Kevin Mary ran to the room. "God, Clarabelle, now you did it this time! She'll kill you," warned Mark.

"Oh, Clare, look at your glasses!" said Freddie.

"I can't see my glasses, Freddie. Where are they? Wa' hoppened?" asked Clarabelle.

By this time, Sister Jean Martin, in her robe and nightcap, came into the room, hands on her hips. "I wish some people would grow up! This is utterly disgusting! She wouldn't get away with this at any other place I've ever been! Grow up, Clare, just grow up for a change, will you please!" She turned on her heels and walked out of the room.

"Ignore her, Clare," said Freddie softly, helping Clarabelle up and picking up her broken glasses. Let me help you take off your stuff."

Clarabelle began coughing and sneezing and crying. "Dear God, I can't seem to do anything right. Jean Martin is right, and Sister will kill me! This is all she needs; she hates me anyhow!" Sister Kevin Mary handed her some Kleenex. Clare blew her nose and cried harder.

Sister Julia Mary stopped by their door. "Hmmm, Humpty Dumpty had a great fall, eh, Clarabelle? Just pretend you live in Tokyo and sleep on the floor . . . Tokyo Rose. It's great for the back." She held up her glass of ice cubes and her *Saturday Review* for all to see. "Well, I'm going to enjoy myself tonight. See ya, girls. Bye, bye."

Mark looked up from the pile of wood. "Smart and drunk. She won't be able to see straight by 5:30."

"Mark, just mind your own business, will you please?" asked Freddie. "Help us clean up this mess before Sister gets home." Clarabelle blew her nose. Mark and Kevin picked up the pieces and carried them down to the basement. Freddie helped Clarabelle get ready for bed and went down to the kitchen to bring her something to eat.

The back door flew open and Sister Helen Francis came in with two of the eighth grade boys, who were carrying her small briefcase. The nuns hid so the boys wouldn't see them without their habits on. She thanked them effusively, hung up her cloak, and came into the kitchen. Freddie, who was fixing something for Clarabelle to eat, told Sister Helen Francis that Clare had had an accident up in the room, had broken her glasses, and was not feeling well.

Sister Helen Francis looked disgusted and made her way quickly up to the room. Clarabelle heard her Superior coming down the hall, jumped out of bed, pulled on her robe inside out.

As Sister Helen Francis came into the room, Clare knelt down. "Oh, Sister Helen Francis," she began, her voice quivering, "may I please have a penance? I broke my bed. I'm so sorry, I didn't mean to do it. I'm sorry." She coughed and sneezed.

"How did this happen, Sister?" asked Sister Helen Francis sharply.

"Ah, Sister, I don't know. I guess I was just in such a hurry to get into bed that I broke it."

"I don't understand, Clare. How did you ever *break* your bed by being in a hurry?" she asked as she looked at the heavy young nun with contempt, never wanting to miss an opportunity to further her humiliation.

"I ran."

"You can say three rosaries, Sister, and you can sleep on the floor for the rest of the year. We don't have that kind of money to have you jumping on the furniture." She turned and left the room, as Clare shouted, "May God reward you, Sister," after her. Clarabelle got back onto the mattress and began crying again.

The following morning after breakfast, Sister Helen Francis delivered a sermon on the use of community property, of the vow of poverty, of the responsibility they all had, whether young or old, to safeguard the worldly things that had been entrusted to them for their use. Sister Jean Martin shot a dirty look at Clarabelle. Big Max folded her arms and frowned in her direction. Aggie's face reddened. Sister Marie Marcel appeared to be sneering again. Freddie's eyes filled with tears as she looked at Clarabelle. Willie stared at the crucifix; Mark stared at the floor. Theo didn't know what she was talking about. Sister Kevin Mary thought she was going to vomit. Clarabelle began coughing and couldn't get her breath. She ran out of the refectory and up to her room.

Sister Kevin Mary went to chapel. She couldn't go to school the way she felt. Oh, Dear God, I don't believe this. Vipers and bands of vipers! See these Christians, how they love one another! That poor nun. I don't know how she can take it.

She sat back at her place in chapel. Thoughts of God and holy things just didn't come. Life wasn't ethereal, abstract anymore. No, life was just a bunch of bodies, all huddled together, sick. Of the seventeen nuns, thirteen had something seriously wrong with them. When they took out their dishes at the table, the bottles of pills and tonics in the drawers came out before the silverware. It looked like a drugstore, with the little brown bottles all lined up, as they waited for the water to be poured so they could all take a pill or two.

Sister Jean Martin had ulcers, peptic ulcers. She always got a special order, minus the spices. When anything fried was served and the cook forgot her needs, she would storm into the kitchen, boil up the tea kettle, make herself some Cream of Wheat or Quaker Oats, bring it back, plunk it down heavily on the table, and ask dramatically for the cream and sugar. Marce said she deserved a bad case of ulcers because she was so generous in giving them to the rest of them.

Marce seemed to be better. Maybe. For the first two weeks after school resumed in January, she taught only half days until Sister Helen Francis caught her uptown at the record store at 1:30 in the afternoon when she was supposed to be resting. Marce told her that she just needed some fresh air and thought the walk would be good for her, but Sister Helen Francis knew when someone was making a fool out of her. The lay teacher was told that her services would not be needed any longer since Sister Marie Marcel was better. Marce went back to teaching full days.

Sister Maximillian, Max, Big Max, almost six feet tall, had a back problem. She wore a big plaster back brace under her habit, and when she got nervous she'd knock on her sides. She left the brace on her desk when she wasn't wearing it, and every time Sister Kevin Mary passed her room, the big white form, sitting on the desk by the door, made her jump. Max had ordered some orthopedic bras from a catalogue company. They were padded and contoured to form two sharp points in the front. When Sister Helen Francis suggested that perhaps she might not want to wear them to school, Max replied, "Oh, yes, Sister. And when the little monsters bump into me, I can poke their eyes out!" Max wore her contoured bras.

Aggie was getting deafer and deafer; her sixty-three fourth-

graders were getting louder and louder. Sister Helen Francis
kept warning Aggie that she would have to take her out of the
classroom if she couldn't control them. Aggie was "well into
her seventies," as Sister Helen Francis frequently reminded the
nuns. Her blood pressure was high and her handwriting was
getting shaky. Aggie kept promising Sister Helen Francis that
her class would be just fine; she'd taught for forty-five years
and these little suburban kids were easy to handle. Aggie
refused to wear a hearing aid, either from a sense of pride or
because she would have been too embarrassed to have a doctor
check her ears. He'd see her hair. The younger nuns kept
Aggie's classroom in perfect order and would go in and bark at
her kids once in a while, telling them that they had to be as
good as they could for Sister Agnes Patrick. Aggie had survived
the Titanic, and a few little kids were not going to pull her
under.

And Sister Julia Mary was acting nuttier than usual. When
she was up, she was utterly hysterical, a "raving maniac,"
Lillian Barrett would have called her. And when she was down,
or "hung over," as Mark said, she wouldn't come out of her
room. She was lapsing into a French accent frequently; she had
never been to France in her life. The Somebodies were meeting
on a regular basis in the French provincial parlor. The setups
had been moved in there, so they didn't have to make trips back
into the kitchen. Jules was the "mover and shaker," as she'd
say, behind these things.

Now that Marce was feeling better, she was a regular with
the Somebodies. She and Jules were getting real chummy.
When the nuns went downtown to see *Vertigo* with half the
nuns in the city, she and Marce ditched the group and went
across the street to see *Cat on a Hot Tin Roof*. In the evenings,
Sister Kevin Mary could hear Jules and Marce roaring and
shouting above all the other Somebodies. The Superior was
always a part of the Somebodies; first of all, they liked her, she
was their age; and second, they had to have her on their side so
she wouldn't ring the bell. The bell for Profound Silence.

As she sat in chapel that morning, Sister Kevin Mary felt that the whole thing was going to hell. The meaning of Profound Silence was the first thing she had learned the day she entered the community. There had been more than 250 novices and postulants visiting together in the Novitiate garden. As the Novice Mistress stood at the top of the steps and rang the little brass bell, everyone stopped talking immediately, even in the middle of a sentence.

If a novice was ever caught talking during Profound Silence, she could be sent home. *Magna Silentia,* the Great Silence ". . . during which the Sisters should not only avoid every disorder but they must make every effort to keep their souls in union with God. . . . They should be mindful of the other Sisters' need for rest and silence." She remembered the time last April when the Novitiate basement flooded, and they all had to get out of bed and bail it out. Over thirty nuns, in their nightgowns and robes, passing buckets, dragging mops, squeezing rags, all in total silence. And at St. Paul's, they didn't even ring the bell if the Somebodies were meeting for their "little somethings." She wondered if she ought to report that when Mother Jeremiah came in spring for visitation. Well, that decision didn't have to be made this morning.

Oh, Dear God, how harshly I judge people. I can't even take care of myself. Fat and ugly. I've gained over twenty-five pounds. Chin broken out. Cramps every month, so badly that I have to leave school and get my Schnapps—my medicine from the Monsignor. And these headaches, maybe my headgear is just too tight. The little white dots, then it feels like half my head is going crazy—over my eye, my cheek, neck, mouth, and then it shifts to the other side. Nuts, that's what I am. Who ever heard of a headache being only on one side? I can't tell her. She'll put me in a category with Clarabelle, and I just couldn't take that.

The house had grown quiet. She was the only one home. Her bed hadn't even been made. The first bell rang for school. She tore upstairs, grabbed her books and papers, picked up her shawl, and ran over to school. Mark hadn't made her bed either. She had to get over to church to play the organ for the

8:15 Mass. Sister Kevin Mary usually made both beds when Mark had to play, but this morning she just closed their door. The room looked a mess because they both didn't feel well, they had both been in bed early, hadn't had time to straighten it up. Today was Friday, so tonight they'd give it a good cleaning.

At 10:30 that morning, there was a sharp knock on her door. It was Sister Helen Francis, angry.

"Get home and clean your room this very minute!! The pipes froze and I had to take the plumber over there. I've never been so embarrassed in my life! And you're supposed to be so smart. You know, Sister Kevin Mary, you are very particular about some things, and about some other things you are not the least bit particular! There were dirty socks in the sink, a sanitary belt hanging on your doorknob, books, papers, magazines. I'll never be able to look that man in the face again. Get home right now and clean that dump!!"

Sister Kevin Mary, shaken, gave her class an assignment, pulled on her black shawl, and, greatly chastized, made her way across the slippery playground. Father Doyle was backing his car out of the priests' garage and honked at her. She ignored him, walked up the steps of the convent and into the kitchen to get a cup of coffee before beginning the cleaning. She greeted the cook, who gave her a disapproving look, for Margaret knew how embarrassed the poor Superior had been with the plumber.

She didn't intend to stay in the kitchen and take Margaret's dirty looks. She carried her cup of coffee up to her room, spilling some down the front of her habit. She walked into the disaster area at the top of the stairs and saw Mark picking papers up off the floor. Mark looked up and said nothing. She stood at the doorway and began laughing, laughing so hard that she spilled more coffee. She couldn't control herself, doubling up with gales of laughter, unable to catch her breath. She walked unsteadily over to her bed, sat down, and continued to holler.

Mark quickly left the room and went back over to school. Sister Kevin Mary sat on the bed, trying to compose herself.

The stockings were still in the sink, soaking. The sanitary belt hung defiantly from the doorknob. Her covers were half on the floor.

As she looked out the window, she could see pallbearers carrying a gray coffin into the church for a funeral. The family walked in slowly behind. Other cars pulled up in front of the church. If they only knew, if they only knew, she smiled to herself, as she began to wash out her stockings.

16.

It was the dead of winter, the middle of the school year. The point of no return. Yet the days seemed to be getting somewhat longer; it wasn't dark at 4:30 anymore. This was the week of the conferences between the parents and the teachers that Sister Carlotta, the supervisor, wanted to experiment with. Sister Carlotta wanted the community to be first with anything new in the field of education. She had heard about Parent-Teacher Conferences in the East and wanted "to lead the way" in the Midwest.

Sister Carlotta envisioned the ten-minute conference as a model of "a new joint venture between parent and teacher," a coming together to discuss the child, a time to enter into a colloquium with the parent, "with those who have the primary responsibility for the child's education." She envisioned the conferences as an opportunity for insight into the family, for garnering new information about each child's development, as a chance to educate the parents about what the school was attempting to do.

Sister Carlotta, not leaving anything to chance, had strongly *suggested* that the conferences begin on Sunday afternoon, from

154

1:00 until 5:00, and continue during the week after school, from 3:00 until 5:00 and then from 7:00 until 9:00 in the evening. Each conference should take no longer than 10 minutes, followed by a 2½-minute break, whereby the first set of parents would be ushered out of the room and the second set greeted, showed around the classroom, and seated by the sound of the bell. Sister Carlotta's suggestions were followed. She would be asking each principal for an evaluation; Sister Helen Francis was not about to appear with missing data.

From the moment the first parents were greeted on Sunday afternoon until she staggered out of her classroom Thursday night at 9:45, it was more like a struggle for power rather than a "joint venture" in the child's interest. It reminded her of the cartoon in her textbook on European history—the balance of powers, the seesaw, with the Allied powers on the one side and the Axis powers on the other. To some parents, she was the enemy, pure and simple; to others, she was someone to be co-opted, cajoled, teased—"You are awfully young, aren't you, Sister?"; to others, she was nothing but a nuisance; to some, a friend. She had a feeling that it didn't have too much to do with her personally, maybe something about their feelings toward their kid or the Church or other teachers that they had when they were in school.

In one way, she wished that these conferences had never taken place. She could never "unknow" these people, parents of her students. Some she liked very much; others she wished she had never met. And every time she looked at the kids, she saw the parents.

The first people scheduled were the Carmodys. They were late. Cowards. She had the gold pen and pencil set on her desk to hand back to them. It was against her vow of poverty to keep such an expensive present, and she was going to let them know. They only had ten minutes scheduled, and it was already 1:06. She went again to the door, looked up and down the hall. No Carmodys. She walked over to her desk, looked through Peter Carmody's papers, all Ds and Fs, closed the folder, opened the slender black case with the gold pen and pencil, snapped it shut, walked back out into the hall.

Mrs. Douglas had been waiting for her 1:12 appointment

since 1:05. She greeted Mrs. Douglas as the bell rang, brought her into the classroom, showed her Maureen's papers hanging on the corkboard, and asked her to be seated.

Maureen Douglas was a bright, beautiful little girl, an only child. Mrs. Douglas was in her early forties and had Maureen when she was thirty-seven, after many miscarriages. The doctors told her not to try to have any more children. Sister Kevin Mary was embarrassed as Mrs. Douglas explained her gynecological problems and how precious Maureen was to them; she never thought she'd hold a baby, have a child of her own. Yes, Mrs. Douglas, I know just how you felt—the empty arms; never to watch anyone grow and develop; no one ever to call you "Mom"; always an "auntie," never a mother. I'm glad you had Maureen, Mrs. Douglas.

Sister Kevin Mary showed Maureen's papers to Mrs. Douglas. Mrs. Douglas glowed with pride, thanked Sister Kevin Mary for being such a wonderful teacher, and told her to be sure to contact her if anything was wrong, if Maureen didn't do her work. Sister Kevin Mary wanted to tell her to call Sister Carlotta and tell her how wonderful she was but decided against it. At 1:22, the bell rang, and Sister Kevin Mary escorted Mrs. Douglas to the door and greeted the Kamowskis.

The Kamowskis owned the local bakery, Bernice's Baked Goods. They were in their late thirties and smiled a lot and sat close together. Broad cheeks, blond wispy hair, and light blue eyes. Sister Kevin Mary sat down with them and broke into a big smile. "I don't know who Joyce looks like. Both of you—I guess you look alike." The Kamowskis beamed, glancing at each other shyly. "How's our Joycie doin', Sister?" asked Mr. Kamowski.

"Joyce tries harder than anyone else in the class, Mr. Kamowski," offered Sister Kevin Mary.

"Is she goin' to make it, Sister?" asked Mr. Kamowski again.

"Well, she's in the lowest group. She has trouble with her sounds, her vowel sounds. But she tries very hard."

"Well, Sister, we know she tries hard. Where does she need help? Can we help her?" asked Mrs. Kamowski.

Sister Kevin Mary opened Joyce's folder and began showing

the Kamowskis the quality of Joyce's work. The smiles faded from their faces as they looked at the corkboard and saw some of the better papers.

"I guess Joycie just isn't too smart, Sister. We want her to do well in school. School was hard for me. I don't want Joycie to have to go through what I went through. That's why we're sending her to a Catholic school. We thought the nuns would be kinder and would understand. We're glad Joycie has you, Sister."

Sister Kevin Mary's face grew red. They were complimenting her, and she really didn't deserve it. She wasn't honest with them about their daughter. The bell rang. Joyce was doing very poorly in school. She was at the bottom of her class and Sister Kevin Mary just couldn't tell them that. It would crush them if they ever knew. She walked the Kamowskis to the door, checked the next appointment, and greeted the Clarkes.

As she was about to close the door, the Carmodys appeared, wanting to know if they could have just two minutes of her time, time that belonged to the Clarkes, she thought. She told them that she had waited for them at 1:00, and that she really couldn't take time from other parents. Mr. Carmody winked an understanding wink at her and guided Mrs. Carmody toward the office. They can just go to hell, she thought as she readjusted her attention to the Clarkes and their Robert.

Bright, funny Robert. Too mature for first grade, too young for second. Robert was bored with school and she knew it. And the Clarkes knew it. But Sister Kevin Mary didn't know what to do with Robert Clarke except to discipline him. Mrs. Clarke was a small, serious woman, the straight man for Mr. Clarke. He unconsciously tapped his fingers on her desk, and Sister Kevin Mary knew that his foot was going, too. He shifted in his place on the stiff metal chair; Mrs. Clarke sat still. It was as if Mrs. Clarke were the mother and Mr. Clarke and Robert were her sons. Sister Kevin Mary asked them to discipline Robert more because he was disruptive, inattentive. "The apple doesn't fall far from the tree," muttered Mrs. Clarke, as she motioned for Mr. Clarke to get going. The bell had rung. She had forgotten to tell them about Robert's handwriting.

As she ushered the Clarkes out, she looked for the Maios. Dr. and Mrs. Maio, Mimi's parents. Mimi was unconscious most of the time, and Sister Kevin Mary was all ready for the Maios. No mincing of words, no embarrassment, no soft pedaling. She was going to hit them right between the eyes. If Mimi didn't start to move, she'd find herself in first grade again next year. They took her out of school for two weeks at Thanksgiving, three weeks at Christmas, and she was sure they were headed to Florida for Easter, two weeks early. The Maios didn't show up. Too much trouble.

At least that gave her a break. She took a dime from the Mission money, ran into the mimeograph room, and grabbed a Coke from the machine. Then she darted across the hall and into the clinic to the bathroom, splashing some water on her face, her fat, red face. God, how I wish I were pale and skinny, then I'd look like a real nun. I'd look smart and holy and prayerful, if only I were skinny. She dried her face with a hard, brown paper towel, straightened her veil, and headed back to Room 103, feeling very hot and fat.

By 3:30, parents began to blur. She found herself saying the same thing. "You have a lovely child . . . Robert or Karen or Patrick needs some more work on his or her . . . Yes, I'll be sure to let you know if there is any trouble with . . ." In and out, in and out. Some with whom she had really wanted to speak seriously, she didn't; she found herself glossing over their problems just to get them out of the room. She couldn't concentrate, too tired. Too many people.

At 4:52, her last parents, Mr. and Mrs. Dill, Martin Dill's parents. She had met them early in the year at the Parents' Open House. Mrs. Dill frequently substituted in the middle grades—she was never too busy to drop everything and come over and help. She took no money, telling Sister Helen Francis to get something for the school. Mr. Dill never spoke. She seemed to be propping him up like a wooden soldier. Mrs. Dill always prefaced her remarks with "Mr. Dill and I feel" or "Mr. Dill and I have often discussed." Mr. Dill did not look like he felt or discussed very much. There was talk that he had been injured in the war and had a plate in his head. No one knew exactly what he did for a living, but there apparently was money in the family.

Mrs. Dill was charming and peppy. The kids took after her, all six of them. Their oldest, Jack, was a freshman in high school; the twins were in eighth grade; and the others were at St. Paul's. Martin was the youngest, and he seemed to take after Mrs. Dill as well. Mr. Dill continued to stare throughout the conference, Sister Kevin Mary picking up on Mrs. Dill's cues to include him in the conversation. When she showed Martin's arithmetic to Mr. Dill, he looked at her as if the paper were written in Sanskrit. Mrs. Dill said that she and her husband were happy with Martin's progress, and if he got out of hand, to please call them and his father would certainly take care of him. She smiled cordially, picked up her husband, and gracefully left the room.

As Sister Kevin Mary straightened her desk and prepared the room for the morning's class, she could see the Dills getting into the car. Mrs. Dill drove home.

Monday morning was an especially difficult Monday morning. She was tired, slightly irritable. Peter Carmody acted sheepish. Did he know that his parents had missed their appointment? Did he know that they were trying to pay his way through school? Sister Kevin Mary grew angry with the very thought of it. She looked at little Peter, little Peter Carmody with the red hair and freckles, little Peter Carmody with the blank expression and dull eyes. She resolved not to take it out on him. A kid couldn't help it if his parents were creeps.

After school, she gathered the papers, straightened the desks, and got ready for more parents who would enter into a colloquium with her. At 3:20, Mrs. Schultz, with a baby in her arms, a two-year-old hanging on her skirt, and Connie, the first-grader, came into the room. Mrs. Schultz had on no makeup and her hair was falling into her eyes, just like her daughter's. Connie took her two-year-old brother to her desk while her mother rifled through her papers on the teacher's desk.

Sister Kevin Mary started to tell Mrs. Schultz about Connie's reading when the two-year-old darted for the mother. His nose was running. The baby started to scream. Connie grabbed the two-year-old by the neck. He screamed louder. Sister Kevin Mary smiled at Connie's papers, trying to let Mrs. Schultz know that she understood family matters as well as those of the classroom. The bell rang, and Sister Kevin Mary hustled the Schultzes out.

They kept coming. Mostly mothers, explaining that their husbands, Jack or Tom or Frank, had to work. Sister Kevin Mary understood. When Sister Kevin Mary complained to Mrs. Miller about Alex's handwriting, Mrs. Miller just laughed. "Why, Sister, I could care less. I expect that Alex will be using a typewriter for really important things." Yes, Mrs. Miller, this stuff really isn't very important, is it? That's why I'm batting my brains out from 8:00 until 3:00 every day, just so Alex can use a typewriter. Sister Kevin Mary said something about it being hard on the child when the parents and the teachers had different values, different goals for the child. She got Mrs. Miller out before the bell rang. Mrs. Miller, pulling her fur tightly around her face, smiled arrogantly at the young nun.

The nuns went home for dinner at 5:00 and had to be back for the evening appointments, from 7:00 until 9:00. Then another full day of teaching, and then it would start again— parents, parents.

The last appointment on Thursday evening was with the Kempers. She was hoping that they wouldn't show up because she knew that she would have to say something to them. She didn't want to, but she knew that she had to. Jimmy Kemper acted like a girl. He walked funny, with his hands out at his side. When he sat down, he'd cross his legs daintily. When he stood in line to go to the bathroom, she frequently saw him dancing in the back of the room, pirouetting on one foot. The kids hated Jimmy Kemper: the boys made fun of him; the girls laughed. Jimmy had no friends, and his schoolwork was suffering. He gave the impression of being relatively intelligent; he scored high on the IQ test, but was not doing well at all.

The Kempers were an older couple, well built and well dressed. She expected tall, willowy people, since Jimmy was thin and dark. The Kempers were stocky and seemed somewhat distracted. Jimmy had two sisters in high school, and it appeared that he was an afterthought to their lives. After they discussed Jimmy's papers, Sister Kevin Mary grabbed for the crucifix on her rosary, cleared her throat, and told them that Jimmy seemed to have no friends, that the kids did not seem to like him and that he was not happy in school. Mrs. Kemper appeared surprised; Mr. Kemper looked at his nails. Mrs. Kemper wanted to know if she had any idea why that was true, if, in fact, it were true.

"Well, you know," Sister Kevin Mary began, "Jimmy is not like the other boys. He appears to be rather effeminate. The other kids have noticed."

"Why, Sister, I don't know what you're talking about. Jimmy's just a little boy," commented his mother.

"Just let her talk, Irene. I want to hear what she's saying," interrupted Mr. Kemper.

"Well, he walks and talks and acts like a girl. He never plays with the other boys. He's dancing around here all the time. He just doesn't act like a boy. I think you're going to have trouble with Jimmy if you don't do something very soon."

The Kempers frowned. Sister Kevin Mary looked at them. No one spoke. Thank God I said something. He'll probably punch me in the nose. I don't care. Something had to be said. Sister Kevin Mary broke the silence. "Haven't you noticed anything peculiar about Jimmy's behavior? I know that you don't have any other boys at home, but you must know how little boys are supposed to act?"

Mr. Kemper looked up. "I just don't know. I guess I don't pay too much attention to him. I'm gone most of the time and really don't have time to spend with the kids."

"You can say that again," interrupted Mrs. Kemper.

"Ahh, what I meant to say is that I leave the kids to the wife. I take care of the money and things like that, Sister," said Mr. Kemper defensively.

The bell rang. The end of conferences, of joint endeavors, of colloquiums. Sister Kevin Mary turned toward Mrs. Kemper. "Have you noticed anything strange about Jimmy's behavior, Mrs. Kemper? Does he play with the other little boys in the neighborhood? I just want you to understand what I'm trying to say to you. I don't like to have to do this, but I feel that I have to talk to you about Jimmy."

Mrs. Kemper sat back in her chair. She stared out the dark window. "Well, he likes to play dress-up. He likes to put on my things, you know, my dresses and heels. He likes to put on my makeup. The girls think it's cute, and all their friends laugh at him. They think Jimmy is real cute when he gets dressed up." Mrs. Kemper began laughing loudly.

Mr. Kemper buried his head in his hands. "Irene, Irene, please don't! Please, Irene! You never told me that. Oh my God, Irene, I can't believe this." Mrs. Kemper continued to laugh, saying something about how cute Jimmy was with lipstick and high heels.

Sister Kevin Mary looked out the window. Some of the lights from the other classrooms were going out. She could hear the nuns in the hall, starting home. Mrs. Kemper was still laughing.

Mr. Kemper stood abruptly, knocking over the gray metal chair. He grabbed his wife's wrist, squeezing it to make her stop laughing. Sister Kevin Mary looked up at the strange couple.

"Thanks, Sister. I know that it was hard for you to talk about this. I think it's my fault. I haven't paid any attention to him. I let the wife handle the kids. I just ignored him. I'm so busy. I let the wife do it. Now look what she's done . . . I'm sorry, Sister, thanks." He turned to his wife. "Come on, Irene. We've got to get home."

Sister Kevin Mary walked the Kempers to the door. The hall lights had been turned out. Freddie was waiting for Sister Kevin Mary by the door to the nurse's clinic. As they walked down the hall, Mr. Kemper turned and waved. Mrs. Kemper was still laughing.

17.

Sister Kevin Mary walked slowly around the classroom, stopping to warm her hands on the radiator. The owner of the local Texaco station was plowing the latest snowfall off the playground, piling it into huge mounds that the kids would level by noon.

It was a dark Friday in February, the end of February. No relief in sight from the cold and the snow and the winds and the ice. And the heaviness. This would probably be the best Lent in her life, she thought, mortifications and penances that were given, not sought. How easy Lent used to be when she was a kid—not going to shows, giving up candy. She smiled as she thought of how she got rid of an old boyfriend. "I'd love to keep going out with you, Eddie, but I'm giving up dating for Lent." Maybe now she was having to make up for that.

The class was coloring a page from their religion books, a picture of the apostles dropping the fishing nets they were mending and running after Jesus. "Come, follow Me and I will make you fishers of men" was the title of the page, and at the bottom were the words, "You have not chosen Me, but I have chosen you, for many are called, but few are chosen." The apostles had dropped what they were doing and responded to the call of Christ, "leaving father and mother."

Sister Kevin Mary loved the story, and as she looked at her class, she wondered how many future priests and nuns were sitting in front of her; she wondered if she were helping to sow the small, delicate seeds of a religious vocation in their hearts. You can't go back on a vocation; there is no going back at all. The apostles couldn't have decided that they made a mistake and what they really wanted to do was to fish and mend nets for the rest of their lives. No, there was no going back, no retracing of her steps. She thought of how Sister Duns Scotus would warn them in her chilly voice: "He who puts his hand to the plow and then turns back is not worthy of the kingdom of Heaven." She had never even seen a plow, much less a fishing net, but she got the idea. You just don't quit. You say good-bye, walk out the door, don't turn back. You keep on going.

She thought of her mother and of the terrible fight they had about her entering the convent. They were doing dishes one night when she turned to her mother and said, "Mother, I'm going to be a nun." Lillian Barrett, without the slightest elevation of her voice, responded, "Oh, no you're not." They continued the dishes as Maureen stated firmly, "Oh, yes I am." Her younger sister Molly came into the kitchen and they stopped talking for a moment but began a fight that would last for the next two years. The tears, running out of rooms, slamming doors, Mrs. Barrett being called over to school to be intimidated by the nuns—a breach between mother and daughter that would never heal. Her mother wanted her to finish college, wait "until you're old enough to know your own mind." Maureen Barrett knew her own mind only too well. She knew what God wanted from her, and that her mother was simply standing in the way of God in her life. God's grace knows of no age or race but moves freely to whomever He chooses.

Her father stepped in and said that Maureen could go into the convent right after high school, if that was what she wanted. He told his wife that she had no right to interfere in her children's lives. Lillian Barrett gave in. A melancholy came over her. She had another miscarriage, didn't seem to talk as much as she had. Maureen would catch her mother looking at her with a certain pain in her eyes; she ignored her mother for there was nothing she could do about her mother's reaction. She knew that she had to be obedient to something higher than the authority of her mother; she could not ignore the call within her.

She remembered the sad farewells to her family and friends, most of whom did not understand what she was doing or why she was doing it, but they respected her. Her aunt acted rather deferentially; the Jewish neighbors were embarrassed; a friend of her father kept saying, "Oh, no, what a waste." Regardless of how she was treated, it was different from before.

A week before she entered, she had folded on her bed all the clothes that she was to bring to the Novitiate, among them a pair of black stockings. She couldn't bring herself to try them on—it was something about pulling all that thick, heavy black cotton over her legs that seemed the ultimate in mortification, self-abnegation, self-denial. Her five-year-old sister Molly came into her room to look over all the strange new clothes. Maureen picked up a stocking, threw it at Molly, shouting, "Look out, Molly, it's alive!" The stocking looked like a long black snake about to strike. Molly ran out of the room screaming, and Maureen rolled on her bed, laughing hysterically.

Lillian Barrett came up the stairs, holding Molly's hand. Her little face was streaked with tears. "That was a cruel thing to do, Maureen, a very cruel thing to do to this little girl. You're the one who decided that is what you want. Now you live with your decision. Don't be imposing your decision on your little sister." Lillian Barrett took Molly into the bathroom to wash her face; Maureen sat on the edge of her bed, staring at the black snake in her hands.

She thought of her black stockings. They always gave her trouble, even though she had worn them for 2½ years. She thought of those stockings and of how the nuns in the Novitiate would sit around at night, darning the stockings with a big darning egg. She thought of her feet, always asleep. As she walked around the classroom, they would feel numb, lifeless. Maybe I'm just dying, feet first. My knees will be next. In the afternoons, when she would sit on the little reading chair in front of the reading group, her feet would get prickly, like an arm that had been slept on. Probably the black deadly stockings, seeping through my skin.

The class had finished coloring the apostles and their nets, the gas station man had finished plowing the playground, and it was time to get on with arithmetic. Then spelling, writing, then, finally, home for lunch. Friday, so it would be fish. And the fast. Even though she was not twenty-one yet, she still observed the Lenten fast of the Church: one big meal and two smaller "colations," which together could not equal or exceed the big meal. And no eating between meals. So the secret was to eat as much as you could at the main meal so you had some latitude at the breakfast and supper.

Sister Kevin Mary planned to fast intently during the Holy Season of Lent, and, hopefully, lose some of the weight that was piling around her hips, on her cheeks, everywhere. She envisioned the weight falling off, looking gaunt and thin, everyone whispering how very ascetic, mortified she was. She would even get pale and finally start looking like a real nun and not this chubby, self-indulgent adolescent walking around in a habit. As a matter of fact, she was never really fat as a teenager. But by now, the second week of Lent, she had gained another three pounds. By Easter, she'd be over 140 pounds.

Monsignor Ryan called for her as she crossed the playground. He held a letter in his hand, waving it in the air in feigned anger. "Kev, you gals are going to put me in the poorhouse."

"I don't understand, Monsignor."

"Just got this from the Cardinal. I've got to increase your salaries by 10 bucks. That's 170 a month more. I'll go broke!"

"Are you kidding? I didn't know we got paid. I never knew we got money."

"What do you think you live on, the love of God?" Monsignor Ryan laughed heartily and told her to hurry so she wouldn't miss her lunch.

Sister Kevin Mary walked quickly through the back door,

hung up her shawl, genuflected in the chapel. "Dear God, don't let me make a pig of myself," she prayed and headed for the kitchen. Margaret, the cook, had a platter of deep-fried shrimp, French fries, cole slaw, hot rolls, green beans, and a relish dish out on the counter. Sister Kevin Mary filled a plate with generous helpings, forgetting that she could come back for seconds. She had to get everything on there at once.

Mark, Freddie, and Clarabelle, all sitting at the younger end of the table, greeted her, telling her not to be so bashful in the kitchen, just take what she wanted, help herself. Sister Helen Francis, who usually ate before or after most of the nuns, when she wasn't eating at the priests' house, was already seated at the head of the table. The nuns at the top of the table were laughing about something.

Sister Kevin Mary stuffed her mouth with two shrimp, motioning to Clarabelle that she had some shrimp sauce on her collar. Clarabelle dipped her napkin in her glass of water and smeared the shrimp sauce around. Freddie had already finished her dinner and was enjoying a second cup of coffee before she went out for playground duty; Mark, who never seemed to like food, was playing with a green bean.

"Hey, nuns," said Sister Kevin Mary, addressing Clarabelle, Mark, and Freddie. "Guess what I just found out? Did you know that we make a salary? We get paid for teaching. I thought we did it for God."

Before any of the younger nuns could respond, Sister Helen Francis, at the head of the table, cleared her throat and stated loudly, "Sister Kevin Mary, if you or if anyone else in this house is accusing me of not handling community funds properly, just say it! You have clothes on your back, a roof over your head, food in your stomach! You are wanting for nothing! Community funds, our salary, is handled by me and you get what is your due!"

There was not a sound at the table. Freddie gulped her coffee audibly. Aggie blushed furiously. Sister Kevin Mary put her fork down, turned in her chair to face her Superior directly. "No, Sister Helen Francis, I was not in any way accusing you of any impropriety in the disbursement of community funds. I was simply stating the cold, hard fact that I was unaware that we received a remuneration for our service to St. Paul's parish. In no way am I questioning your integrity. I am stating a fact to these three nuns with whom I am eating." She picked up her fork and stabbed the French fries.

Mark smiled broadly, picked up her plate, kicked Sister Kevin Mary under the table, and went into the kitchen to wash her plate. Clarabelle stared blankly through her thick glasses, not quite sure of what had just taken place. Freddie gulped down the rest of her coffee and knocked over her chair in a rush to get in and out of the kitchen before Sister Helen Francis went in. Aggie walked past Sister Kevin Mary, knocking her on the back of her head with her elbow. Aggie's going to give me hell, she thought. The rest of the nuns finished their lunches in silence. Willie, who was on first duty, came into the silent refectory. "Who died?" she asked Margaret. Margaret continued chasing the grease around the bottom of the deep fryer, ignoring Willie's question.

Out of respect, Sister Jean Martin grabbed Sister Helen Francis's dishes from her, took them into the kitchen and washed them. Sister Kevin Mary continued to eat, chomping down on the shrimp and French fries with a newfound freedom and determination. Willie came into the refectory and looked at Sister Kevin Mary. "What's going on around here, Kevvie? Nobody's saying a word. Did something happen?"

Sister Kevin Mary continued to eat, smiling to herself. "I guess something did, Willie. Don't ask me, it was all so fast. I'm not really sure." As she finished her dinner, having stock-piled her food to last her until 5:30, she went into the kitchen to do her dishes. Margaret ignored her. Sister Julia Mary, at low ebb, ignored her; she was beginning to smell like old booze or Listerine mouthwash all the time.

Sister Kevin Mary stopped in chapel to make a short visit before heading back out to the slippery playground. Sister Marie Marcel was sitting in her place, holding her head. She looked up as Sister Kevin Mary genuflected. "Go get her, Tiger! Go get her! Don't ever let her try to pull that on you again, Kevin."

Sister Kevin Mary smiled, "Thanks, Marce. I won't. She won't, I mean." She walked over to school, thinking, "Go get her, Tiger! Go get her, Tiger! Go get her!"

Friday after school, the nuns changed into their aprons to begin the end-of-the-week scrubbing on the house. They prayed privately on Fridays. At 5:30, the bell rang for supper. They gathered, said grace in English before eating, and sat down. Neither Sister Helen Francis nor Sister Julia Mary was there. Frequently, two or three of the nuns would not be at the table, since most of them scheduled shopping or doctor appointments after school. Whenever the Superior was absent, it was assumed that she was somewhere with the pastor; Sister Helen Francis usually made it in time for dessert.

After dinner, Sister Lucy, an older nun who was in charge when the Superior was not there, said she had something to say. She had been a Superior in four different places and had a reputation for her strictness, her letter-of-the-law attitude toward obedience, and her sense of community, tradition, and history. Perhaps of all the nuns, Sister Lucy was the closest to Mother Jeremiah and to the nuns at the motherhouse. While Sister Lucy disapproved of, or at least did not take part in, the evening parties of the Somebodies, and had very little use for Monsignor Ryan and his antics, she was a good nun and never for a moment criticized the Superior. Of all the rules and traditions, obedience was the primary one—respect for the *office,* if not the person, of the Superior.

Sister Lucy, still dressed in her habit, looked around the refectory slowly, making eye contact with each nun. "Sisters, I have an announcement. Sister Helen Francis and Sister Julia Mary are not here. They left this afternoon for Florida. Sister Julia Mary is not well. They will be gone for a week. Everything is going to go on just as if Sister Helen Francis were here. If there are any permissions that you need, you can ask me." Sister Lucy stared at each nun in turn, daring them to make any remarks about this highly irregular situation. She continued, "Are there any questions?"

Sister Jean Martin looked up disgustedly. "How'd they get there, walk?"

"No, Sister, they left on an early afternoon flight."

"I mean, how did they get to the airport?"

"Monsignor Ryan drove them out there, Sister."

All the nuns assumed that, but Sister Jean Martin took particular delight in making Sister Lucy spell out the details of their departure.

"What's the matter with Jules?" asked Clarabelle.

Freddie pinched her elbow, telling her to shut up.

Sister Lucy looked at Freddie and Clarabelle. "She's not well, Sister Clare Elliot. She is just not well, and that's all there is to it. Do you understand, Sister?" asked Sister Lucy.

Clarabelle nodded, but she did not understand what was the matter with Sister Julia Mary. The nuns left the refectory, the Somebodies staring at each other in disbelief, the Nobodies smiling. Everyone knew what was the matter with Sister Julia Mary; however, it was not to be mentioned.

After dinner, Sister Mark asked Sister Kevin if she would come over to church with her at 8:00, for she had to play the organ for the Stations of the Cross. The two nuns climbed into the choir loft as Father O'Mahoney came out onto the altar with three altar boys. Two were carrying candles; the tallest one was carrying a bronze crucifix and led the procession to the side of the church. Father O'Mahoney said loudly, "The first Station of the Cross, Jesus is condemned to death." He prayed, "We adore Thee, O Christ, and we bless Thee," to which the congregation responded, "Because by Thy holy cross, Thou hadst redeemed the world."

After each Station, Sister Mark played a verse from the *Stabat Mater:*

> At the Cross her station keeping
> Stood the mournful Mother, weeping
> Close to Jesus at the last.

Sister Kevin Mary felt her insides harden again. She couldn't breathe deeply. The darkened church, the purple on the priest, nails and whips and thorns, the spear in Jesus' side, vinegar to drink, his mother left alone. "Father, into Thy hands I commend My spirit."

She thought of suffering, of agony, of life and how very hard it could be. What did the resurrection mean? What was the matter with Jules? Was she insane? Was she too brilliant? Was she just an old drunk, as Mark called her? Jules suffered; she suffered a lot. Maybe when she drinks, it makes her feel better for the time. Maybe she thinks that her head is going to explode and maybe the booze makes her not feel it as much. Dear Jesus, as you walked to Your death, falling and stumbling and getting kicked and beaten, please help Jules. Help her not go crazy. Help the nuns not talk about her. Help the sun heal her. Maybe Sister Helen Francis can even help her.

Father O'Mahoney concluded the Stations and returned to the sacristy with the altar boys. Sister Mark locked up the organ, turned out the lights, and the two nuns walked home as the sharp February winds tore at their thin cloaks. The convent was quiet as they came in the back door. Most of the lights were out; the nuns were in their rooms. The Somebodies were not meeting in the parlor that evening.

18.

The nuns filed out of chapel and into the refectory. The reader read the saint of the day and then began the Holy Rule, which was read weekly. All the nuns knew it by heart, or at least knew its rhythm and meaning, its archaic words and cadences, its European concepts and traditions. The thousand-year Rule transcended time and spoke about basic issues such as obedience, charity, purity, poverty.

Big Max was serving, walking from the kitchen with her long, heavy stride, plopping the food down on the table with a bang, sighing as she returned to the kitchen for another serving. The soft-boiled eggs were overcooked and the coffee was weak. Hot and wet, thought Sister Kevin Mary. She liked it strong.

Sister Julia Mary seemed to be doing so well after eight days in the sun, she thought to herself as the reader enjoined them "to subdue your flesh by fasting and abstinence from meat and drink, as far as your health permits." She seemed to be abstaining totally from drink. There were no more meetings of the Somebodies. She seemed to be on a more even keel. Perhaps the valium the doctor prescribed calmed her down. She was only twenty-eight; she could recover. But she slept a lot, heading upstairs right after school, not making it down on time for prayer in the evening, sometimes sleeping straight through until morning. The shrill had gone out of her voice—even her nose didn't seem so pointy.

Sister Kevin Mary felt a thud on the back of her head. Max wanted her to reach for the toast platter. She handed Max the plate, grabbing the last piece before it went back into the kitchen. Now, I'll have to eat more for lunch to accommodate this big breakfast, she figured. She tried to concentrate on the reading and not on the food. The reader began the section from the Rule, *Care of Health and of the Sick:* ". . . if any Sister have a secret pain in the body, let her, being the servant of God, be believed without mistrust, when she declares what she suffers. Nevertheless, if it be not certain that what she fancies is really the best means of removing the pain, let the physician be consulted."

Sister Kevin Mary looked down the table. Sister Marie Marcel was not at her place. She had been teaching full days and for a while seemed to be her old self, wild and free. Sister Kevin Mary had seen her sitting in the chapel, late at night, holding the back of her head. Her left eye was almost totally closed and her complexion looked bad. It was yellow. The doctor had ordered some new glasses and new medicine.

Marce went up to her room every chance she had—at lunch, right after school, over the weekends. She made frequent trips to the refrigerator for ice, pounding it into small chips for her blue icepack. At dinner on the previous Sunday, Sister Helen Francis offered to get the lay teacher back so Marce would only have to teach half days again, but Marce refused.

"Hey, don't worry, Sister Helen Francis, you can't keep a good girl down! It's my class and I'm going to teach them. I'll be OK, and besides, the kids are just great." At that point, Sister Jean Martin groaned, for she thought the kids at St. Paul's were the worst in Chicago.

Sister Kevin Mary wondered if Marce "had a secret pain in her body." What was the matter with her? She's only thirty-four. That's old, but not terribly old. Her mother was forty-three and certainly didn't have the trouble Marce was having with her head, although her mother had suffered migraines for many years. Maybe Marce just had migraines, and no doctor had diagnosed them correctly. Sister Kevin Mary decided that she would mention that possibility to Marce after breakfast.

Sister Kevin Mary left school as soon as she could get out. It was Friday again, and she had to get right down to the basement to start on the wash. It was fun, splashing around in the water, sorting the clothes, mixing the soaps, turning the dials on the big, institutional washers, lifting out the wet, "spun dry" clothes, which smelled so fresh and clean, throwing them into the dryer, and watching them bounce around. Seventeen white nightgowns dancing in the hot air like ghosts out for a night on the town. The handkerchiefs floated in the dryer like white clouds in a storm, feverishly moving back and forth. She would stand in front of the round glass doors, mesmerized by the soap churning and bubbling, the clothes yielding up their dirt so gracefully, so rhythmically.

It was fun to get wet, to do something with her arms and legs besides walk around a classroom or sit and eat. When the clothes were dry, she lifted and carried the heavy baskets into the ironing room where the clothes were sorted on the long green ping-pong table. Aggie was downstairs ironing as always, the steam rising off the board onto her face. She didn't have to worry about the iron making too much noise; no one could fire her or intimidate her about her ironing. Sister Kevin Mary thought that perhaps Aggie was cold, cold down deep in her bones, and the steam and heat from the iron warmed her up. It also raised a good thirst, for Aggie went into the fruit cellar for her daily beer when she was well into her ironing.

After Sister Kevin Mary had washed the underwear, slips, nightgowns, and handkerchiefs, she lowered the water temperature and began to wash the tunics, the long plain dresses that were the basic part of the habit. The nuns scrubbed their tunics before they were washed, coating the bottom with Fels Naptha soap and rubbing them against a scrub board. The bottom frequently dragged on the ground and picked up everything. If the tunic was older and the bottom frayed, the bottom of the habit or the facing was replaced. The sleeves of the tunic were also rubbed and scrubbed, since the washing machine couldn't get out all the dirt. The nuns would then rinse out their habits and hang them, doubled up, on the line until they were machine-washed. After that, they were shaken out and hung with clothespins on the basement line to dry.

When the tunics were cleaned, Sister Kevin Mary washed the collars, cuffs, and finally the scapulars, the most important part of the habit. The scapular was given to the order by the Blessed Virgin and was blessed by a priest. Everytime a Sister kissed her scapular, she received an indulgence of five years, meaning that five years would be cut off her time in Purgatory.

A nun was never to let her scapular touch the ground, never to sit on it. She was to treat it with the same respect as laymen treated the flag. Whenever something happened to the scapular, if it got caught in a door or if a child stepped on it, the nun was supposed to kiss it. A scapular had a life of its own. When they were novices and had to wear dead nuns' clothes, Sister Duns Scotus had reminded them that the blessing had not gone to the grave with the deceased. Their scapulars were blessed and demanded the respect of a sacred object. Even when the nuns wore those nurses' "aprons," they put on their scapulars. A nun was naked without her scapular.

Sister Kevin Mary carefully lifted the scapulars from the big wooden box marked "Scapulars" and placed them in the large washer, which she had already filled with warm water and gentle suds. She closed the heavy door firmly and began sweeping water from the floor down toward the drain. The washing machine growled on, shaking the slush and dirt out of the soiled scapulars. She loved her obedience—all alone with the suds and heat, with the water and the droopy clothesline.

And she loved being able to do something so personal for the nuns. It was March already, and she knew by now whom she liked and whom she disliked, although she tried very hard not to show either. Sister Duns Scotus had drummed into them over and over again that the demands of fraternal charity were such that the nuns were to avoid showing aversion for anyone they disliked and to raise to a supernatural level any natural leaning they felt for anyone. Washing the nuns' clothes gave her a chance to do for some of the nuns what she really couldn't do directly. She could even wash Sister Jean Martin's clothes with love in her heart, even though she was finding her more and more unbearable. And she truly loved Willie and Freddie, Aggie and Mark. This was also a good chance to do something for her friends.

The washing machine ground to a halt. There was just enough time to hang the scapulars before dinner. Dinner smelled like grilled cheese, and she was hungry. Only four more weeks and Lent would be over, thank God. Then she could stop thinking of food. She put the wide broom against the wall, checked which lines were still empty, walked over to the machine, and opened the metal door. She stuck her head through the opening, grabbed the scapulars, and lifted them out to the white canvas cart on wheels.

Sister Kevin Mary grabbed the rim of the cart and looked at the scapulars. Red. They were covered with red. Little red dots, little red ink dots from one of those new ballpoint pens that were striped with red and white to look like a candy cane. Dear God in heaven, all the scapulars are ruined! She grabbed one, ran over to the sink, reached for the drippy bar of Fels Naptha and rubbed it furiously on the scapular. The red ink wouldn't budge. She held it up to the light; the ink was the same on both sides.

She could feel her heart pounding in her ears. She held onto the cold stationary tubs for her life, for her knees were getting weak. Stupid, stupid, dumb, dumb, dumb. Dear God, how could I have been so dumb? I didn't check what I put into the washer. Maybe it was *my* pen—who knows, we all got them for Christmas. Some threads had clogged the drain, leaving the bottom of the tub covered with gray, tired suds. She stared at the drain, not knowing what to do. Each scapular matched the habit it was worn with; each habit was cut from a different bolt of material; some of the nuns were experimenting with a synthetic material; others had the wool blend. A scapular from one habit could never be worn with another habit. And now, not only the scapulars, but the entire habits were ruined—for habits were not worn without scapulars.

The high pitch of the little brass bell signaled dinner. Sister Kevin Mary picked up a scapular, turned and walked hesitantly up the basement stairs. Aggie had unplugged her iron at the very first sound of the bell and was on her way. Hearing someone so close behind, she turned; Sister Kevin Mary held up a red-dotted scapular for Aggie to see. "My Jesus, mercy," prayed Aggie. "You be sure to tell Sister. Oh, that's just terrible. Terrible, terrible, terrible."

"Aggie, it's not just one scapular. It was a whole load of them. They're all red. Somebody's pen got in there."

Sister Helen Francis walked out of her first-floor office that was to the right of chapel. Sister Kevin Mary knelt on the floor, holding up the ruined scapular for her Superior to see.

"Sister, a pen got in with the scapulars. I didn't see it. I'm so sorry. Umm, may I please have a penance for ruining all the scapulars? I just don't know how it happened, Sister."

Sister Helen Francis looked down at the young nun in dismay. "Get up, Sister, and give me that scapular. I've had just about as much carelessness as I'm going to put up with. We'll get to the bottom of this immediately! Where's that pen?"

"I don't know, Sister. I'll go right down and find it."

Sister Kevin Mary ran down the basement steps, turned on the fluorescent lights, and began sorting through the scapulars until she unearthed the thin red-and-white ballpoint pen buried in a scapular. Sister Kevin Mary returned to the refectory with the pen. The nuns were standing in silence, waiting. The wet scapular was in a ball in front of Sister Helen Francis's place. Sister Kevin Mary handed the pen to her Superior, the nuns said grace, and Sister Helen Francis, holding the red pen in her hand, turned slowly from the crucifix and faced the nuns.

"Whose is this?" Sister Helen Francis demanded.

No one answered. Everyone looked around the room to see if anyone was nodding or in any way acknowledging ownership.

"I want to know! Who owns this pen? All the scapulars have been ruined. Whose is this? If it is yours, I want you to speak up immediately. Sister Kevin Mary found it in the wash *after* it had gone through the entire wash and rinse cycle. Whose is this?"

Silence. Max placed her hands on her hips, swollen from the plaster cast, rapped on it, and scowled at Clarabelle. Jean Martin gave Clarabelle a dirty look. Aggie grew red in the face. Sister Lucy stared impassively at the crucifix. Freddie and Willie looked pained. Mark stared out the window, pursing her lips in boredom. Clarabelle folded her arms protectively and looked down at the tile floor through her thick, spotted glasses. Sister Kevin Mary felt nauseated again. Dear God, please let Clarabelle or whomever it is please speak up. I just can't stand all this warfare. Dear God, please help the one it is—please Dear God, please!

"Apparently you have not understood what I have just asked you. This pen, and I want everyone to look at it hard, was carelessly thrown into the scapulars. The scapulars were washed. They are presently ruined. That means you will all have to have an extra habit this year. You can't wear them in this condition. *Whose pen is this?*"

No one answered. No one moved. Max and Jean Martin glared at Clarabelle. Freddie swallowed loudly. Mark shuffled her feet.

"All right. There will be no recreation until one of you owns up to this. We will eat in silence, and that means Easter and Sundays and every day for the rest of the year until the nun who threw her pen in with the scapulars owns up to it. Is that clear?"

"Yes, Sister," the nuns answered in unison. The Superior sat down in silence; the rest of the nuns followed. They took out their dishes, filled their plates, and ate in silence. The dishes were scraped, washed, dried, and put away in silence. They said grace and quietly, chastized, left the refectory.

Sister Kevin Mary followed Sister Helen Francis back to her office. She again knelt and asked for a penance. The Superior said that was not necessary, it wasn't her fault, but just to pray that whomever it was had the courage to come forth and admit it. She told her to dry the scapulars and to put them in the nuns' boxes; they could wear them for cleaning or working in school.

Sister Kevin Mary went into chapel, genuflected, and buried her face in her hands. *I just can't believe this. Maybe whoever did it doesn't even know that she did it. Oh, it's going to go on like this forever. Dear God, I just can't take it. Is this what you want from me, to have to live with this kind of stuff, day in and day out?*

Mark came into chapel and sat down heavily next to Sister Kevin Mary. "I wonder if she ever stopped to figure that there were two people missing from dinner—Julia Mary and Marie Marcel. Jules is in such a fog half the time that she could have done it, and Marce can't see straight, so she could have done it. No, she can't miss a chance to throw her weight around, to show who's boss. God, that damn pen will sit there 'til hell freezes over and she won't give in, and no one knows a damn thing about that damn pen. And we'll sit and chew the damn food like a bunch of mummies, while her highness lords it over us. That woman drives me nuts, Kev."

Sister Kevin Mary did not respond. The door to chapel opened and Sister Julia Mary walked through slowly and went to her place. She had been sleeping, for her face was puffy and flushed. Mark whispered loudly, "Hey, Jules, what did you do with your red ballpoint pen? One got in the wash and we all got hell. Is it yours?"

Sister Julia Mary shook her head sleepily. "Sorry, girls, find yourself another scapegoat. I don't usually wash my pens that way, although it may be a good idea."

Sister Kevin Mary left chapel in a hurry, walked quickly down the basement steps and into the ironing room. Aggie's shoulders were more stooped than ever. Her face was deeply lined and red. As Sister Kevin Mary approached, she cast her eyes down onto the ironing board, shaking her head sadly. Sister Kevin Mary stood next to Aggie, saying nothing. She turned and walked slowly into the laundry room to hang up the spotted scapulars.

19.

The red ballpoint pen sat at the head of the table, the uninvited guest at every meal. Day after day, the Hebdomadarian chanted, *"Oremus, Benedic, Domine, dona tua, quae de tua largitate, sumus sumpturi. Per Christum Dominum nostrum,"* making the sign of the cross. Sister Helen Francis would pause dramatically, look at the pen, and face the community, waiting for the owner of the red pen to acknowledge her thoughtlessness. No one came forth. Throughout the days and weeks of Lent, the nuns ate in total silence, breakfast, lunch, and dinner. The pen became a symbol of the Superior's pervasive power. She had full control not only of their lives, but of their speech as well.

A ritual formed. The dishes were brought out of the drawers, along with the pills and tonics, more noisily than usual. The steps of the server became heavier, the words of the reader more exact. Anger and thoughts of revenge were eaten with the food, chewed with hostile bites and swallowed in lumps. Sister Kevin Mary grew to dread mealtimes. She was filled with a ravenous hunger from the Lenten fast and a nausea at the battle of wills.

Max and Jean Martin had already held court and brought in

the verdict that Clarabelle was the only one stupid enough to have thrown the red pen in with the scapulars and the only one weak enough not to be able to admit it. Others joined them in their judgment, and as the plates of food were passed along the table, many of the nuns scowled, glared, and frowned in silence at Clarabelle. The Nobodies—Freddie, Mark, and Sister Kevin Mary—felt that Clarabelle was innocent. They would scowl back at the others in Clarabelle's defense; Clarabelle could not protect herself.

Clarabelle developed stomach troubles. When the others brought out their medicines, Clarabelle brought out a big pink bottle of Pepto-Bismol, which she gulped straight from the bottle before eating. Sister Jean Martin would nudge Max when she saw Clarabelle drink the Pepto-Bismol and they both smiled.

The middle Sunday in Lent, March 21, was *Laetare* Sunday. *Laetare*: Rejoice! for Lent was half over. Hang on, dear Christians, for all this weeping and gnashing of teeth will soon be over. You made it this far; you can get through the rest. The priest wore pink vestments for the Mass—a slight glimmer of Easter, a glimmer of the joys and beauty of the Resurrection.

The bell rang at 4:47 on Sunday afternoon for Matins and Lauds. The nuns gathered for prayer. Sister Kevin Mary walked quickly into chapel, feeling good. It seemed like the winter was finally over. There was the slightest stirring of spring in the air. The walks and drives were dry, and the wind didn't seem as cutting. She felt that they would finally be able to talk at the table. Sister Helen Francis would give in; none of them could stand the constant warfare any longer. *Laetare, dear nuns,* rejoice, this is all over. Let's bury the old red pen; let's join together in the spirit of the Liturgy, forgetting the pains and wounds of this terrible misunderstanding. Let us open our hearts to forgiveness and humility! Let us rejoice!

Willie was in the kitchen, so Sister Kevin Mary knew dinner would be good. As they chanted the Office, she could smell the ham baking in the oven. Willie had made two cherry pies that afternoon and had fixed sweet potatoes with orange to go with the ham.

Clarabelle was not there for Office. Perhaps she was lying

down. Marce was not there either—up in bed, as usual. She hadn't been with the nuns for some time. She seemed to be getting worse.

After prayers, the nuns filed into the refectory. Grace in Latin. The Superior looked once again at the pen and sat down. The reader began the saint of the day. Two places were empty—Marce's and Clarabelle's. Marce was in her room. Sister Helen Francis motioned for Mark and asked her where Sister Clare Elliot was. Sister Mark said that she didn't know but thought she might be over in her classroom. The server brought out a tray of baked ham with glazed peach halves and parsley. Sister Helen Francis told Mark to go over to school with Sister Kevin Mary and find Clare. The two nuns grabbed their cloaks and ran over to the darkened school.

They opened the back door, turned on the overhead lights of the gym, walked quickly through the gym and down the long green halls, turning on lights as they went. Sister Kevin Mary felt frightened. The halls were long. Someone could be hiding at the bottom of the stairs at the end of the addition. They had to go down to the basement to Clarabelle's room. Their heels clicked loudly on the metal runners on the steps, echoing down the darkened halls. Clarabelle's room was across from the boiler room. The smell of burned paper, cleaning supplies, dirty mops filled the air. Large brown barrels stood in the hall like grizzly bears about to attack.

"Mark, I'm scared! It's dark down here," whispered Sister Kevin Mary, grabbing Mark's arm.

"Leggo me, Kevin. Where the hell is Clarabelle?"

Sister Mark reached for her keys, hanging from her black leather belt, unlocked the basement classroom, and snapped on the light.

"Clare . . . you here? . . . Clarabelle, answer me this minute."

There was no sound. Sister Mark turned to Sister Kevin. "I know she's around here. Let's look in the back."

In the back of the classroom were full-length wooden cup-boards. Sister Kevin Mary followed Mark to the back of the classroom. Mark opened the first cupboards—shelves of books, papers, boxes of scissors, crayons, paste. She closed the first cupboard door and opened the second. Standing next to the wide, oily mop was Clarabelle, a black shawl wrapped tightly around her shoulders. Her glasses were steamy from tears. Her face was puffy and red.

"Clare! What in the name of God are you doing in here?"

Clare turned around in the cupboard to face the back. She lowered her head, mumbling something about not coming out forever.

Sister Kevin Mary felt frightened. Clare was three years older than she. Even if she was Clarabelle, she was still an older nun. Dear God, this is just a terrible thing.

The two nuns reached for Clare, leading her gently out of the cupboard. Clare landed heavily on a child's desk, lowered her head, and began sobbing into her sleeves. Sister Kevin Mary and Mark sat next to her, their hands resting on her shoulders. Clare looked up at her two friends.

"I can't go back there. I just hate them. They hate me. It wasn't my damn old pen. I can't take any more of that . . . I'm going crazy . . . that damn Max and her girlfriend, Jean Martin. They think they're God. I hate them. I'm not going back there," she sobbed. Her words came in a rush. She pounded her fists on the desk, shouting and sobbing, knocking her glasses onto the floor. The glasses broke. "I'm going to kill myself, Mark. I hate them. I can't live this way. I'll kill myself!" Clare raised her foot, stomping on the broken glasses. Her eyes, usually magnified by the thick glass, disappeared into her head.

Sister Kevin Mary wanted Mark to do something. Help Clarabelle. She was frightened by the nun's emotions. What if she kills herself right in front of us? Mark is so hardhearted, so hardheaded. God, what will we do with her? If we bring her home, Sister will kill her. The glasses. She's blind without them. The nuns will have a field day with Clarabelle. Now they have her right where they want her. Dear God, take me out of this situation. Oh, my God, home was never like this!

Mark took a deep breath. "Clare, stop it this minute! Just stop it. You're going right back there and face them. We know it's not your pen! Why did you let them get to you like this?

Look what you did to your glasses."

Clare raised her foot and stomped again on the glass. "I mean it, Mark; I'm going to kill myself."

"You can't, Clare. That's a sin."

The three nuns burst out laughing. Clare began laughing hysterically, muttering something about sin, and what is sin, and love and kindness, and her glasses were broken, and nothing really mattered.

Sister Kevin Mary heard her stomach roar. Mark shot her a look, shaking her head. This is not the time to think of your stomach, Kevin. Think of this poor nun who is hysterical, this poor blind nun who is an emotional wreck.

"Hey, Clarabelle, remember what Sister Duns Scotus used to tell us?" asked Sister Kevin Mary. "She used to say, 'When you get to the end of your rope, tie a knot and hang on.'" Mark looked at Sister Kevin Mary, nodding approval.

Clare blew her nose with a dirty handkerchief. Her red pen, which was in her pencil case hanging from her belt, had leaked onto her habit. "I'm just a mess," said Clare, trying to regain her composure.

"Ya, you are, Clare," agreed Mark. "You're a hell of a mess. But too bad, you've got a right to be. You just have to snap out of it. Tie a knot, Clare. We've got to get you home before Max comes gallumping over here. They'd just love to see you like this, Clare."

Clarabelle blew her nose and wiped her narrowed eyes with her soiled handkerchief. They took her by the arm, led her out of the classroom, shut off the lights, and went up the stairs, down the hall and out of the school.

"Do you have any other glasses, Clare?" asked Sister Kevin Mary.

"Yeah, but they're not nun's glasses. I had them from high school. Pink rims. I'll have to use them. I think they're in my trunk. Will you go down and see if you can find them, Kev?"

The nuns took Clare right up to her room. Mark told her to get ready for bed and they would bring her some dinner. Willie had saved their dinners in the oven. Mark went to Sister Helen Francis and told her that Clare was not feeling well and that she just seemed to be somewhat upset. Perhaps she just needed a good night's sleep. Sister Helen Francis told her not to bring Clare a tray; if she were hungry enough, she could just come down and eat in the refectory like everyone else.

Mark and Sister Kevin Mary ate their dinners in the refectory. The rest of the nuns were finishing up their weekly lesson plans or watching television. The ham was dry and salty; the cherry pie was pasty. Sister Kevin Mary had two pieces, ramming her left thumb between her belt and her habit as she made her way into the kitchen to cut another piece. Mark only played with her food.

They heard Sister Helen Francis start up the front stairs toward Clarabelle's room. Clare's bed was still on the floor, and without her glasses, she didn't know what was going on. Sister Kevin Mary went out to the kitchen again for a glass of milk, picturing the Superior standing with her hands on her hips, Clare not knowing where she was or who was in the room. Blind, deaf, and dumb, poor Clarabelle. She could hear Sister Helen Francis raising her voice, shouting something about disobedience, the bell, and acting like a mature religious. Clare was blowing her nose loudly, an act that Sister Helen Francis found undignified. Sister Helen Francis only wiped her nose gracefully, if needed.

She heard Clare's door slam and Sister Helen Francis marching forcefully down to her own room. Mark had washed her dishes and gone down to Clare's trunk to find her glasses. Sister Kevin Mary had another glass of milk, feeling guilty that Clare wasn't eating any dinner. Willie came into the kitchen to find out what was the matter. Sister Kevin Mary told Willie the story. Willie's eyes filled with tears as she bit her bottom lip. "Damn, Sam," she muttered and tore into chapel.

It was all growing increasingly worse. The Lenten fast, silence at the table, no letters, no phone calls, Clare with her pink glasses. Sister Kevin Mary was getting headaches regularly. And her cramps were intensifying, as well as the numbness in her feet. God, I'm falling apart and I'm only twenty. She thought she was going to explode most of the time, and tears would come when she least expected them: a child bringing her a piece of birthday cake, watching Aggie bending over the ironing board, seeing Marce getting worse and worse and no one doing anything about it. Marce was missing more and more school and rarely showed up for prayer or meals. But she really wasn't missing anything, Sister Kevin Mary thought. If my father ever knew what was going on, he'd drag me home by the nape of the neck.

She could no longer pray. She had said everything that had to be said. Maybe it was just time for her to listen. She loved the passage from Isaiah, about listening for the voice of God in the sound of the sea and the thunderclaps, but finding Him in the still, silent voice within. And she listened for the still, silent voice within and heard nothing. She tried to remember her classes in ascetic theology, Sister Duns Scotus's lectures on the life of prayer. She tried to remember what she had told them about aridity, the dark night of the senses, and the bleakness of the soul that meant you were moving closer to God, that you were becoming proficient in prayer, and that God could now remove the spiritual props that He had to use to entice those whom He especially loved to begin the arduous journey to sanctity.

Laetare Sunday. She knelt in chapel, full of salty ham and cherry pie, and nothing in her soul. She reached back and unpinned her collar; she felt like she was choking. She lifted her headband with her left thumbnail, raised and lowered her forehead, and placed the headband back on her forehead. She sat back and stared at the altar. Nothing made sense anymore. She had no taste for the things of God, just food, food, food, and it was Lent. She wasn't a very good nun and she knew it. Her teaching was mediocre, at best. Prayer was zilch. A big cipher. Life was just one big salty ham and doughy cherry pie.

God, the damn tears are starting again. If I could only pray like I used to. She couldn't even swallow the lump forming in her throat. Some of the nuns were down in the basement watching the "Ed Sullivan Show." Lawrence Welk would be on next, "anda one, anda two, anda tree." She put her elbows on her knees, hiding her face in her hands.

Maybe this was the hardest thing of all, being a nun and not being able to pray. She thought back on how she used to feel when she could pray, of all the Masses she attended from the time she was in eighth grade, getting up every morning, from the dark of winter to the hot, sultry days of August, never missing morning Mass. She loved the Mass, the daily Liturgy, receiving Holy Communion every day of her life. Her life of prayer was the most important part of her day; as a matter of fact, prayer *was* her day, constantly uniting herself with the thought of the presence of God. "Background music" Sister Duns Scotus used to call it.

Before every class, before she went out on a date, she would kneel by her bed and ask the Blessed Virgin to keep her pure, and when she got home, she would thank her that she had committed no sin, either of word or of deed. She thought of her home parish church, St. Mary's, with its white colonial walls and white pews, and of the priests who served there, who heard her weekly confession, always ending with, "Now say three Our Fathers and three Hail Marys, and keep up the good work, my dear."

She loved the smell of that church, clean and airy without smelling like disinfectant or old flowers. There were no stained-glass windows, just glass slightly tinted blue, the color of a clear spring sky. The sanctuary was white and the altar was white, above which a large gold crucifix hung. During Lent, all the statues were covered with a deep purple cloth; the church—blue, white, and purple—held you within itself by its sheer beauty.

She looked up at the little altar in the convent chapel, sterile, just like the nuns. So emotionally sterile, devoid of anything that would evoke a sense of beauty or prayer or feelings. It's just here, that's all. Just like me, just here, in body, not in soul. As a matter of fact, I have no soul left. It just dried up and blew away, like dead leaves. Burned in a big rubbish heap.

Sister Helen Francis genuflected in the doorway of the chapel, reached for the little brass bell, and rang it with four sharp shakes of her wrist. The downstairs television was snapped off. Sister Kevin Mary stood, made the venia, and left the chapel, feeling no better than when she had gone in. Mark was already asleep when she went into their room.

Monday, Tuesday, Wednesday. More of the same. Sister

Kevin Mary always hated Wednesdays. The middle of the
week, locked into time, unable to escape. The nuns gathered
for the chanting of the Seven Penitential Psalms, specially
chosen to express sorrow for sin. Supposedly, St. Augustine
recited these psalms when he was dying, shedding copious tears
for his sins. Sister Kevin Mary always tried to picture a dying
person getting through all the verses; maybe he wasn't all that
sick.

In Latin they chanted:

> I am afflicted and humbled exceedingly;
> I roared with the groanings of my heart.
> My heart is troubled, my strength hath left me;
> And the light of my eyes itself is not with me.

The air was heavy. The words were heavy. And Clarabelle
was not there for the Office. Dear God, is she cowering over in
her classroom again? Another scene, more tears, more suffering.

After the Office, Mark went over to Sister Helen Francis and
whispered something to her, then motioned to Sister Kevin
Mary to come with her. They headed back over to school.
Instant replay of last Sunday—opening doors, turning on the
lights, down the long halls in silence.

Mark rammed her key into the lock of the basement classroom, shouting, "Clare Elliot, come out of there this minute!"
They walked quickly to the back of the room, throwing open
the cupboard doors. Only the oily mop and an empty bucket of
stiff, dirty rags stood in the cupboard.

Mark pursed her lips, muttering about Clare's stupidity. The
two nuns went into both of the bathrooms, shouting,
"Clare . . . Clarabelle . . . Clare Elliot . . . Clarabelle." They
walked slowly into the janitor's room, looking behind metal
shelves and drums of disinfectant, into the broom closet. No
Clare. Mark turned to Sister Kevin Mary. "Kev, we're going
to turn this damn school on its ears until we find her. Let's go!"
They went into every classroom, bathroom, closet, cupboard,
into the office, clinic, storage room, gym, kitchen. No Clare.

"She's not here. Let's go home. Maybe she's hiding in her trunk or in the bathtub," Mark told Sister Kevin Mary. When they came in the back door, the nuns were still at the table, eating in silence. They went down to the basement, checking all the corners and hiding places, then upstairs. No Clare. They went into the chapel and stayed until the nuns left the refectory to avoid making a public announcement of Clare's disappearance.

The door of the chapel opened. "Where is she?" demanded Sister Helen Francis. "Where's that nun?"

"Nowhere, Sister. We've checked everywhere. She's not here."

Sister Helen Francis slammed the chapel door and went into the refectory. She told all the nuns to go over to school and find Clare. The nuns grabbed their cloaks and went, two by two, over to school. Max and Jean Martin, the last to leave, walked over, laughing together. Willie and Freddie went over to the church to check out the sacristy and the choir loft. She might be hiding in a pew.

No Clarabelle. Sister Helen Francis called Monsignor Ryan. He came in the back door, singing, "Where are you, now that I need you?" No one thought he was very funny. He went into Sister Helen Francis's office and closed the door. Sister Kevin Mary heard them laughing, then talking softly, then more laughter. Very funny, she thought. Clarabelle could be lying dead somewhere, and all they can do is laugh. She heard Monsignor dial the phone. Within minutes, two police officers were at the front door. They went into the French provincial parlor. Monsignor Ryan was laughing with the policemen. She couldn't hear Sister Helen Francis.

It was now 7:30, dark for over an hour. Still no Clare. Freddie and Mark walked into town, thinking that she might be in a restaurant or the theater. The nuns had combed the playground, the area behind the school, and the area behind the convent. No Clare. Blue and white squad cars drove up and down the streets slowly, occasionally flashing their lights in the bushes or up and down the walks. No Clare.

By 9:00, Sister Helen Francis was biting her lips and picking at her cuticles. Aggie had been in chapel since dinnertime, saying the Stations of the Cross as she finished a rosary. Marce came down to the kitchen to fill up her ice bag, mumbling about how she hoped they were happy now, since they had poor Clare where they wanted her. On her way back up to her room, she lost her balance and banged into the chapel door.

Everyone seemed to be standing around, in the refectory, in the community room, or in the halls. Sister Lucy looked indignant. She finally went into the office, not excusing herself to Monsignor Ryan, who was still in the office. The office door closed. Soon Sister Helen Francis dialed the phone. In the chapel, her deep voice could be heard, speaking deliberately and confidently to whomever was on the other end.

Sister Lucy left the office when Sister Helen Francis hung up. She came into chapel. Sister Kevin Mary looked at Sister Lucy. Sister Lucy shook her head, warning no one to ask her any questions. Sister Helen Francis came out of her office and led Monsignor Ryan to the door. He was no longer laughing. Sister Helen Francis told the nuns in the kitchen to get everyone together and that she would meet them in the community room. The nuns gathered quickly.

"Nuns," she addressed the community, "we have a problem. Clare Elliot is nowhere to be found. I've just notified Mother Jeremiah at the motherhouse. The police have been apprised of this situation. Now, I want you all to think very hard. Did she say anything to anyone about what she might do? She's been unsettled for a while now, and I have been very worried about her. Can anyone remember anything that she might have said?"

The nuns, standing with their hands folded under their scapulars, shook their heads.

"Nothing, Sister."

"I can't think of a thing, Sister."

"Clare never really told anyone what she was thinking."

Max and Jean Martin both looked piqued, daring anyone to look at them reproachfully. Sister Helen Francis avoided their eyes; Sister Lucy stared at both of them.

"Well, if anyone remembers or can think of anything, come to me. I don't care what the hour is."

The nuns nodded, slowly leaving the community room. The bell for Profound Silence did not ring; it was not necessary. The lights were off within minutes. Clarabelle's mattress was empty.

The bell rang the following morning at 5:10 sharp. Clare had not shown up during the night. Dear God in heaven, not another day, thought Sister Kevin Mary as she climbed into her black cotton stockings. Where will they find Clare? Maybe the kids will find her on their way to school, hanging from a tree. At least it won't be on a Wednesday.

At 5:30, Sister Helen Francis began morning prayers with the sign of the Cross. Even with one of her nuns missing in action, her voice was deep, confident, in charge. The rest of the nuns joined in the prayers.

At 5:35 A.M., the phone rang. Sister Helen Francis, who usually did not answer the phone, rose quickly and picked up the receiver. It was Mother Jeremiah calling from the motherhouse. Sister Clare Elliot was safe. She had gone to her mother's, taking the train into the Loop and a Greyhound bus up to the little town in Michigan where her mother lived. She had used the money the children donated to the poor as their Lenten sacrifice for her ticket. Her mother, knowing that this was irregular, called the local convent; the Superior there called Mother Jeremiah. They were bringing Clare down to the motherhouse that afternoon. She'd stay there until after Easter. Sister Clare Elliot was safe but terribly disturbed.

Sister Helen Francis interrupted the morning prayers to pass on the information. Freddie burst into tears and ran out of the chapel. Max snorted. The morning prayer resumed.

After breakfast, Sister Helen Francis announced that they would have the Chapter of Faults. Dear God, just what we need. A little stress, a little strain, just to keep the girls in shape. We don't have enough already. The dishes had been washed and put away; the red pen sat on the table.

As Willie walked up to the crucifix to confess her faults, she glanced at the pen, biting her lower lip.

"Reverend dear Sister," she began, "I humbly confess that I have not rightly observed our Holy Rule and Constitu-

tions. . . ." Willie listed her faults for all to hear, and as she
was about to ask for a deserving penance, she added, "And I
assume full responsibility for ruining the scapulars with the red
pen, and for this I also ask a deserving penance."

Sister Helen Francis stared at the young nun, inclining
toward the crucifix. Willie was a good nun. If it had been her
pen, she would have owned up to it immediately. And Willie
would never have been so careless as to throw her pen in the
laundry. And she wasn't lying. She didn't say that it was her
pen; she just said she would take the responsibility for it in
order to stop this senseless warfare that had resulted in Clare's
persecution. Sister Kevin Mary smiled, relishing the thought
that the Superior's ego had been assuaged by a person bigger
and better than she was. The Sullivans had class, and even
though Willie was only twenty-three, she had more sense than
her Superior and was big enough to take the rap.

Sister Helen Francis had no choice but to accept Willie's
gesture of peace. "Sister William Ann, you may say a rosary
for your carelessness."

Willie looked up at her Superior. "May God reward you,
Sister."

The Chapter of Faults concluded with Sister Helen Francis
warning them not to say anything about Clare to the lay
teachers or to anyone, including their parents. And they were
not to write about this to any of their friends in any other
convent. What went on within these walls was to remain
inside. They were a family, families have problems, and they
were not to wash their dirty linen in public. This was their
problem, and they would learn to live with it.

The nuns nodded in agreement, thanking her for her words.
Sister Helen Francis picked up the red pen, smiled to herself,
and went into her office to call Monsignor Ryan. As she made
her bed, Sister Kevin Mary could hear the Superior laughing
loudly on the phone.

20.

The fat usher stood at the side door, handing each of the nuns a few palm fronds. He nodded patronizingly, smiling in a fatherly way as they passed in front of him. Some of the nuns smiled back, thanking him for the palm; others studied the brass plate on the door to avoid looking at him. Little China dolls parading in front of the emperor.

It was Palm Sunday, the start of Holy Week. The Gospel was long: a chronicle of the Passion, beginning with Christ's entry into Jerusalem, when the crowd called him a king, waving palm branches as He rode through their midst on a donkey, and ending with His death on the cross. Hosannas filled the air as the priest and the altar boys proceeded around the church, commemorating the triumphal march of Christ, the march of Christ to His death.

Sister Kevin Mary knelt in a pew, understanding the bitter-sweet victory of the day, for Christ knew what was ahead for Him that week but no one else did. He could have gotten out of it so easily. But in another way, He could not have because His Father wanted Him to die on the cross, and the only thing He wanted to do was to obey His Father.

She understood that obedience. It was not weakness; it was strength, for only the strong could obey. She knew deep within her that her life was also bittersweet, a life called to obey, to accept the cross of her life. The bitterness of life with the nuns, the terrible, terrible loneliness at a depth she had never known existed. How could you be so lonely living with sixteen other people, teaching fifty-six kids every day? People, people, people, and she was alone. Abandoned even by God. She loved the passage when Christ shouted at His Father, "My God, My God, why hast Thou forsaken Me?" That was God's way, and when you felt the most abandoned, that was when God was the closest to you, if you had faith.

Something was going on that morning. Long-distance calls, Monsignor Ryan back and forth to the convent, Sister Lucy in the office with Sister Helen Francis for over an hour. Sister Helen Francis picked her cuticles all through breakfast. A call came while they were doing dishes; she ran out of the refectory to grab the phone. She came back into the refectory as the nuns were saying grace after meals.

She addressed the community: "As you know, nuns, Sister Marie Marcel has not been getting any better. She's in a lot of pain. Monsignor has arranged for her to go to Mayo Clinic for some tests. We're sure that it isn't anything serious, but he wants her checked out just to be sure. We're leaving this afternoon for Rochester, Minnesota. Monsignor Ryan will take us to Midway Airport. If there are any permissions that you will need before I leave, you'd better see me now. Sister Lucy will be in charge while I'm gone. And do keep Marie Marcel in your prayers. We've got to get to the bottom of this."

The nuns looked at each other. Sister Kevin Mary felt like she had been kicked in the stomach. The Mayo Clinic? Mayo Clinic? That's only if you are really sick. There are plenty of hospitals in Chicago. Mayo Clinic?

Yet she felt relieved. Marce had unraveled before her eyes. She had never really seen anyone that sick before. Marce used to be so wild—doing what she damn pleased, always having money, blaring her transistor, wearing loafers, no undershirt or cuffs. Now it was just ice packs, missing school and prayers, lying up there in her darkened room like a lizard under a rock.

Her left eye was completely shut; her lip curled in a permanent sneer. She didn't have much to say anymore. When Sister Kevin Mary would bring her a tray or a cup of coffee, Marce would lift her head, attempt to smile, and say faintly, "Just put it there, kid. Thanks." And Sister Kevin Mary, frightened, would put the tray on the desk next to the dusty transistor and return a half hour later to take the untouched tray back down to the kitchen.

"Can I get you anything else, Marce? Do you need anything?"

"No, kid. I'll be just fine. As soon as I get rid of this headache. Can't seem to throw it anymore. Just get me some fresh ice, OK?"

"Sure, Marce, sure."

When they finally got her dressed, downstairs, and out to the car, she seemed to be better. Maybe just the thought of getting some relief from all the pain was enough to make her better. When Freddie carried the suitcases out to the car, Marce asked her if she had packed her transistor. The nuns all laughed, telling her that they were sure she was better already.

Sister Helen Francis ripped at a cuticle, feigning a hearty laugh. Her nails were bleeding and she didn't smell of Shalimar. She was biting the inside of her cheek, the way she did when she was nervous. She called Sister Lucy aside and gave her some last-minute instructions.

Sister Kevin Mary wanted to hug Marce, just a gentle hug to let her know that she cared, to let her know that she wanted her to get better. Marce wasn't the type who went in for hugs. But as she watched Marce, the lump was back in her throat, and she could feel tears welling up in her eyes. God, I've got no control. I can't stop myself. She bit her bottom lip until it hurt, clutching her rosary tightly—anything to distract herself from her emotions. She caught Jean Martin's eye; Jean Martin, who had no use for sentimentality, looked disgusted.

"God bless, Sister," said Aggie softly.

"Take care," called Freddie.

"Keep the Faith, Marce," shouted Willie.

"See ya' later, alligator," Sister Kevin Mary said.

"After a while, crocodile," answered Marce softly.

Monsignor Ryan locked the doors, turned the car around, honked twice, and pulled out of the parking lot, Marce in the back seat alone, Sister Helen Francis sitting in the front next to him. The nuns waved and slowly headed back to the convent.

"Kevin! Kevin Mary!" shouted Theo from the convent steps, "It's your father . . . long-distance. Hurry up!"

Some of the people coming out of Mass looked up. They had heard Theo call her just "Kevin," not "Sister Kevin Mary." She felt embarrassed but tried to smile with great dignity. Why can't she use correct titles in front of lay people? She does that all the time.

Sister Kevin Mary looked at Sister Lucy for permission to take the call. She was embarrassed because it was Lent and they weren't supposed to receive calls or mail. Maybe Sister Lucy would think that she had this planned. Just let Sister Helen Francis get out of the drive and look what happens. When the cat's away, the mice do play. Sister Lucy told her to hurry up, it was long-distance. Sister Kevin Mary ran up the steps of the convent, into the office, and picked up the receiver.

"Dad, what's the matter? Is anything wrong?"

"Hi, Maureen. How ya' doing?"

"Daddy, it's Lent. You're not supposed to call me."

"I know, Maureen, but it's almost over. I just had to tell you something. You know who our next President is going to be? An Irishman. A Catholic. Kennedy, from Boston. I just saw him on "Meet the Press." Maureen, our next President is going to be an Irish Catholic! You just wait and see!"

"I don't believe it. A Catholic can't be President, you know that, Daddy."

"Maureen, I've never lied to you. I know this fellow is going to get elected. They've got loads of money, and this guy is sharp and good-looking. Timmy Byrne went to Harvard with Kennedy's younger brother. He said they've got lots of class. I mean it, Maureen, Kennedy is going to be the next President. I just had to tell you that. Hope I won't get you in trouble."

"No, Daddy. It's OK. How's mother and everybody? How's Kevin?"

"Everyone's just fine. How you keepin', Honey?"

"Just fine, Daddy. Sister Marie Marcel just left for the Mayo Clinic. She's been pretty sick."

"Christ, the Mayo Clinic! It must be pretty serious!"

"Well, they just want to do some tests. Listen, I've got to go. It's Lent, ya' know."

"I know, Maureen. I'm sorry. I just had to tell you about Kennedy. Tell the nuns. I didn't mean to get you in trouble."

"You didn't get me in trouble, Daddy. I just have to go. Thanks for the call."

"Bye, Honey. Take care of yourself."

"Bye, Daddy. Thanks."

She hung up the phone and went to thank Sister Lucy for being able to talk with her father. Sister Lucy wanted to know if anything was wrong at home. She said no, that he just wanted to tell her something about someone.

Monday evening, Sister Helen Francis called from Rochester. She said that Sister Marie Marcel was very tired from the trip and that the next day they were going to start the tests on her. They were doing a spinal tap: take out the fluid in her spine and shoot air up to her brain. They could then see if there was a blockage. It would be painful, but sometimes they had to be cruel to be kind.

They didn't hear anything on Tuesday, but on Wednesday of Holy Week, the Superior called and said that Sister Marie Marcel was very sick from the tests. The spinal tap was very painful; it would take her a few days to get over it. The air had increased the pressure in her head. They had her on a lot of medication but were determined to find out what was the problem. Sister Helen Francis had a lovely room at the hotel across from the hospital, and she was spending her time with Sister Marie Marcel.

On Thursday, Holy Thursday, Sister Helen Francis called again. They had done another test, shot purple dye into her spine and watched it go into her brain. They could follow it on an X-ray machine and see if anything was in the way. It wasn't as painful as the air test. They would have the results the following morning, Good Friday. She'd call them as soon as she knew anything. In the meanwhile, they were to pray very hard that the doctors could find out what the problem was.

The nuns had a great feast that evening after the evening Mass. Holy Thursday was perhaps the most beautiful day of the year, the day Christ instituted the Holy Eucharist, the day He changed bread and wine into His Body and Blood. It was the day that He gave Himself forever to His people. He would die the following day and leave them forever, but through the Eucharist He would remain with them until the end of time.

The bells rang throughout the Gloria of the Mass and then were solemnly put away until Easter morning. After the Mass, the priests had stripped the altars, moving the Blessed Sacrament to a side altar to be reposed throughout the night for adoration. Since there had to be someone with the Blessed Sacrament, the men of the parish were scheduled to come into the church throughout the night, taking turns watching with Our Lord. The men of the parish would give up an hour's sleep to keep vigil, for Christ had chastized His own apostles when they fell asleep when He was in His agony in the Garden, "Could you not watch an hour with Me?" The men of St. Paul's parish would gladly watch an hour with the Lord. The nuns went to bed.

The bell rang at 7:00 the following morning, Good Friday, the most sacred day of the Liturgical year, the day Christ died on the cross. The nuns wore their long black cloaks throughout the day and ate nothing until the noon colation. They gathered in chapel, and the Hebdomadarian read:

> Darkness covered the earth while the Jews crucified Jesus; and about the ninth hour Jesus cried out with a loud voice, "My God, My God, why hast Thou forsaken Me?" And bowing down His head, He gave up the ghost.

> God spared not His own son; but delivered Him up for us all.

More rosaries, the Stations of the Cross, Tenebrae, the Penitential Psalms, kneeling, praying, fasting, silence, darkness covering the earth. The nuns were in mourning with the Lord, hiding their lives with Him in His suffering. Then they would go over to church from noon until 3:00 for *Tre Ore*, the sacred three hours that Christ hung on the cross.

At 11:30, as the nuns sat in silence at the table, eating hot cross buns and drinking black coffee, the phone rang. Sister Lucy rose quickly and went to the office. She returned to the table in silence and waited until the dishes were finished.

"Nuns, that was Sister Helen Francis. They have the results of the tests. Sister Marie Marcel is going to have surgery on Monday morning. They found something at the base of her brain. Sister Helen Francis feels confident that they will be able to remove it and that Sister Marie Marcel will be just fine. She is in considerable pain from all the tests but seems to be resting. Monsignor Ryan is going to fly up there Sunday night. The bell will ring at ten minutes to twelve for *Tre Ore* in church. Pray for Sister Marie Marcel."

No one moved. Something at the base of the brain? One by one, they left the refectory, avoiding each other's eyes.

As Sister Kevin Mary walked through the kitchen, Max was drying the pans for Jean Martin. She heard Max say that it sounded like cancer and that her father died of cancer. Cancer kills quickly, especially in the brain.

21.

Sister Kevin Mary couldn't sleep. She was very tired, exhausted from everything—Lent, the nuns, fasting, teaching, trying to be a good nun. April 4—Easter—would be in two more days. Lent was practically over.

She had always hated Good Friday, even when she was a kid. Her grandfather died on Good Friday when she was seven, and every Good Friday after that, it seemed that the skies blackened about 2:00, and by 3:00, when Christ died, a terrible storm was churning in the skies. She knew that she should be rejoicing, for it truly was a *good* Friday, good since her redemption was won by Christ's death on the cross. She never really knew what that meant—her redemption—she was redeemed, bought back by the death of Christ. She really didn't understand, but she had Faith, and that was all that mattered.

She couldn't get comfortable. She lifted her pillow, punched it twice, and tried lying on her right side. The left side was more comfortable for sleeping, but tonight she thought she'd try the right. Her legs itched, and she rubbed them against each other. That only made them more itchy.

She was beginning to hate her body, her fat body. When she turned to lie on her stomach, her stomach hung down. She pictured herself like a fat banana, head and legs elevated, stomach on the sheets. There was something wrong with her body, but she didn't know what it was. It ached all over and seemed to be screaming from inside. She hated these nights when she couldn't get to sleep; either she fell asleep immediately or she was tormented with thoughts of him over there, and then tormented that she was tormented. Play with fire and you're going to get burned.

Why did God have to send Dan Doyle to the same place at the same time that she was there? There were hundreds of parishes in the city where he could have been sent. There were more than 400 places throughout the country where she could have been sent. The kids were beginning to ask her if she and Father Doyle were brother and sister; they looked alike, acted alike, and they were both getting fat. Doyle was getting a beer belly.

Dear God, how I ache. My arms ache just to hold something. I'm so terribly much alone. No one ever touches me, except the kids. If I didn't have the kids, I'd go mad. At least I can give them a little squeeze or a little hug when they need it. Or when I need it. I feel so hollowed out, scooped out, empty. Dear God, stop this terrible aching inside of me, please stop it. I know Willie and Mark and Freddie don't feel this. Ever.

She looked over at Mark, sound asleep, a brown rosary wrapped around her slender fingers. Sleeping with women the rest of my life, the rest of my life. Eating, living, talking, living and dying with women. Women, wall-to-wall women, who always said, "Oh, pardon me," when they accidentally brushed each other's arms. Oh, pardon me, Dear Lord, for being human. Pardon me for my terrible hunger and loneliness and my screaming emptiness.

Hunger, hunger of the body and of the soul. I'm hungry again! She jumped up, threw on her robe, and made her way down the back stairs. She genuflected in the chapel door, went into the kitchen, and turned on the light. On the counter was half a lemon meringue pie, lightly dusted with powdered sugar.

She was so hungry she was shaking. She took out a long, sharp knife, measured the half into thirds, and sliced herself a piece of pie. One-sixth of a pie; one-third of one-half is one-sixth. She poured herself a tall glass of cold milk and walked into the refectory, not bothering to turn on the overhead light. The slice of pie was consumed in seconds; she jumped up, carried her saucer back to the kitchen, and took another slice of pie. One-sixth plus one-sixth equals two-sixths, reduced to one-third. One-third of a lemon meringue pie, on Good Friday night. Good Friday! Dear God! I'm still supposed to be fasting. Well, I broke it, might just as well finish it.

The milk was gone before she realized it. She went back for more milk, more cold, bubbly milk. She finished the second piece of pie, placed the fork down, and frowned. She was still hungry. This must have been what her ancestors felt when they came over: The Great Famine, but then it was about potatoes; she had graduated to pie. From potatoes to pie in three generations, she thought. She picked up the plate, went into the kitchen for the last piece of pie, and carried her glass so she could fill it up again.

Round Three, all for Good Friday, Good Friday in the convent. What else do you do but stuff yourself with lemon meringue pie when you have a hunger like mine? Her sister Ann would have considered her behavior utterly gross. Too damn bad about Ann; she doesn't know what it is to be this hungry. One-sixth times three equals three-sixths, reduced to one-half. One-half of a pie, and I'm still hungry. Hollow leg, her father would say.

She washed the empty dish and held up the glass. Maybe just a little more milk, one for the road. She filled up the glass with more milk. I just can't drink milk alone like that. She opened the cupboard and found a package of Oreo cookies, her favorite. My Tre Oreo services, she mused. One-half a pie and three Oreo cookies, that ought to see me through the night.

She washed the glass, snapped out the light, and stood in the dark kitchen. I can't go back upstairs. I'm wide awake. She went into chapel, genuflected in the dark, and sat down in her place. She thought again of her stomach. Now that took the wrinkles out, her father would have said. Yes, that took the wrinkles out. Out of my stomach but not out of my soul.

This was supposed to have been such a holy day, but it seemed to be so physical, carnal. Fasting made her so much more conscious of her body, her fat, ugly body. She lifted her nightgown as she sat in the chapel, looking at her legs without the black stockings. She looked like a Russian woman athlete with fat, bulging muscles. Her knees looked funny in the dark, like big, round balls growing at the tops of her calves. Knee balls. In the Novitiate they were thin and cracked from all the kneeling. When she first got there, she had to stick a Kotex in her stockings for little pads, because the kneelers were made of hard wood. She had to kneel for hours at a time. Housemaid's knees. Nun's knees. No one will ever see my knees again. My big, fat knees.

It's Doyle—he's the one that got me started. She thought of the Holy Rule under *Purity of Heart*:

> If your eyes light upon any man, let them never be fixed upon him. Say not that your minds are pure, if your eyes be impure, because an impure eye is the messenger of an impure heart. And when, though the tongue be silent, the mutual looks of both parties proclaim the impurity of their hearts, and concupiscence moves them to take pleasure in sinful desires, though their bodies remain inviolate, yet is the virtue of chastity destroyed in their souls.

The virtue of chastity. Virginity. Today was just so terrible, God hanging on the cross, and me thinking about Doyle. During the service, the three priests had to prostrate themselves in front of the altar to show humility and obedience. And all she could think of was lying next to Father Doyle. Oh, what a terrible thing for a nun to think about! But that's what she wanted to do, and she hated herself for thinking about it.

After the services, they had the veneration of the cross when everyone in the church had to come up and kiss the cross. The people knelt at the communion rail, and a priest walked to each one, offering the cross for them to kiss, then wiping off the kiss and proceeding to the next person.

She hadn't planned it, but Father Doyle had the nuns' side of the church, and she couldn't get out of it. She was kneeling there, thinking that she was going to faint, land in a heap on the church floor. He was coming closer and closer, and all she could think about was that she'd stand up uncontrollably, kiss him instead of the cross, then run out of the church. He was only two people away, and she could see him wiping the crucifix as he made his way toward her. She grabbed the communion rail tightly, hoping that she could hold herself down if her legs went out of control and she jumped up and kissed him.

It was her turn. He was standing right in front of her and she had to kiss the crucifix. She closed her eyes, trying to think quickly of the terrible suffering of the Lord. He seemed to hold it there forever. She couldn't pull herself away from the crucifix; she was stuck. Mark nudged her with her arm. She opened her eyes and looked up at Doyle. He was smiling down at her, and slowly took the crucifix away from her, brushing his hand against her cheek. She thought she was going to faint. Mark kissed the crucifix quickly and gave her another poke with her elbow. "Move it," she whispered. Sister Kevin Mary braced herself on the communion railing, stood, and made her way back to her place. She didn't know if her knees would buckle and she'd disgrace herself. She got back to her place and buried her head in her hands, hoping everyone would think she was upset about Good Friday.

As they finally left the church, Mark looked at her strangely. "What was that about? You really kill me sometimes, Kevin. You really do. What were you trying to do? You looked like a fool, if you want to know. I thought you were having some kind of a seizure. God, I never know what you'll do!"

Sister Kevin Mary shrugged her shoulders. "I haven't the faintest idea, Mark. It just happened. I just don't know."

She turned and looked at the clock: 1:10 A.M. Here she was, sitting in chapel in the middle of the night with her skirts up to her knees. She patted her fat knees, lowered her nightgown, and knelt down.

Dear Holy Mother of God, keep me pure and chaste. I didn't mean to do that today. I don't mean to have this attraction for

Doyle. I didn't look for it. It just came. Take it away from me, dear Mary. Keep me close to you and your son. I love you, and I give my life to you. Help me never to offend you by my passions, my ignorance, my sinfulness. Keep me pure in thought and deed.

She yawned, made the sign of the cross, genuflected, and left the chapel. She went back into the kitchen, grabbed another Oreo, and went to bed.

22.

After the sumptuous Easter breakfast, some of the nuns went over to the basement of the priest's house to help count the collection. It was the second-biggest haul of the year; Christmas was first. Monsignor Ryan delivered all the sermons at the Easter Masses, mentioning the joy of the resurrection and the fact that he hadn't seen many of them since Christmas. With a twinkle in his eye, he would whisper into the microphone, "Now, do let the dear Lord know that you haven't meant to stay away. Reach deep into your heart and show the Lord that you are grateful to Him. And if any of you are so moved to reach deeply into your pockets as well as your hearts, all the better." The congregation would laugh at the Monsignor's gentle humor and reach deeply into their pockets. And since his sermon lasted no more than ninety seconds, they would usually double their offering in gratitude for not keeping them in church too long.

The rectory basement was filled with ushers. The most vocal was Mr. Foley, who had two brothers who were priests. Mr. Foley assumed that he knew everything that was going on and loved to order the nuns around. Monsignor Ryan watched his empire grow under his eyes: the tens, twenties, and fifties piling up in tall green stacks on the tables. By the Coke machine, some high school kids were counting coins and entertaining Father Doyle with stories about school and their latest dates.

Father O'Mahoney, having just finished the last Mass, came down to the basement to see if he could help out. He wore black pants and a starched, white, long-sleeved shirt, open at the collar. He approached Monsignor Ryan, who was entertaining Mr. Foley and a group of nuns with his latest joke. Monsignor Ryan looked up when he saw the young priest. "Father O'Mahoney, go upstairs and put on your cassock."

The tall, muscular young priest looked at the pastor. "Yes, Monsignor," he said immediately, turned, and walked quickly up to his room. Within two minutes he was back down, fully dressed in his long black cassock. "That's better now, Jack. Why don't you and a couple of the nuns start on the singles? They add up too, you know." Mr. Foley let out a roar, nudging Monsignor Ryan in the elbow.

Father O'Mahoney, Willie, and Sister Kevin Mary sat down at a small gray card table and began to count the singles. Father O'Mahoney had hair the color of butterscotch that curled like a cap around his head. His broad, thick hands were covered with curly, sandy hair. Only his black eyelashes, flashing over his light blue eyes, signaled a possible anger hidden within this obedient young man. He was the most priestly of the three priests: Monsignor Ryan loved the power of his priesthood; Father Doyle loved the people; Father O'Mahoney just loved being a priest. He seemed unaware of the possibility of power in terms of money or respect; he thought of the priesthood only in terms of being a servant of the Lord; not weak, just obedient.

Willie, who also had brothers who were priests, knew what to say to them. She was neither in awe of them nor did she take advantage of her position to create a false intimacy, like Mr. Foley did. She looked at him indignantly. "Why'd you let him do that to you?"

Father O'Mahoney shrugged his shoulders. "It makes the old boy feel good. He's got to have someone to boss around. Doyle

will get his turn next. It's just a game. Don't take it so
seriously, Sister."

"It kills me the way he throws his weight around. I can't
understand how he gets away with it!"

"You know the answer to that as well as I do, Sister. Hey,
let's change the subject. I just got some really good news. Mary
Clare is going to be able to come home in July. She's not due
back until next year, but the folks are celebrating their fortieth
anniversary, and they're letting her come!"

"Who's Mary Clare?" asked Sister Kevin Mary.

"Oh, I'm sorry, Sister. I thought you knew. She's my twin
sister. She's a missionary in Nigeria. Works with some Belgian
and Irish priests. She's a nurse in this little village. They don't
even have running water. She's been there for six years now.
They get back every seven years, but they're letting her come
early."

"It's nice to have a sister a nun, isn't it, Father?" asked
Willie.

"Oh, I don't know. Wish I could see her more often. We're
pretty close. They used to call us Jack and Jill. We look so
much alike it's embarrassing."

He pulled out a picture of his family from his wallet. In the
center was a tall, handsome man in a policeman's uniform; a
small woman next to him; four tall young men, one in a
cassock; and a young woman in a habit standing next to the
priest. He pointed to each one.

"There's himself, Captain Timothy J. O'Mahoney, Chicago
Police Department; the Mrs.; Jimmy and Pat, they're lawyers;
Tom, he's a painter; and the two holy ones, Jack and Jill." He
put the picture back into his wallet, shoving it under a small
plastic badge of the Sacred Heart.

"Incidentally, see this?" He pointed to the badge of the
Sacred Heart. "I've had this since eighth grade. Mary Clare
gave it to me when we graduated. That was fifteen years ago.
We're twenty-eight now."

Monsignor Ryan and Mr. Foley came over to the table to see
how the singles were stacking up. They picked up the stacks of
ten $1 bills, took them over to the head table, fanning them-
selves with the money as they went.

"He makes me sick," stated Willie definitively, looking at Monsignor Ryan.

"Now, Sister William Ann, where is your charity?" smiled Father O'Mahoney.

Father O'Mahoney asked them about Sister Marie Marcel and her surgery. They told him they were sure she would be fine—Marce was such an old fighter; you can't keep a good girl down; she'd be up raising Cain within a week. He laughed and told them he would offer his Mass for her in the morning. He had to take Monsignor Ryan to the plane that afternoon. Ryan really was very worried about her. They finished counting the collection. The nuns returned to the convent for the rest of Easter Sunday.

Sister Lucy had posted a notice on the chapel door: "Easter Monday—Natural Rising. Pray for Sister Marie Marcel who is having surgery at 10:00."

Sister Kevin Mary had never heard of natural rising. There was no mention of that in the Rule or Constitutions of the Order. How could she have missed that? Sister Duns Scotus had never mentioned it. She asked Freddie what "natural rising" was. Freddie told her that she could get up whenever she wanted; the bell was not going to ring at all; they could sleep all day, if they wanted.

The nuns stayed up and watched the late movie, and those who could, stayed up for the late, late movie. They made popcorn and drank Coke and beer. It seemed strange for Marce not to be there, for she would have been the one organizing it. Sister Helen Francis had called earlier in the day, assuring them that everything was going to be just fine; she knew that everything was under control. Aggie had been even quieter than usual that day, shaking her head, as the nuns agreed that Marce would be all right. Sister Kevin Mary had asked her what was wrong, and all Aggie would say was that the Lord sends His cross to those He loves, the cross is God's gift to His friends. They told Aggie that she didn't have much Faith, for Marce would be home drinking beer and eating popcorn with them before she knew it. Aggie just shook her head.

The next morning, Sister Kevin Mary was awakened by the sound of the bell. It sounded funny—quicker than usual. She rubbed her eyes. It was bright, very bright, and warm. The window was open, and there was a faint smell of fresh grass in the air. Mark had already gotten up and dressed, for she had to play the organ for the early Mass at 6:30 and the one again at 8:15. Funny that the bell rang: it was supposed to be "natural rising"—you get up with nature, or something like that. The bell rang again, this time faster and louder. She threw on her robe and nightcap and opened her bedroom door.

The nuns were down in the refectory, all dressed. She came into the refectory and was greeted with raised eyebrows.

"What time is it?" she whispered to Freddie.

"After 11:00. How could you sleep so long?"

Sister Lucy's face was drained, paler than usual. She faced the community, wrapped her fingers around her rosary with her left hand, and grabbed the back of the Superior's chair with her right.

"Sister Helen Francis just called. They operated on Sister Marie Marcel this morning. They found the tumor. It's inoperable. They couldn't get at it. They had to close her back up. Sister is coming home tomorrow. Mary will stay with Sister Marie Marcel. I don't know any more than that. Sister Helen Francis will tell us about it when she gets home."

Sister Lucy stared at the nuns; the nuns stared at her. Tears filled her eyes. She turned toward the crucifix, reached for her handkerchief in her sleeve, and blew her nose softly.

"You know, I taught Sister Marie Marcel in second grade, almost thirty years ago. She was as spunky as she is now. She was a beautiful little girl. Her head was covered with golden curls that fell in her eyes. She looked like such a lady, but she was a terrible tomboy with all those brothers. Little Joannie Lacroix, Joannie Lacroix. Her people are so good, so gentle. This will just kill them. Joannie was so special to them."

Sister Lucy smiled sadly as she lifted her glasses to wipe her eyes. Aggie blessed herself, lowering her eyes. Willie ran into chapel. Freddie sat down at her place and began to sob. Max and Jean Martin stared at each other. Sister Julia Mary walked quickly into the kitchen and began filling a glass with ice cubes.

Inoperable. Sister Kevin Mary had never heard the word

before, but she knew what it meant. She sat opposite Freddie, who was sobbing loudly. Sister Kevin Mary felt nothing inside. She was just numb, dead. She couldn't cry. Down deep, she really didn't believe what Sister Lucy had said. It was all just a mistake; Marce would outsmart them; she was just hiding that little tumor to test them, to see how smart those doctors up there really were.

Gently, she kicked Freddie under the table. Freddie didn't look up. Sister Kevin Mary moved next to her, put her arms on Freddie's shoulder, somehow hoping to communicate the strength she thought she felt. Freddie looked up, her face streaked with tears.

"Got a Kleenex, Kev?"

"Sure, Freddie, here. Who's Mary?"

"She's divorced."

"*Who* is Mary? Why is she staying with Marce? I don't understand why Sister isn't staying up there with her."

"Oh, Mary is Marce's sister. She's a nurse. She was married to a doctor who used to beat her up. She's very close to Marce. They are the only girls in the family. Think there's seven or eight boys, hockey players and all that. Her folks are pretty old."

Sister Helen Francis returned with Monsignor Ryan on Tuesday. After dinner, she asked the nuns to remain at the table, and she would explain Sister Marie Marcel's condition. She said that there was a little tumor, about the size of a pea, growing at the base of her brain. It appeared during the tests and on the X-rays, but the doctors didn't know exactly how deep it was. When they opened her up, they saw that if they attempted to remove it, they would either kill her right then or she would lose her sight, her hearing, or her speech.

It wasn't all bad news, Sister Helen Francis said reassuringly, for they did a biopsy and determined it was growing very slowly. On a scale of one to ten, it was a one, the least aggressive of all. She'd have many good years ahead of her, but, yes, it would kill her eventually. She was young, only thirty-four, and in good health; her heart and everything were just fine. But the tumor would grow. They could tell that it was slowly growing. It was resting on the nerve that controlled her sight, and as it grew, it would press against that nerve. Her sight would start to fail.

The most important thing was that *under no circumstances* was Sister Marie Marcel to know that they didn't take it out. They were absolutely forbidden to say anything to her about this and they were to tell no one outside the house, not their families, friends, other nuns, students, lay teachers, parishioners, no one. The priests all knew, and this was as far as it was going to go. She and Monsignor and Mary had conferred with the doctors, who strongly advised them not to tell her. She would give up hope, which would be the greatest injustice of all. While there's life, there's hope.

Marce would not be coming home until April 20, because the doctors wanted her to stay there for a few weeks to recover from the surgery. They wanted to watch her carefully. She reminded them again that *under no circumstances* were they to say anything to Sister Marie Marcel. She knew about the tumor, but she would be told that they had removed it and she would be fine.

The nuns sat. No one moved. Sister Helen Francis smiled confidently, once again telling them they had to carry on like nothing happened. Certainly Sister Marie Marcel couldn't come home to a living funeral. She told them to try not to let this weigh them down, that they owed it to Marce to be happy. The nuns nodded at the Superior, stood, and left the refectory.

"Hey, Freddie," whispered Sister Kevin Mary. "Do you know what April 20th is?"

"No, what's April 20th?"

"Hitler's birthday."

"How do you know that?"

"I dunno. That's just the kind of stuff I know."

23.

April 13, Saturday after Easter. Clarabelle was coming home from the motherhouse; she had been there for over three weeks. A week later, Sister Marie Marcel would be coming back, tumor intact, from Mayo Clinic.

Sister Helen Francis needed two nuns to go downtown and pick Clarabelle up from the Greyhound station. All the cars were being used, their own and all the priests' cars. She asked if anyone knew a parishioner from whom they could borrow a car for the day. Sister Kevin Mary remembered that the Carmodys had told her if she ever needed to use their car, it was all hers. She hated herself for even having thanked them for their offer; just one more bribe to get Peter Carmody through first grade. She had never returned the gold pen and pencil set they gave her for Christmas, the $25 for Valentine's Day, the bottle of Blue Grass cologne for St. Patrick's Day. They were wearing her down with their little gifts. If they'd only spend the time and energy helping dumb Peter with his reading.

Sister Kevin Mary called the Carmodys. They were only too

happy to loan their car to the Good Sisters, anything at all. Anything at all to get your kid through my class, she thought. But I'm just as guilty as you are, acting so damn pious, while all the time keeping my hand out. Well, it's for a good cause; someone has to get Clarabelle.

Edith Carmody pulled up in front of the convent at 10:00 sharp. The nuns, Freddie and Sister Kevin Mary, drove her home and headed for Chicago. Clarabelle wasn't arriving until 3:00, but with the traffic and the errands they had to run for Sister Helen Francis, they needed the extra time.

Sister Kevin Mary loved driving the big gold Chrysler—power steering, power brakes, buttons, lights, automatic this and that. At 67th Street, she moved into the center lane, driving through Jackson Park like she had lived in Chicago all her life. It was a beautiful, beautiful city. And people who lived in it took care of it, and had fun in the city. She looked over at groups playing golf on the public course, kids flying kites, and then past the yacht club and the large white cabin cruisers and sailboats bobbing in their moorings like apples in a tub of water.

She turned up the radio, opened all the windows, and stepped on the gas as they made their way onto the Outer Drive, past the imposing gold statue commemorating the Columbian Exposition of 1893. Lake Michigan appeared to their right, couples walking hand in hand on the beach, kids stripped to their waists, bodies, people, love, touching and holding and being held. So what? This was her life, and they were going to have fun today. Jean Martin and the rest of them were far behind, and the thought of them was not going to ruin her day.

"Kevin," said Freddie, "how'd you like to go to the Conrad Hilton?"

"Why not? We've got loads of time. Tell me where to park. What's at the Conrad Hilton?"

"Let's just get there and then we'll know."

They parked on Wabash in a dark and oily garage. A heavyset man, chomping on a cigar, motioned for them to stop at the line, leave the keys in the car, and asked them when they would be back. The nuns began to giggle, exhilarated at the thought of their freedom, someone *asking,* not *telling,* them when to be back.

"Look, ladies, I gotta know. How long ya' goin' be? Just give me a straight answer. There's tree cars behind ya."

"About four hours," stated Freddie, quickly grabbing control of the situation. "Come on, Kev. We've got work to do!" As they crossed the street, Freddie told her that her father, poor old Bruno, had a girlfriend, someone he met at a church group for widows, and that he seemed to like her. Freddie wanted to check her out; she worked as a manicure girl at the barber shop off the main lobby of the Hilton. Her name was Belle something or other, but she was Polish, so it was OK.

They went to the main desk and asked for the barber shop. The man behind the desk looked up in surprise. He stared at the little hairs sticking out from their headgears.

"I . . . I don't think they give nuns haircuts in there. It's only for people who are here at the hotel. I'm, aahh, sure you can get your hair done somewhere else, ladies."

The nuns doubled over, tears rolling down their cheeks. They tried to tell him that it was not for them, they had to meet someone there. He looked suspiciously, not knowing if he was being taken in or not. He frowned, pointed down a long hall, and went back to his work. The nuns spotted the Ladies Room and made a beeline for it. They had to regain their composure before their reconnaissance flight past the barber shop.

They stood over the sinks, splashed water on their faces, and went over to the towel machine to dry their faces. Two elderly, well-dressed women looked daggers at them, whispering loudly about Catholics. They had Southern accents and were hard to understand but made their point. As the nuns left the washroom, snapping their black cloaks on the second snap, a little girl shrieked, "Mommie, Mommie! Witches! Look at the witches! They're all in black!" She began to scream. Her mother picked her up, holding her close, and gave the nuns a dirty look. Frightening her child like that—they ought to be ashamed of themselves. The nuns smiled faintly, trying to imply that they meant no harm, they really were nice people, if you only knew.

They walked slowly down the long marble hall, somewhat chastized. The world seemed much bigger here than at St. Paul's parish, where people were falling all over them, the Good Sisters this and the Good Sisters that. Until it made them sick. But this was something else. People just hating them for *what* they were, not for *who* they were. Sister Kevin Mary thought about the sign of the cross being a sign of contradiction: the early Christians were stoned and put to the lions for their beliefs. Freddie could only think of Belle in the barber shop, perhaps her future mother.

They walked past a women's clothing shop, red and black negligees, some no bigger than a bikini, in the window. Sister Kevin Mary nudged Freddie's arm. "Get a load of that." Freddie whispered, "Madam Fufu . . . at your service, sir."

They passed the Fannie May candy shop displaying summer chocolates—white, pink, yellow, and green. Chocolates should be brown, she thought. They do a trick in your mouth, not really tasting like chocolate if they're not brown. There was another shop, a travel agent with large posters of beaches, palm trees, sailboats, women and men lying around or walking and holding hands. Oh, Dear God, here we go again. Please keep me pure, in thought and deed.

They came to the barber shop, four black leather and cream-colored chairs elevated in front of four oval mirrors. Some were facing in toward the mirrors so the men could see themselves. One man was sitting with his face wrapped in a steamy towel. He looked like he was dead. A barber was slapping the back of another man's neck with a large shaving brush, clouding the air with talcum powder. He rose, nodded, paid the barber, and left. In the corner, opposite the shoeshine stand, was a chunky woman, full-breasted, with bright strawberry blond hair. She was sitting so they couldn't tell how tall she was, but she looked short. The nuns walked slowly past the window, maximizing their peripheral vision.

"What do you think of her, Freddie? What about that hair?"

"I couldn't tell. Let's walk back again, this time more slowly."

The nuns walked to the end of the corridor, looked out the glass door, turned, and walked slowly back toward the lobby. Belle, legs crossed under her manicure table, was sitting at the edge of her chair. She was holding a man's hand and buffing his nails. He seemed to be enjoying himself. The man's knees were touching Belle's knees. Belle was laughing. The man was laughing. The nuns, accustomed to keeping track of fifty-six first-graders all at once, didn't miss a detail of the interaction between Bruno Petrowski's girlfriend, Freddie's potential stepmother, and the man getting his nails done. They walked silently into the lobby and sat down on one of the blue leather couches. An elderly man, reading *The Wall Street Journal,* folded his paper quickly and moved to another place, away from the nuns. A woman in uniform dusting the tables gave them a dirty look.

"God, you'd think we have leprosy."

"Listen, Freddie, this is a public place, and we have as much a right to be here as those creeps. Ignore them. What do you think of the girlfriend?"

"I don't like her, Kev. Not at all. The way she was flirting with that guy. Did you see what was going on under that table? She was making a fool of herself. I just hate to think of my father with someone so cheap as that."

"Freddie, get off your high horse! Maybe she's the only bright light in your father's life. Besides, it'll take you off the hook. You're all he has, and what if you get sent to Florida or California? You going to bring your father with you? Want to take another look? This is your last chance."

"Yeah, let's go."

They began their pilgrimage back down the long corridor, past the black and red negligees, the pink and white chocolates, the travel posters, to Belle, now polishing the man's nails with clear lacquer. He said something to her and she looked up quickly. The nuns were looking at her. Belle smiled slowly, almost bashfully, uncrossed her legs, moving away from the man. Freddie and Kevin looked away and walked quickly past the barber shop and out the side entrance of the Conrad Hilton.

"God, she caught us looking at her! Now she'll know my father said something to me about her. How many nuns in the city would be hanging around a barber shop on a Saturday morning? Kev, I just don't like her. That would hurt my mother so—if she thought a woman like that was going to take her place."

"A woman like what, Freddie? What the hell are you talking about? If she's good to your father, what more do you want, for God's sake? Freddie, you ought to get on your knees and thank God that he found someone. You're acting like a child, like a spoiled child! You're just jealous, Freddie!"

"Why don't you shut up, Kevin. I'm the one who asked you to come here. I didn't ask you for your advice."

"Tough toenails, Freddie. I'm giving it to you, whether you like it or not. You've got it coming, Freddie."

The two nuns walked down Michigan Avenue in silence. Freddie was mad and hurt; Sister Kevin Mary was just plain mad. Michigan Avenue, with its broad sidewalks, was growing hot. A sign on a bank said 12:58, 62°. They turned in front of the library and walked west down Washington to the Pittsfield Building and to the little restaurant in the basement where Sister Helen Francis told them to eat. It was discreet, out of the way, and the hostess was beginning to know them.

They said nothing to each other—Freddie, pouting; Sister Kevin Mary, indignant. As the hostess led them to a little booth, they smiled cordially, not wanting to reveal the fact that they had been fighting. They sat opposite each other, studying the menu intently. Sandwiches: tuna, grilled cheese, BLT, and cream cheese and jelly. They were both scowling, as if the weight of the decision as to what kind of a sandwich to have for lunch was unbearable.

The waitress stood by their booth, pencil poised. "What'll it be today, girls?"

"I'll have a grilled cheese, on rye, with a Coke," said Freddie, not looking at her companion.

"I'll have the same, but could you add a few pieces of bacon?" asked Sister Kevin Mary.

"That'll cost you twenty cents more. It's more with the bacon."

"Then just forget the bacon. Plain grilled cheese. *Not on rye, though. Just white.* And a Coke," stated Sister Kevin Mary. She had to establish her distinction from Freddie. Two nuns, looking exactly alike, ordering the same thing. The waitress wouldn't know where one stopped and the other began. Besides, she had to let Freddie know that she didn't agree with her about Belle.

They took turns looking at the fresh yellow tea rose in the frosty silver bud vase, carefully avoiding each other's eyes. The waitress brought the Cokes. They thanked her in unison; she looked at them strangely, thinking perhaps that they were joined at the hips. Sister Kevin Mary drained her Coke with one gulp; Freddie nursed her Coke like she was nursing her wounds. Finally, she looked at the yellow tea rose and, with the whisper of a conspirator, said, "Who's that remind you of?"

They both burst out laughing, relieving the tension of their battle over Belle and Bruno.

"Freddie, I'm sorry. I shouldn't have been so hard on you."

"No, I had it coming, Kev. You're right. Who do I think I am?" answered Freddie.

"Let's just forget it, Freddie. This is our one day out, and we're not going to ruin it. We still have a good hour before Clare comes in. I'm getting nervous about her. What are we going to say to her—'Glad you ran away from home'?"

"We'll know what to say, Kev. It's only Clarabelle. Just wait until Marce gets home . . . that's when the fun will start."

"Yeah, I know. Let's just enjoy our lunch."

After their lunch, they decided to have a cup of coffee. A couple in the adjoining booth were smoking, and the smoke was drifting over to their booth. They sat, inhaling the exhaled smoke, both wishing that they could have just a puff. They finished their coffee, left the waitress two dimes for a tip, and went to pay their bill. The waitress, who was clearing their table, gave them a dirty look. "What's her trouble?" asked Freddie.

"Sore feet, probably," answered Sister Kevin Mary.

They went over to Marshall Field's to check out the latest in greeting cards. Sister Kevin Mary had asked to get a birthday card for her mother's birthday later in April. There was a new section of cards, with a sign that these were the newest ideas in communication and were called "contemporary cards." She picked up a long white card with thick red writing, "I wanted to get you a Chinese backscratcher for your birthday." On the inside was inscribed, "But she got away," with a picture of a man chasing a naked Chinese girl.

"Dig this, Freddie," whispered Sister Kevin Mary, handing the card to Freddie and looking to see if anyone was looking at them.

Freddie burst out laughing. A pale, wrinkled clerk peered over the rack of cards, "May I help you, Sisters? The religious cards are over on the other side. Next to the sympathy cards. If you'll come around, I'll show them to you." She spoke slowly, articulately, deliberately, as if she thought they would get lost going around the counter.

"She needs a Chinese backscratcher, Kev. Might loosen her up a bit," muttered Freddie, as the nuns obediently followed the pointed finger to the religious cards.

"Here's a lovely one with lillies and a rosary. Or another with the Sacred Heart of Jesus. That's a get-well card. What did you have in mind, Sisters? Was it for anything in particular, or hadn't you quite made up your minds?" she asked patiently.

"Oh, I just have to get something for my mother's birthday. Do you have a section for family birthdays, just something nice for my mother? It doesn't have to be holy," stated Sister Kevin Mary defiantly. No old bag is going to make me buy one of those creepy cards for my mother. She'll think I'm going off the deep end with this religious stuff.

The clerk pointed a long, wrinkled finger at the end of the row. The two nuns walked quickly down to the family section, grabbed a card, looked at the price, and handed the woman a quarter.

The clerk took the card, opened it, and slowly read the message. "I know your mother will like that very much, Sister.

That is a lovely selection. That's twenty-five cents, and *no tax*. I know, you don't have to remind me."

"I don't mind paying the tax, Ma'am," stated Sister Kevin Mary flatly.

"No, now, Sister, you're not supposed to pay and you're not going to pay, not as long as I'm behind this counter. There are enough of them that make it as hard as they can for us. We Catholics have to stick together, don't we, Sister?"

The nuns forced a smile, not wanting to scandalize the poor woman. The Good Sisters were giving her a hard time; they ought to let up. The clerk smiled appreciatively, recognizing the collusion that those of the Faith had to share if they were to survive in this hostile world. Sister Kevin Mary took the thin brown paper bag from the woman, thanked her, and headed out the Randolph Street exit toward the Greyhound station.

They walked quickly, dodging people sauntering down the streets, stopping to look in the store windows. They looked down to avoid looking at everyone's eyes. Too many different expressions—awe, surprise, hostility, affection, disbelief. A policeman on State Street tipped his hat. Kids greeted them, "Good afternoon, Sister." An old man, talking to himself, shouted, "There they go, the angels of the Lord. Have mercy! Have mercy!"

Crossing at the light at Dearborn, a curly-haired young man grabbed Sister Kevin Mary by the elbow and whispered in her ear, "Want a good screw, baby?" She shook his hand off her and jumped into the street. A car jammed on its brakes and the driver shouted, "Why the hell don't you nuns watch where you're going!" The curly-haired man laughed. Freddie caught up with Sister Kevin Mary, who was hot, angry, and ready to punch someone. They said nothing but walked westward to the station as fast as they could go.

Clare was already off the bus and leaning up against some large gray metal lockers. Her veil was crooked, as usual; her glasses steamed with perspiration. She seemed to be staring at nothing. When the nuns approached her, she looked at them without smiling.

"Let's go," she said flatly.

"Clarabelle, how are you?" asked Freddie, smiling warmly. "We missed you. Have a nice rest?"

Sister Kevin Mary said nothing. She was frightened.

"Let's go," repeated Clare.

The three nuns retraced their steps, walking east on Randolph, south on Michigan Avenue, and then back to the oily, dark garage to get the gold Chrysler. Sister Kevin Mary handed the woman in the office the ticket, paid the money, and waited for the car to arrive. There were three honks, a high-pitched screech of the brakes, and the fat man with the soggy cigar got out of the car, motioned for the nuns, and asked for the stub from the ticket. She had thrown it away. He shook his head as they climbed into the Chrysler, slamming the door of the driver's side. "Catlicks! Damn Catlicks! That's all they are," he said loudly to himself. Sister Kevin Mary waved to him as she pulled out of the garage and headed south out to the Drive.

The nuns said little, commenting only on how hot they were with their cloaks on. It was after 4:30. They would be missing prayer. Boats were heading for the harbor and families were crossing the overpass, heading home after a day at the beach. Sister Kevin Mary looked in the rearview mirror and saw Clare staring out at the lake.

"How ya' doin', Clarabelle?" Sister Kevin Mary asked.

"Do you really want to know, Kevin? If you do, I'll tell you. Do you know where I've been? Do you *really* want to know?"

Freddie turned around, facing Clare directly. "Yes, Clare, we do want to know. We care about you. We've been worried, and we are glad to have you home. Tell us what you want us to know, Clare. We're your friends, remember?"

"Home. Ha! That's a laugh! You think that's a home? Freddie, you have no idea what a home is, if you think that place we live in is a home. It's nothing but a hellhole, as far as I'm concerned."

"Clare, I'm not going to get into that with you. Do you want to tell us where you've been?" asked Freddie.

"I've been in the looney bin! The nut house! Cracker factory! Shrinks have been looking into my head, looking for demons.

They call it Mercyhurst. Ha! Mercy! They wired my head and gave me electricity, just like those guys going to the chair! Zap, zap, zap—one, two, three! One for the Father, one for the Son, and one for the Holy Ghost. A little jolt for the bad nun who couldn't take it anymore! Nothing like a little jolt of electricity—it's good for what ails you. Girls, you really ought to see if you can't get some."

"Clare! Clare! Oh, dear Clare, I didn't know anything about that," sobbed Freddie.

Sister Kevin Mary snapped off the radio and clutched the steering wheel. Freddie was crying, looking at Clare and then out to the lake. "Clare, that's terrible! I didn't, we didn't know. We knew you were having a hard time. They didn't have to do that to you. You're not crazy, Clare."

"Yeah? Tell that to the judge," said Clare bitterly.

Sister Kevin Mary snapped the radio back on. Doris Day was singing, "Que Sera, Sera"—the future's not ours to see, que sera, sera. If this is what you will do in the green wood, what will you do in the dry? Brides you are, and brides you will be. When you get to the end of your rope, tie a knot and hang on. The cross is God's gift to those He loves. I promise obedience to Almighty God, the Blessed Mary, ever Virgin—three jolts, one for the Father, one for the Son, and one for the Holy Ghost. Inoperable. Inoperable. Just a little low-grade tumor, just like a little low-grade infection, like a little low-grade temperature. How about a little screw, honey? I promise obedience to Almighty God, to the Blessed Mary, ever Virgin.

They were almost home. Sister Kevin Mary looked at the fuel gauge; it was near empty. She drove into the local Gulf station where they could fill it up and put it on Monsignor Ryan's charge. She had to humiliate herself enough with the Carmodys; she wasn't going to return their car empty. She told the man to fill it up and to check the oil and water. The nuns sat in the car in silence, the windows down. They were hot, dry, drained.

Barreling around the corner of the station in a small jeep was one of the owner's kids. She saw him coming right at the front of the gold Chrysler, the Carmodys' gold Chrysler. Her heart jumped. "*Son of a B!*" she shouted at the boy. He swerved, missing the Chrysler by a hair. The owner came running out. Mechanics came running out. Two cars on the other side of the pumps looked at the nuns. Freddie put her face in her hands. Clare smiled.

"Oh, dear God, Freddie, do you think they heard me?"

"I had no trouble. Absolutely no trouble, Kevin. You made your point—loud and clear. Everyone is looking at us! I'm so embarrassed, I could die. Let's get out of here!"

She told the man to charge it to Monsignor Ryan and shot out of the station. Looking in the rearview mirror, she could see the men, their faces smudged with oil and dirt, slapping their knees and laughing.

24.

It was a hot, scary Saturday afternoon, April 20, Hitler's birthday, and Sister Marie Marcel was coming home with her sister Mary. The nuns had been instructed again by the Superior to protect Sister Marie Marcel from the truth of her tumor. She had been informed that she had had a tumor that had been benign, and they had gotten it all.

The tension rose in the house as the early spring heat clung to the jonquils and tulips growing alongside the convent. The windows of the convent were open. The noise from the electric lawn mower added to the clatter of dishes and elevated voices. Aggie dropped a glass on the floor. Willie, carrying a dishpan of dirty water back into the kitchen, tripped, sending a gallon of sudsy water across the kitchen floor. She knelt in the soapy water, laughing hysterically. Sister Helen Francis was once again at her cuticles, tearing them off and chewing the removed cuticle with her front teeth.

Three short honks of the horn was the signal. She was home. The nuns ran out of the house, down the back steps, and out to the playground. Monsignor Ryan was opening the trunk to remove the suitcases. As he saw the nuns coming toward him in a herd, he dropped the suitcases, spread his arms, and began to sing. "Now laughing friends deride, tears I cannot hide. So I smile and say . . ." The nuns tried to hide their annoyance at his characteristic injection of levity. He shrugged his shoulders— what was he supposed to do, wear a black armband?

Willie opened the car door. A gaunt, yellow-skinned nun smiled at them. Her eyes were black, as if someone had smudged ashes onto a yellow board. She looked very thin and very sick.

"Hi, kids," Sister Marie Marcel said faintly, smiling.

"Marce, how are you?"

"God, are we glad to get you home!"

"Get out of that car immediately, so we can see you!"

Marce, smiling broadly, said, "Hey, ya can't keep an old fighter like me down! I knew we'd lick this damn thing! I'm so glad to be out of that place. If you weren't sick when you went in, they're sure to hand something out to you."

The nuns laughed, nudging each other at Marce's high spirits. Everything was going to be all right, and besides, doctors don't know everything. They're just human beings, and with her spirit, she will be OK, she'll get better, the tumor will just shrivel up and not bother her anymore.

"Hey, meet Mary, my private bedpan pusher," said Marce, introducing her sister to the nuns. The nuns introduced themselves, thanking her for taking such good care of Marce.

"I don't think I can remember all your names, Sisters, it's good to be here. Joan has told me about so many of you. Listen, I think we ought to get her to bed. It's been a long trip. We had to get out of there at 8:00 this morning."

"Hey, Mary, I just got home! Don't start ordering me around now. I just want to see the old place." She turned to the Superior, "Sister, tell her to get off my back!" The nuns laughed heartily, still ignoring Monsignor Ryan. He quietly closed the trunk, visibly hurt by his exclusion from the community.

Sister Marie Marcel went into the chapel for a short visit, then walked around the house, smiling, relieved to be home.

Mary was going to be staying in the spare bedroom, which was also used as the Superior's office. A desk, the phone, and some files were in the room. Freddie put Mary's things in the guestroom, showed Mary where the kitchen and community room were, and told her to make herself at home.

The nuns agreed that Marce's spirit was just great, she was her old self, but she looked worse than any of them had expected. Marce was home and Clare was home and the year would end up just fine, a few wounds, a little scar tissue, but that was life, and together, as a community, sticking close to each other, they would make it. To the end of the year.

On Easter Sunday, Sister Kevin Mary had sat at her desk with a calendar, figuring how many days were left until she could get out of there. Easter was April 7; they were to leave for the motherhouse on June 10, four days after school was dismissed. Sixty-four days, sixty-four days and she would be free, back at the motherhouse where she belonged, where her real friends were, where she could pray and study and think, where she could lose her obscene obsession with food. The last time she got on the scale, she was over 145 pounds. She weighed 112 last August; 33 pounds in eight months, an average of over four pounds a month; a pound a week.

She rarely looked in the mirror anymore and had taken to wearing a stretchy belt. Her heavy black leather belt dug into her hips, and since it was on the last notch, there was nowhere for it to go but back into her trunk until she lost some weight. And her feet were still numb, clear up to the ankles. It would happen in the afternoon, when she would sit down for a few minutes, then get up. She felt she was walking on the stumps of her legs, like a double amputee. The cross is the gift God gives to His friends.

Secrets are hard to keep. Sister Marie Marcel was living with a time bomb in her brain, and she was not to be told, under any circumstances, under pain of obedience. Holy obedience. But Marce and the tumor were all they could talk about when she wasn't around. "Why doesn't she wear a bell around her neck?" asked Sister Julia Mary. "Then we'd know where she was."

Marce was still not up for prayers, nor was she in her classroom, despite her campaign to get back. She went over to the room three or four times a week to see the kids, but she would return within minutes. She made the substitute nervous, because the kids liked the nun better.

Marce was back, playing the transistor, louder than she had before. Max was losing patience, stomping up to her room, closing the door forcefully, muttering about the work she had to do and couldn't do with all that racket.

Her sister Mary had gone back to Detroit, and Marce's parents were driving in to see her within the week. It was already May, and the chances of a snowstorm were nil. Her parents were in their late seventies and couldn't chance bad weather. They had never flown and were not going to begin at this hour of their lives.

Marce rarely dressed. She wore a stiff white nylon robe and a little white nightcap that sat like a beanie on the top of her head. The hair on the back of her head was starting to grow back, but the deep purple cut from the surgery, the hoax of a surgery, was clearly visible. Her eyes retained the black, ashy look, and she frequently seemed to be looking at an invisible bull's-eye in front of her.

A hot Tuesday afternoon. The kids all had spring fever; the nuns and lay teachers had spring fever. The first bell rang, and within seconds, the school emptied out; the teachers closed and locked their classroom doors and headed home. Parched and dry, the nuns threw their books and papers on the back steps and went to the kitchen for something cold to drink—Dr. Pepper, a Coke, or 7-Up.

"Hey, nuns, only thirty-five more days left, less than twenty more days for school. I can't wait," said Sister Kevin Mary.

"You can say that again," added Clarabelle.

"What I'd like right now is a little trip out to check on Mrs. Thornton. I'd love to be in that pool right now," Mark commented.

"You can say that again," repeated Clare.

Jules came into the refectory. "Whew! It's hotter than Dutch love. Give me something to drink before I croak!"

They looked up at the kitchen door. Sister Marie Marcel, white robe blowing in the air from the fan, stood in the doorway. The talking stopped. The laughing stopped. The nuns looked down at their glasses, avoiding her eyes. Marce, realizing that she was not wanted, turned and walked back up to her room. The nuns glared at each other.

"Why'd we stop talking?"

"We weren't saying anything about her. Why did we do that?"

"We do that every time she comes around," stated Mark. "I can't figure out why we have to continue this little game with her. She's got a right to know. It's her life."

"You're wrong, Mark," said Willie softly. "It's our place to protect her. If she knew the truth, it would kill her."

"Listen, Willie," Mark said firmly, "do you think she's stupid? What the hell kind of a message do you think we give her? Shutting up every time she appears, avoiding her. I don't think we are one bit fair to her, nor to ourselves. I think this is wrong." Mark got up and left.

"She gives me the creeps," said Clare.

"You give me the creeps, Clare," laughed Jules. "You really do."

Tension in the house continued to mount. Willie was tripping and falling, Aggie was breaking glasses, the nuns were becoming more and more abrupt. Sister Helen Francis had no cuticles left. Margaret, the cook, stopped speaking altogether.

One morning before school, Sister Kevin Mary stopped in to see Marce. Her door was slightly open, so she knew Marce wasn't asleep. Marce motioned for Sister Kevin Mary to come into the room.

"Hey, Kevvie, how do you think I'm doing?"

"Just great, Marce, just great. Why do you ask?"

"I don't know. Something just doesn't seem right. There's something going on around here. Have I been told everything, Kevin? I want a straight answer. I think I can trust you for a straight answer. Have I been told everything?"

"Marce, would I lie to you?" Sister Kevin Mary responded.

"I just hope that you guys aren't keeping anything from me.

It's my life, you know," Marce said softly. She turned, pulled the sheet up over her shoulder, and closed her eyes. "Pull the door closed when you go out. And thanks, Kev."

Sister Kevin Mary stood up, walked out, and closed the door tightly. She closed her eyes, profoundly embarrassed. I lied, I lied, I lied, all in the name of Holy Obedience. I lied to her; I looked a dying woman in the eyes and lied to her. I just plain lied. She ran down the stairs and over to school.

She was late getting over to school. Freddie had unlocked her door, and the kids were running around. Two boys were standing on top of their desks, throwing bits of chalk at the girls. "Bombs over Tokyo!" one shouted, as he pummeled the first row with the chalk.

"Robert Plunkett, get down from there this minute!" shouted Sister Kevin Mary. "And the rest of you, pick up that chalk and throw it in the basket!" She wondered how she would make it through the day. Her feet were already numb and her head throbbed.

Her desk was a mound of lilacs and tulips for the May altar. Some of the flowers had leaked onto the teacher's manuals, left open in her rush to get home the day before. Sandwiched between the flowers was a large slice of coconut birthday cake. The frosting had run onto a stack of corrected arithmetic papers. A mother was at the door with a cage of gerbils, wanting to know if she could leave them there for the day. There were three notes, excusing absentees from the previous day, asking for make-up work. Sister Kevin Mary had just gotten her period; she knew she was going to have cramps, real bad.

The classroom was a sea of heads, bobbing and talking and laughing. Charts, books, flashcards. Only thirty-four more days and I'll be on retreat, far from the madding crowd.

She opened the religion book. It was the story about our Lord's ascension into heaven. They said prayers and she began to tell them the story. Jesus had spent forty days walking the earth after His resurrection, and now it was time for Him to join His Father in heaven, for His Father had been waiting for Him. She told them Jesus told His apostles, "Where I am, you cannot go." He was lifted up, body and soul, right before their very eyes, into heaven to sit at the right hand of His Father for all eternity. Every time she said "for all eternity," she sounded like Sister Duns Scotus: "for all eternity . . . for all eternity." There was something so theological, so esoteric, so abstract about the phrase "for all eternity." Inoperable tumors, cramps, electric shock treatments will cease to exist in the vast, vaulted cathedral of eternity.

Hands shot up from the class. "You mean like a helicopter? How'd He get up there?" asked a boy.

"No, stupid," came a voice from the back of the room. "It was like a hot-air balloon. Pssss . . . up, up and away . . . to heaven."

The class was looking at the ceiling, imagining the Lord ascending into heaven, into the realms of the Trinity in a balloon. Sister Kevin Mary closed her eyes and walked slowly to her desk. She sat down heavily; the cramps were starting. She jumped up, knocking her chair against the blackboard. Someone had placed fresh roses, wrapped in foil, on the seat. The thorns sticking through the foil clung to her habit. She wheeled around, trying to grasp the bouquet hanging behind her like a tail. The kids laughed, watching their teacher in obvious discomfort. A little girl in the front row quickly pulled the roses off the back of her habit. She scowled and told them to open their religion books to page 73 and begin coloring Jesus going up into heaven. She told them to be quiet, that she had to leave the room for a moment on important business. She opened her desk, took out a dime from the milk money, and left the room.

Sister Kevin Mary opened the door to the supply room, put the dime into the Coke machine, and sat on an unopened carton of paper, drinking the Coke. I wish I could go up to heaven in a balloon, just to get away from all of this. She sat, just looking into the green bottle, trying not to think of her cramps. Her dead feet. Her pounding head. The door of the supply room opened. Sister Helen Francis walked in with two of the poachers. Sister Kevin Mary jumped up, drained the bottle, nodded, and went back to her classroom. She could hear the three of them snickering as their dimes fell into the Coke machine.

As she walked back into the room, the arithmetic timer on the windowsill buzzed loudly. The class jumped and started laughing. She tore over to the windowsill, turned off the timer, and shouted, "Who did this? Who did this? Who set this timer?"

The class pointed to a little boy with thick glasses in the row by the window. "Mark did it! Mark did it!" they chanted in unison.

"Mark Crangle, get up here this instant!" Sister Kevin Mary shouted. She reached for the thick wooden paddle hanging on a nail behind her desk and directed the little boy to bend over his desk. She lifted her arm and swatted him five times on his seat, his dark brown corduroy pants flattening with each blow.

His glasses fell off and onto the floor. She told him to stand. He stood, crying and jumping, holding his bottom. "Stand still!" she shouted at him. He reached for the front of his pants, trying to hold himself so he wouldn't have an accident. The front of his pants was wet, and on the floor was a small puddle around his shoes. He looked up at her, holding himself, his face red and streaked with tears.

"I'm sorry, Sister . . . I'm sorry," cried Mark.

The class was in an uproar, hooting and hollering at Mark and his wet pants. His face, his pants, his shoes and socks were soaking. Sister Kevin Mary looked down at the little boy, standing in the puddle, crying. She looked down at herself, holding the big wooden paddle. She was twice his size. She began to shake, not knowing if she was going to faint or vomit or cry.

She directed Mark to the door, passed out papers for the class to do, and led him into the nurse's room, holding him by the hand. She took off his wet clothes and reached into the emergency box for some dry ones. She told him to lie down and she put a wet cloth on his head. Then she went to the office to ask if she could go home and wash the little boy's clothes. She washed them by hand, threw them into the dryer at the convent, and politely asked Margaret if she would take them out when the dryer buzzed. Margaret snorted some answer. Sister Kevin Mary returned to the class and warned them not to say one single word to Mark Crangle when he came back into the classroom.

After lunch, Sister Kevin Mary dressed Mark in his own clothes. She told him she was sorry, but that he shouldn't have set the timer, especially when she had asked them to stay in their seats when she had to leave the room on serious business. Mark understood and said again that he was sorry. She hated herself for being such a bully, for spanking the kids all the time. But it was a Catholic school and that was the way things were. All the nuns in the lower grades spanked the kids, either on the bottom if they were really bad, or just on the hands if they needed it there—if they scribbled or did a messy paper.

She remembered the first time that she had to hit a kid. She was correcting papers at home and Willie saw one that was a mess.

"What are you going to do with that?" she asked.

"Just give it back to her and make her do it over," Sister Kevin Mary replied.

"Yeah, and then, what about next time? She's got to be taught that messiness is unacceptable, totally unacceptable, and the rest of the kids get the point. You should have cracked her on the hands the minute you saw that mess. Nip it in the bud, Kev. Nip it in the bud!"

That was at the end of September. She spanked the little girl and made her cry. And after that, hardly a day went by when some child did not get a good crack on the hands or a swat on the bottom. If they were very bad, they had to go into the clinic, take down their pants, and get a really good spanking. You have to be cruel to be kind, they always said.

After school, as soon as she got in the door, the phone rang. The nun on doorbell called her to the phone.

"Yes, this is Sister Kevin Mary speaking. May I help you?"

"Yes, you can, Sister. I'm Mrs. Thompson, Mark Crangle's grandmother, Mrs. Crangle's mother. Mark is here crying, and his bottom is all red. I know what happened today, Sister, and I just want you to know that I cannot believe that a Sister would do that to Mark. He has been hysterical ever since he came in the door, Sister. I just can't believe it."

"I'm sorry, Mrs. Thompson. I told Mark that I was sorry."

"You know, Sister, and I wrote you at the beginning of the week. His mother is in the hospital with another baby. Mark is only six, and there are five others younger than him around here. I'm sure you have noticed that Mark is a very high-strung child, and there has been a lot of strain around here lately. Mark is the most sensitive of all the kids, he's not doing well in school, and I would have expected a little kindness, a little sympathy for this child. I just can't believe that a Sister would have beat this child so. I just can't believe it, Sister. You hurt him, Sister," Mrs. Thompson said slowly. "You hurt Mark."

"I don't know what else to say, Mrs. Thompson. I, I was just not feeling well myself. I . . . I don't know what to say to you . . . I'm sorry that that happened."

"I am sorry, too, Sister. I'm sorrier than you'll ever know."

"Good-bye, Mrs. Thompson."

"Good-bye, Sister."

Sister Kevin Mary ran up the stairs, past Marce who was coming out of her room, down the long corridor, and into her room. She threw off her veil and landed on her bed, sobbing hysterically. I beat him, I beat him, I beat him. A child of God, a little boy, a helpless little boy, and I beat him, almost killed him. I'm a bully, a big, fat, ugly bully who beats little helpless kids, all in the name of God and the Catholic Church.

She thought of her little brother Kevin, the same age as Mark Crangle, and of some fat and ugly nun pounding Kevin, beautiful little Kevin. Oh, dear God in heaven, forgive me, please forgive me for being so hateful, for being such a bully, for being such an awful human being. She tore her headgear off, threw it on the floor, and cried harder, feeling like her chest was caving in and that she was going to die. Dear God, make me die, take away my life; I deserve it for beating a child.

There was a knock on the door. "Kevin Mary, you OK?" someone asked. She was crying too hard to answer. The door opened. Freddie stood, assessed the situation, and came into the room, closing the door behind her.

"What happened, Kev? Jean Martin getting to you again?"

"No, Freddie," Sister Kevin Mary sobbed. "I hit a kid, almost killed him, and his grandmother called me. They have all kinds of trouble with the family, and I just added to it. . . . I just beat the kid . . . I didn't feel well, and I really don't like him anyway. But he's just a child, and I beat him, and I'm a nun."

Her face was in her pillow, weeping and sobbing. Freddie went to the sink, took a washcloth, ran the cold water on it, and brought it over to the bed.

"Here, Kev. Put this on your head. Take it easy. Take it easy. You didn't mean to hurt him. Just take it easy."

"But I'm a nun, Freddie. He's just a little boy, just like my brother." She began crying louder, thinking of her brother getting beaten by a nun.

"So, big deal! You're a nun. So who says you're not a human being? Did you give up your right to make mistakes when you took your vows? You're awfully hard on yourself, Kev. Just take it easy; loosen up a bit."

"Freddie, I did a *terrible* thing. That's why people turn against the Church, because of people like me. In twenty years, he'll be at a cocktail party, telling a group of people how this fat, ugly nun almost killed him when his mother was in the hospital. He'll leave the Church, I just know it, Freddie, I know it."

"Hey, hey, take it easy, old girl. You're not that powerful, not yet. Give the kid some credit, too. Have you ever done anything nice for him?"

"Yeah, the days when I didn't hit him," she cried.

"Listen, Kevin, we've all been under a lot of strain with Marce and trying to hide this thing from her. We're like seventeen corks, ready to pop. We're walking on egg shells, dynamite. This is your first year; it's almost over."

"Yeah, I know. Only thirty-four more days."

"Listen, you know about forgiveness? You know, letting things go? Why can't you just forgive yourself, tell yourself,

God, the parents, whoever, you can even tell me. Just tell yourself you're sorry; forgive yourself, Kevvie. Let it go, let it go. . . . Come on, put your stuff back on. I've got to go to the foot doctor. My corns are killing me. Sister said that you were supposed to go with me. Get your stuff on. I have to be there in fifteen minutes. Meet you downstairs?"

"OK, OK, Freddie, give me time to pull myself together. Thanks, Freddie."

The two nuns walked into town, stopping to watch some ants climbing on the pink and purple peonies in the front of the convent. They turned into the doctor's office, grateful for the blast of cold air from the air conditioner. The waiting room was filled, so the doctor asked Sister Kevin Mary to step inside the examination room while he took care of Sister Frederick.

Freddie's shoes were off. The doctor was holding her foot up to the light, probing her corns while Freddie tried not to register discomfort. Sister Kevin Mary sat in a chair in the corner, trying to give Freddie as much privacy as she could. She thought of her own feet, numb most of the time. Should she say something to the doctor? She hadn't asked permission to have an appointment; she had never mentioned to Sister Helen Francis that she was having trouble with her feet.

Freddie's feet were soaking in a basin. The doctor told her that they would have to wait a short while, that he had to soften them up and then he'd be able to get at them. Sister Kevin Mary rose, walked over to the doctor, and asked him if he would be able to look at her feet even though she didn't have an appointment. They were always numb. They were all right in the mornings, but by 1:00, there was no feeling in them at all.

The doctor was sitting on a short stool, the kind used in shoe stores. He frowned, poked at her shoes, squeezed the instep, frowned some more, shoved at her big toe, and finally looked up. "Is this the way you tie your shoes all the time?" he grunted.

"Yes, Doctor, I do," she answered.

"You're tying your shoes too tight and cutting off your

circulation. Sit down and loosen them up. You want to get gangrene?"

The nuns avoided looking at each other, fearful that they would disgrace themselves by laughing in the doctor's office. Sister Kevin Mary sat down, untied her shoes, loosened the laces, and retied them. She wiggled her toes inside her shoes to get the blood moving, feeling slightly silly.

The two nuns left the office in a hurry and burst out laughing right outside the office door. Freddie slapped Sister Kevin Mary on the back. "See! What'd I tell you? You gotta loosen up! Loosen up! Even the doctor knows! Loosen up! Loosen up!"

25.

Only twenty more days, twenty more days to keep the secret, to keep on stretching the skin over the swelling drum. The skin was ready to tear, grown thin from pulling and stretching the truth. Sister Kevin Mary resolved to keep her silence, to obey the dictates of her Superior, if not of her conscience.

As she was leaving school, Father O'Mahoney came out of the office and shouted for her to wait for him. He asked if they could go back into her classroom for a minute, he had to ask her about something. He wanted to know what was the matter with all the nuns—they were short with him, distracted; he couldn't get a laugh out of anybody. Had he done something or said something to offend them? He certainly hadn't meant to offend, but if he had, he wanted to know.

Sister Kevin Mary looked at the priest, in earnest, and knew that she could at least tell him the truth. It would even feel good to talk about this with someone outside of the house.

"It's Sister Marie Marcel. You know what's the matter with her?" Father O'Mahoney nodded. Sister Kevin Mary continued,

"Well, we're not supposed to tell her. They think it would kill her to know the truth, so we all have to keep this big secret. We're all ready to explode."

Father O'Mahoney sat on the edge of her desk, nodding his head. "Oh, I see, I see. That must really be tough. No wonder you're all acting that way. God, that's just terrible."

"Yeah, but the worst part is that I don't know if she should be told or not. She asked me the truth and I lied to her. I lied to her. I looked her straight in the eyes and lied."

"Take it easy, Sister. You were only doing what you thought you had to do, weren't you?" Sister Kevin Mary nodded ambivalently, not proud of her obedience. Father O'Mahoney picked up a paper clip and began twisting and bending it. "You know, Sister, you have to ask yourself: 'Does she have a *need to know*? Does she have a *right to know*?' Think about that."

"It's *her* body, *her* tumor, *her* life. It's not mine, not the rest of the nuns. It's all hers, Father."

"Well, I guess that's your answer, Sister." He smiled kindly, reaching for another paper clip.

"It's not that simple, Father. What do you do when you are expressly forbidden, by your lawful religious Superior, to whom you have vowed unquestioning obedience? Just what do you do?" she asked angrily.

"You get down on your knees and pray, Sister. You ask for an answer, and you tell the Good Lord that you need an answer soon. You don't have that much time, Sister."

"I know. We leave in twenty days. Thanks a lot, Father. Say a prayer for us, OK?"

He handed her the paper clips, shaped into two interlocking circles. She turned the circles slowly, thinking about the dilemma—trust versus obedience—and decided to pray.

That evening, the nuns had pork chops, wild rice, spinach, and fresh strawberries with brown sugar and sour cream. Marce was at the table, and her very presence changed the tone and tenor of their conversation: high-pitched, curt, and giddy, all at the same time. Aggie characteristically said little, placing the burden of the conversation on Sister Lucy, Sister Helen Francis, and the other older nuns. Marce was enjoying being at the table, out of her cell with its drawn shades, bottles of pills, ice bag, stacks of unread magazines and get-well cards.

The server came around with a pot of freshly brewed coffee. Sister Helen Francis took some, Aggie waited for the tea, and Marce held out her cup. She asked Aggie for the cream. Aggie reached across the table, grabbed the creamer, turned the handle to Marce, and handed it to her. Marce took the creamer and poured the cream. The cream missed the cup by two inches, spilling on the table and running onto the floor. Aggie gasped, throwing her hand over her mouth. Sister Helen Francis bit the insides of her cheek. Sister Lucy stared at Sister Helen Francis.

Willie ran into the kitchen for a cloth, whispering to the server, "My God! It's her sight already! She couldn't find the cup!"

Marce felt embarrassed and began teasing Aggie. "Aggie, did you move that cup on me? That's a dirty trick, Aggie!" Aggie muttered, "Yes, Sister," unconvincingly. Willie wiped up the cream and said, "There's no use crying over spilt cream." She poured Marce another cup of coffee and added a little cream. The rest of the nuns finished their coffee in silence, not trusting themselves to say another word.

After dinner, Sister Lucy followed Sister Helen Francis into the office and closed the door firmly. They stayed in the office for over an hour; they emerged shortly before night prayer, both obviously agitated. After night prayer, Sister Helen Francis stepped out into the hall, motioning for the nuns to stay in their places. She walked halfway up the back stairs, looked toward Marce's room, and came back down to chapel, closing the door. She stood by the holy water font, addressing the community.

"Nuns, Sister Lucy and I have discussed this. We are going to tell Marce tomorrow. She's got a right to know. The rest of us will be dead by June from all this tension. Monsignor Ryan and I will tell her tomorrow. Have your classes pray that we say the right thing. And all of you pray. Pray hard, for this is the most difficult thing I've ever had to do. Just pray."

The nuns nodded to the Superior. Freddie wiped her eyes.

Aggie sighed. She hadn't heard exactly what the Superior had said but knew what was going on. The bell rang for Profound Silence, a relief from all the words, spoken and unspoken.

The nuns got home early after school the following day. They had seen Monsignor Ryan and Sister Helen Francis heading toward the convent at 2:30. Sister Kevin Mary had her class stop their work and say three Hail Marys for a special intention.

At five minutes after three, Monsignor Ryan and Sister Helen Francis came down the back stairs. Monsignor Ryan's face was drawn. He nodded to the nuns and walked quickly out the back door. Sister Helen Francis came into the refectory, looked at the nuns, and said simply, "She knows . . . she knows." The nuns looked at each other, not knowing if they wanted to laugh or cry.

Within a minute, Marce, in her flowing white robe and little nightcap, came into the refectory. The nuns jumped up and ran to her, all of them crying and laughing. She was smiling broadly, embracing the Sisters, all so relieved to have been delivered from the lie, from the burden of continuing the lie.

"Hey, why didn't you guys tell me? I wish you had told me. I knew that there was something going around."

The nuns, crying and laughing, told her they were sorry, that they thought they were doing the best for her. She nodded and smiled, "Yeah, I knew. I knew it all the time. Guess I was just as much a part of it as you. Let's never do that to each other again. I forgive you this time, but don't let it happen again."

The nuns hugged Marce, telling her they loved her, that they were sorry. Sister Helen Francis came into the refectory, smiling at the nuns, sharing in their relief. She told them that there wouldn't be any prayer tonight, their life was a prayer, and they should just relax.

Marce turned to her Superior. "Hey, Sister, that's more like it! The White Sox are leading Cleveland, 8 to 3. Whitey Ford's pitchin'. Can we watch the rest of the game on TV? I'm gettin' sick of sticking that damn transistor under my pillow every time you come to my door!"

The White Sox won, 12 to 10, in extra innings.

26.

June 6, D-Day. The last day of school, books cleaned, counted, wrapped for another school year. Report cards and records in the office. Peter Carmody was passed to second grade on the condition that he attend remedial classes at the public school during the summer. The Carmodys gave Sister Kevin Mary a check for $25 to pick up some little thing she needed for her classroom. She turned the money in to the Superior, saying that she thought Peter would do fine in second grade. The second grade teacher could stand up to the Carmodys and fail Peter the following year, she thought.

The buses arrived at the regular time, left, and were back within two hours, just long enough for the final report cards to be given out and for final farewells. A little red-haired girl, Annie, gave Sister Kevin Mary a dime from her piggy bank with a note thanking her for teaching her how to read. Mrs. Thompson, Mark Crangle's grandmother, sent a note to the office, requesting that Mark have a different teacher next year, since he was being held back in first grade. Mark had had enough of Sister Kevin Mary.

Sister Kevin Mary blessed herself slowly as they concluded their final Hail Mary. She told them to get into line, more curtly than she had planned, for the old lump was back in her throat. She just couldn't say good-bye to them; they had saved her life this year. If it hadn't been for the kids, who or where would she be? If she couldn't have run over to them, literally run for her life, what would have happened to her? She thought of the many little hugs that had nourished her in an emotional desert, of the many tears they had shed which taught her that it was OK to cry.

Their temper tantrums that showed her anger was healthy. The way they learned and showed her that she had so very much to learn. The way they forgave her ineptness, her lack of experience and preparation, her shortness. She looked at her class, marveling at how they had formed their own little community, their little power groups, how they nourished and tempted each other, how they fought and forgave each other and shared with each other the magic of learning.

She just couldn't say good-bye, for once they walked out that door, their little community would vanish like an early morning dream, and someday they would forget her name. She loved those kids, especially when they would forget and call her "Mom." She hated it when they corrected themselves, "Oh, I'm sorry. I mean Sister."

The kids taught her the meaning of loyalty. They were loyal to her, she knew it. They didn't take advantage of her the way they could have. When she didn't feel well, when the cramps or the headaches hit, they backed off, didn't push.

And, most of all, they taught her the meaning of prayer. They understood the power of God, perhaps at a depth she never would. They loved the Mother of God at a depth she could only envy. Poverty, chastity, and obedience. Dear God, what did those words mean, except that a child would understand, for was not a child poor, chaste, and obedient? Without the struggles, complexities, theology that confused everything. The raw, pure innocence of a child, of my kids, my first class.

They will grow up and lose their innocence, but while it is here, it is Your gift to me, Dear Lord. They have taught me more than all the Novitiates in the world, all the prayers and retreats, all the books and writings of the saints. Dear Lord, thank you for my kids. But they're not mine any longer.

"Hey, Sister," interrupted a little girl, "we're going to miss our bus!"

"We gotta go, Sister. Bye!"

"Bye, Sister, have a good summer!"

She waved at them as they hurried for their buses. They didn't see her wave.

The kids were gone. She picked up a box of lemon drops and a little bunch of yellow and purple pansies, straightened her chair, locked the windows, closed the door on Room 103, and returned to the convent.

27.

Three days left to clean, pack, and get ready for the summer. Everything had to be out of their bedrooms, for no one knew where they would be the following year. Some would return to St. Paul's; some would be sent to other places. What was not going with them for the summer was to be packed neatly, tightly, in their trunks, in case they were changed and their trunks had to be shipped to their next appointment.

Before they left for retreat, the seven days of silence, prayer, and conferences that preceded summer school, each nun went to everyone with whom she lived and knelt down, saying:

> Please pardon me, Sister, if I have offended or scandalized
> you in any way during the past year. Pray for me during
> this retreat and I shall do the same for you.

Some of the nuns were hard to approach; some were easy. Freddie burst into tears; Willie burst out laughing. Clarabelle stared. Aggie blushed. Sister Helen Francis bit her lip, smiled, and thanked her for all she had brought to St. Paul's. Sister Kevin Mary didn't know what she was talking about and decided not to ask.

Sister Kevin Mary just could not go up to Jean Martin or Max. She knew that they hated her, and if the truth be known, she didn't care for them one bit. They had brought her nothing but pain. She forced herself, stopping Jean Martin in the basement as she was placing some clothing in her trunk.

"Jean, I'd like to say the pardon prayer with you, if you have the time."

"Go ahead."

Both nuns knelt down. Sister Kevin Mary began, "Please pardon me, Sister Jean Martin, if I have offended . . ." Sister Jean Martin was looking into her trunk to see if she had put her clothes in the right spot. She looked bored. Sister Kevin Mary continued, ". . . or scandalized you in any way. . . ." Sister Jean Martin reached for her cuffs, straightening them. Sister Kevin Mary finished, "Pray for me during this retreat and I will do the same for you." Sister Jean Martin put her cuffs in a different pile and shifted on her knees. "OK, now it's my turn." She said the pardon prayer with one breath, not looking at Sister Kevin Mary.

"Thanks, Jean. Have a nice summer."

"Yeah. If I can."

Sister Kevin Mary clenched her fists and went up to the kitchen for a Coke. Damn, she can't resist sticking it to me at the last second. She just can't smile and say good-bye. Let her wither in her own bitterness, poisoning everything in her way. She went up to her room for another load of books to bring down to her trunk. Sister Marie Marcel's door was open, and tomorrow they would all be leaving. Dear God, I have to go in and say good-bye to her. I can't do it; I just can't. She turned, knocked on the partially opened door.

"Marce . . . Marce . . . you awake?"

"Hi, kid. Come on in. What's on your mind?"

"I just want to say the pardon prayer, Marce."

Sister Marie Marcel lifted her head from the pillow and motioned for her to come in. Sister Kevin Mary knelt down next to her bed. "Please pardon me, Sister Marie Marcel, if I have offended or scandalized you. . . ." She completed the pardon prayer. Sister Marcel told her to close the door and to come back in and sit down.

"Sit down, Kevin. Sit down. I am not angry with you. I just have something to say to you. You have offended me, you have offended me greatly. You lied to me, Sister, you lied to me when I asked you if I was OK, and you said I was. I'm not. I'm dying, and you knew it, and you lied to me."

Sister Kevin Mary thought she was going to faint. The room was airless and dark. *I'll land in a ball and they'll never find me until next September.*

"I don't want you to misunderstand what I'm going to say to you. I am not angry. I would be doing you a grave disservice if I did not tell you this. I know that you thought you were doing the right thing. You weren't."

"But Sister Helen Francis had forbidden us to say anything to you," protested Sister Kevin Mary.

"Listen, kid, there is a higher obedience, an obedience to truth, to your conscience. Didn't you have any inkling that what you were doing was wrong?"

"Yes. I spoke to Father O'Mahoney. I told him that this was your life and that I felt I didn't have any right to keep this from you. But then she said that we couldn't tell you and I didn't know what to do." Sister Kevin Mary began to cry.

"Stop crying, Kevin. This is a very serious issue, and you're not going to learn it any other way. I want you to understand."

"OK, Marce. Let me have it."

"What I'm talking about is basic justice. I needed to know that I am dying. I'm going fast. You know that and I know that. There are things that I have to settle, issues within me that have to be resolved. You have no right to take that opportunity away from me, no matter how well intentioned you are. *Thinking* you are doing the right thing isn't enough. You have to *do* the right thing, especially in issues of life and death. Do you understand?"

"I'm trying to, Marce. I'm listening."

"You violated my integrity. You violated your own integrity with your lie. I realize that you are young, very young, and that they are filling you with all that new stuff about the supremacy of the Superior. 'When the Superior commands, God commands.' Right?"

"Yes, that's what I've been taught."

"Well, that's only partially right. There is the supremacy of your conscience, and you violated it, right?"

"Yes, I did."

"You tried to take away from me my integrity, my right to the truth about my life and my death. You violated me, Kevin. You violated me, all in the name of Holy Obedience."

Sister Kevin Mary was sobbing, holding onto the desk. She reached for the Kleenex and blew her nose.

"Why are you telling me this, Marce? You must hate me. How can you stand to be in the same room with me?"

"Hey, kid, how can I hate you? You're my good friend, and good friends have to be honest with each other. What kind of a friend would I be if I kept this from you? And there's another reason."

"What? Just what?" Sister Kevin Mary asked.

"You're going to go places in the order. You're smart, articulate, aggressive, from a good family. You'll be a Superior one of these days and have responsibilities over other people. Or you might have to face this with your own parents. You're going to have to use this experience someday, I know you will, and I don't want this to be lost on you."

Sister Kevin Mary smiled at the compliments. Maybe Marce didn't hate her after all.

"I think I understand what you've said, Marce. I'll think about what you said. Can you ever forgive me, Marce? What I did was terrible, I realize. All I can say is that I'm sorry."

"Hey, kid. Your slate is clean. Of course, I'll forgive. Listen, someday when you get in a jam, remember me. I'm your friend, kid. I'll be with God before you get back here next August, and when you really need something, just ask Old Marce. Trust me, I'll deliver for you. I won't let you down, Kevvie. I won't let you down."

"Marce . . . Marce, don't talk like that!"

"Listen, I'm tired. I'm very tired. Close the door and let me get a little sleep. Bye, kid. Take care."

Sister Kevin Mary leaned over, kissed Marce gently on the forehead, closed the door, and walked slowly down to chapel, smiling.

Epilogue
1981

Sister Helen Francis finished her term of office at St. Paul's and was appointed Superior at two other convents. She then became a major officer in the Order in charge of public relations.

Sister Agnes Patrick (Aggie) taught for three more years at St. Paul's, her hearing becoming increasingly worse. She retired at the age of seventy-eight and died at the motherhouse two years later, in January 1965.

Sister Lucy died in her sleep on Christmas Day, 1972.

Sister Maximillian (Max) had surgery on her back in 1959. The surgery left her paralyzed from the waist down.

Sister Jean Martin remained in the community, providing many of the Sisters with a living cross.

Sister Theodore Marie (Theo) remained in the community and went to live with her mother.

Sister William Ann (Willie) became a Superior at the age of twenty-seven. She was then sent to the Novitiate to replace Sister Duns Scotus. At the age of forty-three, she became Mother General of the Order.

Sister Mark Stephen (Mark) left the order in 1967 at the age of twenty-eight. She married an attorney, had two children, and withdrew from active participation in the Church. She is presently active in the Junior League in Winnetka.

Sister Clare Elliot (Clarabelle) was not given permission to renew her vows. She left the community in August 1959 and married a Michigan dairy farmer a year later. They had seven children. Clarabelle became President of the LaLeche League in her community, as well as President of the local Catholic school Parent-Teacher Organization.

Sister Julia Mary (Jules) was diagnosed as manic-depressive and alcoholic. She pursued a doctoral degree in clinical psychology and withdrew from the community in 1969. She then joined Alcoholics Anonymous. She is presently in private practice with alcoholic nuns and priests in the New York area.

Sister Frederick Ellen (Freddie) requested to leave teaching and go into nursing. She fell in love, left the Order, and married a doctor whose wife had died, leaving him with five children. They had three additional children. She presently lives in La Jolla, California. Bruno Petrowski married Belle.

Sister Marie Marcel (Marce) died on August 4, 1959, at the age of thirty-four. Prior to her death, she refused all medication, saying that she wanted to know where she was going.

Father O'Mahoney suffered a nervous breakdown after his twin sister, Mary Clare, was raped and murdered in Nigeria a week before she was to return to the States. Father O'Mahoney was made Chancellor of the Archdiocese in 1976.

Father Daniel Doyle left the priesthood and married a nurse. They had six children. He is presently a salesman for World Book Encyclopedia in the Chicago area.

Monsignor Ryan stayed at St. Paul's until his death in 1980 of a heart attack on the fourteenth tee.

Sister Kevin Mary remained in the order for 13 years. She became active in the anti-war and civil rights movement, withdrawing from the order in 1969 after a dispute with community officials over racial matters. She married in 1974, had two children, and became a writer.

Also Available from Whales' Tale Press

WHATEVER
HAPPENED
TO THE GOOD
SISTERS?

·A COLLECTION
·OF REAL LIFE
·STORIES

EDITED BY:
KATHLEEN W. FITZGERALD, PH.D.
CLAIRE BREAULT, M.A.

Whatever Happened to the Good Sisters?

Too much has been written about nuns. Far too many tasteless jokes have peppered conversations at Catholic gatherings about "Sister Mary Holy Water" or, worse, "Sister Mary Pew". Enough you may say. Enough already.

It is time to tell the simple story. Hundred of thousands of adult Catholics were educated by religious women. For every horror story told about nuns there are ten memories of warm, caring women who taught us to read, to write and yes, even to love God and our fellow men and women.

Who were these women? What were their emotions, masked as were their bodies in those mysterious black and white robes. Which of the stories we were told were the truth? Will we allow John Powers' book *Do Patent Leather Shoes Reflect Up* serve as our collective memory or is there another story to be told?

Let's take a walk together. The path is personal; the story as complex as the church we served. The journey is meant to satisfy the curiosity of those who have questions yet to be answered. For those other readers who were characters in the plot it will be, hopefully, a nostalgic trip into the not so distant past.
    Joanne Rooney

ISBN: 1-882195-00-0
$19.95 USA
$24.95 Canada

WHALES' TALE
P · R · E · S · S

P.O. Box 27
Lake Forest, Illinois 60045

Publication Date: August 2002

Also Available from Whales' Tale Press

Alcoholism: The Genetic Inheritance

by Kathleen W. FitzGerald, Ph.D.

For over thirty years the AMA has recognized alcoholism as a disease with identifiable and progressive symptoms that, if untreated, lead to mental damage, physical incapacity, and early death. Yet we still do not treat alcoholism as a disease, but as a sin, a social stigma, a moral aberration."

FitzGerald traces the roots of this disease to the alcoholic's unique and unusual body chemistry, laying to rest arguments for weakness of will or "alcoholic personality." *Jellinek's disease* is used as a synonym for alcoholism.

This sound and sensitive book addresses the very real pain that those who love an alcoholic must bear.

With compassion and honesty, the author speaks to these other victims — the family and friends — and gives voice to its silent victims — the children. Moving stories illustrate the universal suffering that everyone whose life is touched by alcoholism knows so well, inviting them out of isolation into their own recovery.

Rarely does a book on alcoholism focus its attention on the family and friends of an alcoholic; this one does, and it does so with depth and understanding. It translates the cold, scientific pathology of alcoholism into meaningful human terms.

No matter how alcoholism has touched your life, this is the one source book that offers you complete understanding, sound medical facts, and, most important, realistic help.

This revised paperback edition includes new chapters on Codependency, ACOA issues and other addictions.

ISBN: 1-882195-01-9
$22.95 USA
$26.95 Canada

WHALES' TALE
P · R · E · S · S
P.O. Box 27
Lake Forest, Illinois 60045

Publication Date: September 2002

Women In AA

By Kathleen W. FitzGerald, Ph.D.

In June, 1996, the National Center on Addiction and Substance Abuse at Columbia University published the landmark study, "Substance Abuse and the American Women," stating that women were as vulnerable to, and participated in alcoholism to the same degree as men. Alcoholism could no longer be accused of gender bias.

Every Friday morning for years I have attended a wonderful Big Book AA meeting for women in recovery. We read stories from *Alcoholics Anonymous*, affectionately called the "Big Book" by AA members. Many of the stories are written by women. We seem to read and discuss these stories with more knowing, with deeper humor and with greater identification.

And so it was one cold winter night, as I sat on our front porch and watched the stars, the idea for *Women in AA* dropped into my lap. For years I had intuitively known that women were equally represented in the manifestation of the disease of alcoholism. I saw with my own eyes that half the folks in AA were women, and it was time for their stories of trial and triumph to be shared.

The Irish say, "When you pray for potatoes, pick up a hoe". So I sent a "Call for Manuscripts" to 900 newspapers throughout the US and Canada, assuring potential contributors of our adherence to Tradition 12, wherein each woman's anonymity would be protected.

Eighty women from 26 states and throughout Canada trustingly sent us their stories, each in her own way articulating the issues that we, as recovering women, must integrate into our recovery if we want a peaceful, joyful recovery.

These stories and reflections invite you to use them to examine some of your own thoughts and feelings and possibly to discover the special meanings that these stories may hold for you. Take from them what you want and leave the rest.

So in giving to you this little book, we are giving back in some way what we have received from AA. Namely, our lives.

WHALES' TALE
P · R · E · S · S

ISBN: 1-882195-03-5
$18.95 USA
$20.95 Canada

P.O. Box 27
Lake Forest, Illinois 60045

Now Available from Whales' Tale Press

Codependency...
PowerLoss
SoulLoss

By Dorothy May, Ph.D.

"When we cry all our tears, laugh at ourselves, and playfully thumb our noses at the world, then we know we are living life as it was meant to be lived. "

Dorothy May, Ph.D. received a Doctorate in Psychology from Northwestern University in Evanston and a Master of Arts degree from Northeastern Illinois University in Chicago.

As a Clinical Psychologist, her professional expertise includes work in her private practice for the past 15 years with Codependents, Adult Children of Alcoholics and Adult Children from Dysfunctional families. She has served as community advisor and supervising teacher/psychologist and has taught at local colleges and universities.

Years ago, she began her personal quest for meaning to her life experience. When Codependency was identified, she knew that the ideas generated by the discovery applied to her own life as well as to the thousands of clients she was seeing. What she had thought was an idiosyncratic problem was in truth a societal/cultural problem.

The research for this book came out of her classes, lectures, workshops and practice, but the heart of this book lies in her own personal quest.

ISBN: 1-882195-02-7
$12.95 USA
$14.95 Canada

WHALES' TALE
P · R · E · S · S

P.O. Box 27
Lake Forest, Illinois 60045